Daughters
of
Fortune

Daughters
of
Fortune

TARA HYLAND

**SIMON &
SCHUSTER**

London · New York · Sydney · Toronto

A CBS COMPANY

First published in Great Britain by Simon & Schuster UK Ltd, 2010
This edition published by Simon & Schuster UK Ltd, 2011
A CBS COMPANY

Sydney

A CIP catalogue record for this book is available
from the British Library

ISBN 978-1-84739-852-9

This book is a work of fiction. Names, characters, places
and incidents are either a product of the author's imagination or are
used fictitiously. Any resemblance to actual people, living or dead,
events or locales, is entirely coincidental.

Typeset by M Rules
Printed in the UK by CPI Cox & Wyman, Reading, Berkshire RG1 8EX

To Tom

Acknowledgements

I owe heartfelt thanks to:

My agent, Darley Anderson, for his unswerving enthusiasm, patience and guidance; I would never have got here without him. And everyone else at his agency, particularly Maddie Buston, who read my manuscript in its earliest – and lengthiest – form, and whose feedback at that stage improved the next draft immeasurably.

My editors at Simon & Schuster: Suzanne Baboneau and Libby Yevtushenko in London, and Sarah Durand in New York. All three have been a pleasure to work with, and their intuitive comments have certainly made this a far better read. Also my copy editor, Joan Deitch, who spotted so many irritating repetitions and inconsistencies, and polished up my French.

And last, but certainly not least: my husband, Tom, for believing in me from the beginning, and providing financial and emotional support throughout the entire process. I hope we have a long and happy life together.

Daughters
of
Fortune

Prologue

London, December 1974

The young woman hurried along the street. It was the fourth time she'd passed through Eaton Square in the last hour. She knew that because she'd kept count, and she had a nagging suspicion that the policeman on the corner had, too. She tossed her head back, trying to look as though she belonged here, among the elegant rows of stucco townhouses that characterised Belgravia. But she had no hope. In her cheap coat and threadbare mittens, it was clear Katie O'Dwyer had no business in a place like this.

As she reached the middle of the street, her pace slowed until she came to a halt outside one of the grand Georgian residences. A clone of its neighbours, it stood six storeys high and was painted virgin white. Wrought-iron railings separated the neat front garden from the pavement. At the top of five marble steps there was a formidable black door with a heavy brass knocker, which the housemaid polished every Wednesday without fail. Katie knew the routine well, even though she had never lived in the house – never officially been a visitor there, if she was honest.

She saw straight away that he still wasn't home. The only light came from the basement, the staff quarters, where a television could be seen flickering through the net curtains. Upstairs, where he lived, remained in darkness. Part of her wanted to knock and ask if she could wait in the warmth, but she knew her presence would raise questions, and she wouldn't risk doing that to him. Instead she crossed to the park bench opposite. The wooden seat was cold and hard, but with a clear view of the house, it was as good a place as any to wait.

A light drizzle began to fall. Despite herself, Katie smiled. It had been raining the night she'd arrived in England, a little over a year ago. She remembered stepping off the boat at Holyhead, her stomach still churning from the journey, and feeling the first droplets on her skin. She had thought of it as a cleansing rain, washing away the memories of her life in Ireland and opening the way to the future.

Not that life back home had been bad – it was simply dull. She had grown up in a small village in County Mayo, the conservative west of the country, the only child of overprotective parents. Having spent fifteen years trying to conceive, they had pretty much given up hope of ever having a baby when little Katie came along, just after her mother's fortieth birthday. Their Miracle Child, they'd treated her as though she was liable to break at any moment. By the time Katie turned eighteen, she craved freedom and excitement; longed to go to London, to see Carnaby Street and the King's Road. Telling her parents wasn't easy. But after weeks of pleading and shouting, they finally bade her a tearful farewell at Dún Laoghaire docks.

Katie arrived at the Catholic hostel in Kilburn full of excitement. But finding work proved more difficult than she'd imagined. The optimism of the early seventies had faded. Inflation and unemployment were on the rise; the IRA's terror campaign was in full swing, making it even harder to find a job if you were Irish. She was on the verge of giving up and going home, when Nuala, one of the girls in her dorm, mentioned hearing about a vacancy where she worked.

'The hours are long and the pay's shite,' Nuala said cheerfully. 'But it's a job, right?'

In fact, Katie thought it sounded terribly glamorous, working as a sales assistant at Melville. The exclusive English fashion house was internationally renowned for its handmade leather shoes, exquisite bags and delightful scarves, its name synonymous with taste and breeding. Katie's heroines, Audrey Hepburn and Jackie Onassis, had both recently been photographed clutching Melville handbags sporting the signature M-shaped clasp.

The following morning, Katie put on her smartest clothes and headed over to Old Bond Street, home to the most elegant and exclusive shops in London. Wide-eyed, she passed art galleries and fine jewellers, designer shops like Gucci and Chanel . . . until she finally found Melville. Even from the outside it was intimidating. Darkened glass and huge velvet curtains at the windows made it impossible to see inside. A liveried porter held the gold-crested doors open for her. Taking a deep breath, Katie walked inside.

That was her first mistake.

'Salesgals must use the rear entrance,' Anne Harper, the Store Manager, told Katie later that morning as she gave her a brief tour of the store. Nuala had put in a good word for her and, after a cursory interview, Mrs Harper had agreed to take Katie on for a trial period. It was said in a way that suggested she didn't expect Katie's employment to last any longer than that.

'If I catch you coming in through the front entrance again, you will be dismissed,' Mrs Harper went on. 'You will also be immediately dismissed if you are late or if a customer complains about you.'

Katie was quickly cured of the notion that working at Melville would be glamorous. Nuala had been right: the hours were long, the pay poor, and the people unfriendly – customers and colleagues alike. She hardly ever saw Nuala, who worked as a secretary in the adjoining Head Office building, and the other shop girls were for the most part from wealthy families, the job merely a diversion until they were married off. Katie knew they looked down on her, the simple Irish country girl. When they made plans to go out at the weekend – plans that never included her – Katie pretended not to hear.

In the face of such open hostility, Katie probably would have looked around for a position elsewhere. But then something unexpected happened. She fell in love.

It began with a spate of thefts. Five handbags disappeared from the stockroom, followed by a dozen silk scarves. But when twenty pounds went missing from the till, Management finally decided to crack down. Mrs Harper called a staff meeting as soon as the store closed, warning that a spot check would be carried out on all bags as employees left that night.

Katie joined the queue with everyone else. As she waited, someone jostled her arm. She looked round to see Fiona Clifton, a horse-faced country-set type, who was always especially unpleasant to her. Fiona's narrow face split into a toothy grin. 'Sorry, darling,' she brayed.

Katie was about to tell her not to worry. But just then she was called forward to open up her bag. Katie looked on as Melville's Head of Security removed her umbrella, Max Factor lipstick and hankie. Finally, he went through her coat pockets. With Mrs Harper and the other staff looking on, he pulled out a twenty-pound note. He turned it over to reveal an orange highlighter mark slashed across it, identifying it as the float from the till.

'That isn't mine,' Katie protested.

But no one believed her story. After all, why would any of the well-to-do young ladies who worked in the store steal money and then plant the evidence on her . . .

Mrs Harper hauled Katie up by her arm. 'You'll have to come with me. Mr Melville wants to deal with this himself.'

Katie's heart sank. She had heard whispers about William Melville, the great-grandson of the founder. Rumoured to be a formidable man, he never made time to visit the shop floor, and the store staff only ever saw him at the Christmas party, at which he made the briefest of appearances. Katie had never even laid eyes on him before, but she couldn't imagine he was the type to give her a fair hearing.

Melville's Head Office was located directly behind the store. Katie had never had any reason to venture over there before, but she had expected it to resemble the stark, soulless backrooms of the store. Instead, it was like stepping into a stately home. She followed Mrs Harper along dimly-lit corridors, complete with deep-pile carpets and original oil paintings adorning the walls. Finally, they reached a heavy door at the top of the building. A gold-lettered nameplate announced that it belonged to 'William Melville, Chief Executive'. Mrs Harper rapped loudly, and a gruff voice invited them inside.

The room was every bit as imposing as the hallway. Walnut wainscoting, polished floorboards and a bookcase crammed with first editions gave a grand, impersonal feel. In the centre stood a handsome Louis XIV desk, made of solid dark oak, the top covered in burgundy leather. Katie guessed correctly that the man sitting behind it was William Melville. Tall and well-built; strong, serious and uncompromising: the kind of man born to run a company like this. He didn't look up as they entered.

'One moment,' he murmured.

Katie shifted uneasily. Mrs Harper still had a firm grip on her arm and it was beginning to hurt, but she didn't dare twist away. It felt like forever before Mr Melville closed the file in front of him and deigned to look up. 'So what can I do for you, Anne?' His voice was strong and clear and, to Katie's ears, terrifyingly posh.

She stared straight ahead as Mrs Harper ran through the events of the evening. William Melville didn't glance in her direction once. She couldn't help feeling despondent. He would undoubtedly believe everything Mrs Harper said, and probably call the police. The thought of being sent back to

Ireland in disgrace, of her parents' shame ... She felt tears welling in her eyes, but blinked them away. She wouldn't give them the satisfaction.

Mrs Harper finished speaking. William's eyes flicked to Katie. She made sure to meet his gaze – after all, she had no reason to be ashamed. He was only in his early thirties, but his sober face, bespoke Savile Row suit and greying temples made him seem older. He stared at her for a long moment, as though getting the measure of her. Finally his eyes dropped to where Mrs Harper still had hold of Katie's arm. He frowned. 'I think you can let go of the young lady, Anne,' he said mildly. 'I doubt she's going to run off.'

The Store Manager did as she was told. Then William turned to Katie, and what he said next took her completely by surprise.

'Now, Katie,' he addressed her as though they were old acquaintances, 'why on earth did you put Mrs Harper to all this trouble?' His tone was filled with mild reproof.

He waited for a moment, as if expecting her to answer. Katie stayed silent. She had no idea what he was talking about. When she didn't speak up, he shook his head and turned to Mrs Harper.

'I'm so sorry about all this, Anne. But I know for certain that Katie didn't steal this money. You see, I gave it to her from the petty cash box myself so that she could pick up my dry cleaning on her way into work tomorrow morning. My secretary would usually do it, but she's been away.'

Katie looked on in disbelief as he forced a reluctant Mrs Harper to apologise to her. She had no idea why he would lie for her, but if it meant she got to keep her job then she was happy to keep quiet.

Mrs Harper didn't stay around for very long after that. Clearly humiliated, she bade William a brisk goodnight, and then hurried off. Katie waited until the other woman's footsteps had faded, before turning to the Chief Executive. 'Why did you do that?' she asked.

William shrugged with the nonchalance of a man who is used to having his orders obeyed without question. 'You looked as though you could use someone on your side.'

She took a moment to digest what he'd said.

'Thank you,' she said finally.

'You're welcome.' His eyes hardened. 'Just make sure nothing like this happens again. I won't be so lenient next time.'

It dawned on her then that he still thought she was guilty.

'I didn't—' she began to explain. But he cut her off.

'All I ask is that it doesn't happen again,' he repeated crisply.

He turned back to his file, signalling that as far as he was concerned, the conversation was over. Katie wanted to say more but knew there was no point. Instead, she slipped from the room.

As she hurried down the stairs and out into the brisk winter night, she knew she should feel relieved – she'd had a lucky escape. But for some reason the incident depressed her. She hated to think that this kind man, who had taken a chance on her, still believed that she was a thief.

A month later, the real culprit was caught. Security discovered Fiona Clifton in the stockroom sneaking five pairs of shoes into a backpack. Apparently, Daddy's monthly allowance wasn't enough to fund her burgeoning cocaine habit. She was sacked on the spot.

With her name fully cleared now, Katie received a second, somewhat stilted apology from Mrs Harper . . . and a handwritten note from William Melville inviting her to dinner that night.

He hadn't asked her to keep their rendezvous quiet. But Katie didn't share her news with the other girls, not wanting them to gossip. Instead, she stuck to her routine, leaving the shop at seven, then whiling away the next hour in a nearby café.

Katie couldn't help feeling nervous as she waited. She had little experience with men. She'd had her share of admirers, drawn to her striking Gaelic looks – glossy blue-black hair and snow-white skin – as much as her full figure, but she'd never had a proper boyfriend. Back home, her father's fierce stare had kept suitors away. London had brought more freedom, but her strict Catholic upbringing meant any dates always ended the same – with Katie pushing away eager hands and then being walked home in sullen silence. She had already decided that if William acted in any way forward she would head straight home – even if it meant losing her job. After all, she wasn't *that* type of girl.

She was back outside the shop entrance by five to eight. William was already there. Early, she noted, and looking fabulously affluent in a navy cashmere coat. She glanced down at her own attire. Dressed in her polyester bow blouse and calf-length cord skirt, she wasn't exactly an ideal dinner companion for him. She waited, uncertain how to greet him.

'I'm glad you came, Katie,' he said, in his deep, cultured voice that made her so aware of her own Irish lilt.

'It was nice of you to invite me, Mr Melville.'

He smiled down at her. 'If we're going to have dinner together, then I must insist you call me William.'

She hesitated for the briefest of moments before smiling back at him.

'Thank you . . . William,' she said.

It was a magical evening for Katie. William whisked her off to the Ritz. Given its proximity to the office, he dined there often, apparently. At first, when they entered the hotel's rather formal dining room, Katie felt a moment of dread. She was bound to do something stupid, commit some awful social gaffe.

But William, seeming to sense her fears, went out of his way to put her at ease. He directed the maitre d' to seat them at a table tucked into a discreet corner, away from the prying eyes of other guests. And he must have seen her look of horror, upon realizing the menu was in French, because he offered to order for her. 'I'm here so often that I know what's good,' he said smoothly, clearly wanting to spare her any embarrassment.

After that, she began to relax. She devoured every bit of the delicious food – lobster bisque followed by Boeuf Bourguignon – and even allowed him to pour her a small glass of the Bordeaux he'd carefully selected. Talking to him was easier than she'd expected, too, since he seemed so genuinely interested in what she had to say. She found herself telling him about her upbringing, how stifled she'd felt at home; he reciprocated by opening up to her about the pressure he had always felt to go into the family business. It was strange to find they had more in common than she could have ever imagined.

At the end of the evening he insisted on having his chauffeur drop her home. As they leaned back against the smooth leather seats of the Rolls-Royce, watching the bright lights of the West End fade into the less salubrious surroundings of North London, Katie was certain that she would remember this as one of the best nights of her life.

When they reached the hostel, he got out of the car to open the door for her, like a real gentleman should.

'Goodnight, Katie,' he said.

He bent to kiss her hand. She felt his lips brush against her skin and shivered. Without another word, she turned and ran into the house, carrying her memories with her.

They made no plans to meet again. But the following Thursday Katie received another note from William in her staff pigeon-hole, asking whether she was free for dinner that night.

This time, she hesitated. She knew he was married. She also knew he had an eighteen-month-old daughter. He had told her all about his wife and child last week. They resided at his country estate in Somerset. During the week he stayed in his Belgravia residence, and at weekends he travelled down to be with them. Katie had no idea what this invitation meant to him, but she knew what it meant to her. And that was enough to make her consider turning it down.

But, despite her good intentions, she found herself standing outside the shop entrance at ten to eight that evening. Once again, he was already there, and he smiled when he saw her.

'I thought we could go somewhere else tonight,' he said, as they walked along the street. 'Somewhere . . . less formal.'

She guessed he meant somewhere that they were less likely to be spotted.

The little French bistro was, as he had promised, less formal. And, whatever his reason for choosing it, Katie found she felt more at ease.

When another invitation arrived the following week, she wasn't remotely surprised.

They ate dinner together every Thursday for the next two months. On the surface, they had nothing in common. But they found each other mutually fascinating. William never mentioned his wife again, and Katie saw no reason to bring her up, either. In fact, she was surprised at how easy it was to forget who he was. She would find herself telling him about her day, about the other girls being horrible to her, as though he was a friend.

'I could do something,' he said once. 'Have you moved to another section . . .'

'No,' she said firmly. 'No. I don't want you to do anything.' What she meant was that she didn't want him to do anything that would draw attention to them.

Katie had no idea what he saw in her, or where he thought they were headed. Other than kissing her hand, he never made any move to touch her. The only person she had confided in about their meetings was Nuala. Her friend made no secret of her disapproval.

'There's only one thing he'll be wanting from you, Katie,' she told her time and again.

'No,' Katie insisted. 'It's not like that.'

Nuala gave a sceptical sniff. She was in the midst of planning her wedding to a young chap she'd met at one of London's many Irish clubs, and didn't like hearing about a married man wining and dining a pretty single girl. 'Ah, Katie, you eejit. You don't really believe that now, do you?'

In fact, Katie *had* almost convinced herself that she and William were friends, nothing more. Then one bitter January night they were walking back to his car when she slipped over on the icy pavement. He helped her up, but when she looked down to check the damage, she found her tights were torn and her knees skinned. Tears filled her eyes.

'Are you all right?' he asked, concerned.

'I'm fine,' she sniffed.

'No, you're not.'

As if to prove her wrong, he reached out to brush a tear from her wet cheek. That only made it worse. Suddenly she couldn't stop crying.

William didn't say anything. He simply put his arms around her and drew her to him. She knew she ought to resist, but for some reason she couldn't pull away. Instead, she closed her eyes and relaxed against his chest.

'Oh, Katie, Katie,' he murmured into her hair. 'What are we going to do?'

That night, instead of having his driver drop her home, William brought her back to his place.

Katie knew it was wrong. She knew that she was likely to burn in hell for eternity, but she couldn't stop herself. That night, Katie O'Dwyer, who had sworn to the nuns that she would save herself for her wedding night, gave herself entirely to another woman's husband. On the embossed silk sheets of a strange bed, with his wife and child gazing down at her from the photos on the wall, she opened herself up to William.

The blood and pain disappeared after the first time. And from then on they stopped meeting in restaurants. He rented a little flat for her in Clapham and every Thursday – and Monday, Tuesday and Wednesday, too – they would skip dinner and head straight back there to spend the evening in each other's arms.

They had eight months together. Eight blissful months pretending the world didn't exist.

Then one night he told her about his forthcoming trip to Italy – the annual family holiday. He couldn't get out of the two weeks at Lake Como, somewhere she hadn't even heard of. The thought of not seeing William for fourteen days bothered Katie more than knowing he would be with his wife. Kissing away her tears, he promised to come and see her the night that he returned.

That was Katie's first experience of men's duplicity. Two days after William left, she was summoned into Anne Harper's office and told that she was being let go.

'But that can't be right!' she burst out. 'You can't do that. Just ask—' She was about to say 'William', but caught herself in time.

The Store Manager smiled unpleasantly. 'Ask Mr Melville, is that what you were going to say?' Katie could see that she was enjoying herself. 'I don't think that's going to do you any good,

Miss O'Dwyer. After all, he was the one who instructed me to get rid of you.'

Katie listened in a daze as the woman told her that, along with losing her job, she would also be expected to vacate her flat by the end of the week. The manageress then slid an envelope across the desk. 'This should compensate you for any undue distress,' she said coolly. 'And I'm sure I don't need to tell you to keep this conversation to yourself?'

Katie heard the warning note in Anne's voice. Somehow she managed to mumble something about not wanting to cause any trouble, and then, still in a daze, she got to her feet and stumbled to the door.

Upstairs, alone in the staffroom, she opened the heavy cream envelope. Some part of her had hoped it would contain a letter from William, with some explanation for what he had done. But there was only a brisk, formal note on company headed paper from Personnel, outlining the terms of her termination, and pointing her towards the enclosed redundancy cheque for one thousand pounds. It was clearly such a ridiculous sum relative to her pay and duration of employment that she nearly laughed. Instead, she tucked the envelope, letter and cheque into her pocket, and cleared out her locker. Then, without speaking to another soul, she left Melville for good.

That night, Katie did what William wanted – she got out of his life. He was right, she decided, as she packed her belongings. A clean break was the best way. If she wished he'd had the courage to tell her face-to-face, she consoled herself with the thought that he had feared his resolve would weaken. It was easier than thinking the alternative: that he had never cared.

She never went back to Melville. She found cheaper lodgings and convinced the owner of a small café to take her on. And William was right, she told herself every night as she cried herself to sleep. It had had to end between them. She needed to forget him so that he could forget her, and be with his wife. However much it hurt, it was the right thing to do.

That had been three months ago. And now here she was, waiting outside his house, where they had spent that first night together.

The familiar purr of a car engine broke into Katie's thoughts. She looked up from her place on the park bench. Sure enough, it was William's Rolls. Her heartbeat quickened. Despite everything that had happened, she was longing to see him again.

The car slowed, pulling up in front of his house. The chauffeur got out first, putting on his peaked cap before going round to open the rear door for William.

Then William stepped out onto the pavement. In the shadowy light from the streetlamp, Katie could still make out his broad shoulders and solemn expression. She stood up, shivering with cold and anticipation. She was about to call his name – but then he turned back to the car and held out his hand. Katie watched as slender fingers gripped his strong wrist.

She recognised the elegant blonde in the fox fur straight away: it was his wife, Isabelle. Katie wondered idly where they had been tonight. The opera? Dinner with friends? Not that it was her business.

She watched as they walked up the steps together and disappeared into the house. A moment later, the Christmas-tree lights flickered on in the front window. In the half-light, she saw William draw Isabelle into his arms. He pointed up at the mistletoe above them and she giggled. He brushed her fair hair back and bent his head.

Katie couldn't watch any longer. She closed her eyes, trying to block out the image of them together. Then she reached down to touch the gentle swell of her belly. She could never tell him now. She had been foolish to come here tonight; just as she had been foolish to get involved with a married man. Now she would have to deal with the consequences alone.

PART I

June – December 1990

Chapter 1

Katie O'Dwyer died on a Tuesday. She was buried three days later, on a warm June morning, Valleymount's first glimpse of summer. The whole village turned out for the funeral, testament to her popularity with everyone who'd ever met her.

Her fifteen-year-old daughter, Caitlin, stood by the graveside, watching the pallbearers lower her mother's coffin into the ground. She'd made it through the Mass without crying but now, as the priest began the Rite of Committal, it finally hit her. Mam was gone and, for the first time in her life, she was all alone.

For as long as Caitlin could remember, it had just been the two of them, her and Mammy. She never realised how close her mother had come to giving her up.

Alone and pregnant in London, Katie's options were slim. She knew girls who had got themselves 'fixed up', but her Catholic beliefs forbade it. Telling her parents wasn't an option, so she resolved to have the baby in London, put it up for adoption and then go home. No one would ever have to know . . .

When it came time for the birth, she went into a home for unmarried mothers in the East End. There was little kindness or sympathy among the staff. They encouraged the young mothers to give up their babies and then sent them off, warning them not to sin again.

After a surprisingly easy five-hour labour, Katie took one look at her daughter's wide blue eyes and knew exactly what she should be called.

'You look like a Caitlin to me,' she murmured to her newborn.

A nurse overheard her and sniffed disparagingly. 'Don't matter what you call her. Her new mother will decide that.'

But I'm her mother, Katie thought.

Two days later, after a huge argument with Matron, she left the hospital with Caitlin in her arms. It was a brave decision. One that meant she had no choice: when she was recovered from the birth, she would have to return to Ireland.

Caitlin couldn't remember her grandparents, which was probably just as well. When Katie turned up on the doorstep of the little house in County Mayo with her two-month-old baby, her mam and dad did nothing to disguise their dismay. They gave Katie and her child a place to sleep, but little else. Caitlin was treated like their dirty little secret. It was just as well they never knew that the father was married, Katie often thought.

When they died two years later – her father first, after a stroke, followed by her mother, whose heart gave out just a few weeks later – Katie decided she needed a fresh start. The thin gold band on her left hand hadn't fooled the neighbours, and she didn't want Caitlin growing up in a place where everyone called her a bastard child. Katie had kept in touch with Nuala over the years. She'd moved back to Ireland, too, with the man she'd met in London, and they were now raising their young family in a picturesque village called Valleymount, in County Wicklow. Known as 'the garden of Ireland', with its lush hills, cascading waterfalls and glassy lakes, Katie had thought on the two occasions that she'd been to visit that it would be the ideal place to raise Caitlin. So she sold her parents' property, and used the proceeds to buy a tiny cottage near her friend.

It turned out to be a good move. Caitlin's early years were spent with a pack of other village kids, running barefoot through the pretty glens and swimming in the nearby Blessington Lakes. Work was hard to come by in eighties

Ireland, but Katie managed to find a job as a cleaner in one of the upmarket hotels nearby. Each day, after school, the little girl would help Katie dust the bedrooms and restock the toiletries. And, even though there might not be much money, mother and daughter were happy. Twice a year, they would make the hour's bus ride into Dublin, and spend the day shopping on Grafton Street before taking afternoon tea in Bewley's. But the rest of the time, they were content with Valleymount — and each other.

'You're so lucky, Katie,' Nuala would remark enviously. 'Caitlin's an angel.' Her own daughter, Róisín, was anything but.

When Caitlin turned twelve, it was time for her to go to the local secondary school, Holy Cross. With less than twenty pupils per class, most of whom she'd grown up with, it was like spending each day with a large extended family. She was bright, but not especially academic. Her real talent and interest was art. She spent hours drawing, and could capture a likeness with a few brief pencil strokes.

Of course, her adolescence brought more changes. With her Snow White looks — jet-black hair and milk-white skin — she was rapidly becoming a beauty, much like her mother. And as the puppy fat melted away, leaving behind womanly curves, the boys she had once played easily with turned shy around her. Tongue-tied, they took it in turns to ask her to the pictures, but she always refused. Boys were the one area forbidden to her.

She had no idea why she wasn't allowed out on dates. All her friends were. Saturday nights, they would head into town to go bowling with their latest boyfriends.

'Sneak out after yer mam's asleep and join us,' Róisín said. Like their mothers, the two girls were best friends.

But Caitlin never did. As always, she obeyed her mother. It was because it was just the two of them. They had to pull together, couldn't live in a permanent state of war like Róisín and Nuala. Róisín never understood. But that's because she *had* a father, Caitlin reasoned, while hers had died before she was born, leaving her mother to raise her singlehandedly. Financially, it had always been tough. Caitlin wasn't about to add to her mother's worries.

Sometimes Caitlin wondered why Katie hadn't ever remarried. There were plenty of men around the village who seemed interested. But her mother would always clam up whenever she asked, and Caitlin guessed that she still hadn't gotten over her father's death. She never pressed the subject, and mother and daughter lived happily and effortlessly together. That was, until six months ago.

Caitlin first realised her mother was ill one night after dinner. As she emptied the leftovers into the bin, she noticed that her mam had barely touched the shepherd's pie she'd made that day in Home Economics. It might not be a fantastic effort, but her mother was the type to clear her plate, if only to save her child's feelings.

Over the next few days Caitlin monitored what went into the bin. Sure enough, each night Katie barely touched her meal. When Caitlin asked if anything was wrong, she dismissed it as a spot of indigestion. Caitlin said no more – but she couldn't help noticing how, instead of insisting that she went to do her homework, these days Katie was happy to let her daughter wash up while she dozed in front of the television.

As the weeks went on, her mother's appetite didn't improve. It was getting increasingly hard to ignore her sunken eyes, dull hair and the way her once-plump cheeks were now almost concave. But whenever Caitlin suggested going to the doctor, Katie dismissed her with increasing irritation.

'Give over, Caitlin,' she snapped one Thursday night. 'I'm fine – it's just—'

But she never finished the sentence. Instead, she ran for the bathroom. Caitlin waited outside, listening to her bring up the supper that she'd managed to swallow earlier. Finally, when everything went quiet, Caitlin pushed open the door. Her mother had collapsed, exhausted, on the floor. Caitlin went over to the basin and started to wash it out. This time she couldn't ignore the blood. She didn't say a word until she'd helped her mother upstairs and into her nightdress. Then, once her mam was settled in bed, she said: 'Please go to the doctor. You're not well.'

For the first time, her mother didn't argue back. And that was what worried Caitlin most.

Dr Hannon smiled at them both and said there was probably nothing to worry about, but he'd like to send Katie for tests. His smile couldn't hide the worry in his eyes.

A few weeks later they sat down with a specialist. He told them that, although the pancreatic cancer had been diagnosed at a late stage, there was still hope. Like Dr Hannon, he couldn't fool the O'Dwyer women. He said they would use chemotherapy to shrink the tumour and then operate. What he actually meant was that at the moment, there was no point operating and they would have to pray for a miracle.

When Caitlin wasn't holding the bowl for her mother to be sick in or helping her wrap the scarf to cover her bald head, she was on her knees in the hospital chapel praying for that miracle. It never came. When they finally opened her up, it was too late. The cancer had spread. There was nothing to do but wait.

Caitlin tried not to show her shock when she walked into the ward. Even though she saw her mother every day, was accustomed to the smell of antiseptic and death, she still couldn't get over how quickly she had gone downhill. Unable to eat for weeks now, Katie had shrunk to a skeletal figure, hardly taking up any room in the tiny single bed. Only her distended belly, full of cancer cells, gave her any shape under the stark white sheets. Her eyes were closed and she was so pale that if it hadn't been for the gentle rise and fall of her rib cage, Caitlin would have assumed her mother was gone rather than simply asleep.

Caitlin busied herself by looking for a space to put the vase of bluebells which she'd picked that morning. It was no easy task. The bedside cabinet was already filled with half-dead flowers, futile *Get Well Soon* cards and grapes that would never be eaten. She was halfway through clearing away the faded blooms when she heard her mother calling for her.

'I'm here, Mammy,' she said. 'Can I get you something? Some water perhaps?'

'No . . . No . . . Nothing like that.'

Katie paused. The only sound was her laboured breathing. She reached out and took Caitlin's hand. Her fingers were thin and cold as death.

'I don't have long now, Cat,' she began. Caitlin opened her mouth to deny this truth, but a look from her mother stopped her. 'Don't be contradicting me. I need to tell you something.'

'What is it, Mam?'

'It's about your father. I never told you much about him. I should have.'

'Let's not be worrying about that. He's gone. There's nothing more to say.'

Her mother closed her eyes, and when she opened them again Caitlin saw they were glistening with tears. 'But that's it, my child,' she said. 'That's what I'm trying to tell you. He isn't dead.'

For the next half an hour, Katie explained to her daughter how she had met William Melville and fallen in love. She told her about his wife and daughter. And how even though they had both known the affair was wrong, they could do nothing to stop their feelings for each other. She spoke with a clear determination to get it all off her chest. As others before her had found, the deathbed made a good confessional.

'He ended it before I found out I was pregnant,' she said, avoiding the precise details of the break-up. 'And we were happy, weren't we?' she continued when Caitlin still hadn't said anything. 'Just the two of us. I wouldn't have had it any other way.'

Caitlin managed to nod in answer. She knew she should say something, offer some comfort to her mother. But she was still too stunned.

'I've written to him, love.'

Caitlin's head snapped up. 'You've what?'

'I wrote to tell him that he has a daughter. A beautiful, fifteen-year-old daughter.'

Caitlin pulled her hand away and stood up.

'He's been in touch, too,' Katie said quickly. 'He left a message to say he's coming to see us.'

Caitlin saw her mam's eyes dart over to the door, as though she expected him to appear at any moment. She realised then why her mother had never married. She still loved *him*. Even after all these years. Hurt and confused, Caitlin turned away.

'Cat?' She heard her mother's voice, weak and pleading. She could feel her reaching out. 'Please don't be angry, pet. I'm sorry I didn't tell you about him. I should have said something sooner.'

She stopped, and Caitlin knew that she was waiting for her to say something. But she couldn't. Not yet.

'Forgive me, my darling. Say that you forgive me.'

Caitlin closed her eyes and swallowed back the tears. All she could think about was how her mother had been lying to her for fifteen years. It was too much for her to process. But she knew she had to.

'It's OK, Mam,' she said finally, opening her eyes. 'I

understand.' She took a deep breath, turned around. 'I forgive you.'

The final word died in her throat. She stared down at her mother. Katie's lips were parted, as though she was just about to say something, but her eyes stared ahead unseeing. It was too late for forgiveness.

Caitlin sat with the body as long as she could. Finally the Staff Nurse persuaded her to get a cup of tea. She was on her way back to the ward when she spotted him – a tall, well-dressed man, talking to the Matron. He must have sensed her presence, because he looked up. For a moment his expression faltered.

'Katie?' he said.

The refined English voice left her in no doubt as to who he was.

'No. It's Caitlin.'

'I thought—'

Caitlin nodded. She had seen enough pictures of her mother as a young girl to know that it was an easy mistake to make. He hadn't seen her mother for sixteen years. To him, she hadn't aged a day since then.

'She's already gone,' she told him.

William Melville booked into the Grand, the hotel where her mother had worked, and took charge of organising the funeral. The more Caitlin saw of him that week, the harder it was to believe that he was her father. It was harder still to understand how her mother had ever got entangled with him. She'd insisted that they had loved each other. So far, in the few days Caitlin had known him, William had been far more reticent about their relationship.

On the day of the funeral, he maintained a dignified distance, standing discreetly to one side during the service and burial. Caitlin half-expected him to leave straight afterwards, but to her surprise, he came to the Clover Leaf for the reception. The pub was packed by the time they got there, everyone tucking into plates of sausage rolls and ham sandwiches. All the men were getting stuck in, having a good drink at someone else's expense. William – Caitlin couldn't yet bring herself to call him 'Father' and he hadn't invited her to – looked stiff and uncomfortable throughout the increasingly raucous proceedings.

By five, everyone began drifting home.

Róisín came over to Caitlin. 'We're off outside. Are you coming?'

Caitlin saw a group of girls lurking by the door. They'd been let off school for the occasion and were aching to get away from the adults. Caitlin longed to go with them, to forget everything for a little while. But she saw William standing nearby, and guessed he was waiting to talk to her.

'I'll be out in a bit,' she said reluctantly.

Róisín went to join the others. The girls had been staring unashamedly at William all afternoon. His identity was meant to be a secret, but Caitlin guessed that Róisín had told everyone. Best friend or not, she never could keep anything to herself. William didn't seem bothered by the interest, though. He didn't even mention it when he took Caitlin over to one side, away from curious eavesdroppers.

'I have to get back to England now,' he informed Caitlin, 'but I'll be in touch with Nuala in a few days to arrange your flight.'

'Flight?'

'Yes,' he said briskly. 'I presumed you'd want a few weeks here, to finish off the school term and say goodbye to your friends. Then you'll come to England – to live with me and my family.'

This was the first Caitlin had heard of it. 'But I don't want to leave Valleymount.' She noticed Nuala hovering in the background. When her mother had gone into hospital, Nuala had kindly taken her in. Caitlin had assumed that now her mam was gone, she would continue to live there.

'You can't stay here alone, Caitlin,' William told her.

'But Aunty Nuala—'

'Nuala isn't family,' he interrupted. 'I am.'

Caitlin glanced over at Nuala, who tried to give her a reassuring smile. But Caitlin could tell that the older woman was as unhappy about the arrangements as she was. Unfortunately, neither of them seemed to have any choice in the matter. If William Melville wanted her to come and live with his family, then she would have to.

Later that night, Caitlin lay awake in bed. Across the room, Róisín snored gently. It was a sound she'd got used to these past few weeks, when sleep had stopped being easy to come by. Watching her mother grow weaker, being in constant pain, the morphine no longer working . . . those images were hard to forget. But none of that could compare with today. Seeing her mother in the open casket, looking the same as she always had, but knowing that she *wasn't* the same. Knowing that the body was simply an empty shell and that however much it resembled her mam, it wasn't her.

The memory set off her tears again. Rolling over to face the wall, Caitlin covered her mouth with her hand to muffle the sobs, so she didn't wake Róisín. Her friend had been brilliant these past weeks. She couldn't count the number of times Róisín had sat up with her, had held her while she cried. Nuala, too.

And now she was going to have to leave them, and the village which she had grown up in, the people that she thought of as her family and the house that had become her home – she was going to have to leave everything that connected her to her mam. And instead go to live with a father she didn't know, who hadn't even known that she existed until a fortnight ago, in a place she knew nothing about.

'Mam, why did you have to tell him about me?' she whispered into the darkness.

The thoughts brought a fresh wave of angry tears, and the guilt and confusion that came with them. Sleep was a long time in coming that night.

Chapter 2

Somerset, England

Elizabeth Melville smashed the ball across the court, determined to make this the winning shot. But James Evans, her tennis coach, ran forward and managed to intercept it with a smooth backhand. She returned with a volley and their lightning-quick rally continued.

They had been playing for an hour and a half now, in the blistering mid-afternoon heat, neither of them willing to yield a point. To the casual onlooker, James had every advantage in the game. At six foot two, he was four inches taller and twenty-five kilos heavier than Elizabeth. But the girl possessed one important quality that he lacked: a burning desire to win.

Long golden hair swished and tanned limbs rippled as she drove home another strong forehand. Caught offguard at the net, James sprinted back to catch it. But he was a fraction too slow and it bounced out of his reach.

Elizabeth let out a triumphant whoop. 'Game, set and match, I believe,' she called across the court.

James shook his head in mock despair. 'What's that – the third time this week? You're making me feel old, Elizabeth.'

She laughed. The one-time seeded player had celebrated his fortieth birthday a month earlier, but he was still in great shape, and they both knew it.

'That's right,' she teased. 'It's time to put you out to pasture.'

They strolled up the great stone steps that separated the tennis courts from the rest of the grounds, chatting and laughing with the ease of two people who had known each other for years. James had first started coaching Elizabeth when she was five. She'd stopped needing his help long ago, but whenever she was home from school he dropped by, 'to keep you on your toes,' he always joked.

Not that he ever minded coming out to Aldringham, the magnificent stately home Elizabeth's great-grandfather had purchased over one hundred years ago. Located in the rolling Quantock Hills of Somerset, overlooking the Bristol Channel and the Welsh valleys beyond, it was a quintessentially English estate, complete with croquet lawns, hidden walks and a deer park. James had been a guest in many exclusive homes, but Aldringham remained by far the most impressive.

He and Elizabeth headed up to the Georgian Orangery, which stood adjacent to the main house. In the citrus-scented room, they found a jug of homemade lemonade that Mrs Hutchins, the housekeeper, had left out for them. James flopped into the nearest chair, content to watch Elizabeth pour the drinks. She handed him a glass and sat down opposite, crossing her long, shapely legs at the knee and looking every inch the well-brought up young lady.

At seventeen, Elizabeth was smart, poised and fiercely competitive. Whether it was on the tennis court or in the classroom at her exclusive boarding school, she had to be the best. A statuesque blonde, she wasn't beautiful exactly – her nose was a little too long, her chin too pointed – but she *was* attractive, in that slightly snotty, untouchable English way. There was something about her – a cool inner confidence, a sense of total self-possession unusual in someone her age. James could just imagine her in bed, snapping off orders at some hapless boy, refusing to settle for anything other than the perfect orgasm. The thought made him grin.

Elizabeth smiled back. 'What nasty little thoughts are going through your head?'

He ignored her almost uncanny ability to read his mind, and instead asked the question that had been bugging him all afternoon. 'Actually, I was wondering when your half-sister is arriving. It's sometime today, isn't it?'

Elizabeth's expression didn't waver. 'That's right,' she said neutrally.

James was disappointed, but not surprised, that she wasn't giving anything away. Like everyone else, he had read about William Melville's lovechild in the tabloids. Elizabeth must have taken the news hard – he knew how much she looked up to her father. But so far she hadn't let on how she felt towards the new arrival. She was one cool customer.

Before James could probe any further, a shadow fell over the table. He looked up to see William Melville standing above them. He was in his weekend smart casual look: carefully pressed chinos, button-down shirt and loafers. But dressing down didn't make him seem any less imposing.

'Daddy!' his eldest daughter beamed up at him, her adoration clear.

'Elizabeth,' he responded, in his typically restrained manner. James noted that William didn't bother to acknowledge him – the hired help, he thought cynically. 'Caitlin will be arriving here shortly. I've told your mother to have Amber ready and in the drawing room by four. I expect you to be there, too.'

The smile vanished from Elizabeth's face. 'Of course,' she said, holding out her hand to study her perfectly manicured nails. 'But we've just finished a game, so I need to take a shower first.'

'Well, make it quick,' William ordered. 'Caitlin is part of our family now and I want everyone to be there to meet her.'

Elizabeth dropped her gaze. 'Yes, Daddy.'

It was said almost apologetically, but James wasn't fooled for a second. He saw the faintest flicker of emotion cross Elizabeth's face as she watched her father head back to the house. Irritation, he decided; anger even. It was there for a second and then gone. If he hadn't known her so well, he would have missed it.

'I'm afraid you'll have to excuse me now, James,' she said, as though nothing out of the ordinary was happening. 'But let's make sure to have that rematch next week.'

'Whenever you want,' he said, wishing he could stick around and see for himself what this new addition to the Melville household was like.

Elizabeth stood up and smoothed down her tennis skirt. 'Good. Now why don't I show you out?'

Upstairs, from her bedroom window, Isabelle Melville watched her eldest daughter follow her husband into the house. She knew why William had summoned Elizabeth in. And she also knew that she should be making her way downstairs to join them. But she needed a few more moments to compose herself.

She walked over to her dressing-table and peered into the vanity mirror, trying to decide what – if any – make-up she needed. At forty-two, she was still an attractive woman. With her fair colouring and delicate build, she was lucky enough to have the kind of English rose looks that didn't date. There were a few telltale creases around her eyes and mouth, but she had stopped trying to cover them up a long time ago, deciding they added character to what would otherwise be a beautiful but somewhat bland face.

After a few seconds' thought, she opted for the natural look – a light covering of tinted moisturiser and the barest lick of lip gloss. It went well with the cream linen suit that she had picked out for the occasion. She had felt it was appropriate, smart but not too formal – although who knew what the etiquette was for meeting your husband's illegitimate daughter.

Fortunately for Isabelle, it wasn't in her nature to be bitter. A lesser person might have objected to having another woman's child come to live in her home. But she had accepted the situation without question, her main concern being for the poor young girl who had just lost her mother. She supposed it helped that over the years her relationship with William had matured into one of friendship. Not that she had fooled herself into believing that it was a love match – well, not on William's part, at least.

Isabelle had known William all her life. Her father – one of Melville's main cotton suppliers – had been great friends with his mother Rosalind, and their families had frequently socialised. Growing up, Isabelle had always been fascinated by the enigmatic William Melville. To a girl of thirteen, the dashing twenty-one-year-old Cambridge undergraduate had been the stuff of adolescent crushes.

By the time she turned eighteen, Isabelle suspected she'd already been half in love with William. He'd had little time for her, though; she was far too frivolous for his tastes. While many of her friends had embraced the sixties' feminist spirit – striking out for careers as doctors, lawyers and businesswomen – Isabelle never harboured any such ambitions. Her greatest achievement in life was making her debut, at a time when that no longer meant very much. She was aware that William, who was even then a very serious young man, found her terribly silly.

That all changed the year she turned twenty-three. At the ball held to celebrate her birthday, for the first time ever William had sought her out, dancing with her and paying attention to her in a way she couldn't remember him doing before. That summer, he escorted her to the social events of the season – Henley and Ascot; Goodwood and Glyndebourne. At the time, Isabelle hadn't wanted to question his change of heart. It was easier to assume that she had simply matured in his eyes; that he was finally seeing her for who she really was. But looking back now, she could see that it was Rosalind, her formidable mother-in-law, who had encouraged their courtship. Isabelle guessed that, to Rosalind, she would have seemed like the perfect choice of wife for William: a pretty, docile little thing – and, most importantly, sole heir to her father's factories.

William's reasons for going along with his mother's wishes were less clear. He'd spent his twenties parading an ever-changing cast of long-limbed models through Tramp and Annabel's. None had held his interest. By that time, Isabelle suspected, he'd resigned himself to never falling in love, so making a good match with her probably seemed like the best alternative. Whatever his motivation, he'd finally proposed to Isabelle in the autumn of 1970, and she, happy to have William on any terms, had readily accepted.

In hindsight she realised that her unhappiness had started long before his affair. The loneliness had begun that first year of marriage. Stuck on her own at Aldringham during the week, she could still remember her mounting excitement as Friday evening approached, waiting for William to come home; only to be fetched to the phone at the last minute and told that there had been some emergency at the office. 'I've decided to stay in London for the weekend. You don't mind too much, do you, darling?'

'No, of course I don't,' she'd always said bravely, ignoring the crushing disappointment at the thought of spending yet another weekend alone.

Of course she'd had friends around – like-minded women whom she'd met through the endless charity committees that she sat on. But they'd always seemed to have so much else going on. 'Now I've had the children, I'm quite happy to see the back of Tim on Monday morning,' Penelope Whitton, one of her old school pals, had confided. And so it was that Elizabeth was born, a respectable eighteen months after William and Isabelle's marriage.

But for Isabelle, having a child didn't ease her loneliness. William's trips back to Aldringham remained infrequent. And Elizabeth didn't fill the void in her life as Isabelle had hoped. In fact, the little girl seemed rather more taken with her father than her mother. 'Daddy home soon?' she would ask hopefully once she was able to talk, her little face brightening on hearing that he would be. Sunday evenings became a battle to calm the child down as she cried for hours after William's departure. Once again, Isabelle was left with an overwhelming sense of inadequacy.

She remembered feeling hurt, but not surprised, when she learned of William's affair. It was Penelope who'd told her; Penny, who'd spotted William on the street the last time she'd been in London. 'Called out to him of course, darling, but he didn't seem to hear me,' she'd told Isabelle, before adding that he'd been far too engrossed in talking to the person he was with . . . the *girl* he was with. 'Didn't know her myself,' she'd said, watching Isabelle's reaction carefully. 'Frightfully young, though – and pretty, too . . .'

It had made sense, of course. Deep down, Isabelle had known there was someone. Over that long hot summer of 1974, her husband's trips home had been even less frequent than usual, and on the rare occasions he was around, he'd stopped sharing her bed. It was almost a relief to know there was a reason behind his growing distance from her.

But even once his affair had ended – which she'd intuitively sensed it had, a few months later – things hadn't improved. He might have been home more often, but everything she did seemed to irritate him. She wasn't sure if it was this in itself that had tipped her over the edge. She hadn't exactly been happy before that, but as 1975 wore on, she began to have *episodes*. They would start innocuously enough, with her breaking out in a cold sweat. But then she would begin to tremble, her chest would tighten, and she would find it hard to breathe.

On Penelope's suggestion, she went to see a discreet young doctor in Harley Street. He listened sympathetically to Isabelle's symptoms, gave her a thorough examination, and told her that it sounded as though she was having panic attacks.

'Everyone has stress in their lives, Mrs Melville, and we all cope with it in different ways. Some of us need more help than others.' He began to write out a prescription. 'A lot of women in your situation have found that this helps them through the difficult periods.'

He tore off the paper and held it out. It was for Valium. He advised her to take one pill every time she felt an attack coming on, and to come back within a month so he could check on her progress.

When she woke the following morning, and felt the familiar tightening of her chest, she reached into her bedside drawer for the bottle. One little white pill later, she was much calmer. To Isabelle, it was a miracle.

She hadn't told William about her visit to Dr Hayward or the tablets that she was taking. She knew that he wouldn't approve. But, even if he didn't know what she had been up to, he was delighted with the results. 'I'm so pleased you're feeling better, darling,' he said on Christmas Eve, as they watched Elizabeth hang up her stocking.

She smiled dreamily at him. The past few weeks, the drugs hadn't been working as well, and so Dr Hayward had suggested upping the dosage. She had been a little worried at first but now, seeing how pleased William was with her progress, she knew it had been the right thing to do.

Over the next few months she graduated from the white to the yellow pills, and then onto the blue. Maybe she was a touch drowsy and confused sometimes, her reflexes perhaps slower than normal, but at least the crippling anxiety was gone.

She remembered little of the day that Elizabeth, not yet five years old, had found her unconscious. As usual, the child had been picked up from school by her nanny, and as soon as they'd got home, she'd raced upstairs to her mummy's bedroom, eager to recount her latest adventures. Even at that age, she had known something was very wrong when she couldn't rouse her mother, and had gone to fetch the housekeeper. An ambulance was called, William summoned home. And, after several fraught conversations, Isabelle spent the next few weeks in a private clinic.

No one was especially surprised when she announced, six months later, that she was pregnant again. Some people have another baby to save their marriage; for Isabelle, it was to save herself.

If Elizabeth was a Daddy's girl, from the start Amber was very much her mother's daughter. While their first child had been called after William's paternal grandmother, this time Isabelle chose the name herself.

Rosalind was appalled. 'Amber? I've never heard such a ridiculous name. What about Anna or Amanda instead? Something more sensible.'

But, for once, William let his wife have her way. 'It's her choice, and I won't have you upsetting her,' he told his mother, with uncharacteristic firmness.

Amber was in every way the perfect daughter for Isabelle. She even looked like her mother – with her white ringlets and peaches and cream complexion – and was far more delicate than her robust older sister. Unlike Elizabeth, she wasn't strong and independent – from the start she *needed* Isabelle. When a boy pushed her over in the playground, she cried for her mummy; if it had been Elizabeth, she would have stood up and pushed him back harder. With Amber, Isabelle was able to do all the things that she'd never been able to do with Elizabeth: shopping, gossiping, discussing falling-outs with friends.

Since Amber's birth eleven years ago, the Melville household had settled into a state of equilibrium. Isabelle wasn't sure if she'd have described herself as *happy* exactly, but she'd found peace.

And then Katie O'Dwyer had come back into their lives.

Isabelle still couldn't find it within herself to be angry with William. She had seen how distraught he was when he'd received Katie's letter. She had witnessed his anguish at the years he had missed with her and their child. She knew the pain he'd felt at not being able to see Katie before she died. And she had comforted him as best she could. Isabelle knew she would never be the love of her husband's life, but she was his confidante, his best friend and the only person who ever saw his vulnerable side, and that was enough for her.

Now, in half an hour's time, his other daughter would arrive. Isabelle hadn't questioned William's decision to bring the girl to live with them, and she would do what she could to make the child feel at home. But, however understanding Isabelle might be, she couldn't help feeling apprehensive. Caitlin's presence would disrupt everything at Aldringham. And she wasn't sure it would be for the better. Especially not for Elizabeth, who so adored her father and was so disappointed by what he had done.

Elizabeth stood on the North Front, watching James's motorbike disappear down the driveway. It was only once he was out of sight that she finally allowed the smile to slip from her face.

God, how she was dreading this afternoon. It had been bad enough learning about her father's *indiscretion*. But having her half-sister come to live with them, a constant reminder of his weakness, made it all so much worse. It irritated Elizabeth no end, the amount of fuss he seemed to be making over this girl – mostly because her own life had always been a constant battle to win his attention. It was a fight Elizabeth had been losing since the day she was born.

While Caitlin had grown up in a house filled with love but not much money, Elizabeth's experience had been diametrically opposite. Materially, she had never wanted for anything. Her birth had been fit for royalty: a private maternity wing of St Mary's Hospital, London, with a world-renowned Professor of Obstetrics and Gynaecology on hand at the delivery. The one crucial element missing from the scene had been the proud father.

'I've been delayed in New York,' he'd told an exhausted, tearful Isabelle over the phone. He'd eventually arrived a day later than his firstborn. This careless neglect set the tone for the future relationship between father and daughter.

Elizabeth grew up with every privilege and advantage money could buy. A new horse every year; tennis lessons with an ex-seeded player; taught to ski by a one-time Olympic champion. But what she didn't have was the one thing she yearned for: her father's attention. To the young girl, he was an enigmatic figure, holding the kind of fascination that came from a lack of availability. She understood from an early age that he was an important man, busy running the family business.

'Daddy had to work,' Isabelle would say when he failed to make another prize-giving, carol concert or ballet recital. But, even though he never turned up, Elizabeth never stopped hoping he would.

To Elizabeth, her father's blatant disinterest had always seemed curious as well as hurtful. From an early age, she was aware that she was his firstborn child, which meant she would one day inherit the controlling stake in Melville. Surely that meant she should be important to him? Her grandmother and Uncle Piers, her father's younger brother, certainly doted on her – lavishing far more attention on her than on her younger sister Amber. What was she doing wrong that made her father so ambivalent towards her?

God, how she loved her father – and how she ached for his approval. She wanted to please him, to prove that she was worthy of taking over from him one day, so she reacted by becoming a compulsive over-achiever. To Elizabeth, second place meant failure. Even if she wasn't naturally gifted at something, she would work hard to become the best. Nothing ever got in the way of achieving what she wanted. When she was just ten years old, she fell off her horse while trying to jump a new fence. The groom rushed over to her.

'Are you OK, Miss Melville?'

But she was already on her feet, gathering the reins. 'Just help me back up.'

Only once she'd jumped the fence did she finally let him examine her arm. By then it was purple and swollen – broken in three places.

This determination translated into every aspect of Elizabeth's life – even her appearance. She used expensive make-up to emphasise her best features, and found out which clothes suited her figure. She had a standing six-weekly appointment at Hari's in Chelsea, to have her mouse-brown hair precision cut and highlighted golden blonde. Hours of sport gave her slender figure definition and muscle tone, as well as a year-round tan. It was a high maintenance look, but Elizabeth didn't resent it. Nothing worthwhile ever came easy, that was her motto.

It was this attitude which had made her the winner she was. She always came top of her class at Greycourt, had been unanimously elected Head Girl, and everyone expected her to get an offer from Cambridge that Christmas. Everything in her life had been perfect until her father, the one person she looked up to most, had let her down. Unfortunately, unlike most other aspects of her life, there was nothing she could do about his failings.

With a sigh of resignation, she walked back into the house and headed upstairs. She was halfway along the corridor when she spotted her bedroom door ajar. She frowned. She was certain that she remembered closing it on the way out – which left only one explanation. Amber, she thought to herself, quickening her pace.

Sure enough, inside she found her eleven-year-old sister

standing at her dressing-table, with Elizabeth's antique jewellery box open in front of her.

'Amber!' Hearing her sister's voice, Amber looked up guiltily. 'What did I tell you about asking permission before you start going through my stuff?'

'I was going to ask,' Amber said, with a touch of petulance, 'but I looked really hard for ages and couldn't find you. And I thought you wouldn't mind.'

Elizabeth had heard all the excuses before. She stalked over and slammed the lid closed. The box was hand-crafted ebony, dating back to the nineteenth century. Her grandmother, Rosalind, had given it to her, along with several pieces of jewellery, for her last birthday. The present had great sentimental as well as monetary value to Elizabeth, and she had forbidden her careless younger sister to play with any of the pieces. But that didn't seem to stop Amber.

'And you can give those back, too.' Elizabeth reached out for the rope of pearls around her little sister's neck.

But as she started to take the necklace off, Amber made a grab for it, as well. For a split second, they were both tugging in opposite directions, and then the string snapped. Pearls clattered across the polished wood floor.

'Oh, for God's sake!' Elizabeth cried. 'Look what's happened now.' She knelt down and started to gather up the pearls. 'Come on, the least you could do is help.'

'It wasn't my fault,' the younger girl insisted, a slight tremor in her voice.

'Of course it wasn't,' Elizabeth muttered. 'It never is.' She scowled up at her sister. 'Wait until I tell Granny about this.'

With that, Amber burst into tears.

'Girls? What's going on?'

Elizabeth and Amber both looked over to see their mother in the doorway. Before Elizabeth could explain, Amber fled from the room, howling loudly.

'Amber!' Isabelle called, but the girl didn't stop. After a moment, her bedroom door slammed shut.

Isabelle turned reproachful eyes on her elder daughter. 'What on earth's the matter with Amber?'

'She's being a drama queen. As usual.' Elizabeth explained about the broken necklace.

'Well, it sounds to me as if it was an accident,' Isabelle said tentatively, once she'd finished.

Elizabeth made no effort to disguise her outrage. 'An accident! You know full well that she shouldn't have been going through my stuff.'

Elizabeth wondered why she bothered. It was just like her mother to turn a blind eye to anything Amber did wrong. Three nannies had told Isabelle that she was far too lenient on her spoiled younger daughter. 'You're storing up a lot of problems for later on,' the last one had warned. 'She can't be allowed to feel that acting out is an acceptable way to get your attention.' Elizabeth had wholeheartedly agreed – but, yet again, Isabelle had failed to listen, allowing Amber to wear make-up and clothes that were far too old for her, no matter what William said.

Now Isabelle lowered her voice. 'Please, Elizabeth. You know this . . . well, none of this has been easy on her.'

'It hasn't exactly been easy on any of us, has it, Mummy?'

Elizabeth waited for an answer. When none was forthcoming, she sighed. That was the problem with her mother – she was weak. She always took the path of least resistance. Like having this Caitlin O'Dwyer come to live with them. Elizabeth didn't understand why she couldn't have just said no to William – told him that it was unfair on her and his two legitimate children. But, as usual, she let herself be walked all over. What kind of woman stayed with someone who had humiliated her like that?

The girl gave an impatient shrug. 'Anyway, I should have a shower.'

'Yes, of course.' Isabelle glanced at her watch. 'You'd better get ready quickly. Caitlin—'

'—will be here soon,' Elizabeth cut in. 'Yes. I know.'

Isabelle looked pained at the scornful tone in her child's voice.

'I'll leave you to it, then,' she said quietly.

Elizabeth was about to snap off a reply, when a sound from outside – car tyres creeping up the gravel driveway – stopped her. Instinctively, both mother and daughter turned towards the window. Damn, Elizabeth thought. There would be no time to shower or change now. *She* was here.

Chapter 3

'Miss?' The chauffeur glanced in the rearview mirror. The girl was lost in a daydream, staring blankly out of the tinted car window as she had for the past three hours, during the long drive west from London to Somerset. Of course now they were off the motorway, the scenery had improved. But even as the Bentley sped past lush green fields dotted with fat sheep and grazing cows, Perkins had a feeling that the view was the last thing on his charge's mind. Hunched up by the door, chin buried in her hand, she looked very young and very sad, her grey mood at odds with the bright summer's day outside. He almost felt bad disturbing her.

'Miss?' he said again, more loudly this time.

She started at his voice, automatically turning dull eyes towards him.

'Hope I'm not bothering you, Miss Caitlin,' he said gently. 'But I thought you'd want to know that we'll be arriving at Aldringham soon.'

'Thank you,' she said, polite but listless, then resumed look-ing out of the window before he could try to engage her in any further conversation. She hoped he didn't think she was rude, but she couldn't care less about reaching the Melvilles' estate. She didn't care about any of it. How could she, when the only reason she was here in the first place was because of what had happened to her mam? She felt her eyes filling with tears and impatiently brushed them away. She'd promised herself earlier that she wouldn't cry again. Not until she was alone, at any rate.

It was six weeks since her mother's funeral. Everyone had told her that it would get easier after that. What did they know? The previous evening, she'd gone to pack up the cottage. Under William's instructions, it was to be sold as soon as possible. Going through her mam's belongings had stirred up so many memories. When she hadn't been able to face it any longer, Nuala had offered to take over. 'I'll know what she'd have wanted you to keep,' the older woman had said kindly.

However, if Caitlin had thought that was bad, it couldn't compare to today: to leaving Valleymount. Róisín hadn't understood why her friend wasn't more excited about getting out of their dull hometown and starting on a glamorous new life with a wealthy family. But for Caitlin, saying goodbye to all the places and people she knew was like losing the last connection to her mother. The flight – her first; the seat in business class; being met at Heathrow by the Melvilles' driver with his sleek black car . . . All those luxuries meant nothing given the circumstances. No wonder she didn't feel like making small talk.

They drove on in silence for a while longer, through market towns and picture postcard villages and onto a series of increasingly winding lanes bordered by pretty stone cottages, until Perkins finally pointed into the distance.

'That's where we're 'eaded.'

Out of courtesy rather than any real interest, Caitlin leaned forward to get a glimpse of her new home. But then, as it came into view, she let out an involuntary gasp. To Caitlin, Aldringham looked like a Roman palace. It was a more acccurate description than she realised. In fact, it was a Palladian mansion, typical of the lavish countryside estates built during the eighteenth century, when the newly excavated ruins at Pompeii fostered a neo-classical revival in England. Perkins saw her reaction and grinned. 'Impressive, ain't it?'

Imposing, more like. Set on the crest of a hillside, it seemed to dominate the surroundings for miles. Late afternoon sunshine glinted off the white Portland stone and marble façade, blinding Caitlin for a moment. She blinked, trying to focus her vision. She couldn't decide if she liked the building or not. On the one hand, it was undeniably beautiful. The vertical lines and symmetry of the architecture gave the house a feeling of grace and elegance. But there was also something cold about the strict geometric design, as though nothing out of the ordinary would be tolerated.

Five minutes later, Perkins turned onto a private road that led up to the entrance to Aldringham. Electronic gates swung soundlessly open and the Bentley pulled into the sweeping carriage driveway. Great cedars lined the pathway. Through their branches, Caitlin caught a brief glimpse of the grounds: fifty acres of untamed parkland rising to meet formal, manicured gardens leading up to the back of the house. A moment later, the landscape passed out of sight again and the car finally came to a stop.

Up until that point, Caitlin hadn't given much thought to what her new situation would be like; she'd been too preoccupied with her grief. But suddenly, for the first time, she felt a shiver of trepidation run through her. However bad everything had been over the past few months, at least then she had been surrounded by friends, people like Nuala who cared. Now, she was going to live in a house full of strangers, who probably didn't even want her there.

William stood on the North Front waiting to greet her. He looked just as intimidating as she remembered. Growing up, whenever she'd imagined what her father would be like, she'd always thought of someone like Róisín's dad – a simple, kind man, someone familiar. William Melville was nothing like that. He was distant and aloof, with his cut-glass accent and stiff manner. Caitlin still found it hard to believe they were related.

She stood awkwardly as he bent to kiss her on each cheek. 'Welcome to Aldringham, Caitlin.' He turned to a well-kept woman who hovered a little way behind him. In an expensive-looking cream suit, her fair hair tied neatly back in a French pleat, she looked terribly elegant. 'This is my wife, Isabelle.'

Caitlin felt a fresh set of nerves ripple through her. But, while she had been expecting a hostile greeting, Isabelle surprised her. Without any prompting, she walked forward and embraced Caitlin.

'We're so pleased to have you here, my dear.' Her tone was soft and surprisingly sincere.

'Good,' William said, clearly pleased by the display. 'Let's go inside. My daughters are waiting to meet you.'

The hallway was every bit as magnificent as Caitlin had imagined, with a flagstone floor, oak panelled walls and a grand staircase that disappeared up into the rest of the house. She had no time to take it in, though, as William whisked her through a labyrinth of long, dark corridors. She tried to memorise her way back to the main hall, but eventually gave up.

Caitlin couldn't help wondering what Elizabeth and Amber would be like. Growing up, she'd always wanted brothers and sisters, but she wasn't sure she would have anything in common with girls who had been brought up in a place like this. As William pushed open the heavy mahogany doors to the drawing room, Caitlin plastered on a friendly smile and hoped she was about to be proved wrong. She wasn't. Two resentful faces greeted her.

'This is Elizabeth.' William indicated a haughty blonde, sitting straight-backed on the velvet chaise longue.

Caitlin felt at once intimidated and envious. She couldn't believe Elizabeth was only seventeen, just two years older than her. She looked so *sophisticated*. Even in her tennis outfit, following a gruelling afternoon on the court, she looked immaculate, not a hair out of place. Caitlin suddenly felt ashamed of her own slightly shabby appearance, her hand instinctively reaching up to smooth down her unruly thick locks.

'Hi, Elizabeth.' She gave a tentative smile. 'It's nice to meet you.'

Elizabeth smiled coolly up at her. 'So nice to meet you, too.' There was the faintest hint of sarcasm in the clipped upper-class tone.

Caitlin's smile wavered. Elizabeth made no move to say anything else. She continued to stare up from her seat, flicking her long, fair hair back in a dismissive gesture.

Amber was another matter altogether. While Elizabeth seemed hostile, Amber clearly had no interest in the new arrival. As soon as she'd said hello, she asked to be excused.

Isabelle shot an apologetic look at Caitlin. 'No, of course you can't go yet,' she said, clearly embarrassed. 'Caitlin's only just got here.'

Amber scowled in answer. Caitlin couldn't believe it. Mam would never have allowed her to be so rude at that age. But then Amber was like no eleven-year-old she'd ever met. She was a beautiful little girl, her porcelain skin and pretty white-blonde ringlets making her seem almost cherubic. But her natural beauty had been spoiled by the way she'd been done up – to look like an adult. Her off-the-shoulder sundress looked out of place on her prepubescent body, as did the hot-pink lipstick and blue eye shadow. The whole effect was grotesque and unsettling.

There was a long silence. Caitlin studied the floor. William looked at all the three girls in turn, frowning as though he couldn't quite understand why they weren't bonding immediately. It was Isabelle who jumped in to cover the awkwardness.

'Why don't I pour everyone some tea? Caitlin, you must be hungry after your journey. Can I get the cook to fix you a snack?'

Caitlin, who had lost her appetite during the uncomfortable

introductions, said she really wasn't hungry, but did accept a cup of tea in a ridiculously fragile cup. As she sipped it carefully, terrified she might spill something on the expensive-looking rug, she wondered if this was going to get any easier.

It didn't. Caitlin couldn't help feeling relieved when, half an hour later, William finally suggested she go to her room to unpack.

'That will give you a chance to settle in before dinner,' he said. His gaze landed on Elizabeth, who was already on her feet. 'Why don't you show your sister to her room? She's going to be in the Rose Suite. And perhaps you could give her a quick tour of the estate as well, so she can get her bearings.'

For a horrible moment, Caitlin thought that Elizabeth was going to object – but a look from William silenced her.

'Fine.' Sharp green eyes flicked onto Caitlin. 'Well? Are you coming?'

Caitlin had to run to keep up with Elizabeth, as the older girl hurried her along another maze of corridors and then up two flights of stairs. These were a different set to the sweeping staircase in the hallway. Steep and covered in a dark-blue carpet – 'the staff staircase,' Elizabeth explained briefly. They were only using it because it was the quickest way to the East Wing, where Caitlin's room was situated. Other than that, she didn't venture any small talk along the way.

They finally reached a cream door. Elizabeth stopped outside and handed Caitlin the key. It was almost like being in a hotel.

'I'm sure you're exhausted, so why don't we skip the tour?' She didn't give Caitlin a chance to reply. 'Dinner's at seven-thirty. Oh, and whatever you do, don't be late. It's the one thing that pisses Daddy off.'

She turned away, with a toss of glorious honey hair, leaving Caitlin standing alone in the hallway.

As Caitlin watched her go, tears welled in her eyes. She hadn't thought she could feel any worse than she had these past few months. But being treated like that, with such utter disdain, made it all so much worse. In that moment, she'd never wanted her mother more.

Shoulders hunched, she unlocked the door to her new room. It was beautiful, of course – huge and luxurious. But Caitlin had no interest in the antique furniture or the breathtaking view across the gardens and parklands. Instead, she went to lie down on the four-poster bed, curled up into a ball, and cried.

'She's *so* weird.'

'Amber!' Elizabeth's reproach was only half-hearted.

'But she *is* weird,' Amber insisted. 'I mean, did you see that cardigan she was wearing? And those *jeans*. They were so shapeless. Definitely not Levis.' She wrinkled her nose. 'God, I wouldn't be caught dead looking like that.'

Despite herself, Elizabeth laughed. She didn't usually like to gossip, considering it beneath her. But even she couldn't resist discussing the new arrival. That was why she'd allowed Amber to come into her room despite the earlier incident with the necklace.

'I know what you mean,' Elizabeth mused. 'She could do with a haircut, too.'

Long hair was all very well if you looked after it. But that tangle of black curls wasn't doing Caitlin any favours. Not that she was unattractive. In fact, she was quite pretty, Elizabeth admitted grudgingly, in that very wild, Celtic way. It was just hard to tell when she did so little with herself.

Amber leaned across the bed. 'You know,' she stage-whispered, 'I think she might be a bit slow, too.'

Elizabeth laughed again. 'Why on earth do you say that?'

'Because she was so quiet. She hardly said a word.'

Elizabeth considered this for a moment. 'She's probably just still upset about her mother.' As she vocalised the thought, Elizabeth felt a sudden pang of guilt about the way she'd treated Caitlin so far. But she quickly quashed it. 'Not that it's got anything to do with us,' she added hastily.

Amber nodded solemnly. 'That's right,' she parroted. 'It's got *nothing* to do with us.'

Looking back later, Caitlin wasn't sure how she got through that first month at Aldringham.

William disappeared the morning after she arrived. 'He had to return to London,' Isabelle informed her apologetically over breakfast. 'Some emergency at the office. But I'm sure he'll be back when he can.'

The last part was said unconvincingly. So much for wanting to get to know me, Caitlin thought, wondering why on earth he'd been so insistent about her coming to live with them. Maybe if he wasn't that bothered about her being here, then he might let her go back home to Valleymount. But even as she let the hope enter her head, she somehow knew it was too much to wish for. For whatever reason, William wanted her here. She knew if Nuala could have changed his mind, she would have.

Later that morning, Elizabeth came to her room. She was clearly under instructions from her father to entertain their guest, and just as clearly not happy about the situation. 'So what do you want to do today?'

Caitlin said, quite honestly, that she didn't mind.

Elizabeth sighed. It obviously wasn't the answer she'd been after. 'Well, do you ride?' she asked impatiently.

Caitlin shook her head.

'Play tennis?'

Again, Caitlin shook her head.

'*Great*,' Elizabeth muttered under her breath. 'Fine. Well, I guess I'll have to teach you, then.'

Predictably, it was a disaster. After an hour of Elizabeth's ill-tempered coaching, a red-faced and breathless Caitlin suggested going in. Elizabeth readily agreed. After that, Caitlin didn't ask for any more lessons, and Elizabeth didn't offer. They were just so different. Caitlin frankly found Elizabeth's effortless confidence intimidating.

Surprisingly, it was Isabelle who was most kind to her.

'Do you want to call that lady you were staying with?' she offered a few days after Caitlin arrived. 'Your mother's friend – what was her name?'

'Nuala. Aunty Nuala.'

'Yes, of course. Nuala. Well, you know you can call Nuala whenever you want,' Isabelle said kindly. 'You don't need to ask permission. There's a phone in your room, so you can have some privacy.'

Caitlin decided to wait until the evening, when the family were more likely to be home. For the first time since she'd arrived at Aldringham, there was something to look forward to.

When she heard Nuala's voice, she felt herself start to choke up.

'Ah, it's so good to speak to you, pet,' her mother's friend said warmly.

'You, too,' Caitlin sniffed. She didn't trust herself to say anything else in case she started crying. She felt overwhelmed and embarrassed at the intensity of her emotions – after all, she hadn't even been away a week.

'Róisín's here,' Nuala said, seeming to sense that she was just about to break. 'Why don't I put her on?'

Talking to her friend was easier. 'What's the house like?' she wanted to know. 'Is it huge? Does it have a pool? When can I come to stay?'

'The house is nice,' Caitlin said vaguely, not wanting to talk about it. 'Tell me what's been going on with you instead.'

Róisín needed no further encouragement. 'Ah, everything's much the same here. Mary's got herself a bloke, and her mam's in bits about it . . .' She chattered on happily for the next half an hour, until she was called away for her tea.

'Ring me again soon!' she said breezily.

Caitlin slowly replaced the receiver. The conversation had made her feel worse rather than better. It was horrible, knowing that all her friends were back in Valleymount and that she couldn't be there with them.

To Caitlin's relief, Isabelle tactfully avoided asking her about the call. She could be quite sensitive, Caitlin realised during those first few weeks. In fact, she wondered sometimes if Isabelle was as unhappy as she was at Aldringham. With William away so much, his wife filled her days lunching with friends or with charity work. She also spent a great deal of time shopping with Amber in London. More than once she invited Caitlin along. 'We'd love you to come with us,' she said, ignoring the face that Amber pulled. 'And you must need a few new things before school starts.'

'That's an understatement,' Amber muttered under her breath.

But so far, despite Isabelle's repeated invitations, Caitlin hadn't felt like going with them. Even though she was aware that her clothes were far cheaper and less trendy than those of the other two girls, it would seem somehow disloyal to replace her old things. Her mother had worked so hard to pay for them – it would be like a betrayal.

Apart from that, the family had pretty much left Caitlin to her own devices. It was still the summer holidays, and so she had endless hours to explore the house and grounds, and to indulge in her favourite pastimes of reading and sketching.

But she wasn't happy. She missed her mother and Valleymount every day. Aldringham was beautiful but cold, like its inhabitants. Her room might have a walk-in wardrobe, separate sitting room and a luxurious marble bathroom, but every night Caitlin climbed into the four-poster bed, with its Frette bedlinen and goosefeather pillows, and then lay awake, longing for the simplicity of her old life and her real home.

She wondered when – or if – that feeling would ever go away.

Chapter 4

Caitlin's difficulties settling in hadn't gone unnoticed. William was aware of the problem and keen to resolve it. But right now, seated in his office at Melville's London headquarters, he was concentrating on the business at hand: the quarterly performance figures.

Sitting with him were the two people he trusted most in the world: his mother, Rosalind, and brother, Piers. Forty per cent of the company might be listed on the London Stock Exchange, but Melville still operated very much as a family business. The main decisions were taken here, in William's office, away from the boardroom – and the board, too.

Piers adjusted his glasses and began. 'Obviously we're still waiting for the final figures to come through. But the first cut of numbers looks promising.'

At thirty-nine, Piers Melville was a decade younger than William, but his slow, staid manner made him seem older. Like William, he was well-dressed and well-spoken, a true English gentleman, but that was where the similarity ended. While William was a strong, dark, imposing figure, with a sharp mind and commanding presence, Piers's fair colouring and fine features gave him an air of fragility, especially when combined with his slightly plodding ways and distinct lack of charisma. But despite these failings – or perhaps because of them – Piers was ideally suited to his position as William's right-hand man. His lack of personal ambition and unconditional loyalty to Melville meant he had never once questioned the fact that it was William, not he, who had been chosen to head up the family business.

'Like-for-like sales are up five per cent,' he went on now. 'And there's been an improvement of fifty basis points in the gross margin.'

William listened carefully as his brother ran through the numbers. Piers's youthful shyness had grown into a thoughtfulness and attention to detail that made him the perfect Finance Director.

'And where exactly is the growth coming from?' William asked. It was a question he could guess the answer to, but he wanted to hear it anyway.

'Mainly Melville Essentials.'

William flicked a pointed look over at his mother, Rosalind. The matriarch of the Melville family, she was a formidable lady. In her day, she had been singlehandedly responsible for taking the moderately successful English company and growing it into an internationally-renowned name. Now, at seventy, she looked a decade younger and was as sharp as anyone half her age.

She inclined her head, acknowledging his point.

'I know, William.' She sounded amused. 'Yet again you've proved that Melville Essentials was an excellent idea.'

It was ridiculous, William knew, to want her to acknowledge that he was in the right. At fifty, he should be past such childish behaviour. But taking over from Rosalind hadn't been easy for William. She might have been a Melville by marriage rather than blood, but she had more claim to this company than anyone else. For three decades, Rosalind had run Melville with indisputable success. She was always going to be a hard act to follow.

When William had finally taken over from her in 1972, he had been determined to make his own mark on the company. He was over thirty and felt like he had no time to spare. By then, Melville had fourteen stores in major cities throughout the world. With the oil crisis and subsequent recession in the US and Europe, William had decided against further store openings. Global expansion had been his mother's innovation – he needed a new strategy.

So he'd taken stock of Melville's strengths and weaknesses. The ready-to-wear line had never performed brilliantly; the bulk of sales had always been from accessories – handbags and shoes. With this and the poor world economy in mind, William had decided to produce a range of products at a lower price point than the traditional handcrafted leather goods. Still bearing the Melville monogram, the new line of cosmetic cases, purses and bags would be manufactured using lower-cost materials, and sold in department stores and perfumeries. The idea was to bring Melville products to a new set of consumers – those who would be too intimidated to enter a designer store.

Rosalind had opposed the idea, arguing that a cheaper line had no place in a luxury goods firm, but William had forced the change through – and his strategy had worked. Melville Essentials was such a success that it began to rival the traditional goods. When Melville's sales hit £300 million in the late eighties, Rosalind had finally admitted she had been wrong. It was a great moment for William. In less than twenty years, he had tripled sales and quadrupled profits. As Forbes had observed last year: *William Melville is the linchpin of the world's foremost fashion dynasty.* He still kept a copy of that article in the top drawer of his desk.

'Thank you for that, Piers,' William said ten minutes later, when his brother had finished running through the rest of the financial report. 'Can I take it home to read this weekend?'

'Of course.' Piers handed over his bound copy. William put the report in his briefcase and snapped the lock closed. He stood up and reached for his jacket.

Rosalind placed a bony hand on his arm. 'Darling, do you

really have to rush off now? I hoped we could all go for an early supper.'

'Sorry, but I want to get back to Aldringham, to check on Caitlin.'

Keen now to get away, William turned and headed for the door. His abrupt departure meant he missed the troubled look that passed between his mother and brother as he left.

Outside, Perkins was waiting for him in the Bentley. It was Friday evening and William didn't relish the task ahead of him. When he had called Isabelle last night to get an update on Caitlin's progress, he hadn't been happy with what she'd told him. It seemed Caitlin was still spending most of her time alone.

He'd always known it wouldn't be easy for her, adjusting to this new life, but he wanted to help her fit in as much as possible. One of his greatest regrets was how things had ended with Katie. All he could do now was make sure her child – *their* child, he corrected himself quickly – had every possible chance at a happy life. He was aware that he'd always been a somewhat distant father to Elizabeth and Amber, unconsciously taking out his frustrations over his unhappy marriage on them. With Caitlin, he didn't want to make that same mistake. He wanted to get to know her and to look out for her in her new life with them at Aldringham. It was the least he could do for Katie.

Later that evening, Rosalind Melville sat alone in the dignified quiet of her Mayfair flat. Situated within a luxury portered block on Grosvenor Street, it was one of the most prestigious addresses in London but tonight she took no comfort in her surroundings.

On the writing table in front of her stood a half-finished tumbler of Hennessy Ellipse, her favourite tipple. Next to it were the documents she had asked her solicitor to prepare.

'Are you quite sure about this?' Gus Fellows, her friend and legal adviser for over thirty years, had asked when he'd dropped the papers over that evening. Sure? She took a large swig of cognac. Of course she wasn't sure. But unfortunately she had no choice. Not when she cared so much about Melville, the company she had nurtured and grown.

The story of Melville had always fascinated her. It had begun in 1860, with the birth of John Miller into a family of Northampton shoemakers. Back then, shoemaking was little more than a cottage industry, but John wanted more. Smart and ambitious, he knew that the only way to make serious money was to cut out the middlemen. So he banded together with other tradesmen and started supplying direct to retail outlets in London. Any additional profits, he reinvested in the business, expanding operations without sacrificing quality.

Like all good businessmen, John was attuned to his target customers: the well-heeled members of Victorian high society who were prepared to pay through the nose for his high-quality, handmade leather shoes. Deciding that his own name didn't sound sufficiently grand, he officially changed it to Melville in 1900. Melville became one of the first brand names to be registered in 1910. John also opened his first shop that year, in the illustrious location of Old Bond Street. Above the front door he hung a brass plate, inscribed with the words *Meliora Conor*. Latin for *I Strive for the Best*. It was to become the company's motto.

A lifetime of smoking finally took its toll when John died of lung cancer in 1925. It was his son, Oliver, who took over from him. A serious, considered man, he was the right person to steer the company through the tough years following the Crash of '29, and Melville continued to prosper during the thirties.

Rosalind – or Rosie Flint, as she was known then – came to work at Melville in 1938, on the eve of the Second World War. Rosie was from a working-class family: her father was a docker, her mother a cleaner. At seventeen, she went for an interview to work as a sales assistant at Melville. The Manager was reluctant to employ her at first — she seemed far too common for the illustrious store. But once she started talking he changed his mind.

'I'm used to hard work, and I'm never sick,' she told him, sensing his doubts. Then she looked him straight in the eye and said with total honesty, 'Look, I need this job and I'm not about to mess you around.'

He hired her on the spot. Anyone who could argue her corner like that would be a natural saleswoman. And the gentlemen customers would no doubt appreciate her looks.

But Rosie was smart and ambitious, and had no intention of remaining a shop girl for the rest of her life. Working at Melville was her opportunity and she intended to make the most of it. It didn't take long for her to lose the Cockney accent. Nor did it take long for her to capture the attention of Edward Melville, the eldest son and heir apparent to the business.

Rosie had heard all about Edward. Handsome, charming and good-natured, he was a notorious playboy, known for taking girls out, showing them a good time and then dumping them quickly afterwards. Rosie wanted more from him than that. When he asked her out, she politely declined his invitation.

'I'm engaged,' she lied.

Unused to rejection, Edward was intrigued. By the time Rosie finally despatched with the imaginary fiancé and agreed to go out with him, he was already falling in love with her.

That was the summer of 1939. There were already murmurs of unrest throughout Europe. When Chamberlain finally declared war on Germany in September, Edward was one of the first to sign up for the RAF. All that time, Rosie had been carefully withholding her favours from him. That night, in the alley at the back of the dance hall, their kisses were hot and urgent. Rosalind pulled away first.

Breathless, she said, 'I wish I could be with you . . . properly.'

'There's a guesthouse nearby,' Edward eagerly suggested.

She looked up at him with wide, innocent eyes. 'But it's a sin.'

Swept up in the romance and bravado of the times, Edward proposed on the spot. They married on special licence that weekend, with two strangers for witnesses. By the time his family found out, there was nothing they could do about it.

'How could you be so stupid?' his father, Oliver, roared. 'She's nothing but a common tart!'

'She's my wife, sir,' Edward replied calmly. 'And you will have to accept her.'

When Edward went off to war the following week, Rosie took up residence in the Melvilles' Belgravia house. It wasn't as pleasant as she'd imagined. Oliver refused to acknowledge her. Mealtimes were silent. More than once she considered moving back to her parents' little house in the East End. But she had worked too hard to give up that easily. Instead, she looked for a way to ingratiate herself with Oliver. The war gave her the opportunity she'd been looking for. With Oliver's three sons and many of the staff signing up, she could sense her father-in-law was struggling to cope at Melville. Rosie knew the store well and reckoned she could help. So she turned up at the Head Office one day, found herself a desk, and set to work.

Gradually, she began to earn Oliver's respect. When the Blitz began, his wife and other daughters-in-law retreated to Aldringham.

'I suppose you'll be off down there, too, Rosie,' Oliver said dismissively.

'No. I'm staying put in London.' She paused. 'And in future, please call me Rosalind.' After all, it felt more appropriate to her new status.

When Edward came home on furlough for Christmas 1941, he was pleased to see his father and wife getting along. A month after he went back, Rosalind was delighted to find that she was pregnant.

Her happiness was shortlived. In late August, a telegram arrived. Edward's plane had been shot down over France. The shock of the news, combined with the subsequent air raid, sent Rosalind into premature labour, in the very public surroundings of London Bridge Underground. When she finally gave birth to a healthy baby boy, she felt a rush of euphoria that overrode all thoughts of her missing husband. She named the boy William: a grand, respectable name, fit for kings. Firstborn of the firstborn; heir to the Melville fortune. Her position was secure.

Word eventually reached them that Edward wasn't dead. He was a prisoner-of-war in Kreuzburg, an *Oflag*, or officer camp, in Poland. He finally returned home in early 1946. Rosalind and Oliver, along with young William, went to meet him off the boat. They had heard he wasn't injured – but the Army only meant physically. When he stepped onto the dockside, Rosalind rushed forward to embrace him. He stood limply as she put her arms around him. It was the first time he'd met his three-year-old son, but he stared blankly at William and didn't once ask to hold him.

It was a precarious time for Rosalind. Edward's two brothers circled like sharks.

'He's useless now,' they told their father. 'You can't leave the business to him.'

But Rosalind was determined that Melville *should* pass to William. So she left her son with the nanny and accompanied Edward into the office every day, where she acted as the puppet-master behind him.

'See? Edward's perfectly fine,' Oliver would say to his other two sons, as Rosalind presented yet another idea as her husband's. 'Quit grumbling and bring me innovations like this, and I might consider leaving you the business. But otherwise . . .'

Knowing when they had been outsmarted, the two brothers did what Rosalind had hoped they would and left, vowing not to speak to their father until he saw sense. Oliver's wife tried hard to broker a reconciliation between her sons and her husband, but when she died in her sleep the following year, it seemed the rift would never be healed.

Meanwhile, Melville was thriving. The optimistic post-war years were a good time to be in the fashion business. In Paris, Christian Dior's haute couture designs were ushering in a new era in fashion. Rosalind looked around for opportunities to benefit the company. The factory next door to Melville's had been making parachutes during the war: Rosalind decided to buy it up and use it to produce silk scarves and coats to the same high standards as Melville shoes. She also started using the leather factory to make bags and suitcases.

In 1951, Rosalind became pregnant again. Rumours flew around. Everyone suspected Edward hadn't visited her bedroom since his return – but there was no proof. She finally gave birth early the following year. This time, the labour was long and painful. While William had come out fighting, her second son was a weak little thing, jaundiced and scrawny. She called him Piers. Ten days after the birth, she was back at work.

Five years later, poor, tragic Edward died. The obituary in *The Times* reported the Coroner's verdict of death by misadventure. The Melvilles' connections had ensured that no one got wind of the fact that Edward had used his service revolver to blow his brains out. Rosalind didn't cry. It was hard to shed a tear for someone who had been effectively dead for over a decade.

The funeral was held on an ice-cold day in February. Against his doctor's advice, an already frail Oliver insisted on attending the burial of his favourite son. Two days later he came down with pneumonia.

Oliver knew he was dying long before the end. Lying on the

Porthault sheets of his canopied bed at Aldringham, coughing and hawking through his final days, his thoughts turned to his two remaining sons. He hadn't seen them for years. Now, sensing his time was coming to an end, he wanted to make amends. He asked Rosalind to contact them. She assured him that she would.

'Are they coming?' he asked hopefully every day.

'Tomorrow,' she told him, as she sponged his brow. 'Tomorrow they'll be here.'

He clung on for a week waiting for them, lonely and frightened, confused about why no one apart from Rosalind had visited him. On the eighth day, he passed away. Only then did Rosalind get in touch with his sons. After all, she couldn't have risked him relenting and changing his will to their favour.

Now, finally, she had full control of Melville.

But that alone wasn't enough for Rosalind. She had big plans for the company. She had no intention of simply preserving the business for William – she wanted to grow it.

Up until then, Rosalind had stayed away from clothing, knowing Melville had no hope of rivalling the Parisian fashion houses. But the sixties brought radicalism and sexual liberation – and, with them, a fashion revolution. Expensive, staid haute couture fell out of favour. Cheaper, cutting-edge ready-to-wear became all the rage, reflecting the fun and excitement of the streets. Mary Quant and Ossie Clark; the King's Road and Carnaby Street . . . subversive, Swinging Sixties London had ousted Paris as the fashion capital.

For Rosalind, it was the perfect opportunity to launch Melville Apparel. Although she never managed to attract the hip young talent to make it truly cool, the buzz around the rest of the Melville goods – particularly its exquisite handbags and shoes – meant demand was still there. Shirts, dresses and trousers emblazoned with the Melville logo were splashed across *Vogue* and *Vanity Fair*. The world had an insatiable appetite for Melville.

In a bid to capitalise on this popularity, Rosalind opened stores across Europe and North America. To finance these expansion plans, it was suggested that she sell part of the company on the London Stock Exchange. At first she resisted, not wanting Melville to pass out of the family's control. But her advisers reassured her that she could just sell part of the company and retain the majority voting rights.

On 25 January 1964, 40 per cent of Melville was floated on the London Stock Exchange, with the remaining 60 per cent split between the family: 45 per cent for William, a nominal 10 per cent for Rosalind and the remaining 5 per cent to Piers. The money funded her dream of taking the company international. When the New York store opened on Fifth Avenue in 1965, Melville became a truly global brand.

By 1970 Melville was at the peak of its popularity. The name had become synonymous with glamour and status, an upmarket English brand sought after by movie stars and jetsetters. Rosalind could be proud. She had grown Melville into a much greater business than Oliver had left, and it was a legacy she felt proud to hand onto her elder son, William.

Of course, the rise of Melville hadn't been without its sacrifices for Rosalind. With her efforts concentrated on the business, raising her two sons had been left mainly to nannies and boarding schools. But she felt it was worth it to secure such a wonderful legacy for them both. And it hadn't seemed to do them any harm. They were still a close family; no sons thought more of their mother; and they had grown into bright, handsome boys. Perhaps Piers was a little shy and quiet, more a follower than a leader. But while he'd grown up in the shadow of his successful older brother, he never seemed to resent his lesser role. Rosalind had seen to that. 'William might be the figurehead of Melville, but you are the heart,' she'd told him time and again as he grew up. 'You must watch over your brother. It's up to you to help preserve the family name.'

So, as had always been Rosalind's wish, her sons had both come to work at Melville. When she'd decided to reduce her duties, William had taken over from her as Chief Executive, although she had continued to advise him, along with Piers. The business remained prosperous and successful.

In fact, everything had been perfect until a few months ago, when this O'Dwyer business had come to light.

Rosalind had made it clear from the beginning that she didn't like the idea of William bringing his illegitimate child to live with the family. 'It isn't fair to your wife – nor the girls,' she'd said at the time. 'If this woman Nuala is prepared to look after her, then why not let her? Provide for Caitlin, by all means, but don't disrupt her life. And don't disrupt your family.'

William had looked her straight in the eye and said, 'Caitlin *is* my family, Mother.'

It was all he'd said on the subject, but it had told Rosalind everything she needed to know. William intended to treat the girl as part of his family, whereas to Rosalind, she would always be an outsider, nothing to do with her. And the old lady didn't like the idea of an outsider getting her hands on any of the Melville business. Originally, she had planned to leave her entire 10 per cent share-holding to William, but Caitlin's arrival had changed that.

Now, she picked up the document in front of her. It wouldn't hurt to read it one last time. Just to be sure.

Sitting in her father's study after dinner that night, Elizabeth tried not to show her irritation as he quizzed her about how much time she'd spent with Caitlin since she'd arrived.

Too much, Elizabeth thought to herself. 'As much as I can,' she said out loud. Well, what did he expect? It wasn't as if they had anything in common. Caitlin couldn't ride or play tennis – all she was interested in was reading and drawing. Dull. She didn't *belong* here at Aldringham. She didn't even *look* like a Melville. With her raw Gaelic looks, she bore no resemblance to Elizabeth and Amber, who had inherited the fair hair and patrician features of their grandmother.

'I've tried my best,' Elizabeth insisted, 'but we've got different interests.'

William gave a curt nod. 'I know that, but you are the older one here and you need to make allowances. Caitlin's had a hard time, what with her mother dying and having to leave everything she knows behind.'

For a second, Elizabeth felt sorry for Caitlin again. But still, it wasn't as if that was *her* fault.

'I appreciate this hasn't been easy for you,' William continued, 'but that's no reason to take it out on Caitlin. She isn't as strong as you, Elizabeth. She needs your help and protection.'

The girl dropped her gaze, deciding the quickest way out of here was to act chastened. 'Of course, Daddy, I understand. I'll try harder.'

'Good.' He paused for a moment, and Elizabeth suddenly had a feeling that she had walked into a trap. Her fears were confirmed a moment later, when he said, 'Then you won't mind about next weekend.'

'What about next weekend?' she asked warily. Every year, the Melvilles spent the August Bank Holiday weekend at their villa in Lake Como. This time, Elizabeth had negotiated to stay behind at Aldringham and invite fifteen of her friends from school to stay.

'I've decided to leave Caitlin with you. She'll be starting at Greycourt this autumn, and I think it would be good for her to meet some of the other pupils. Give her a head start on the term.'

Elizabeth stared at him, horrified. Thankfully, years of practice kept her from revealing her true feelings.

'Of course,' she managed. 'That sounds like a good idea.'

'Excellent,' William said brusquely. 'I knew I could count on you.' He returned to the documents on his desk.

Realising she'd been dismissed, Elizabeth got up to leave. At the door, she turned back.

'Oh,' she said, almost as an afterthought. 'Did you ever get round to reading my Personal Statement?' It was the essay for her Cambridge application. She had given it to her father to look at the previous week.

'Not yet,' William told her, without even bothering to glance up from his work.

Typical, Elizabeth thought as she left the study. He had all the time in the world for the Irish stray, and none for her.

By the time Elizabeth got back to her room, she was already plotting how to keep Caitlin as far away as possible from her friends the following weekend.

Chapter 5

On Friday morning, William, Isabelle and Amber departed for Italy, leaving Elizabeth and Caitlin alone at Aldringham. By three that afternoon, the estate's extensive driveway was filled with Porsches, Mercedes and Ferraris, the vehicles of Elizabeth's classmates. Out on the sun deck, a dozen of Greycourt's most popular students lounged in the afternoon heat. The girls wore string bikinis and lay stretched out on sunbeds, watching the boys show off in the pool. All excellent sportsmen, the stars of the rugby and rowing teams, they were trying to outdo each other with double and triple back-flips.

'So are we going to meet your stepsister this weekend?' The question came from Morgan Woodhouse, Elizabeth's sometime friend and rival. The two girls were lying side by side, turning golden in the heat of the afternoon sun.

'Half-sister,' Elizabeth corrected automatically. 'And no, you won't be meeting her.'

Elizabeth had spoken to Caitlin that morning. She'd told the younger girl that she was welcome to come along, but that she'd probably be bored, listening to them catching up, although she could always join them for the water polo tournament later. By the time Elizabeth had left Caitlin's room, she was positive the younger girl had got the message: that she wasn't wanted.

'And what's the little country bumpkin like?' Morgan asked. Most people would have taken the hint that Elizabeth didn't want to dwell on the subject of Caitlin. Morgan didn't.

'Fairly dull.' Elizabeth flipped over onto her front to signal her lack of interest in the topic. 'Can someone put suncream on my back?' she asked, smoothly changing the subject.

'With pleasure.'

Unsurprisingly the offer came from Elliott Falconer. Elliott was Greycourt's top rugby player and widely considered to be the best-looking guy in school, something of which he was all too aware. He was also a notorious womaniser. Elizabeth didn't need to ask him twice. Within seconds, he was kneeling over her, massaging the cool suncream into her shoulders.

'Untie my bikini, will you?' she murmured. 'I don't want a tan line.'

He did as he was told and squeezed more lotion onto the small of her back. His hands moved upwards and outwards, grazing purposefully against her breasts, lingering a fraction longer than necessary. Elizabeth hoped Morgan didn't notice.

Elliott and Morgan had been a hot item until he'd dumped her at the beginning of the summer. Since the split he'd devoted himself to cracking onto any female with a pulse. Elizabeth was forever giving him the brush-off, but Elliott wouldn't take no for an answer. As if on cue, she felt the beginnings of his hard-on against her thigh. She guessed he was doing it deliberately. Subtlety wasn't his strong point.

'That's enough, thanks,' she said. When he didn't stop immediately, she elbowed him sharply in the ribs.

'Jesus!' he complained. 'That hurt.' But it had the desired effect. He sat back on his sunbed, grabbing a towel to throw over his lap. He didn't look remotely embarrassed. Pushing his Ray-Bans onto his head, he regarded her for a moment. 'You know what your problem is?' he said.

She bit. 'What?'

'You need a good, hard shag to loosen you up.'

'Fuck you, Elliott.'

The boy stretched lazily. 'Whenever you want, Elizabeth.'

She didn't bother to dignify him with an answer. Instead she closed her eyes, signalling the end of the conversation.

Lying on the sunbed next to Elizabeth, Morgan looked enviously at her friend. In a crowd of beautiful people, Elizabeth stood out as usual. The white Dolce & Gabbana bikini showed off her tanned, toned body to perfection, the halterneck top and tiny short bottoms giving her a wholesome, sporty look. Morgan had been sunbathing topless all afternoon, enjoying the blatant stares from the lads. But now, looking at Elizabeth, she suddenly felt cheap in her leopardskin thong and reached for a T-shirt to cover up.

However hard Morgan tried, Elizabeth always managed to out-do her. Like her friend, Morgan was tall, thin and blonde. But Elizabeth had something crucial that she couldn't replicate – effortless cool. She really couldn't give a damn what anyone thought of her. Morgan always tried a little too hard, which meant she was destined to be the number two in the group. She was as horribly aware of her status as she was determined to change it.

She wondered for a moment if there was any truth to what Elliott had said, about Elizabeth still being a virgin. There had been those rumours last year, about her and Mr Butler, the school's tennis coach. But she'd remained tight-lipped about the whole incident. Morgan knew there was no point asking. Elizabeth never confided in her. It was one of the many inequalities in their friendship. But, for all Elizabeth's sophistication, could this be the one area where Morgan trumped her?

Certainly Elizabeth had never shown much interest in having a boyfriend. Morgan was the opposite. She hated to be without a man. Wistfully, she looked across the deck to where Elliott was now chatting up Lucille Lewis, a pretty redhead. Deep down Morgan knew he was a bastard, but that was part of the appeal. Now Morgan watched as he picked up the platinum Zippo she'd given him for his birthday and leaned over to light Lucille's cigarette. The gesture was unnervingly intimate. Jealousy snaked through her. She knew it meant nothing – it was just the way he was with women, an instinctive flirt. But it still hurt. Elliott said something and Lucille laughed prettily, throwing her head back. Morgan's eyes narrowed.

She got up. The other thing about Elliott was that he had a short attention span. It was something that had irritated Morgan about him when they were in a relationship, but now she could use it to her advantage. Easing herself into the pool, she swam over to where he was sitting, precariously near the side. He had his back to her and didn't notice her swim up. She scooped up some water and threw it at him. It was a childish ploy to get his attention, but it worked.

'Hey!' he protested. Morgan had aimed well. He stopped talking to Lucille and turned to see who had attacked him. When he saw it was Morgan, he grinned, recognising the prank for what it was – a mating call.

He stood up, pulling off his T-shirt to reveal a perfect six-pack beneath. 'You're going to regret that, Morgan Woodhouse,' he said, his voice playfully threatening.

Behind him, Lucille scowled, irritated that she'd lost his attention so quickly. Elliott dived into the pool, his taut, tanned body slicing through the water. Morgan made a half-hearted attempt to swim away, yelping theatrically when he grabbed her around the waist.

'Elliott, don't!' she protested weakly, as he picked her up easily in his strong arms. 'Put me down! Now!'

But she didn't mean a word of it. She loved being the centre of his attention. She just wished he felt the same way about her.

Upstairs, Caitlin put her hands over her ears, trying to block out the screams of excitement coming from the pool below. It made no difference. She had reread the last passage of her book three times now and she still had no idea what it was about. An Agatha Christie mystery had seemed a good way to pass the long afternoon, but it was impossible to concentrate with all the shouting and laughing, the sounds of people having fun.

She had retreated to her room when Elizabeth's guests had started arriving. 'Don't feel obliged to come down,' her half-sister had said that morning. 'You're probably sick of meeting new people, and they'll all be in a different year to you anyway.' Caitlin had known what *that* meant. So Elizabeth didn't think she was good enough to introduce to her friends? Well, frankly, if they were anything like Elizabeth, she wouldn't want to hang out with them anyway. With that mutinous thought, Caitlin determinedly flipped the page of her book.

A moment later, another shriek of excitement pierced the air. Caitlin sighed. She folded down the corner of the page and put the novel down. Who was she kidding? She was dying to see what was going on downstairs.

Pushing back the duvet, she walked over to the windowseat. Below, were around a dozen of the most beautiful people she had ever seen. They held themselves with a confidence that up until now she'd thought only adults possessed. She might not be able to hear the details of their conversation, but she knew instinctively that the jokes were sophisticated, the banter witty.

Her eyes were drawn to a couple in the pool – it was hard not to be, given they were making the most noise. Even from up here, Caitlin could tell what was going on between them. The boy was chasing the girl through the water. She was yelping and squealing, splashing him, but clearly loving every minute of it. The girl was a thinner, blonder version of Elizabeth. She was very pretty, Caitlin thought with a touch of envy. She'd thought it was just her half-sister who looked and behaved in such a sophisticated manner. But now it turned out that there were others like her. What if all the girls at Greycourt were clones of Elizabeth?

But it was the boy who caught her attention. With dark, floppy hair and chiselled bone structure, he was as good-looking as a model or a pop star. He was also tall and obviously strong, lifting the blonde clean out of the water as though she weighed nothing, holding her firm as she squirmed against him and struggled to get free. Then he ducked her into the water, laughing as she surfaced and shouted a threat at him. Caitlin wished for a moment that she could be like the pretty blonde, confident and outgoing, completely at ease with someone as good-looking as him.

She didn't fit into this rich, privileged world. But nor was she the same person she'd been back in Ireland. She'd continued to phone Róisín regularly since coming here. At first they'd made plans for Caitlin to go back to visit, and Róisín had been excited about seeing Aldringham. But recently Caitlin had got the feeling Róisín was a little jealous. She'd tried to explain that she hated it here, but Róisín couldn't see what she was complaining about. It all seemed so glamorous to her: the big house, the pool, the tennis courts . . .

'I can't talk now,' Róisín had said last time she'd phoned. They'd only been speaking for about two minutes. 'I'm off out to the cinema with Mary and Theresa.'

Caitlin had put down the receiver feeling empty and sad. Valleymount had moved on without her. She could never go back. She was stuck between two worlds – not fitting in with the Melvilles but also no longer being an O'Dwyer.

She took one last envious look at the couple playing in the pool below. There was no point wondering what it would be like to hang out with them. She would never get the opportunity to find out.

Caitlin stayed hidden in her room for the rest of the day. Mrs Hutchins, the housekeeper, brought her up a plate of food at dusk.

'I'd stay and chat, love,' the woman said, placing the tray on the dressing-table, 'but the kitchen's flat out, getting dinner ready for seven-thirty. I best get back.'

Mrs Hutchins shot her a sympathetic glance as she left the room. Caitlin was a nice kid, all the staff thought so. In fact, she was the only one of the three children with decent manners, never missing her pleases and thank yous. It just went to show that money didn't buy you everything.

Caitlin ate the food hungrily. She hadn't had anything since breakfast and Mrs Hutchins had prepared a delicious spread – a plate of cold cuts, hams and cheeses with freshly baked bread. She devoured every scrap before going back to her book.

An hour later, Caitlin finally finished the mystery. It was only then that she realised how quiet it was outside. She crossed to the window. The patio was deserted. Elizabeth and her friends must be eating at the moment. It was the ideal opportunity to get some air.

She took the back stairs down to the ground floor. The dining room was at the rear of the house, so she had no choice but to pass it. She sneaked by as quietly as she could, although the sounds of chatter and laughter, glasses and cutlery clinking, were so loud that she needn't have bothered.

Outside, the sun was setting. But even though it was growing dark, the air was still warm. Caitlin walked by the pool and down the stone steps. At the bottom, instead of turning left onto the path that led to the floodlit tennis courts, she headed in the other direction, down the sweeping lawns and on towards the walled garden.

She entered the garden through the Acorn Gates. She loved it in there, preferring the haphazard displays to the manicured beauty of the rest of the grounds. There was something romantic about the high stone walls covered in ivy; roses, clematis and honeysuckle tumbling over each other, filling the air with perfume, attracting bees and butterflies.

Caitlin made her way towards the centre of the garden, her favourite place. Hidden in a circle of beech trees was a small clearing, with a pretty pond. No one else ever went there. It had become her hideout, where she would go to sketch, or just escape from the house and the Melvilles. There was an old swing, made with heavy ropes tied onto a strong branch. The first time she'd seen it, she'd been worried it might not hold her weight. But the ancient tree had stood true. After that, she often went to sit there when she was feeling miserable, swinging gently back and forth, staring into the deep waters of the pond. It was the one place she felt at peace.

But tonight, as she pushed through the leafy branches and emerged into the clearing, she found someone was already there. Sitting on the swing, moving back and forth in the cool evening breeze as he smoked, was the young man she'd seen frolicking in the pool earlier.

He was even better-looking close up: tall and stocky, with the imposing build of a rugby player; dark eyes to match his dark hair; a strong jaw and symmetrical face.

Suddenly she caught herself. What was she thinking? She began to back away. He was so engrossed in his cigarette he hadn't looked up. She was nearly back within the cover of the trees when she trod on a twig and it snapped, breaking the silence. Damn. There was no way he could miss that.

She was right. He – whoever *he* was – looked up, alerted to her presence. She stared at him, her blue eyes wide like a startled deer's. He stared right back, although a lot more calmly. In fact, he didn't seem the least bit unnerved by her presence. He took another long drag on his cigarette as he looked her over, his eyes lingering on her breasts. She felt her cheeks heating up and instinctively pulled her cardigan closed across her chest.

'And who, may I ask, are you?' he said finally. He spoke in low, unhurried tones, pronouncing every word with slow deliberation, an upper-class drawl.

'Caitlin.' The word came out almost like a squeak. She felt herself turning an even deeper shade of red.

He grinned then, as though something had amused him. 'Ah,' he said. 'So you're Caitlin.' He sounded her name very precisely. In fact, he took his time over every syllable he spoke, as though he was used to the world waiting for him to finish whatever he had to say. 'As in Elizabeth's mysterious half-sister.'

She nodded. It seemed as good a description as any. 'That's right,' she said, smiling awkwardly at him.

'Well, Caitlin,' he drawled, 'it just so happens that I am one of Elizabeth's very closest friends. So why don't you come over here.' He patted the seat of the swing next to him. 'And we can get to know each other a little better.'

She hesitated for just a moment, and then did as he'd asked. All thoughts of getting away had magically disappeared.

'I'm Elliott, by the way,' he said, as she sat down next to him. 'Elliott Falconer.'

He said his name as though it should mean something to her. It didn't. But he didn't seem too bothered by her lack of recognition. In fact, he looked decidedly unbothered about everything. She realised for the first time that he was wearing jeans and a rugby shirt. She wondered how he'd gotten away with that. From what she'd seen since arriving at Aldringham, everyone dressed formally for dinner.

He transferred his cigarette to his left hand and offered his right to shake. She took it, surprised at how cool his skin felt despite the warmth of the evening.

'So why haven't I seen you around so far this weekend?' he asked.

She stayed silent, not sure how to answer. He seemed to sense her dilemma and his grin widened.

'Let me guess. Your lovely half-sister decided that it would be better for all concerned if you stayed hidden away in your room?'

Caitlin smiled a little, but still said nothing.

'Hmmm.' He took another long drag on his cigarette. 'The silence tells me everything.' He looked sideways at her, fixing those dark, penetrating eyes on her. 'Well, try not to take it too hard. It's nothing personal. Lizzie's like that with everyone.' Reaching into his pocket, he produced a packet of Marlboros and held it out to her.

She shook her head. 'Thanks, but I don't smoke.'

He chuckled softly. 'Good for you. Terrible habit. I keep meaning to quit.'

But his reassurances had the opposite effect on Caitlin. She suddenly felt naïve and uptight. As Elliott smoked in silence, she tried to think of something intelligent to say. Nothing came to her. She was almost on the verge of changing her mind and accepting a cigarette, just to make conversation. But before she could, there was the sound of twigs breaking as someone else came through the bushes.

They both looked up to see who was there. Caitlin recognised her straight away. It was the blonde girl from the pool, the one who had been horsing around with Elliott. In a short, glittery dress that Caitlin would never dare to wear, she looked wonderfully glamorous. Caitlin felt a twinge of disappointment at the interruption. The blonde didn't seem very happy either.

'Bloody hell, Elliott, there you are,' she snapped. 'I've been looking everywhere for you.'

He looked unperturbed. 'I've only been gone twenty minutes, Morgan. There was no need for a shagging search-party.'

Morgan's eyes narrowed. She turned her attention to Caitlin then, looking her over carefully. Caitlin got the feeling she didn't like what she saw.

'And who's this?' Her gaze was still on Caitlin, but the question was clearly directed at Elliott.

'This is my new friend, Caitlin.' Elliott looped his arm around Caitlin and squeezed her shoulder. 'You know – Elizabeth's half-sister.'

'Right.' Morgan sounded unimpressed. 'Well, anyway, I just came out to tell you that Elizabeth wants to serve dessert. Everyone's waiting on you.'

'I'm sure five more minutes isn't going to kill them,' he replied.

Morgan's jaw tightened a fraction. 'Fine,' she said shortly. 'Do whatever you want. But I'm going back in.' With a disparaging glance at Caitlin, Morgan flounced back towards the house.

Elliott turned to Caitlin and rolled his eyes theatrically.

'Ah, well. Duty calls.' He took a final drag on his cigarette and then threw it onto the ground, stubbing it out under his shoe. He stood up and gave her a little half-bow. 'It was a pleasure to meet you, though, Caitlin.'

She watched as he strutted back towards the house. Suddenly the prospect of going to Greycourt didn't seem be so bad after all.

Chapter 6

The second Sunday in September brought with it the first fall of leaves and a chill to the air that signalled the end of summer. It was also the day that the three Melville girls packed up their belongings and set off for Greycourt Independent Co-educational School.

Elizabeth was the first to leave Aldringham, speeding off early – alone – in her silver Porsche 911 Carrera, a seventeenth-birthday present from William. That left Perkins to drive Caitlin and Amber later that morning. There was the predictable last-minute tantrum from Amber. She had three trunks and four suitcases, packed full of clothes from the almost daily shopping sprees she'd been on with her mother during the holidays. Unsurprisingly, they wouldn't all fit into the boot.

'Darling, you can't take everything,' Isabelle tried to reason with her. 'There simply isn't enough room in the car.'

Amber's mouth set in a stubborn line. 'But I don't want to look like a dag.'

The argument went on, until William was eventually called in.

'You can't seriously need all these clothes,' he said wearily. 'Five days a week you wear your uniform.'

Backed into a corner, Amber did what she always did in these situations – burst into tears and ran into the house.

Isabelle followed her. As she passed Caitlin, standing quietly by, waiting for the fireworks to subside, Isabelle couldn't help wondering what Katie O'Dwyer's secret had been. How had the single mother managed to raise such a sweet, placid child, who was never any trouble? Compared to her own two children ... Sometimes Isabelle despaired. Elizabeth might be smart and sensible, but she was also a cold fish. And Amber ... well, she was turning out to be a brat. Where had she and William gone wrong?

Half an hour later, a compromise had been reached. For practicality's sake, one of Amber's trunks would remain at home and then be sent on to Greycourt the very next day. The girl's tears miraculously dried up and they were on their way.

Caitlin's first glimpse of Greycourt sent a shiver of anticipation through her. It was everything she had imagined an English boarding school to be. The ivy-clad stone buildings were old and dignified; the lawns immaculate; the playing fields stretched to the horizon. In the cold, bright autumn sun, it was beautiful in an imposing way.

Greycourt was the fourth largest boarding school in Britain, after Eton, Millfield and Oundle, and by far the most illustrious. It commanded fees of thirty thousand pounds a year and had an attitude to match. Founded in 1840 by David Greycourt, a philanthropic industrialist, to 'educate the sons of gentlemen', it occupied 100 acres of greenbelt, a picturesque mile and a half walk outside the pretty market town of Towcester, in Northamptonshire.

While Greycourt prided itself on its strong sense of tradition, it had also learned over the years that the key to survival was to move with the times. Like many of its brethren, it had decided – after much heated debate – to admit girls in 1983. The Board of Governors had never had any cause to regret the decision. Now, Greycourt provided a first-class education to just under a thousand pupils between the ages of eleven and eighteen, seven hundred boarding, the rest day pupils. The school's record spoke for itself: 25 per cent of last year's Sixth Form went up to

Oxbridge; it regularly topped *The Times*' annual league tables for exam results; and it had just been given a glowing write-up in the *Daily Telegraph*'s educational pages.

William had explained all of this to Caitlin when he'd first broached the subject of sending her to Greycourt. Being educated there was a Melville family tradition and one not to be argued with.

Usually, pupils were only accepted if they passed an entrance exam and an interview with the Headmistress, Dr Phillips, but William managed to have the rules waived in Caitlin's case. And, as the day for starting at Greycourt drew nearer, the girl found herself almost looking forward to it. After a summer spent in the claustrophobic confines of Aldringham, she was longing for a change of scene. Plus, she would get to see Elliott Falconer again.

Greycourt's glossy prospectus proudly informed parents that the school was made up of fourteen Houses: eight for boys and six for girls. Caitlin had been assigned to Berrylands House. She couldn't help feeling disappointed when she first saw it. Buried as an afterthought at the far end of the campus, it had been built during that architectural nadir, the sixties. It had none of the old-fashioned charm of the magnificent buildings that lined the entrance. The only redeeming feature seemed to be the rows of blackberry hedges that fringed the small garden, and which lent the House its name.

'You weren't expecting somewhere so modern, were you?' Mrs Collins, Berrylands' Housemistress, gave her a knowing smile. 'Most people prefer to be in Gladstone or Pankhurst, the original Houses. They're beautiful inside, full of oak panelling and spiral staircases. But trust me,' she said conspiratorially, 'in this case, looks really aren't everything. We may not have original wood beams in Berrylands, but we do have power showers, and that's far more important. The plumbing in those Victorian buildings leaves a lot to be desired.'

Caitlin warmed to Mrs Collins straight away. A rotund woman in her mid-fifties, she chattered non-stop as she showed Caitlin to her room. Every House had a set of Houseparents, she informed Caitlin; a married couple who taught at the school. She was a Home Economics teacher and her husband headed up the Physics Department. 'Eamon will pop round to introduce himself later.'

Caitlin was relieved to have met someone so open and friendly. Predictably, neither Amber nor Elizabeth had shown any interest in helping her settle in. Elizabeth was too busy, her afternoon filled with hosting a meeting of all the prefects, her first duty as Head Girl, followed by tennis practice. Amber, who was also a newcomer to Greycourt, already knew a lot of her year through the feeder prep school that she had attended. That meant, as soon as she arrived, she'd immediately been surrounded by a group of girls, all eager to hear about her holiday.

Caitlin's room was on the fifth floor. As they passed a large window in the hallway, she saw that Berrylands had a dazzling view across the grounds. Buildings from every decade over the past 150 years lined the campus, clashing architectural styles documenting the history of the place. Outside, Greycourt was in the throes of moving-in day. Pupils had started arriving from eight that morning. Harried parents and children rushed from cars to buildings and back again, carrying boxes, trunks and suitcases up long, narrow flights of stairs.

'Here's your room,' Mrs Collins said, stopping outside an anonymous beige door labelled 5c. 'I'll leave you to get acquainted with your roommate. Her name's . . . er . . .' she quickly consulted a list '. . . yes, you're with Georgina Mitchell. Lovely girl. I'm sure you'll get on.'

Inside, the new roommates eyed each other warily. Caitlin relaxed first. She took one look at Georgina and decided she had nothing to worry about. If appearances were anything to go by, Georgina wasn't anything like Morgan. A thickset girl with short, wiry hair and a ruddy complexion, she clearly didn't give a damn what anyone thought of her. Dressed in loose-fitting jeans and a baggy T-shirt, she seemed almost masculine.

Caitlin nodded at Georgina's side of the room. 'I guess you like horses, then.'

It was an understatement. The walls, desk and cupboard were covered with equestrian paraphernalia – posters of Grand National winners, photos of Georgina in gymkhanas and trophies celebrating her wins.

Georgina grinned. 'You could say that!'

It did the trick. Within half an hour, the two girls were friends. It turned out Georgina – or George as she preferred to be called – had been equally worried about sharing with one of the Melville girls.

'But you seem like a good sort,' she declared. 'Nothing like Elizabeth.'

Caitlin smiled. She'd been right. Being at Greycourt wasn't going to be so awful after all. She wondered briefly if George knew Elliott, but decided to wait until later to ask.

Greycourt tried hard to foster a sense of community among its pupils. As such, mealtimes were formal occasions, served in the school's magnificent dining hall. The Lower School – Years One to Four – sat down at six on the dot. The Upper School, the Fifth and Sixth Forms, then convened at the more civilised hour of seven-thirty.

The dining room itself was a re-creation of a Tudor banqueting hall, with vaulted ceilings, massive wooden beams and large arched windows dividing the stone walls. Huge candelabras lit the room – a health and safety nightmare, but why let that get in the way of tradition?

At twenty past seven that night, George and Caitlin filed into the hall with the rest of the Upper School. George pointed to the far end of the room. 'My lot always sit over there.' She waved at one of her friends, who had been instructed to save them places.

The air crackled with excitement. It was the first dinner of the term, so everyone was milling around, taking a while to catch up and settle in. George and Caitlin had to force their way through the crowds to get to their seats. As Caitlin squeezed between the wall and a burly rugby player's back, she caught sight of a familiar face in her path. It was Elliott, leaning casually against the wood panelling, chatting to a couple of girls. She wiped her sweaty palms on her jeans and tried to think of something intelligent to say. Nothing came to her. Instead, as she drew level with him, she slowed down and gave him a shy smile.

'Hi, Elliott.'

'Hey.' He looked blank for a moment, and then there was a flicker of recognition. 'It's Elizabeth's sister, right?'

'Caitlin,' she filled in, trying not to feel disappointed that he'd forgotten her name.

'Right, right. Caitlin. Sure.' He gave her a lazy grin. Her stomach turned over. 'I knew that. Good to see you again.' Then he turned back to the pretty redhead next to him and resumed their conversation.

Caitlin stood there for a moment, feeling foolish. She'd spent weeks fantasising about the moment when she saw him again. And that was it. He'd barely glanced at her. She was trying to think of something else to say to him, but before she could, George grabbed her hand.

'Come on. The teachers will be here soon. We ought to sit down.'

Caitlin had no choice but to follow.

'Do you know Elliott?' she asked, once they were away from his group.

'Everyone knows Elliott Falconer.' The way George said it didn't sound especially complimentary. She paused and looked back at Caitlin. 'Why? When did you meet him?'

Caitlin quickly explained. 'He seemed really nice,' she added, wanting to get the other girl's opinion on him.

George snorted. 'Yes. Elliott can be awfully charming when he wants to be.'

'So, how well do you know him?' Caitlin pressed. 'Are you friends?'

George didn't answer straight away. By now, they had reached her group. Once they were seated, and quick introductions made, George gave Caitlin a sidelong look. 'Look, there's something you ought to understand about Greycourt. There's a strict social hierarchy. People like us,' she indicated her set of friends on the bench, 'aren't friends with the Elliotts and Morgans of the school. And, to be honest, that's no bad thing.'

Before Caitlin could ask what she meant, a gong sounded, silencing the chatter. Benches scraped as the pupils got to their feet. A moment later, the teachers filed in and walked towards the high table. Once they were settled, Elizabeth went to the front of the hall and everyone bowed their heads. As Head Girl, she would start the year off by saying Grace. She began to speak Latin in her strong, clear voice.

'*Benedic, Domine, nos et dona tua . . .*'

The rest of the meal, Caitlin tried to concentrate on what George and her friends were saying. They seemed to be nice, down-to-earth girls, like George herself. But every now and again, Caitlin's gaze would stray to Elliott's table. Everyone around him seemed so cool. The guys were good-looking, the girls slim and pretty. Caitlin looked at the slightly dishevelled lot that surrounded her. She could suddenly see George's point about the two groups not mixing in. It hadn't been like this back in Ireland at Holy Cross. The school had been too small for cliques. It was yet another change she would have to get used to.

Chapter 7

Caitlin's first month at Greycourt passed at breakneck speed, mostly because there was so much to get used to. Privilege surrounded her at every turn. The facilities were unbelievable. There was a Fencing Salle, a Judo Dōjō, an Olympic-sized indoor pool and a nine-hole golf course. She couldn't help comparing it to Holy Cross. The two places were worlds apart.

Never was that more apparent than in lessons. At Greycourt, academic prowess was highly prized. The school's motto, *Sapere Aude*, Dare To Be Wise, said it all. Classes were brutal. Caitlin found that out on Day One. The School Secretary handed her a badly photocopied map, and she promptly got lost in the maze of dark corridors. None of the pupils rushing through the cloisters seemed interested in helping her, the new girl.

She was fifteen minutes late to her first lesson, which was English. Mr Reynolds, a rodent-like man with a penchant for tweed, brushed aside her breathless explanation. 'In future, make sure you arrive at my class on time, Miss Melville,' he said, his tone filled with ennui. 'Otherwise Berrylands will be docked ten House points.'

Caitlin found a seat at the back. She didn't recognise any faces in the room. Classes were streamed, and unfortunately, George and her friends were in the top set. Caitlin had been slotted into the bottom – 'until we see what you're made of,' the Headmistress had said at their meeting that morning. Caitlin already suspected she'd be staying put.

The lesson was on the Metaphysical Poets, and it gave Caitlin an insight into Greycourt's Darwinian approach to learning: only the fittest survived. Mr Reynolds read out one of Donne's sonnets, 'A Valediction Forbidding Mourning', picking randomly on pupils to explain particular parts of the poem. If someone didn't answer correctly, the teacher would groan loudly while the rest of the class sniggered.

Finally, Caitlin's turn came. Mr Reynolds stood over her desk and barked, 'Miss Melville! The final three verses. What can you tell me about them?'

Eleven pairs of curious eyes turned to stare at Caitlin, eager to evaluate her. The girl gazed down at her notepad, trying to collect her thoughts. But Mr Reynolds didn't give her a chance.

'Come along now, weren't you listening? Time's up, Miss Melville!' He turned to the rest of the class. 'Anyone else care to venture a guess on this?'

A dozen hands shot up.

'Yes, Miss Adams.' Mr Reynolds moved on to a striking brunette. 'Would you care to enlighten us where Miss Melville could not?'

'We see Donne's most famous Conceit being introduced here,' the brunette said with an air of superiority. 'The two lovers are likened to the two points of a compass. At first this seems like a ridiculous comparison, but Donne goes on in the rest of the poem to show us how it makes sense.'

Mr Reynolds nodded along as she spoke.

'Good, good,' he said. The brunette preened under his praise. 'And how does he do this?'

Caitlin spent the rest of the lesson trying to keep up, but feeling as if she was falling further and further behind. And this was supposed to be the slow class . . .

'I'm never going to be able to do all this homework,' Caitlin remarked to George during that first week. She was trying to get to grips with trigonometry. She'd spent twenty minutes on the first problem and still had no idea how to solve it. There were fifteen more to do before she could even think about going to bed.

George looked over at the question she was struggling with. 'Don't worry. I can help you with that.' She nodded down at her geography textbook. 'Just give me five minutes to finish this.'

She was true to her word. In no time, she'd simplified the maths concepts so that Caitlin knew exactly what to do. Caitlin wasn't surprised, since George was naturally academic. It was only because she didn't have a competitive bone in her body that she had ended up in Berrylands.

Caitlin had discovered that every House at Greycourt had its own distinctive character. The Head made a judgement at each pupil's interview about where they would be best suited. To most of the other Houses, Berrylands was a joke. Inter-House competition was actively encouraged, with points being handed out for academic achievements and sporting wins. A league table was published annually.

'Berrylands is always bottom,' George told Caitlin cheerfully.

There was a pecking order for everything at Greycourt. As Caitlin had observed that first night, there was a clear divide between the popular and unpopular pupils. That meant Elliott was out of her league. Not only was he two years older, he was part of Greycourt's in-crowd. Being friends with George and her group meant Caitlin didn't even appear on his radar.

It worked both ways. George and her friends had no time for them, either.

'Look at Barbie,' George would say scornfully, nodding over at Morgan in hall. 'I don't know why she bothers putting food on her plate. She's only going to throw it up in half an hour.'

The table would laugh along with her, but Caitlin couldn't help looking over wistfully at Elliott. There was part of her – a shallow, superficial part, she knew – that wondered what it would be like to be accepted by his group.

Art lessons were the one part of the week Caitlin enjoyed. It helped that she got on well with Mr Wright, the Head of the Art Department. A gentle man in his early forties, he was a gifted teacher. The Head, it was rumoured, wasn't happy with his somewhat unorthodox appearance – he favoured Black Sabbath T-shirts and black jeans, and had a diamond stud in his left ear – but he got results, so she put up with it.

At the end of Caitlin's first lesson, Mr Wright asked her to stay behind. She half-expected him to say she wasn't up to the acceptable standard. Instead, he asked if she'd like to join the class he taught out of hours on Wednesday and Friday afternoons.

'It's mainly for the Sixth Form,' he told her, 'but I think you'd really benefit from coming along. It's purely optional, of course.' What he meant was that it was a privilege to be asked.

The classes turned out to be more fun than Caitlin had imagined. The A-level course was 'Art School' orientated, with students encouraged to experiment and explore their own style. For the first time, she had an opportunity to shine.

The only problem with joining the Sixth Form class was that Morgan Woodhouse was taking Art, too.

As the lessons were out of school hours, uniforms weren't required, so on the first afternoon Caitlin turned up in a maroon floor-length gypsy skirt and olive-green long-sleeved T-shirt. As she walked to her easel, Morgan leaned over to the girl next to her.

'God, what *is* she wearing?' she said in a stage whisper.

'I don't know,' her friend giggled. 'She must think the hippy look is back!'

Caitlin ignored the jibe, thinking that eventually Morgan would grow bored of being horrible to her. But she was wrong.

It didn't get any better, especially once it became apparent how talented Caitlin was. Morgan was used to being the best in the school at Art, and she didn't take kindly to this scruffy kid usurping her title.

Caitlin stood back from her easel so Mr Wright could see what she had been working on. A fortnight earlier he had set the class a new project, with the prompt 'To create an Alternative Self-Portrait'. Caitlin had decided to explore the changes that had happened to her over the past few months. She had split her canvas into a grid of nine boxes, each square showing a different scene from her life. All nine pictures then cleverly came together to form one large portrait of her.

This was the first time Mr Wright had seen it, and she was impatient to hear his thoughts. He stared at the canvas for a long time, and then finally started to nod.

'It's good,' he said, almost absent-mindedly. Then went on: 'I mean, it's more than good. It's exceptional.' He squatted down beside her. 'You know, the Saatchi Gallery run a competition each year for schoolkids. I really think you should consider entering. If you win, your work gets displayed in the Gallery and you'll be considered for a bursary to one of the major Art Schools.'

He spoke just as there was a lull in the class's conversation, meaning that everyone heard the unprecedented praise. Morgan's head snapped up and she scowled over at Caitlin.

After chatting to Caitlin about her work for a few more moments, Mr Wright moved on around the class, offering praise and advice as it was due. He finally came to Morgan, who had a confident smile on her face. Her painting was an oil-on-canvas piece, similar to a Picasso self-portrait from his Cubist period.

Mr Wright looked at it for a moment, frowning. 'Morgan,' he said at last, 'I think you've missed the point of the exercise.'

The girl's smile faded.

'While technically this may be good, a self-portrait is supposed to be about self-expression and exploration,' he explained gently. 'It's meant to reflect the very essence of you. What you've shown me here is a picture of you in the style of Picasso. That doesn't tell me anything about you as a person.'

Morgan's face reddened, but Mr Wright didn't seem to notice.

'Class is nearly over now,' he concluded. 'But maybe take this weekend to think about what you want to say about yourself and the best way to express it.'

Before Morgan could respond, the bell rang. The class started to tidy away, chattering about their weekend plans. Caitlin was the last to wash up her brushes. She had just got back to her easel when Morgan walked by with one of her cohorts.

'I don't see what's so great about her picture anyway,' she sneered, making sure to speak loud enough for Caitlin to hear.

'Mr Wright probably just feels sorry for her,' her friend responded.

George had arrived at that exact moment to meet Caitlin after class. It was Friday afternoon, and they planned to head into town for hot chocolate and cake at the Little Tea Shop on Watling Street. She overheard Morgan's bitchy comment and shook her head.

'Don't worry about them,' she told Caitlin. 'They're just jealous.'

Caitlin gave a weak smile. Somehow the knowledge didn't make it any easier.

There were plenty of quaint country pubs around Towcester. The Brass Monkey wasn't one of them. A dingy establishment on the outskirts of town, the floors were sticky, there was never any loo roll in the toilets, and it stank of stale cigarettes and beer. But the landlord wasn't fussy about ID and so Greycourt's Sixth Form patronised it despite these obvious faults.

It was Friday night and, as usual, Elliott Falconer was holding court at one end of the bar. Beneath the scarred table, where no one could see, he could feel Morgan's hand sliding up his leg, her knuckles grazing his groin. He sighed. The last thing he needed right now was another random hook-up with his psycho ex.

He reached down and pushed her hand away. 'Leave it out, Morgan.'

He made his voice deliberately harsh so there could be no misunderstanding. Not that anything he said seemed to get through to her these days. How many times could you tell someone it was over? Although maybe getting drunk and sleeping with her every few weeks was sending out mixed messages . . .

'Why don't you hit on someone else?' He nodded across the smoke-filled room. 'What about that bloke in the corner? He looks desperate enough.'

The entire table turned to see where he was pointing – at an overweight, bald man in his fifties. Everyone, apart from Morgan, laughed. She scowled at Elliott.

'Fuck you.'

The obscenity sounded out of place coming from such a refined voice, and everyone laughed again.

Elliott set down his pint. It was unusual for Morgan to react so strongly to his jibes. Usually she put up with any crap he threw her way. He was the only person at Greycourt who could treat her like dirt and get away with it.

'What's up with you, then?' he asked.

Morgan looked away. 'Nothing.'

He was about to let it go – frankly, he didn't give a shit. But then Lucille Lewis, Morgan's sometime best friend, said something interesting.

'It's Caitlin Melville.' Like most of the girls at Greycourt, Lucille was prepared to betray a confidence if it meant getting

Elliott's attention for even a moment. 'She's Mr Wright's new pet and Morgan's jealous.'

Morgan shot Lucille a furious look. She had no desire for the humiliating incident in Art class to become public knowledge.

'Don't be stupid,' she said quickly. 'I'm just tired.'

But Elliott sensed she was lying and couldn't help adding salt to the wound.

'Caitlin Melville?' he drawled, a slow grin spreading over his face. 'Oh yeah, I remember her. She's pretty hot.'

Beside him, Morgan stiffened. 'Don't be so ridiculous.'

He shrugged. 'I'm not. She's a babe.'

The guys around the table murmured their agreement. Caitlin had unknowingly become an object of lust among the hormonally charged adolescent boys at Greycourt. She wasn't their usual type, they all agreed in the locker room. She was quiet, shy even. And the company she kept – all those geeks and dykes like George Mitchell. She didn't do much with herself either. Other girls shortened the hem on their regulation skirts, or bought their shirts a size too small. Not Caitlin. She didn't make any effort: no make-up, raven hair tied back in a pony-tail. But that didn't matter. She had a natural beauty that needed no enhancement: creamy skin, deep blue eyes and full, pouty lips. And a knock-out body. While Elizabeth was lithe and compact, Caitlin was all Rubenesque curves.

'Yeah.' There was a faraway look in Elliott's eyes. Earlier that evening, in the dining hall, he'd deliberately stood in Caitlin's path as she'd walked to her seat, forcing her to squeeze past him. He could still remember the feel of her breasts brushing against his chest. She had to be a 34D at least, he reckoned. In a school where most of the girls either didn't eat or threw up what they did, a decent rack was rare and highly prized. 'She's definitely hot.'

Morgan pursed her lips. She always hated hearing compliments about another girl. But for it to be about that stupid little county bumpkin really got to her.

'Well, it's not like you'd ever get anywhere with her,' she retorted. 'The Virgin Mary isn't about to put out.'

Elliott grinned with the easy confidence of someone who had slept with half his class and knew the rest wouldn't need much persuasion. He'd noticed Caitlin's puppy-dog eyes following him around school.

'Oh, I wouldn't be so sure about that,' he said, with a touch of his trademark arrogance.

There was a chorus of catcalls around the table.

'Sounds like a challenge.' This came from Sebastian Ashford, Elliott's best friend and roommate.

'Fifty quid says you can't shag her by the Snow Ball,' Seb's identical twin brother, Nicholas, added.

With their delicate bone structure and floppy fair hair, the Ashford twins were good-looking to the point of being almost girlish. But their beauty was only skin-deep. Intensely cynical and morally bankrupt, more than one girl around the table couldn't quite be sure which twin she'd slept with, or whether it was both. Their sharp minds were in constant need of diversion, and this seemed as good a game as any to keep them amused – for a little while at least.

Elliott gave a quick glance around to make sure Elizabeth Melville wasn't within earshot. She might not have much time for her half-sister, but he had a feeling she'd still draw the line at this. Only once he was sure she was nowhere near did he give the nod. 'You're on.'

Half an hour later, the bets had been placed. Elliott stood to win – or lose – about a grand. The money didn't bother him. His generous allowance would cover the financial hit. It was more about keeping his reputation. And there was no way he intended to lose that.

It wasn't hard for Elliott to engineer a reason to talk to Caitlin. Monday lunchtime, he was in the Sixth Form common room when he overheard two nerds in the Drama Club talking about her. They'd apparently roped her into doing the scenery for the next school play, *The Winter's Tale*. She'd told one of them, Rob Cooper, that the seven-foot papier-mâché pillars she'd designed for Act I in the palace were now dry. They were meeting her in the Art Room after lessons ended, and then carrying them downstairs to the school hall. Elliott saw his chance. It didn't take much to persuade Rob to let him take his place.

Elliott walked into the Art Room and greeted Caitlin like an old friend, even going so far as to complain that he hadn't seen her around much since term had started. Caitlin thought of the dozen or so times she'd walked by Elliott and he'd ignored her, and promptly forgot all about them.

She watched as he effortlessly picked up one of the pillars. Next to him, Paul Edmunds, the other half of the team responsible for shifting the scenery, was struggling with his.

'I didn't realise you were involved with the Drama Club,' she said to Elliott as he headed towards the theatre.

He shrugged nonchalantly. 'Oh, I help out from time to time.' He grinned. 'Mainly when they need some heavy lifting done!'

Behind them, Paul sniggered. Elliott shot him a glare and glanced quickly back at Caitlin, but she hadn't noticed. She was too busy wishing that she'd worn something other than her paint-spattered jeans and a shapeless T-shirt.

'Well, let's start carrying these downstairs . . .'

Caitlin didn't want the afternoon to end. Fortunately, Elliott didn't seem in any rush to leave, either. After they'd finished their task, and Paul had tactfully departed, Elliott leaned against the wall and gave Caitlin a slow grin, the one that made her stomach flutter.

'So are you free now for a coffee?' he asked. 'We could drive into town.'

Caitlin hesitated. 'I can't,' she said regretfully. 'I told George I'd watch her ride. She's competing at four.'

So blow her off, Elliott was on the verge of saying. But he stopped himself. Most girls would happily dump their friends to spend an hour with him. But his gut told him Caitlin wasn't that type.

'So when are you free?' He tried hard to look vulnerable. 'Unless that was just a polite excuse, and you don't really want to go out with me.'

'How about Saturday?' she suggested quickly. It was hard to keep the enthusiasm out of her voice.

He heard it and grinned lazily. 'Saturday sounds perfect.'

Her face lit up, her expression confirming everything he'd thought.

This was going to be too easy.

Chapter 8

Elizabeth wasn't sure when she first noticed Caitlin and Elliott together. She had been so busy that term: what with studying for four A-levels, her Head Girl duties, extracurricular activities, applying to Cambridge and organising the Snow Ball, inevitably she had less time to socialise. She hadn't even wanted to go along to the rugby match that Saturday. She could think of far better things to do than stand in the November drizzle and watch thirty men running through the mud. But it was a home game against Oundle, Greycourt's biggest rivals, and as Head Girl she should show school spirit. So she huddled up on the sidelines with the other diehard supporters.

With two minutes left in the game, Greycourt were three points down. Sebastian, one of the forwards, made a pass to Elliott, the fly-half. He tore along the pitch, passing Oundle's defence . . . The crowd roared as he grounded the ball in the in-goal area, scoring a try and pulling Greycourt two points ahead as the whistle blew.

Elizabeth clapped and cheered with the others, watching as Elliott ran across the pitch, high-fiving the team as he went. Elizabeth rolled her eyes. God, how he loved playing the hero. She watched in amusement as he headed towards a little knot of adoring girls. He picked one of them up, swung her round in victory. So Elliott has a new girlfriend, Elizabeth thought. Poor cow. She wouldn't last long, that was for sure. Finally Elliott put the girl down. They spoke for a couple of moments, and then Elliott kissed her and started to jog towards the changing rooms. He'd gone twenty metres when he turned and shouted something back. The object of his attention looked round, finally giving Elizabeth a glimpse of her face.

Elizabeth blinked once, then again. Now what the hell's going on *there*? she wondered.

Refreshments were served in the school canteen after the game. As soon as they got inside, Elizabeth cornered Morgan. If anyone would know what was going on between Elliott and Caitlin, it was her.

'So is it true?' she demanded.

Morgan followed her gaze towards Caitlin and Elliott. 'Is what true?' she asked, stalling for time.

Elizabeth's eyes narrowed. 'Are Caitlin and Elliott going out?'

'I guess so,' Morgan hedged.

'And how long have they been together?'

'A couple of weeks,' she admitted reluctantly. 'Maybe longer.'

Elizabeth couldn't believe it. How had she missed this? OK, so she hadn't spent much time with her old crowd this term. But still . . .

She thought guiltily about the promise she'd made to her father. He'd called her into his study the night before term started and asked her to keep an eye out for Caitlin at Greycourt. But she'd barely spoken to her half-sister since they'd got here.

'Why didn't you say anything?' Elizabeth asked Morgan.

'I don't know. I suppose I didn't think it was important.'

'Not important?' Elizabeth scoffed. 'Usually another girl only has to look at Elliott and you're screaming blue murder.'

Morgan's lips tightened. 'I must be over him, then, mustn't I?'

Elizabeth thought about it for a moment. She wasn't sure she believed Morgan – but what possible reason did she have to lie? 'So, is it serious?' she asked finally.

'How should I know?' Morgan fired back. She didn't like all these questions. She knew Elizabeth was smarter than her, and was worried that she was going to trip herself up and reveal something she shouldn't. 'Why don't you ask them instead?'

Elizabeth glanced across the canteen to where Elliott and Caitlin were drinking juice together. For once, Morgan was right; she needed to hear this straight from the horse's mouth. But something told her it would be best to wait until later, when she could get Caitlin alone.

Caitlin pulled away in his arms.

'Elliott, no.' Her glance went to the door, a chair wedged under the handle in case his roommates came back. 'I think we should stop.'

'Really?' He looked down at her. In the soft light of the bedside lamp, she could see the amusement in his dark, intelligent eyes. He could tell she didn't mean it.

He bent his head and kissed her again. After a moment, she sighed softly against him, and he knew that he had her. Slowly, skilfully he manoeuvred her onto her back, his single bed creaking under their combined weight. This time, when she felt him pushing up her grey wool skirt, one hand gently caressing the soft flesh of her inner thigh, while the other unbuttoned her blouse, she didn't tell him to stop.

That was because she didn't want him to. In fact, a pretty big part of her wanted him to keep on going, to know what it felt like to have his fingers reach inside the white cotton knickers that were standard issue at Greycourt, to have him touch the dull ache between her legs that was there whenever he was around. A month ago, she'd never have imagined feeling this way. Up until then, Caitlin had always considered herself to be a sensible girl. But when it came to Elliott Falconer, she couldn't think straight.

And he knew it.

It had started that afternoon in the Art Room. The following Saturday they'd arranged to drive into Northampton after lunch. Caitlin had devoted the morning to getting ready. It was the first time she'd ever bothered with her appearance. George was no help, so she ended up asking Lucille Lewis, Berrylands' resident fashion-plate, for advice. Even though Lucille was a friend of Morgan's, she'd been surprisingly nice. By eleven, Caitlin was squeezed into Lucille's Levis, rather than her usual shapeless Dunns' jeans, and wearing a shamelessly tight sweater. Lucille helped blow-dry her wild hair straight and silky, a shimmer of ebony falling almost to her waist, and she was even wearing make-up for the first time. Looking in the mirror, she felt pleased with the results. She could almost have passed for one of the girls Elliot usually hung out with.

They were supposed to meet in her room at two. She had waited and waited, ignoring George's told-you-so looks. He finally turned up a little before three – something to do with rugby practice over-running. Any disappointment she'd felt evaporated when his eyes ran appreciatively over her. She'd been a bit worried about the low-cut top, but Lucille had been insistent that she make the most of her 'best assets' as she called them. Elliott seemed to agree.

'Looking good, Melville,' he said, his eyes straying to her chest.

She glowed under the praise, pleased she'd made the effort.

By the time they got into town it was nearly four, and Caitlin was already fretting about getting back. For Fifth Formers, Saturday's curfew was six. If she wasn't there for dinner, she'd get detention. But Elliott was characteristically laidback. He knew Hannah Goldman, the Head Prefect at Berrylands House, he told Caitlin, promising he'd call and make sure she turned a blind eye . . .

Caitlin hesitated, torn. She didn't want to get into trouble, but nor did she want to look like a baby in front of Elliott.

He saw her wavering and grinned. 'Trust me. Would I get you into trouble?'

It was easy to give in. Being with Elliott always made her feel careless and daring. He was so sure of himself, nothing like the boys she'd known back in Valleymount. They had been nervous around her, overly considerate. Elliott Falconer, the big shot rugby player, the most popular guy in school, took control. He showed her round the pretty market town of Northampton, with its medieval architecture and quaint cobbled back streets. But he tired of sightseeing quite quickly, and suggested they get some food instead. She was happy to go along with whatever he wanted.

They drove out to a country pub that he apparently liked. If she noticed that he'd booked a table even before she'd agreed to stay out, she didn't say anything.

Back in Ireland she'd rarely gone out to restaurants, and she felt a little uncomfortable at the Swan, as if she was playing at being a grown-up. Elliott had no such qualms. He ordered a bottle of red wine without consulting her, then went ahead and ordered food for her, too. It all felt so dangerous and exciting. During dinner, when his leg accidentally brushed against hers under the table, she felt something stir within her, something she hadn't ever felt before.

They finally got back to Greycourt at eleven. Elliott walked her to the door of Berrylands and, without asking for permission, proceeded to kiss her with a skill and confidence that left her breathless. When he finally pulled away, cool and collected, she stared at him for a long moment and then, without another word, fled inside.

Elliott was an expert in these matters. He knew the best course of action was to do nothing. He'd felt her response and knew he had her. The following day was Sunday. The whole school went to Chapel. When he walked by her to his pew, he simply gave her a slow, knowing grin. And she felt a lick of desire so deep and strong within her that she shuddered. When she got back to her dorm later that morning, she wasn't surprised to find him there waiting for her.

They had been an item since then.

Being Elliott's girlfriend changed everything. Caitlin was suddenly part of his inner circle. She sat with him in hall; went with the other girls to watch his rugby matches. Every Friday and Saturday night they would go out for the evening – to the cinema, maybe the Brass Monkey or a party at one of the Houses. Her new status hadn't gone unnoticed, of course. Pupils who had previously ignored her now went out of their way to say hello.

At first it was difficult, hanging out with his crowd. She didn't have much to say to them – or to Elliott himself for that matter. She especially didn't like his roommates, Sebastian and Nicholas Ashford. The three of them had snared the best accommodation – a triplex in the old belltower of Heath House. With its large communal sitting room, kitchen and a bathroom each, it was far more luxurious than the average student rooms. But Caitlin still never enjoyed going round there. There was something slightly creepy about the Ashford twins, something she couldn't quite put her finger on. They mostly ignored her, but sometimes she'd catch one of them looking at her – and she could never figure out which one – with a look of amusement on his face, as though there was some joke which she wasn't in on. They'd also walked in on her and Elliott a couple of times, and she was sure it hadn't been an accident. That was why she now insisted on him wedging a chair under the door handle.

She knew most of the school were talking about them. No one could quite understand what they were doing together – or, more accurately, what Elliott saw in her. Caitlin could guess what they were saying. So she started making an

effort to fit in with his group. William had given her a generous weekly allowance at the start of term, which she'd hardly
touched. But now she went shopping with Lucille and invested
in a new wardrobe. She found she had a good eye for what
suited her. While Lucille would slavishly follow the latest fashion, whether it looked good on her or not, Caitlin was more
discerning.

'What do you think?' Lucille asked, as she stepped out of the
changing room. They were in Peacocks, a department store in
Northampton. Lucille had on an A-line skirt and T-shirt, with
heavy dark tights and DM boots. The outfit was all wrong for
her: making her look chunkier than she was. The two girls had
similar builds – small and curvaceous, rather than long and
lean – and Caitlin wouldn't have dreamed of wearing something like that. But she didn't want to hurt her new friend's
feelings.

'You look good,' she said tactfully, 'but I saw something else
that you might like more . . .'

Five minutes later, Lucille came out wearing a jersey dress in
deep reddish purple, almost the colour of aubergine. It clung
tightly to her curves, emphasising rather than hiding. Lucille
looked sensational in it.

'I love it!' she said, twirling around to admire herself in the
three-way mirror.

Caitlin smiled at her obvious delight. She'd been planning to
buy the dress for herself, but she knew Lucille was going out
with Nick Ashford that evening. She'd had a crush on him for
ages and wanted to look special. Caitlin couldn't begrudge her
the outfit. She'd always find something else.

Later, as she paid for her dress, Lucille couldn't help thinking that being friends with Caitlin Melville wasn't as bad as all
that. Morgan would never spend time helping her decide what
to wear. She felt a sudden twinge of guilt about the bet, but
quickly put it from her mind. If she was starting to like Caitlin,

then maybe Elliott was, too. And maybe he wouldn't go through with it, after all.

Caitlin knew she was dumping her friends, but somehow she always wound up sitting with Elliott's group in hall or going out with them after school. More than once, George tried talking to her about it. She couldn't understand why Caitlin was with Elliott and wasn't afraid to tell her.

'He's the kind of guy who's only after one thing,' she said, one night when they were in their dorm room.

Caitlin blushed. 'It isn't like that,' she said unconvincingly.

George raised a sceptical eyebrow. 'Yeah, sure.'

Now, as Caitlin felt Elliott easing down her bra strap, George's words came back to her. She might be naïve, but she wasn't an idiot. She knew Elliott was experienced and wanted more. But she wasn't sure she was ready to give it to him yet. It might be the nineties, but Caitlin had been schooled by nuns. She shared the same fear and ghoulish fascination with sex as thousands of young Catholic girls before her. Not that Elliott was pressuring her. Well, not with words, anyway.

But she couldn't think about that any longer. Not when his fingers were easing her right breast out of its cotton cup, stroking her the way she liked, caressing her nipples erect. It was hard to think about anything when he was doing that.

She could feel his other hand moving from her inner thigh, trailing lightly across the gusset of her panties. Usually when he got anywhere near her underwear she would make him stop. But today she'd left it too late. She squirmed under his touch, pressing down against his palm, wanting him to keep going. The thin material was growing damp, and he liked that she was already wet. But he refused to be hurried. He kept his touch light and teasing. Enjoying the way she was the one writhing now.

She pretended not to notice his hand finding its way inside her knickers, cupping her bush as his index finger came to rest on a particular spot. Slowly, gently, he began to rub back and forth. She could feel the pressure beginning to build between her legs, like she wanted to pee, but better. A low groan escaped from the back of her throat.

He heard it and chuckled softly. 'You like that, huh?'

She didn't say anything. She didn't need to: her reaction spoke for itself. He knelt over her, his other hand pushing the elastic of her knickers out of the way. She tried not to think about what he was doing as he slipped one finger inside her. He hesitated for a moment, as though waiting for her to tell him to stop. When she didn't, he slid another finger in.

The first had been a tight fit, the second hurt more. But it was a good pain. His co-ordination was perfect, his fingers moving in and out, while he continued rubbing her clitoris. She felt a fresh rush of moistness between her legs. Her hands gripped the edges of the duvet. Her knees clamped together – not to stop him, but to try to increase the intensity. She could feel that she was on the brink of something.

Elliott froze, feeling the change in her. This was exactly what he'd been waiting for, getting her to the point where she didn't want to go back. Encouraged, he withdrew his hands and started to undo his jeans.

The sound of the zipper snapped her back to reality. The fog of desire lifted and suddenly all the good feelings were gone.

'Elliott, no,' she murmured. But he wasn't listening. Instead, he was busy trying to ease out of his jeans.

'Honestly, Elliott. I think we should stop now.'

She tried to pull her skirt back down, to cover herself up, but he reached out and caught her wrist. There was no reasoning with him, and the knowledge made her start to panic. With every bit of strength in her, she put her free hand on his chest and pushed him hard.

'*No!*'

This time there was no mistaking the command in her voice. He lurched back, banging his head on the bedside lamp.

'Fuck!' He scowled at her, rubbing his head. 'What the hell did you do that for?'

'You wouldn't stop,' she mumbled.

'Well, it didn't seem like you wanted me to,' he shot back.

Caitlin looked away, all too aware that what he said was true. Instead, she concentrated on straightening her skirt and doing up the buttons on her blouse. The guilt was back again. Now she felt dirty, ashamed. How could she let him do those things to her?

In the silence of the room, she could hear his breathing gradually return to normal. Only then did he reach out and take her hand.

'Look, I'm sorry. I got carried away. You know how it is. I just find it hard to control myself around you.'

They were the magic words she loved to hear.

I can't help myself, you're just so beautiful.

God, you turn me on.

I want you so much.

However much she hated to admit it, she liked what she did to him. Seeing him out of control, his breath laboured, struggling to contain himself . . . It gave her a feeling of power that was addictive. Once, in a moment of anger, he'd called her a pricktease. She'd cried. He'd apologised. But there was part of her that was beginning to wonder if he was right.

She didn't know how long she could keep on saying no. Every time she did, she worried that he was going to say it was over between them. She wanted him to like her. She wanted to stay being his girlfriend, being part of his group. For the first time since coming into the Melville family she felt accepted into this elite, privileged world. She didn't want that to stop.

At first she refused to look at him. She wasn't even sure how she felt. Angry, frustrated, confused . . . After all, was it even that wrong between them? Mam might have raised her with all these strict Catholic morals, but it wasn't like *she'd* practised what she preached.

Elliott reached out, gently lifting her chin until their gazes met. 'Look, I'm really sorry.'

She saw the sincerity in his dark eyes and, as always, melted. 'It's OK. But we'd better go now. We don't want to be late for hall.'

He smiled then, and she relaxed a little. She couldn't believe how understanding he was being. She just wondered how long he was prepared to wait – and, more importantly, how long she could hold out.

Half an hour later, Elliott sat opposite Caitlin in Greycourt's dining hall, pretending to listen as she chattered on about her Art project. Instead, he was silently willing her to lean forward across the table again, allowing him to catch a glimpse of her creamy cleavage.

After six weeks together, today was the first time he'd managed to get past first base. Six long weeks of being on his best behaviour. Opening doors. Pulling out chairs. Helping her on with her coat. Listening attentively as she droned on about her shagging Art class. Getting her all hot – and himself in the process – only for her to pull away at the last minute, all wide, frightened eyes. And then having to pretend to understand what all the fuss was about. He'd never gone to so much trouble for one lousy lay before.

He'd thought he had her today. He'd waited until she was just about to come, thinking she'd be too far gone to pull back when he tried to take things further. But, no. He stabbed at a green bean, taking his frustration out on the overcooked vegetables. He was very aware of his deadline. Three weeks to go until the Snow Ball. Most of the Sixth Form seemed to be in on the pool now. Worryingly, two-thirds of the money was riding against him. Everyone thought she was too prissy to put out. But he had his plan all mapped out. He would invite her to the Snow Ball, spend the evening romancing her, and by the end of it she'd be begging for it. He felt his dick start to twitch just thinking about it. That was what had surprised him most: this wasn't just about money or reputation any more. He actually wanted her. More than he'd ever wanted anyone in his life before. Maybe it was because she was the first girl to say 'no' to him.

He watched as she tucked her heavy dark hair behind her ears and looked up at him with those huge, violet eyes. There was an innocence there that couldn't be faked. He liked the idea that he would be her first. She would be timid at first, shy even. But once he warmed her up, he bet she would love it . . .

He was suddenly aware that she was looking at him quizzically. Shit. He hadn't been listening.

'So what do you think?' she asked.

He looked at her rosebud mouth, pouting softly at him. At that moment, he thought how nice it would be, to have those plump lips wrapped around his hard cock.

She frowned. 'Elliott? Did you hear me? Should I use oils or acrylic?'

He forced himself to snap back to the present. 'Whatever you think's best,' he said, and then changed the subject. 'Any idea what you'd like to do later?'

They spent the rest of the evening cuddled up in front of a video in the common room – her choice of activity. By the time they finally said goodnight, he was ready to explode. As he got in his car and headed into the Cave Club in Northampton to meet up with the gang, he was still thinking about Caitlin. As usual, she'd got him all riled up and he needed relief – fast. His eyes fixed on a drunk and desperate Morgan. Two more

rum and Cokes – and the vague suggestion that he might consider getting back together with her – and she was happy to
follow him into the Gents.

There were a couple of guys at the urinals who gave them a
knowing glance as they came in, but either she didn't notice or
didn't care. He pulled her into one of the tiny cubicles and
locked the door. The smell of urine and worse inside wasn't the
greatest aphrodisiac, but he was too far gone to care. He shoved
her up against the graffitied wall, grabbed one of her boobs and
squeezed hard. That was as far as foreplay went. She pulled
down her knickers and hitched up her skirt, resting one foot on
the loo seat to give him access. As he finally plunged into her
soft, wet warmth, he closed his eyes and pretended that it was
Caitlin.

Elliott was in two minds about taking Morgan back to his room
that night. After all, it wouldn't do for Caitlin to see them
together. But in the end he was pleased he'd taken the risk.
Later, after she'd finished giving head, she gave him a heads-up
on Elizabeth.

'Be careful,' she warned. She took a sip of water, gurgled, then
spat into the sink. 'She's onto you guys.'

'So what? It's a free country. She can't stop us going out.'

'If that's what you think, then you've been smoking too
much of that stuff.' She gestured at the spliff he was just about
to light up. 'Come on, you know Elizabeth. If she thinks something dodgy is going on, she'll do whatever it takes to stop it.'

After Morgan had gone, Elliott spent a long time thinking
about how to deal with this little hiccup. The solution was
really quite simple.

Chapter 9

The afternoon following the rugby game, Elizabeth went round to Caitlin's room, to talk to her about Elliott.

Both Caitlin and George looked surprised to see her there. It was a stark reminder for Elizabeth that it was the first time she'd been to see her sister all term. She felt a stab of guilt again and then pushed it away. Well, she was here, now, wasn't she? That was what counted.

She asked George if she'd mind leaving them alone. Only once the other girl had grabbed her books and headed off to the prep room, did Elizabeth finally sit down on the bed. Caitlin perched on the desk.

'What did you want to talk to me about?' she asked, clearly curious about the reason for Elizabeth's sudden interest in her.

'Elliott,' she said, deciding it was best to be blunt.

Caitlin frowned. 'Elliott? I don't understand.'

Elizabeth tried to be as gentle as possible. 'Look, I noticed you two have been spending a lot of time together, and I'm worried about you.'

'Worried about me? Why?'

'Well, it's just that I don't think he's really the type of person you should be with. He's two years older than you, for a start. And he's got . . .' She stopped, wondering about the best way to phrase this. Caitlin was so desperately naïve that she wasn't sure how well she'd understand someone like Elliott. 'Well, he's got something of a bad reputation. With girls, that is.'

Caitlin smiled. 'I know he's had a lot of girlfriends,

Elizabeth. And I know that he's . . .' She blushed. 'That he's experienced.'

Well, that was something of a relief, Elizabeth thought. She wasn't totally green, then.

'But he's been really kind to me,' Caitlin continued.

Elizabeth gave a short, cynical laugh. 'Yeah, so far, maybe. Elliott can be the perfect gentleman when he wants. But it's all an act. He only does it as long as it suits him. Once he's got what he's after . . .' She trailed off, letting Caitlin draw her own conclusions.

But the younger girl was already shaking her head. 'He really isn't like that,' she said.

Elizabeth gave an exasperated sigh. 'Look, Caitlin,' she said impatiently. She hadn't anticipated having such a battle with her half-sister over this. 'I think I know him a lot better than you do.'

There was a silence. No one said anything for a minute or so. Then Caitlin tentatively asked, 'Do you like him yourself?'

Elizabeth was speechless. 'Do I *what*?' It was such a ridiculous notion that she almost laughed. Almost. 'You think I'm saying all this because I *fancy* Elliott?' She snorted. 'Please. Is that what *he* said?'

In fact, Elliott had mentioned something to Caitlin that morning. He hadn't said outright that Elizabeth was jealous – just implied that she'd stopped hanging out with him once he started going out with Morgan. But Caitlin couldn't tell Elizabeth that. After all, Elliott had sworn her to secrecy. 'No,' she said instead, hating herself for lying. 'He didn't say any-thing—'

But Elizabeth wasn't listening. 'And you believe him, I suppose?'

Caitlin hesitated a fraction too long. She wanted to find a way to answer without offending Elizabeth or being disloyal to her boyfriend. But it was already too late. Elizabeth had heard enough. She got to her feet.

'You know what?' She held up her hands in mock surrender. 'If you don't want to listen to me then that's your problem. Learn the hard way.'

She slammed the door hard on her way out.

Elizabeth resolved to put the whole unfortunate incident from her mind. She had far more important matters to worry about than what her half-sister was up to. She'd said her piece, and if Caitlin wanted to ignore her advice, there wasn't much she could do about that. Her Cambridge interview was scheduled for early December, only two weeks from now, and so all her energy needed to go into that.

She had arranged to meet her father in London the weekend before the interview. As a Christ's College graduate, he had been through the whole process and would hopefully have some wisdom to impart. Plus, it was an excuse for Elizabeth to spend some time alone with him.

The week before they were due to meet, she called several times to check he was still on for Friday night. William's PA assured her with increasing amusement that yes, her father had the whole evening penned in for her. After classes ended on Friday afternoon, she departed Greycourt in high spirits. Opening up her Porsche on the M11, she covered the distance to London in less than an hour and a half, arriving at Eaton Square in time to take a long bath and freshen up for the evening ahead.

They had arranged to meet at Le Caprice, off Piccadilly, at seven-thirty. With its convenient location near Melville's office, the glamorous brasserie had become a favourite with William ever since it had opened nearly a decade earlier. Elizabeth was ready by seven, elegant in a black strapless Versace dress, blonde hair freshly washed and falling neatly to her shoulders. She was about to leave when the phone rang.

He was cancelling. Apparently his old friend, Magnus Bergmann, was in Town and had contacted him at the last minute to see if he was free that evening.

Elizabeth thought quickly. 'Can I come, too?'

'For God's sake,' William made no attempt to hide his irritation. 'You must be able to think of something far better to occupy your evening.'

'But what about going over my interview questions?' The words were out before she could stop them. She hated having to beg for his time.

William gave an exasperated sigh. 'We'll talk tomorrow over breakfast,' he said shortly.

After they said goodbye, Elizabeth sat on the stairs, thinking. Then she picked up the phone and called Claridge's. She remembered Magnus saying once that it was the only place he would countenance staying when he was in London. She had remembered correctly. The helpful receptionist told her that Mr Bergmann had just departed for the evening, but if she would like to leave a message . . .

Elizabeth demurred, saying she would call back later. In fact, she had no intention of doing anything of the sort. She would much rather see him in person.

Elizabeth's early memories of Magnus Bergmann were sketchy. He and William had first met in the late sixties, when a young, hungry Magnus had become the Melville heir's stockbroker. The two men's professional relationship had swiftly developed into a close friendship, and as they grew older, acquiring wives and then children, it was only natural that their families should socialise, too. When it came time for Elizabeth's christening at Wells Cathedral, Magnus stood at the font as her godfather. Not that he ever made much effort to fulfil his duties. He wasn't the type to show a great deal of interest in children, even his own. The appropriate gestures were made – his somewhat insipid wife sent cards and gifts of expensive jewellery on birthdays and at Christmas – but other than that he remained a distant figure in Elizabeth's life, rather like her father.

Elizabeth was eight years old when Magnus relocated to New York, to set up a hedge fund. It was a busy time for him. The rare trips he did make to London didn't factor in time to get down to Somerset. Elizabeth, who had barely known him anyway, hardly noticed his disappearance from her life. That all changed the year she turned sixteen, the year before Caitlin arrived at Aldringham.

As usual that summer, the family had been holidaying at Villa Regina, the Melvilles' elegant stone villa located on the shores of Lake Como. In the Lombardy region of Northern Italy, Lago di Como was less than an hour from Milan and mere moments from Switzerland, which meant it benefited from lush, green Mediterranean mountains rising straight from the water's edge as well as a backdrop of snow-capped Alpine peaks. It was an idyllic place to be.

That summer, however, Elizabeth had been having a far from idyllic time. By the third day, she was already bored. Her mother and sister were busy sunbathing and shopping – neither of which interested Elizabeth – and her father was almost constantly on the phone to his office. Uncle Piers, her usual ally, had stayed in England to look after Rosalind, who was recovering from a fall. Elizabeth felt trapped and couldn't wait for the fortnight to end.

That particular day, she woke from her *riposo* before the rest of the house. Slipping into a light summer dress, she stepped out onto the balcony. The oppressive heat of the August afternoon had subsided into the cool of the early evening: the perfect time to wander around the grounds.

She managed to sneak through the house without disturbing anyone and headed outside. Immediately, she felt better. Like most of the exclusive properties that fringed Lake Como, Villa

Regina had charming gardens, stretching down to the lakeside in a series of terraces. She strolled by olive, citrus and cypress trees, and down the villa's winding cobbled pathway. On impulse, she continued through the cool, damp underground tunnels, which led to the dock where the Melvilles' sail- and speedboats were tethered. She walked to the end of the jetty and sat down, dangling her legs over the side, her toes dipping into the cool water. She closed her eyes, content to listen to the rhythmic sounds of the lake lapping against the great stone walls that surrounded the villa.

So lost in thought was she, that she didn't realise someone had joined her on the dock until she felt the wood creak under the new arrival's weight. She turned, expecting to see her father. Instead, she found herself staring up at a tall, good-looking man in his mid-forties.

'Hello, Lizzie,' he said with a familiarity that threw her. He saw her confusion and smiled. 'Don't worry, I hardly recognised you either – I forgot you'd be all grown up! It's your Uncle Magnus.' He offered Elizabeth his hand to help her up. As she stood and he fully took in the sixteen-year-old girl, showing off her newly developed figure in a flimsy cheesecloth dress, something in his expression changed. 'Although perhaps it's time we dropped the Uncle bit now.'

Elizabeth felt her bad mood lifting. At last the holiday was beginning to look up.

Magnus's decision to come to Lake Como had been a last-minute one, he told her, as they walked back to the villa. He had just been through a messy divorce, and his ex-wife had taken the children to their house in the Hamptons for the summer. He'd fancied some time to himself, and when William had suggested joining them in Italy for a week or so, it had seemed exactly what he needed.

Elizabeth listened attentively to everything he said. She had never shown any interest in the opposite sex before that summer. At Greycourt she had a reputation for being an ice-queen: standoffish, serious . . . clearly frigid. It was the only way her spurned suitors could justify being turned down. But she simply wasn't interested in schoolboys, who only cared about getting drunk and laid. Magnus Bergmann was nothing like them. He was clever, urbane and – having amassed a personal net worth of $1.5 billion – highly successful, too. He was someone Elizabeth could look up to. The fact that he was forty-four didn't even cross her mind.

Over the next few days, Elizabeth conspired to spend as much time as possible alone with Magnus. It wasn't difficult. They both loved the outdoors, so during the day they left the others sunbathing by the pool, and went windsurfing and water-skiing on the lake. Evenings in Como were low-key, nightlife at a minimum. So after the obligatory three-hour dinner, they would adjourn to the billiards room or the den, and stay up late into the night, talking. How well they got on didn't go unnoticed, but no one thought anything of it. Elizabeth had always been mature for her years, and Magnus a father-figure to her. It didn't occur to them to read anything into it.

Elizabeth waited politely for Magnus to make a pass at her. But as the days dragged on and nothing happened, she began to grow impatient. Had she misinterpreted the signals? She was sure he was attracted to her. With the holiday nearing an end, she knew that if she didn't make something happen soon, then it never would.

It was the last day of the holiday. There was no question that Magnus and Elizabeth would spend the day together. On Elizabeth's suggestion, they took the boat out early, the best time to be on the lake. They sailed across to the town of Menaggio and spent the morning hiking up the mountainside, admiring the pretty villages that dotted the way. By midday, the blazing sun was high in the sky. They found a shady spot under the leafy boughs of a giant redwood to eat the picnic Elizabeth had brought along: homemade salami, polenta, pecorino and perfectly ripened tomatoes grown on the estate, all washed down with a bottle of the somewhat average red wine that seemed to be characteristic of the Lombardy region.

Back on the boat, neither of them was eager to head home to the villa, as though they knew that would signal the end of the holiday. Instead they sailed towards a deserted cove, where they anchored the boat and went for a swim to cool off after the morning's excursion.

Magnus was the first to get out of the water. Elizabeth watched as he hauled himself onto the deck, his strong arms ripping under his body weight. She stayed in for a little longer, happy to show off, aware of his eyes on her as he stood on the deck drying himself. She splashed around, floating on her back, swimming back and forth from the boat, knowing her bronzed body looked at its best slicing through the clear water. She dived under, peering down into the depths of the lake. Then finally surfaced, pushing her wet hair back from her face and effortlessly treading water with her strong legs. She was pleased to see he was still watching her.

Finally, when she'd shown off enough, she hoisted herself gracefully out of the water.

'Wow, Lizzie, where do you get the energy?' Magnus joked, as she towelled off. 'I felt exhausted just watching you in there.'

'Anything to keep in shape,' she said, deliberately drawing attention to her long, lean body. He swallowed hard and quickly looked away.

By mutual agreement, they decided to laze in the sun until they'd dried off. Magnus stretched out on his beach towel, one hand shading his eyes from the glare of the mid-afternoon sun reflecting off the water. Elizabeth flopped down next to him.

They lay in silence. The only sounds punctuating the quiet were shouts of laughter coming from other boats criss-crossing the lake. After a while, Elizabeth rolled onto her side, so she was propped up on one elbow, looking down at Magnus. His eyes were still closed. It was now or never . . . After a moment's hesitation, she reached out and trailed her fingers across the flat of his stomach. Her touch was feather-light, almost a question. She waited a moment to see if he was going to turn away, signal to stop. But he didn't. Instead, he stayed very still, as though he hadn't felt anything at all.

Feeling braver now, she repeated the action, brushing her fingers back and forth across his firm belly. She heard his breathing deepen. Slowly, deliberately, her thumb circled his belly button, once then twice, before boldly following the spattering of sun-bleached hair that trailed down, down into his trunks.

When she reached the waistband she paused tantalisingly, and then pressed on his warm flesh to allow her hand to slip beneath the elastic. As she found the hollow of his hipbone, he gave a little contented sigh, almost a moan deep in the back of his throat. They both heard it and froze. They stayed like that for a moment, neither of them moving. All that could be heard was their breathing and the waves gently lapping against the edge of the boat. Elizabeth knew she needed to do something, and do it quickly, if she didn't want the moment to slip away. So she leaned over and kissed him full on the mouth.

There was nothing platonic about this kiss, she made sure of that; no mistaking what she wanted to happen. Even if she made a fool of herself, it would be worth it, just to know how he felt.

But the risk paid off. Because Magnus was kissing her back. He reached up, pulling her down on top of him. Then his lips skilfully parted her own, his tongue moving gently, probingly against hers. It wasn't the first time Elizabeth had been kissed, but it was by far the best. A kiss full of experience.

They rolled over on the beach towel, sun-warmed limbs tangled together. Somewhere along the way Elizabeth felt the strings of her bikini top fall away. Not that it mattered. In their bathing costumes, they were already practically naked. It would have been impossible for Magnus to pretend he wasn't interested. She'd spent the last ten days imagining this moment, and she was eager now to get on with it. She hooked her fingers into the sides of her bikini bottoms, ready to wriggle out of them. But before she could do so, he reached out and grabbed her wrists, stopping her.

'Don't,' he said.

He pulled away from her and sat up abruptly. She stayed lying on the beach towel, unsure what was happening. He took a moment to compose himself, before turning back to look at her.

'God, Elizabeth. I'm sorry.'

'Don't be.' She grinned up at him. 'I was having fun.'

He laughed a little. 'I know,' he said, running a hand through his hair. 'So was I. But . . . well, you're a kid and I'm forty-four. And I don't want to take advantage of you.'

'You wouldn't be.' She meant it, too. Having sex for the first time didn't scare Elizabeth. Once she'd made her mind up about something, she wasn't the type to turn round and regret it later.

He gave her a wry smile, before growing serious. 'You say that now, but I'd hate to think you'd regret it later on.' He paused. 'I care too much about you, Lizzie.'

She regarded him for a long moment and decided he was serious. She suddenly felt very naked and very young. She sat up then, desperate now to find the T-shirt that she'd discarded earlier.

'Fine,' she said, trying to look as though this was no big deal. 'I understand. You're probably right.' She flicked her hair back nonchalantly. 'Why don't we head back to shore?'

Magnus opened his mouth as if to say something more. But then he seemed to change his mind.

'Of course,' he said finally. 'Let's go.'

Elizabeth would always be proud of the way she acted that day. After she'd pulled her T-shirt on, she held out her hands for Magnus to help her up. Then, in a surprisingly neutral voice, she suggested stopping to get *gelati* in Bellagio before heading back to Villa Regina.

She managed to behave with quiet dignity until they parted at the airport the following morning. It was only once she was on a plane back to England that she admitted to herself how humiliated she felt. After years of being told she was mature for her age, someone had finally told her otherwise. While she might be academically ahead of the game, she still had a lot to learn before she would truly be a woman. And she was determined to do something about it.

She approached the matter of finding an appropriate partner to divest her of her burdensome virginity with the same calm logic that she applied to tackling Physics problems. She knew she could have her pick from the boys at school, but Greycourt was an incestuous place. Whoever she chose would be bragging about nailing the uptight Melville heiress before she'd had time to pull her knickers back up. No – she needed someone who valued discretion as much as she did.

Giles Butler, the school's tennis coach, was the obvious answer. At thirty, he was by far the hottest member of the faculty. Each year, at least a dozen Greycourt girls tried to seduce him, and failed. It wasn't that he wasn't tempted, but sleeping with a student was a sackable offence. So he stuck to the bored housewives he tutored on weekends instead. But he hadn't reckoned on Elizabeth Melville. Once she put her mind to something, she always got what she wanted.

Seducing him wasn't difficult. As Captain of Tennis, it was

easy enough to make an appointment to go round to his rooms to discuss the term's fixtures. While she was there, she complained of a strained ligament in her right calf. If it had been any other girl, Giles might have been more wary about examining an injury in his private rooms. But sensible, trustworthy Elizabeth was the last person anyone would expect to behave inappropriately.

'It doesn't seem swollen,' he said, his cool hands running the length of her lower leg. He was so busy searching for the problem, that at first he didn't notice her flexing her foot, burrowing deep in his lap, softly massaging his groin with her toes . . .

He froze. 'Elizabeth!' He sounded shocked, outraged even. But she noticed he still had hold of her calf, and was making no effort to remove her foot, which was working away at his now semi-erect penis.

Slowly, she removed her leg from his grasp, got up and walked over to the door, flicking the lock. When she turned back, he was already removing his shirt.

Her first time was surprisingly easy. She even managed a small orgasm, although it was nothing compared to what she could achieve alone under the covers in her dorm room.

As the term wore on, they met at least twice a week in his room. The small fold-out cot was the scene of Elizabeth's sexual education. As in every other aspect of her life, she was eager to learn. But by Christmas Giles was growing clingy, and she was getting bored.

'I don't know how I'm going to stand a whole month without you,' he murmured, as they lay together the night before she was due to go home. His fingers traced the length of her bare spine, and it was all she could do not to shudder.

Later that night, he presented her with a beautifully wrapped Christmas present – which she neglected to take with her when

she left Greycourt the next day. Nor did she bother returning
his increasingly frantic calls to Aldringham during the holidays.
When she got back to Greycourt in January she told him gently
but firmly that it was over.

Giles was devastated. Elizabeth was not. She had already set
her sights on the newest member of staff, the far more aloof
History Teaching Assistant, Tristan Foxworth. Freshly graduated from Bristol, he was passing the time teaching while
pursuing a career in county cricket. She suspected he was
seeing other girls, but didn't much care. She wasn't in love with
him and had no desire to make their relationship exclusive.

After Tristan, there were others. No one of any conse-
quence.

She hadn't seen Magnus since that humiliating day back in
Italy over a year earlier. Now, with her newly acquired experience, she was ready to finish what they had started.

Having reconciled herself to not seeing her father for dinner,
Elizabeth spent the evening reading in the first-floor sitting
room at Eaton Square. When she heard the antique grandfather
clock finally strike eleven, she put her Physics textbook away,
left the house and headed up to Belgrave Road, where she
easily caught a cab over to Brook Street.

Once at Claridge's, she checked with reception: Magnus was
still out. She left word for him to come to the bar when he
returned. She was halfway through her cognac when Magnus
appeared. If he was surprised to see her, he didn't show it.

'You're lucky your father didn't come back with me,' he said,
as they waited for the lift.

Elizabeth gave him a cool look. 'Actually, I think it's you
who were the lucky one. After all, Daddy would be more likely
to blame the responsible adult – don't you agree?'

Magnus was still laughing at that as the lift doors closed.

*

The next morning, Elizabeth woke early in the hotel. After a quick shower, she left Magnus asleep and headed over to Eaton Square. Her father still wasn't up. She wrote him a brief note to say that she needed to get back to Greycourt immediately and would call him during the week to talk.

She never bothered. She went off to Cambridge without the benefit of William's input. It made no difference. At the end of three flawless interviews, she was confident that she had secured a place.

In all that time, Elizabeth hadn't given Elliott and Caitlin another thought. But the following day, as she checked the ticket sales for the Snow Ball, she spotted Elliott's name – and in the adjacent column labelled 'guest', was Caitlin's.

Elizabeth sat back and pondered this for a while. After her last conversation with Caitlin, her instinct was to stay out of it. But despite this, she couldn't help feeling a certain responsibility for her half-sister. Perhaps she needed to try harder to make the girl see sense.

She finally decided she would go round to Caitlin's room later, offer to take her shopping for a ball dress and then, when they were out, she could tackle her on the subject of Elliott again.

Chapter 10

Caitlin stood in front of the full-length mirror, smoothing down the folds of her gown. It was the night of the Snow Ball and all across the school, girls were styling hair, applying make-up and making last-minute adjustments to their outfits.

Caitlin had ended up designing the dress herself after a disastrous shopping trip with Elizabeth the previous Saturday. The two girls had spent the morning trawling round elegant boutiques, Caitlin trying on outfit after outfit. But everything was far too sophisticated for her tastes.

Elizabeth had been getting increasingly irritated when they happened to pass an art shop. In the window, Caitlin spotted a reproduction of her favourite painting, Edmund Blair Leighton's *The Accolade*. It showed a maiden knighting a kneeling warrior. The maiden was clad in a medieval gown of flowing ivory silk with gold Celtic embroidery trimming the waist, neckline and arms. It was a fairytale dress, capturing a long-forgotten age of chivalry and romance, and it gave Caitlin an idea. Dragging Elizabeth to a rundown haberdashery, she bought up yards of cut-price material.

Making the gown wasn't difficult. Her mother had been a dab hand at dressmaking, and Caitlin had often helped her out. Mrs Collins, Berrylands' Housemistress and Head of Home Economics, allowed her to use the school sewing machines in the evenings. Now Caitlin stood in almost an exact copy of the dress in the painting. Swapping the pale silk for green velvet gave it a dramatic, wintry feel, and flattered her pale skin. With her dark hair curling over one shoulder, she could have been Guinevere at Camelot.

'You look wonderful.' George stood behind Caitlin, smiling at her in the mirror.

'Thanks.' Caitlin reached up and touched her curls. 'And thanks for your help.' George had spent hours taming her hair into pretty ringlets. Caitlin wanted to say more, apologise for neglecting her lately, but before she could, there was a knock at the door.

It was Elliott. He did a double-take when he saw Caitlin.

'Wow,' he said, in case there was any doubt what he thought.

Caitlin smiled shyly up at him. She'd been worried he might not like her gown. She knew all the other girls would be competing to reveal as much flesh as possible, but skin-tight, skimpy clothes just didn't suit her figure.

From behind his back, he produced a small bouquet of miniature roses. Elizabeth's wrong about him, Caitlin thought. She frowned at the memory. When they'd gone shopping, Elizabeth had brought up Elliott again, saying all the same stuff as before: that he was using her, telling her how he'd treated Morgan. Caitlin had insisted he wasn't like that; her sister had got angry with her for not listening and they'd ended up driving back to Greycourt in silence.

Now, seeing how sweet Elliott was being, Caitlin knew she had been right to defend him. George took the flowers from her, saying she'd put them in water, and urging them to be off. Even she had managed to put aside her dislike of Elliott this evening and smiled benevolently at the couple as they left for the ball. She had never seen Caitlin look so happy. She hoped her friend had a wonderful evening. She deserved it.

Like everything else at Greycourt, the annual Snow Ball was the ultimate in sophistication and good taste. The boys wore dinner jackets that had been custom made, not bought or hired;

the girls had shopped for their dresses in Selfridges, Liberty and Harvey Nichols. The only hint of Moss Bros and Top Shop was among the scholarship students.

The Ball committee had outdone itself this year. Everyone agreed on that as they filed into the circus-sized marquee that stood on the school grounds. It was only to be expected, of course, given that the event had come together under the expert eye of Elizabeth Melville. Inside, the huge tent had been transformed into a Prohibition era speakeasy, with dark drapes, low lighting and an intimate dance floor. A jazz band, made up of the most talented musicians in the fourth and fifth years, played softly on a raised dais at the front.

Elizabeth herself looked typically aristocratic in a strapless red crêpe gown, her hair swept up into a French pleat and a string of pearls around her swanlike neck. She had stationed herself by the welcome drinks table, so she could greet everyone as they came in – as well as make sure each person only took their one allocated glass of bubbly.

By eight, the Sixth Form and their dates for the evening were all there. The dance floor was full. There was a queue at the buffet – everyone helping themselves to the delicate canapés supplied by Fortnum & Mason – and a crowd was gathered around the roulette table. Caitlin and Elliott were among the last to arrive. Caitlin was unaware of the stir they caused, walking into the tent arm-in-arm. Dressed in a tux, his dark hair still damp from the shower, Elliott looked every inch the upper-class cad. Caitlin, in contrast, was a curious mix of virginal and sexually ripe. But while they were undoubtedly the best-looking couple in the room, that wasn't the reason everyone turned to stare at them. Word had got out about the bet. Most of the Sixth Form – with the marked exception of Elizabeth Melville – knew tonight was the night for Caitlin and Elliott. It was all anyone was talking about.

Morgan's clique stood huddled in a corner, watching their entrance.

'She looks gorgeous,' Lucille Lewis said enviously, glancing down at her own boring strapless black number.

There was a murmur of agreement.

Morgan's eyes narrowed. She was conscious that no one had complimented her on how she looked. Maybe the shell-pink cocktail dress had been a mistake. The shop assistant had tried to tell her that the pale colour washed her out but, as usual, Morgan hadn't listened to the well-meaning advice.

'I think she looks weird,' she said stoutly.

No one said anything. They could sense her jealousy and it made her seem weak.

Standing next to Morgan, Lucy Briars sighed dreamily. An English student with a penchant for romance novels and an overactive imagination, she had been closely watching the burgeoning relationship between Caitlin and Elliott.

'I wonder if they're in love?' she said now.

'Don't be ridiculous!' Morgan replied irritably. 'Elliott's only doing this for the bet.' But secretly, even she was beginning to wonder if Elliott was still play-acting his feelings for Caitlin. She'd caught him staring at the Irish girl when he thought no one else was around. There was lust in his eyes and . . . something else. Affection, that was it. Morgan knew he'd never looked at her that way in all the months they'd gone out, and she burned with jealousy. She just hoped Caitlin finally got what was coming to her tonight.

By eleven, Elliott had to get away. He excused himself to go to the Gents, and instead slipped outside and round to the back of the Science blocks. The teachers were on the war path tonight, and it was the one place they weren't patrolling. Consumption of alcohol was being strictly monitored this year. The School couldn't risk a repeat of last time – when two students ended up being rushed to hospital to have their stomachs pumped. It wasn't the sort of publicity Greycourt wanted.

By the time he reached the Chemistry lab, quite a crowd had gathered. There were smokers, couples making out. One enterprising soul had brought alcohol along and was selling it at a huge mark-up. There were almost more people out here than in the marquee. It was only a matter of time before someone caught onto where everyone was hiding.

A few people acknowledged Elliott as he walked by, but most prudently ignored him. The black look on his face was enough to warn them off. He ducked behind a wall and squatted down.

Tonight wasn't going like he'd hoped. He'd thought it would be easy, fun. He hadn't expected to feel . . . well, quite so guilty. When he'd arrived at Caitlin's door and saw her standing before him, looking so beautiful and innocent, he'd begun to wonder whether maybe he shouldn't go through with this, after all.

But if he didn't, then he would be a laughing-stock. His reputation would be in ruins. And he couldn't have that.

He slipped his hand into his pocket. The pills were still there: GHB, an over-the-counter alternative to anabolic steroids. He'd got them off some bodybuilders from the local gym when he'd wanted to beef up earlier in the rugby season. They also had the handy little side-effect of acting like Rohypnol.

It was a last resort – but one that was looking increasingly necessary. Taking out the silver hip-flask he'd brought with him, Elliott swigged the almost neat vodka. It made him feel better, so he drank down some more. He'd go back inside in a bit. He just needed a little more time to gather his thoughts.

Caitlin was having a glorious evening. This was nothing like the dances back home, where the boys from the nearby school lurked moodily at the edges of the room while the girls stood in small, giggly circles. Here, couples were dancing together properly, attempting the waltz, quickstep and jive, thanks to the compulsory Ballroom and Latin American lessons over the past few weeks. It all felt very grown up.

For the first time since coming to Greycourt, Caitlin felt fully accepted. Loads of the girls had come up to ask her where she'd bought her dress. They'd looked impressed when she told them she'd made it herself.

'Is that what you want to do?' Lucille had asked, fingering the green velvet bodice. 'Be a designer?'

'I don't know.' It was an honest reply. She'd never really thought about what she wanted to do with her life. Other people plotted and planned. She wasn't like that. But it was nice that someone thought she might be capable of doing something so glamorous.

A hand touched her shoulder. It was Elliott. Naturally he looked fabulous tonight, darkly handsome. Without a doubt, Elliott Falconer was born to wear black tie.

'I was wondering where you'd got to,' she said.

'Just needed some air,' he told her. Then he held out his hand. 'Will you dance with me?'

Caitlin smiled. This was what she'd been waiting for all night. She let him lead her onto the dance floor. It was perfect timing. The lights darkened and the song changed to a slower number, Roxette's 'It Must Have Been Love', made famous by that summer's blockbuster movie, *Pretty Woman*. Elliott took her in his arms. She rested her head against his strong chest and closed her eyes. She felt his hand stroking her hair away from her face, as he pulled her closer. Their bodies moved together. Caitlin sighed contentedly. This was everything she'd waited for.

'Let's sit down for a bit,' Elliott said after a while.

Caitlin didn't especially want to. She was happy dancing. But she let him lead her to a table in the corner. It was a dark, secluded spot, hidden behind an ornamental pillar. A moment later she realised why he'd chosen that particular place away from everyone, as he reached into the inside pocket of his jacket and took out a hip-flask.

He unscrewed the lid and held it out to her. 'Ladies first.'

She hesitated for a moment. She'd never really drunk before, and knew it was against the rules. Only Sixth Formers were allowed alcohol tonight, and even that was on restriction: tokens had been handed out for a glass of champagne as they came in and then two more drinks over the course of the evening.

Elliott saw her indecision. 'Hey, don't worry,' he said easily. 'If you don't want to, that's fine. All the more for me.'

She felt foolish then. Why shouldn't she have a tiny bit of alcohol? She always did everything by the book. Maybe it was time to be reckless. 'Wait,' she said, stopping him just as he was about to take a swig. 'I'll try some after all.'

The vodka hit the back of her throat, taking her by surprise. Instinctively, she gagged, and a little of the liquid escaped from the side of her mouth and down her chin. Laughing, she wiped it away.

'Finish it up, if you want,' Elliott said. 'There's plenty more where that came from.'

She forced herself to drink it down, wanting to show him that she could be as laidback as Morgan or Lucille. He watched, pleased, as she finished it up and handed the flask back to him.

'Good girl,' he said, tucking it back in his pocket.

Then he held out his hand and escorted her back to the dance floor.

Elizabeth's crowning glory for the evening was a fireworks display at midnight. She'd managed to persuade a team of professional pyrotechnicians to mount a state-of-the-art display for free. They had been working on it for two days straight, building pontoons stacked with fireworks on the school's playing fields, which would be set off using three computers.

The display was timed perfectly to last fourteen minutes and twenty-three seconds – the full duration of Tchaikovsky's *1812 Overture*, which was to be played over loudspeakers at the same time. The climax of the display was a complex lancework tableau in the shape of the Greycourt insignia.

At a quarter to twelve, Elizabeth started ushering the guests outside. One hundred and fifty students and teachers crowded onto the rugby pitch. Heels sank into the muddy field; the girls shivered in their skimpy gowns, too vain to put on coats, and waited for a chivalrous boy to offer his jacket. Inside the school building, the lower years sneaked out of bed and crowded around the dorm windows, noses pressed against the glass so they could enjoy the fireworks, too.

As Caitlin followed Elliott outside, she stumbled on the steps and he turned to catch her. She mumbled a 'Thank you,' and wondered what was wrong. Her head felt muddled, her legs heavy. But she didn't want to say anything because the display was just about to start.

The countdown to midnight began.

'Ten . . . nine . . .' the crowd chanted.

Caitlin tried to join in, but for some reason no sound came out of her mouth.

'Five . . . four . . .'

Something wasn't right, she was sure of that now. But if she could just hang on for a little while longer, then she could go in, go to bed.

'Three . . . two . . . one!'

The first rocket exploded, a shimmer of red and gold in the night sky. The crowd oohed and aahed their appreciation.

Somewhere at the back, Caitlin tried to focus on the fireworks. Tiredness swept over her. She couldn't keep her eyes open or her head up. Maybe it was the alcohol. But she didn't think she'd drunk that much.

Elliott was saying something to her. She could see his lips

moving, but she couldn't hear the words. Her body sagged, and he put his arm around her waist, holding her up. And then . . . then . . .

Nothing.

Elliott half-dragged, half-carried Caitlin through the school. By the time he got to the spiral staircase that led up to his room, he was out of breath, his dress shirt soaked with sweat. He tried the first step and buckled under her dead weight.

Deciding to take a rest first, he propped her up against the wall. With one arm still supporting her, he started searching for his cigarettes. He was so caught up in his task that he didn't notice the Ashford twins coming up behind him. They saw the unconscious girl in his arms and grinned at each other.

'Where's Lover Boy sneaking off to?'

Elliott jumped guiltily, thinking he'd been caught. It took him a moment to realise it was only his roommates loitering in the shadows. In matching black tie, it was even harder than usual to tell them apart. He relaxed a little, as much as he could when he was struggling to hold Caitlin up. 'What the hell are you guys doing here?'

'We got bored,' Seb said.

Nick held up a bottle of Bollinger that he'd swiped. 'So we thought we'd bring the party up here instead. We didn't expect you to be . . . er . . . *entertaining*, shall we say.' The twins' eyes shifted simultaneously to Caitlin, who was slowly sliding down the wall.

'Oh dear,' Seb drawled. 'Now she doesn't look too good, does she, Nick?'

Nick nodded solemnly in agreement. 'No, not too good at all.'

'She had a bit too much to drink,' Elliott started wittering. 'I thought it'd be easier to bring her back here.'

The twins raised sceptical eyebrows.

Seb stepped forward. 'Why don't we give you a hand?'

With the other two helping, it was easy to carry Caitlin up the stairs and through to Elliott's room. They dumped her face down on the bed and then Seb and Nick left him to it.

It wasn't as much fun as he'd thought it would be. He was used to girls being responsive, wanting it as much as him. A limp body wasn't quite so much of a turn-on. It didn't help that in the sitting room, he could hear the pop of the champagne bottle being opened, the sound of the twins' laughter filtering through the door. He had a feeling they were doing it deliberately.

It was kind of a relief to finally finish. He cleaned himself up, rearranged her clothes and went to join the others. As he came through the door, Seb drained his champagne, stood up and made for Elliott's room.

'What are you doing?' Elliott asked nervously.

Seb stared at him. 'What do you *think* I'm doing?'

Elliott wanted to object, but he wasn't really in a position to start acting morally superior. And what was the harm? Surely she was too out of it to notice. He watched as Seb closed the door to his bedroom, and then turned to Nick.

'So what else have we got to drink around here?' he asked.

There wasn't really anything else to do now, apart from get good and drunk.

Chapter 11

When Caitlin woke the morning after the ball she knew something wasn't right.

On the surface, nothing was out of place. She was in her room, in her bed, safe under her pink duvet, wearing her pyjamas, her gown folded neatly over a chair. But she knew something was wrong. She felt wrong. Her limbs ached for one thing, as though she had flu, and she thought she might throw up. She wondered if this was what a hangover felt like.

She remembered being at the ball, dancing, chatting and laughing . . . then everything faded. She could feel the memories at the back of her brain, waiting to be unlocked. She closed her eyes and tried to remember, but she must have drifted off instead, because the next moment she was dreaming, detached from her body, as though she was watching herself in a movie . . .

She was in a room, a room as dark as a cave, lying on a bed of coats. At first she thought she was alone, but then the mattress sank down and she knew someone else was on the bed with her. The musky odour of aftershave told her it was a man.

'Elliott?' she tried to ask as he moved towards her.

But then she felt his full weight on top of her, forcing her legs apart, and she knew it couldn't be Elliott, because he wouldn't do something like that to her. Through her haze, she felt a tearing pain. And then he was pumping away at her, so hard that she wanted to cry out. But she couldn't. On and on he went, until finally he stiffened and fell limp on top of her.

After a while his breathing steadied and he climbed off. She lay quietly, thinking that at least it was all over now. But then the door opened, there was a hushed conversation, and another person took his place. And then another . . . until every part of her ached and begged for them to stop.

This time when she woke, there were tears on her cheeks.

Everyone knew. Caitlin didn't know how, but they knew. Everywhere she went, people were staring. As she walked along the corridor to the shower, she could feel them watching her. They were talking about her, too. Conversation died when she entered a room and resumed when she left. People's eyes followed her as they whispered and laughed behind their hands.

She clutched her towel around her and hurried back to her room.

She waited for Elliott to come and see her. When he didn't, she wasn't sure what to do. She had no one to talk to. George could barely meet her eyes.

She didn't go to hall that night. She told Mrs Collins, Berrylands' Housemistress, that she wasn't feeling well. In truth, she couldn't face everyone staring at her.

She was sitting alone in her room, staring out of the window into the darkness, when there was a knock on the door. She got up to answer it, thinking that it must be Mrs Collins coming to check on her. But when she opened the door, she found Elizabeth standing there, fierce and unsmiling.

Caitlin's heart sank. *So she's heard too.*

'We need to report what he did.' Elizabeth's voice didn't invite any argument. She'd heard the rumours in the Sixth Form refectory today. Caitlin with Elliott and the Ashford twins . . . Morgan had been gleefully spreading it around.

At first, she'd assumed it was all just talk. She'd come up to Caitlin's room to let her know what was being said, so they could set everyone straight. But as soon as she'd seen Caitlin, eyes red and skin grey, she'd realised there was much more to this. Having forced her sister to tell her side of the story, it was obvious to the older girl what had really happened last night. Caitlin was just too naïve to work it out. She thought she'd got drunk and agreed to do something she now regretted. Elizabeth knew better. She'd heard whispers before, but hadn't believed Elliott would really stoop that low – although she wouldn't put anything past the twins. Well, they weren't getting away with it this time. Elizabeth was going to make sure of that.

'We'll go to Dr Phillips,' she said. 'I'll come with you, back you up.'

But Caitlin was adamant. 'I don't want to do that. I'm fine—'

'You're not fine!' Elizabeth exploded. 'God! Haven't you learned anything from this? If you'd listened to me in the first place, then maybe—' She stopped abruptly, but it was too late. She could see from the hurt in Caitlin's eyes that she'd already finished the sentence for her: *then maybe this wouldn't have happened*.

Damn. Had she really just said that? She hadn't meant to make Caitlin feel even worse. But comforting people simply wasn't Elizabeth's forte. She was only good at taking action. Plus, she felt partially responsible, too. If she hadn't been so busy then she might have guessed what Elliott and the others were up to, and been able to stop it. She had promised to look out for Caitlin, and she'd failed. She had no idea how she was going to make this right.

Caitlin looked up at Elizabeth. She seemed so angry. Caitlin couldn't find it in herself to feel that way. She just felt . . . guilty. Whatever Elizabeth said, she couldn't help believing it was her fault. She'd wanted to do it, hadn't she? All those times she was with Elliott, she'd wondered what it would be like. Maybe he'd been able to sense that.

Elizabeth was staring intently at her. 'This isn't your fault,' she said, as if she was reading Caitlin's mind.

'Maybe,' Caitlin said slowly. 'But please ... you can't say anything.'

'Caitlin—'

'No.' For once, Caitlin was insistent. She wanted to forget this. Dragging the Headmistress in would only make it worse. 'I mean it,' she said. 'You have to swear that you won't tell.' Caitlin could see that Elizabeth wanted to argue with her. But she also knew that her sister wasn't the type to go behind her back. If she made a promise, she wouldn't break it.

'Please, Elizabeth. It's up to me. And this is what I want.'

The older girl sighed, reluctantly giving in.

'Fine. I won't say anything.' Her green eyes narrowed dangerously. 'But I still think he needs to pay.'

A few days later, the gossip about Caitlin was upstaged by a greater scandal.

Dr Phillips, Greycourt's Headmistress, received an anonymous tip that someone in the Upper Sixth was storing large quantities of drugs in their room. The accusation couldn't be ignored. At dawn the following day, four senior members of staff held an impromptu inspection of all Sixth Form rooms.

The search took a little over forty minutes. It was finally called to a halt when half a kilo of cocaine was found in the sitting room shared by Elliott Falconer and the Ashford twins. The three were led away in their boxer shorts and rugby shirts to Dr Phillips's office, protesting their innocence.

No one believed them. It wasn't the first time they'd been associated with rumours concerning drugs. The faculty had turned a blind eye for personal consumption, but this time the boys had gone too far: a Class A drug, plus the quantity involved was far too great to ignore. All three were immediately expelled.

'If they go quietly,' Dr Phillips told both sets of parents, 'the police won't need to be called.'

Elizabeth never said anything about the matter, and Caitlin never asked her outright if she had anything to do with it. But the next time Caitlin passed Elizabeth in the hallway, she smiled at her. And, for the first time ever, the smile was returned.

After that, the last few days of term passed quickly. Caitlin went through the motions, laughing in the appropriate places at the panto put on by the Lower School, singing at the Carol Service, pulling crackers at the Christmas lunch. On the outside, everything was perfectly normal. But inside she couldn't get back to how she had been before that night. George invited her to stay with her family for a few days over the Christmas break, but Caitlin just wanted to be left alone.

Back at Aldringham, she found it hard to settle into the holiday festivities. She felt ridiculous. The *incident*, as she referred to it in her head, was over. *They* were gone from her life for ever. There was no reason to mope. Elizabeth had said once, when they were alone, that if she ever wanted to talk then she was happy to listen. But Caitlin had made it very clear that she didn't. She just wanted to try to put what had happened behind her.

The sound of laughter made Caitlin glance up from her sketchbook. The large bay window in her room gave a clear view across the estate. She looked out at Amber and Elizabeth, who were walking back through the snow-covered grounds to the warmth of the house. Chris, the Melvilles' groom, followed behind them, carrying a six-foot pine from the forest. The girls had gone with him to pick it out. Later that night, over mince pies and brandy, they would decorate it for Christmas. It was an annual ritual for the Melville children, Elizabeth had explained that morning at breakfast, when she'd invited Caitlin to join them. Caitlin had said that she would, but when it had come round to it this afternoon, she hadn't wanted to.

In fact, she hadn't been in the mood to do much recently. Ever since she'd got back for the Christmas holidays she'd just been sleeping and sketching. Elizabeth tried to include her, but Caitlin just wanted to be left alone.

Half the time she felt numb, and she could handle that. But then other times she would feel a rush of anger so violent that it frightened her. The same futile thoughts kept going through her head. If her mother hadn't died . . . if she hadn't been sent to live with the Melvilles in the first place . . . then none of this would have happened. It was slowly consuming her, the knowledge that she should never have come to Aldringham; that she didn't belong in this world.

Instinctively she looked towards the large wooden trunk that stood in the corner of the room. It contained all her mother's clothes and personal belongings. Aunty Nuala had packed it up for her back in June, when they'd needed to clear the cottage out. The chest had been shipped to Aldringham from Ireland when Caitlin had first moved over, but so far she hadn't felt up to looking inside. Now, with everything that had happened, she needed the comfort of being among her mother's things again.

Walking over to the trunk, she knelt in front of it. She kept the key on a chain around her neck. The lock was a little stiff, but finally she managed to open it. Slowly, carefully, she lifted the heavy oak lid. Inside, the lining was velvet and luxurious. It was one of the only pieces of furniture Katie had brought from her parents' house when she'd originally moved to Wicklow. Caitlin remembered how it had sat at the foot of her mam's bed, used for years as a blanket box.

On the top lay two photo albums. She opened up the first one and saw her mother's careful, loving documentation of her daughter's life – Christmases and birthdays; holidays and school plays. Aware that she was already getting lost in the memories, Caitlin closed the albums and put them to one side. She wanted to see what else there was. For the next half-hour, Caitlin sifted through the contents of the trunk. Nuala had put everything she could have wished for in there: from her mother's favourite clothes to the pieces of crockery she'd saved for 'best' – wrapped individually in tissue paper, so as not to break.

At the bottom was a folder stuffed full of official documents – Katie's Leaving Cert, Caitlin's birth certificate, the deeds to the cottage. It was all much as Caitlin had expected to find, until she finally pulled out a little bundle of letters, tied together with a red ribbon. This looked more interesting. She turned the stack over in her hand. The envelopes were all made of the same expensive cream paper, and were an identical size and shape. She loosened the bow of the ribbon and spread the envelopes across the floor. There were sixteen in all.

For some reason, she sensed that what she had found was significant. She hesitated, wondering if her mam would have approved of her going through her personal correspondence. But now she'd started this, she couldn't let it go. Feeling a little guilty, she picked up the first letter for closer inspection. It simply had her mother's name typed on the front, with no postage.

She opened the envelope: there was a letter inside. The paper was cream and stiff, good quality like the envelope. It took her a second to realise that the letter was on embossed Melville headed paper. Caitlin quickly skimmed the words: it was a letter from the Head of Personnel at the company, terminating her mother's employment. A cheque was fastened to it with a paper clip – made out for one thousand English pounds – never cashed.

What did it mean? Caitlin wondered. Her mother hadn't told her much about what had happened between her and

William. She'd simply said he'd ended it with her, before she'd known that she was pregnant. But had her mam been sacked as well? With her heart beating faster, Caitlin opened the second envelope; again, there was no address. And again, there was the same formal covering letter, referencing the cheque *as per our termination agreement*. This time, the attached cheque was made out for five thousand pounds. Caitlin was about to put the letter back, when something caught her eye. The date on the cheque: 3 June 1975. It was her birthday. It took her a moment to process the significance. It couldn't be a coincidence, surely – which could only mean one thing: William had known about her all along.

The rest of the envelopes were addressed and posted to Ireland – first to her grandparents' house, and then forwarded on to the cottage in Valleymount. Caitlin went through each one. They all contained the same thing – a brief covering letter, and then a cheque dated each year on her birthday. The value increased by 5 per cent each year, but other than that, no detail changed.

It was a while before Caitlin finally felt able to pull herself together. She put everything carefully back into the trunk, closed and locked it. Then she went to the wardrobe, took out a backpack and began to stuff clothes inside. It was clear now what she needed to do – she had to get away from the Melvilles and their world.

Leaving here, starting over, was the only way to put this behind her.

Tonight, she promised herself. She just needed to get through tonight and then everything would be fine.

'We missed you this afternoon.'

Elizabeth hurried down the stairs towards Caitlin, Amber trailing behind her. The three of them were on their way to the drawing room for pre-dinner drinks.

'We got a huge tree,' she said, falling into step with her half-sister. When Caitlin didn't say anything, she continued, 'And then we spent the afternoon decorating it.'

Caitlin still didn't speak.

'So – what did you get up to?'

Caitlin looked blank. 'When?'

'This afternoon, while we were out.'

Caitlin shrugged. 'Nothing much.'

'Oh.' Elizabeth wasn't sure what to say to that. 'Well, you should have come along,' she finished lamely.

'Yes, Caitlin, you should have come along,' Amber piped up. She slipped her hand into Caitlin's. Elizabeth noticed and smiled to herself. At the start of the holiday she'd instructed her to start being nicer to Caitlin. 'Why?' she'd asked.

'Because maybe I was wrong about her,' Elizabeth had answered honestly. 'She's not that bad after all.' That had been good enough for Amber.

Now, as the three girls walked towards the drawing room, Amber began to tell Caitlin about the lead role she was sure she was going to get in the spring-term ballet.

'Sienna's telling everyone that Miss Abbot promised to pick her, but I'm a much better dancer.'

As Amber chattered on, Elizabeth darted a glance towards Caitlin. The other girl looked dreadful: tired and pale. In fact, she looked almost as haggard as when she'd first arrived at Aldringham. Elizabeth was worried. She could see Caitlin was desperately unhappy and she was the only person who knew why. But she didn't know what to do with that knowledge.

Caitlin had asked that she respect her privacy and Elizabeth had tried to do that. She'd thought long and hard about whether it was wrong not to report what had happened. But that was Caitlin's wish, and Elizabeth wasn't the type to betray a confidence. She'd done what she could to help – insisting on driving Caitlin to an anonymous clinic in the next town to go through the barrage of pregnancy and STD tests, waiting for her while she was in there and then taking her back for the results – fortunately so far negative. She'd found out from George about any assignments Caitlin had due before the end of term, then completed them herself – something she didn't even think her half-sister was aware of.

But, apart from those practical gestures, she hadn't really known what else to do. So far, all her overtures at friendship had been rebuffed. In some ways, she couldn't blame Caitlin. She'd done nothing to make her feel welcome when she'd first arrived at Aldringham. Looking back, she hadn't stopped to consider how miserable and disorientated Caitlin must have been feeling. So she could hardly be surprised now, when Caitlin didn't want anything to do with her. But Elizabeth wasn't going to let that put her off. She'd made the mistake of giving up too easily last time; she wasn't going to do that again. She just worried that, whatever she did now, it was too little too late: Caitlin was already too damaged to care.

The evening felt interminable to Caitlin. With two days to go until Christmas, Rosalind and Piers had come down to Aldringham. That meant sitting through an even longer than normal five-course meal in the vaulted dining room. Afterwards, everyone took their coffee through to the drawing room, where 'the girls', as Rosalind referred to them, were tasked with arranging the presents under the tree.

'Oh, and you, too, Caitlin,' she said, as an afterthought.

Before, those little digs had hurt. But now Caitlin could brush them off, knowing that after tonight she wouldn't ever have to hear them again.

By ten, she could stand it no longer and excused herself, saying she felt as if she was coming down with flu. Isabelle was the only one to make any fuss, following Caitlin upstairs with some Paracetamol and a glass of water. She seemed reluctant to go, so in the end Caitlin feigned sleep and her stepmother eventually left.

After she had gone, Caitlin opened her eyes. She couldn't risk nodding off. Instead, she lay in the dark, waiting for the house to fall silent. Unfortunately it was impossible to judge in a place as vast as Aldringham, so she watched the clock by her bed, the illuminated digits moving from midnight to one then two . . .

By half-two she decided she must be safe. She pulled on jeans, a jumper and trainers, grabbed her backpack, and took one last look around her room. Then, her heart beating hard from a mix of fear and adrenaline, she opened the bedroom door as quietly as she could, and started down the corridor.

It was impossible to make it to the front door in total silence. However lightly she trod, the ancient floorboards squeaked, the doors creaked. She only hoped that anyone waking would assume they were just the usual noises from the old house and not come to investigate. Walking through the long corridors in the dark, even she had jumped once or twice, feeling as though she wasn't alone, hearing something that could have been another person or just the wind rattling a window.

However, she made it to the ground floor, through the front door and out towards the electric gate without any problem. She had memorised the code when Perkins brought them home from Greycourt and now quickly entered it, praying it hadn't been changed. As the gate opened soundlessly, she felt a rush of relief.

It was a ten-mile walk to the station. A cold, dark walk, along winding country lanes. More than once Caitlin had to dodge into a bush to avoid a car racing back from a Christmas party. She couldn't risk being caught. She was banking on no one missing her until mid-morning at least. That way, she'd have a good head-start.

She finally got to the station just as the cold winter sun was coming up. She found the waiting room and huddled in the corner, as far from the draughty door as possible, trying to warm up.

The ticket office opened just before the first train was due. She had a couple of hundred pounds, taken yesterday from Isabelle's dressing-table. Caitlin O'Dwyer: stealing and running away. Who would have believed it? She'd thought the money was a fortune. But five minutes later, most of it was gone, spent on the last-minute fare.

The man at the counter gave her a curious stare as she walked towards the platform. A young girl on her own, buying a single ticket to London on Christmas Eve . . . As soon as she was out of earshot, he picked up the phone.

When Caitlin stepped off the train at Paddington, she saw them. Three policemen guarding the barrier, two burly men in dark suits with them, scanning faces in the crowd. She knew instinctively they were there for her. She glanced around, looking for an escape route. For a second she thought about getting back on the train, but the disembarking passengers surged forward, carrying her along with them. There was nothing for it – she would have to try to sneak by. She fell in behind a large, noisy family and tried to blend in.

She walked confidently towards the exit. When one of the policemen met her eye, she stared defiantly back, as though she had nothing to hide. But the ploy, clever as it was, didn't work. A hand came over and rested on her shoulder, and someone said, 'Would you mind coming this way, miss?' Caitlin looked on enviously as the large, happy family continued their journey without her.

The two burly men turned out to be associates of William's, tasked to bring her home. Not a word was exchanged on the way back to Aldringham. It was early evening by the time they arrived. William was waiting for her alone.

In the study, he began the lecture he'd obviously been preparing all afternoon. What had she been thinking? The danger to herself, the worry to him and the rest of the family. Caitlin listened sullenly as he talked.

William caught her blank, angry face and despaired. Sullen – Caitlin? It was a word he would never have expected to associate with her. What had happened to the sweet, quiet girl whom he had first met six months earlier? What had made her this way?

'Don't you understand the danger you put yourself in?' he demanded. 'What on earth was going through your head?'

Again, she didn't answer.

William felt his frustration mount. Anything could have happened to her, out there alone. If Isabelle hadn't gone in early this morning to check on her . . . if the man at the station hadn't called the police . . . She was supposed to be his responsibility. And he needed to make damn certain something like this didn't happen again.

'I'm not sure how well I'm getting through to you,' he said finally. 'So let me make one thing clear.' He leaned across the desk, his face suddenly hard, his voice low and uncompromising. 'You can run away as many times as you want, but I promise you that I will keep bringing you back. It doesn't matter where you go or what you do, I *will* find you. Until you turn eighteen, you stay under my roof. Do you understand?' When she didn't respond, he repeated the question again. 'I said, do you understand?'

Slowly, she raised her gaze to meet his. 'Yes. I understand.'

He looked into her eyes. There was resentment there, but resignation, too.

'Good,' he said. He waited a beat before continuing. 'Now,' he allowed his tone to soften a little, 'is there anything else you want to talk about? Perhaps if you tell me why you're so unhappy I can help you.'

He'd been hoping that this might be the moment his clearly troubled daughter would open up to him. But instead she shook her head. 'I'm fine,' she said. 'Just tired. I think I'd like to go to bed, if that's OK.'

Caitlin could tell he was disappointed, but she didn't care. She owed him nothing. She was almost tempted to tell him how she felt – that he had abandoned her mother when she needed him most and that he needn't pretend to care about her now. Except there was no point. Once William had made up his mind about something, there was no changing it. But that didn't mean she couldn't have a plan to get out of here on her own terms.

As she walked back upstairs to her bedroom, her head felt clearer than it had for weeks. She didn't belong here, but if William wasn't going to let her go, then she would have to stay – at least for the next couple of years. But he'd said it himself. Once she was eighteen, once she was old enough to look after herself, she would walk away from the Melvilles. It was that thought, of one day escaping, that would get her through.

PART II

June 1993 – June 1995

Chapter 12

'Steer clear of Belleville,' the other girls at the hostel warned Caitlin. They were very clear on the subject. Belleville was the part of Paris to be avoided. It was rough, tough, dirty and dangerous. It was a Gallic Harlem.

It was also all she could afford.

The agent made that plain when Caitlin told him her budget. Maybe she did want a place in St Germain or the Marais. Who didn't? But Belleville was all he could offer her.

An hour later, standing outside the address he'd scrawled down, Caitlin could see why she was getting it on the cheap. Hidden within the maze of narrow, cobblestoned streets off Boulevard de la Villette, Place Ste Marthe was made up of two rows of faded turn-of-the-century townhouses. It might have been quaint, except most of the buildings were either boarded up or covered in graffiti.

Inside wasn't much better. Five flights of narrow stairs led Caitlin up to the top floor. The agent had optimistically described the tiny attic as *bijou*. It was one small room crammed with a broken sofabed, two gas rings and an elderly fridge. The bathroom smelled of mildew and there was a ring of grime around the claw-footed tub. Caitlin couldn't help thinking of William's sumptuous penthouse on the exclusive Rue St-Honoré. She could be living there in luxury.

Except she didn't want luxury. She wanted freedom and independence. And that's what this represented.

Her mind made up, she turned to the round-shouldered landlady and beamed. '*C'est parfait*,' she declared.

The old woman's eyes widened, but she quickly covered her surprise. If *la belle irlandaise* wanted to overpay for this dump then she wasn't going to stop her. She made Caitlin give her the deposit in cash, then hurried out before the girl changed her mind.

Caitlin opened her backpack and looked for somewhere to hang her clothes. There was a tiny wooden wardrobe and a somewhat unsteady-looking chest of drawers. Luckily she hadn't much in the way of belongings: DM boots, All Star trainers, three pairs of jeans and a bunch of T-shirts.

As Caitlin began to unpack, she caught a glimpse of herself in the mirror. There was no trace of the naïve fifteen-year-old girl who had arrived at Aldringham three years ago. Her look was dark and edgy now: her pale skin and black hair – chopped elfin-short – ideally suited to the nihilistic grunge craze she'd embraced. At Greycourt, where the look had been decidedly preppy, she had stood out. Walking through the school's hundred-year-old corridors, wearing her standard uniform of faded jeans and the T-shirt of some obscure Indie band, she had set herself apart as the rebel, the loner.

Greycourt. Thank God *that* was over. She had kept the promise she'd made to William that Christmas Eve and stayed to finish school. But she'd done so on her terms. She'd gone back with no interest in making friends or being accepted, no longer caring if people gossiped about her. And somehow, once she'd stopped caring, everything had gotten easier. George had still tried to stay friendly with her, but even there Caitlin had kept a distance. She was a nice enough girl, but Caitlin had known there was no point getting close – she had no intention of keeping in touch with anyone who'd known her these past three years.

Now, at eighteen, she was finally old enough to strike out on her own. And Paris was her opportunity to do that. Ironic that it was William who had originally put the idea of coming here in her head. Nearly a year ago now. Back then, like all the other final year pupils, thoughts of the future had been uppermost in her mind. Art was the only subject she made any effort in. A course in Fashion and Design had seemed like the obvious choice.

She'd spent the autumn half-term filling in application forms. Central St Martins in London was at the top of her list. With its reputation for eccentricity, it was a great place to study fashion. She probably would have ended up going there, too, if William hadn't spotted what she was doing.

'I have some excellent contacts at St Martins,' he'd told her. 'Let me know when your interview is, and I can put in a word for you.'

In that moment, St Martins had suddenly lost all its appeal for Caitlin.

When Perkins had dropped her back at school the following Sunday evening, her first stop was the Careers Room. She'd found the folder on Art and Design courses and started checking out the best places to study fashion – outside of London. Within half an hour, she'd been leafing through a prospectus for the *École de la Chambre Syndicale de la couture parisienne* – the famous college of fashion in Paris.

It hadn't taken long for Caitlin to decide that the Chambre Syndicale would be the ideal place for her to learn. Its two-year programme in fashion design and technique was world-renowned, and had been the training ground for so many great designers – Yves Saint Laurent, Issey Miyake, Valentino . . .

That night, she had filled out the ten-page application form. She'd gone to her favourite Art teacher, Mr Wright, for a reference. Since those first few weeks at Greycourt, he'd been her greatest supporter, and he'd known all about her dream of attending St Martins. When he'd seen that she was applying to the Chambre Syndicale instead, he'd made no comment on her sudden change of heart – although he had wanted to know why she was submitting the application as Caitlin O'Dwyer.

'The Melville name's too well-known in the fashion world,' she had told him and anyone else who asked. But the truth was, she didn't see herself as a Melville and she never would. Paris was her chance to start over as O'Dwyer.

She hadn't told William that she was applying to the Chambre Syndicale. She didn't want to risk him interfering. Instead, she had used one of her private study days to sneak over to Paris for the interview. Her French was just about good enough to get her through. A panel of chic Parisians had quizzed her for nearly two hours on her ideas and influences. They'd reviewed her portfolio at length, probing and critiquing her work. She'd emerged from the ordeal exhausted and discouraged. Places were limited and, after the grilling she had received, she didn't rate her chances highly. But then a few weeks later she'd received the call telling her she was in. William hadn't been happy. But in the end there wasn't much he could do about it. Her decision was made.

School had officially finished ten days earlier. She hadn't bothered hanging around for the Leavers' Ball. She'd made a brief trip back to Valleymount – her annual pilgrimage to her mother's grave – although she hadn't gone to see Nuala. Contact between them had dwindled over the past three years, reduced to exchanging Christmas and birthday cards. Caitlin guessed she was mostly to blame. She had just found it too painful to hear about everything going on back there, when she wasn't part of it any more.

She had arrived back from Ireland late Friday afternoon. She'd spent the weekend at Aldringham packing, and then booked herself on Eurostar Monday morning.

Now, her unpacking finished, she walked over to the large

window that dominated the room. From there, she could see across the rooftops, down to Canal St Martin. In that moment she forgot William, Greycourt and everything else. She was finally in Paris. And that was all that mattered.

Having sorted out somewhere to live, the next item on Caitlin's list was to find a job. She'd made up her mind months ago that she wasn't going to take a penny from William. Fortunately, after two years of receiving commendations in the Saatchi competition, she had finally won first place this year, 'the only time in the school's history that a pupil has received such an honour,' Mr Wright had announced proudly in assembly. Apart from a lavish awards ceremony in London, the prize included a generous bursary which would cover the cost of her course. Now she just needed to find the money to pay the rent and eat.

The next morning she got up early and hit the streets to look for work. It also gave her a chance to check out the area. It wasn't anywhere near as bad as everyone had warned. Spread along the hills of north-eastern Paris, in the twentieth *arrondissement*, Belleville might be one of the shabbier corners of Paris but it was also colourfully atmospheric. Originally a working-class quarter, its mazelike streets had served as home to generations of impoverished Parisians and immigrants. As Caitlin walked along, she could see its history in every inch of the place: there were Chinese noodle bars and Jewish book-shops; Arab men smoking sheesha pipes in shop doorways; the cries of North African street vendors selling plantain and sweet potatoes. It was as far away from the wide boulevards and upmarket boutiques of central Paris as you could get. Maybe living here wouldn't be so bad after all . . .

But by late afternoon, her optimism was beginning to fade. It seemed she'd tried every shop, bar and café from Belleville to Canal St Martin, but with no success. Either they'd already hired staff for the summer, or they looked down their noses at her heavily-accented French. Sticky from the July heat, she decided to head back along Boulevard de la Villette towards her apartment.

Along the way, she picked up a copy of *Carrières et Emplois* at a *tabac* and found a low-key café-bar where she could read it. Inside, she ordered an espresso. She didn't especially like the strong coffee, but it was the cheapest item on the menu. As the waiter hurried off to get her drink, Caitlin spread the paper acrosss the table and turned to the section for menial jobs. She was busy reading through the ads when the waiter returned. He set the cup down in front of her, but instead of taking the money Caitlin had laid out, he hovered for a moment. Caitlin looked up to see what the problem was. She found a tall, thin, rather effeminate-looking man of around forty staring back at her.

'Can I help you with something?' Caitlin asked.

The man smiled at the stilted French. '*Non*. But maybe I can help you.' He nodded down at the paper. 'You're looking for work?'

'That's right.'

'One of the waitresses didn't turn up for her shift today. The owner's desperate. If you can start now, the job will be yours.'

Caitlin gulped down the hot coffee and stood up.

'And my French won't be a problem with the owner?' she asked the waiter as she followed him through to the kitchen.

'No, he won't mind.'

Caitlin frowned. 'How can you be so sure?'

He turned and grinned at her. 'Because you're looking at him.'

He introduced himself as Alain Chabot, and over another coffee told Caitlin his life story. A graduate of l'École des Beaux Arts, Paris's Fine Arts school, he had been a well-respected sculptor until an early onset of osteoporosis had ended his career. Rather than mourning his loss, he had looked around for a new opportunity – and a year earlier had invested his life's savings in Café des Amis.

It had been a smart move. Alain had spotted an important trend – Belleville was changing. The area that had always been seen as harsh and uninviting had begun to attract a new breed of migrants: Paris's young, cool, bohemian crowd. Artists, writers and musicians were flooding the area, drawn there by the lure of cheap rents, just as Caitlin had been. And they were rapidly transforming Belleville into the city's newest hotspot for night-life and creativity. Disused warehouses were being converted into cutting-edge galleries. The ethnic restaurants and stores that lined Belleville's thoroughfares were now being joined by trendy café-bars, featuring hip new bands and DJs. And Café des Amis was leading the way.

'Even I'm surprised at how successful it's been,' Alain told Caitlin proudly.

Caitlin looked around doubtfully. It was nearly six now, and the café was pretty much empty.

Alain caught the look and grinned. 'Trust me. In a few hours you won't recognise the place. And you'll be wishing that it was as quiet as it is now.'

He was right. That night was a baptism of fire for Caitlin. By midnight, the place was filled with smoke, noise and an achingly hip crowd. Most had come to listen to the DJ. The room was jammed wall-to-wall with dancers, moving to the electronic beats, warming up to go clubbing later. Table service had been abandoned a few hours earlier, and Caitlin stood behind the dimly lit bar with five others, as the drunken clien-tèle shouted their requests over the chatter and the music. She messed up more orders than she got right, but luckily Alain didn't seem to mind. As soon as he'd found out that she was a design student, he seemed to have decided she would fit right in at Café des Amis.

'Working here will improve your French in no time!' he'd joked, as she struggled to remember a list of six different drinks.

As the most junior member of the team, it was her job to ensure they had enough glasses behind the bar. Whenever they looked in danger of running out, she would dash outside to the huge sidewalk, where cool young things dressed in black lounged at tables drinking red wine and *pastis*, smoking and flirting. She would take a few deep breaths of air, collect whatever empties she could, and then hurry back inside to wash them up, before getting behind the bar again.

By the end of the night she was exhausted.

'Don't worry,' Alain said, as he handed her a wad of francs. 'It'll get easier. I promise.'

It did. As the summer wore on, she found herself gradually settling into the routine. It was hard work and the tips weren't particularly good. But the other waitresses were nice enough. Plus, Alain always seemed to be short-staffed, so she could pick up as many extra shifts as she wanted before term started.

When she wasn't working, she spent time exploring the city. She bought croissants for breakfast in the nearby *boulangerie*, drank *café au lait* in the famous *Les Deux Magots*, and spent hours wandering through the pretty streets of the Marais.

During her third week there, William called to check how she was.

'I'm going to be in Paris next Thursday,' he said, at the end of their short conversation. 'We'll go out to dinner then. I'll have a table booked at *La Tour d'Argent*.'

'Sure,' she replied dutifully.

But the following week when he called, she let the answer machine pick up.

Chapter 13

As summer turned to autumn, it came time for Caitlin to start at the Chambre Syndicale. On the first day of term, she turned up half an hour early. She was still the last student to arrive. It was a stark reminder that this was the pre-eminent fashion school in the world. No one was here for an easy ride.

The School was located at 45, rue Saint-Roch, between the famous Rue de Rivoli, which housed the Louvre and the Tuileries, and Avenue de l'Opéra. The exterior of the building had all the olde worlde charm and elegance that characterised the area. Inside, classes were held in a large, airy workroom, with the obligatory stark white walls, vast windows and fluorescent lights. The space was dominated by huge cutting tables, which came complete with scissors, sewing machines and dressmaking dummies.

There were forty-five students in the year, split evenly into three more manageable groups. Caitlin's fourteen fellow classmates had already taken their places by the time she found the room. Most of the students were dressed extravagantly, showing off their style on the first day. In faded jeans and a T-shirt, she looked comparatively nondescript. Maybe people found it odd, that someone who wanted to be a designer could be so uninterested in their own appearance. But she didn't see the paradox. To her, designing was about creating a piece of artwork from cloth and thread, not slavishly following fashion magazines. The way she looked had nothing to do with her talent.

The class was made up of all different nationalities – Japanese, American and Australian, as well as native French. English seemed to be the common language and a few tentative conversations had been struck up, more to assess the competition than any real attempt at friendship.

'Parsons practically begged me to come,' a pushy New Yorker called Brooke bragged, referring to the famous school of design located in the heart of Greenwich Village. 'But I just couldn't turn down Paris.'

A camp young man from Hong Kong joined in, name-dropping a major designer where he'd interned over the summer. 'They've pretty much guaranteed me a job once I finish here,' he boasted.

Caitlin tuned out. They'd find out who had talent soon enough – talking about it wasn't going to do any good. Fortunately, right then the Course Director, Madame Tessier, arrived, cutting off any further conversation. Madame was unnaturally thin, fabulously chic and utterly terrifying. Her skin was stretched tightly over her face, making it impossible to guess her age. And her clothes were classic black and navy.

'A woman of a certain age should dress *comme il faut*,' she told the class after five minutes. 'Maybe it is the fashion to show off your midriff, but it doesn't mean anyone wants to see mine, *n'est-ce pas?*'

There were tentative giggles, which she stifled with a look. She had a discernible limp – rumoured to be from a childhood case of polio – and an elegantly carved walking stick with a jewelled handle that she liked to use to point at unsuspecting students. She also seemed to enjoy banging it hard on the floor to emphasise her point.

'You all come 'ere wanting to be the next Yves Saint Laurent,' she said in her opening speech, pounding the stick into the floor. The new intakes were already beginning to realise why there were so many dents in the wooden boards. 'But inevitably some of you will end up designing – and I 'esitate to use that word – for the 'igh street. Decide now that it will not be you.'

There was a collective nod from the class.

'There are two parts to the course,' Madame continued. 'Creatively, you will be encouraged to push your mind out of the box that it 'as grown comfortable in. Then technically, you will learn 'ow to transform a few sheets of paper into garments for the catwalk.'

The students hung off her every word. She had headed up the design team at Donna Karan in New York before coming back to her homeland to teach this course, and everyone knew that if they wanted to become the best then she was the person to listen to. She also had phenomenal connections in the industry, and would make sure her favourites were noticed by the major haute couture houses. She was the person they needed to impress – although Caitlin had a feeling that wasn't going to be an easy task.

In fact, over the next few weeks, Caitlin discovered just how hard it was going to be. The course was far more difficult than she had envisioned. The Chambre Syndicale was renowned for its traditional methods and approach to teaching, but she was still surprised by the rigidity of the class structure.

'The first year of the course is about developing technical skills and confidence,' Madame informed them early on. She wasn't lying. Caitlin had come to the school expecting to have her creativity fired, but instead she found she was expected to learn the tedious arts of garment construction and pattern-cutting, endure Computer Aided Design lessons, and write essays on the history of couture.

'When are we going to start working on some of our own designs?' she asked one day.

Madame gave her a cool look. 'When you have finally mastered the simple art of sewing a hem.' To illustrate her point, she picked up the skirt Caitlin had been working on, and in one easy movement pulled the stitching apart. She threw the material back onto the desk in disgust and walked away.

After that, Caitlin sat quietly in class, trying to absorb everything that Madame said and reminding herself that she was here to learn. Her only consolation was that everyone else seemed to be struggling as much as her. All she could do was keep her head down and try her best.

William tried not to feel disappointed as he put the phone down. It had been Caitlin, calling to say that she wouldn't be coming home for Easter. She'd claimed to have too much work. That had been her excuse for missing Christmas, too.

When the phone rang again a second later, he half hoped it was going to be Caitlin, telling him that she had changed her mind. Instead, it was his secretary.

'Everyone's gathered in the boardroom, Mr Melville,' she informed him with her usual brisk efficiency. 'Are you ready for them?'

Years of practice had made him an expert at compartmentalising his feelings. He did this now, putting thoughts of the growing distance between him and his middle daughter from his mind. He couldn't be distracted today of all days.

'Yes. I'm ready,' he said with a confidence that surprised him.

He hoped to God he was.

It was Piers Melville who had first heard about the takeover approach that morning. As Finance Director, he closely monitored Melville's share price. When the stock opened 5 per cent higher than the previous day's close, he knew something was up. A call to the Luxury Goods' analyst at Morgan Stanley had revealed the reason for the movement — rumours were circulating about a possible bid for the company.

'Who?' Piers had demanded. 'Who's behind this?'

The name being mentioned was Armand Bouchard.

Piers had gone cold. The French businessman had a reputation for being a ruthless predator. He'd slammed down the
phone and rushed next door to William's office – barging in
without knocking. William had just been coming off the phone
himself. Piers had taken one look at the grim expression on
his brother's face and known the news had already reached
him.

'That was Armand Bouchard,' William had told him. 'He
wants to meet next week.'

William had immediately put a call into US investment bank
Sedgwick Hart to help with the defence. His contact had
promised to send round its resident specialist in takeover battles:
Cole Greenway.

Now, just one hour later, Melville's eleven directors gathered
in the boardroom, waiting for Cole to arrive. When he walked
in ten minutes later, William was somewhat taken aback. These
days, he mostly dealt with Sedgwick Hart's private banking divi-
sion, which was staffed by portly, middle-aged men, ex-public
schoolboys each and every one. Cole Greenway was the very
opposite of this. Young, black and American, to William he
looked more like a rapper than a banker. Only the thousand-
dollar Hugo Boss suit and smart Emporio Armani glasses gave a
clue to his real profession. William guessed correctly that this
was the reason he wore them.

However, once Cole started speaking, any doubts William
may have had quickly vanished. Given that he'd only started
looking at Melville sixty minutes earlier, Cole already seemed to
have a grip on the company that would rival most of William's
senior management team. Most importantly, though, he had an
encyclopaedic knowledge of the aggressor, Armand Bouchard.

The French businessman was the founder and Chairman
of the luxury goods conglomerate Grenier, Massé et Sanci.
Bouchard had been on the acquisition trail for the past few

years. With a coffer full of spare cash, he was taking advantage of the early nineties' recession – which had hit the luxury goods sector particularly hard – to snap up smaller companies at a bargain price. Over the past few years, William had watched many fashion brands being assimilated into the GMS Group. But he had never expected Melville to be a target.

'Bouchard favours the creeping takeover,' Cole told his fascinated audience, his dark eyes staring at them over his trendy square-rimmed glasses. His accent was pure New York – Bronx rather than Upper East Side. A poor boy made good, William decided.

'He likes to build up a stake until he gets into a position of control,' Cole continued. 'Now, given that sixty per cent of the company is still in family hands, the only way he could do that is by convincing you to sell—'

'Well, we're not likely to do that!' William interrupted.

Cole had been pacing the floor while he talked. Now he came to a halt, placing his hands on the back of a free chair. He gave William a wry smile.

'Hey, I gotta be honest here. You're not the first family-controlled company to say that. Bouchard is a brilliant man. He's not gonna come in here, all guns blazing, demanding that you hand the company over to him. He has a way of, uh . . .' he paused, choosing his words carefully. 'Well, let's say he has a way of persuading people that it's in their best interest to work with him. And yes,' he continued quickly, seeing that William was about to interrupt him again, 'that includes men like you, who were adamant that they'd do nothing of the sort.'

William felt the first prickle of fear. 'So what do we do?' he asked gruffly. He didn't want to let on how worried he was.

Cole straightened up to his full six foot four inches. It was an impressive sight. 'Our best bet is to put him off ever trying to get a toe-hold in Melville. And here's how I propose we do that.'

For once, William shut up and listened.

The banker was certainly a compelling speaker. In fact, there was an energy about him that fired up the whole room. Most of the board were older men, uninterested in fighting battles. They had been selected for their willingness to rubber stamp William's decisions rather than any innate talent. But Cole was clearly here to win. William was grateful. He knew it could be hard for an outsider to understand the importance of the family in a business like this. But the two were inextricably linked.

For a moment William couldn't help wishing his mother was here. But her heart condition kept her confined to bed these days. Obviously he still had Piers to back him up, he thought, glancing over at his brother, who was busy scribbling down every word that Cole said, in his neat, precise handwriting. But while Piers was dependable and competent, he wasn't an ideas man. He would always look to William to provide direction. Whereas Rosalind – she would have put up a formidable fight, even now.

Not that he had any doubts about his ability to see the company through this crisis. Melville had flourished under his tenure and would undoubtedly continue to do so for many years to come. Of course – and he hated to admit this – the sheen had come off the brand a little lately. In the sixties and seventies, the Melville name had been so inextricably linked to glamour in the eyes of the public, that practically anything with the company's label on had sold. However, over the past decade, Melville had begun to lose that cachet. The bread-and-butter accessory lines of handbags and shoes were still doing well – their classic Englishness would never go out of fashion. And the lower-priced goods sold through Melville Essentials were keeping profits up. But the buzz and excitement that had once made Melville *the* name to own was no longer there.

William could live with that, though. He didn't take it as a reflection on his management skills – it was just part of the cycle that luxury brands went through. While Melville might be past its heyday, it was still one of the greatest fashion houses in the world, the brand name associated with class and breeding, old-fashioned English values. He still believed that he had handled his legacy well. William was the fourth generation to run Melville. He was determined not to go down in history as the man who sold out. That was something Armand Bouchard would just have to get used to.

The meeting wrapped up soon after that. As the other board members filed out, William cornered Cole.

'So you think this will work?' he asked Cole eagerly. 'That this is enough to make him stay away?' He had been impressed with Cole's ideas of how to deal with the GMS approach. Already he was convinced Bouchard would back off.

Cole was more cautious. 'For the time being, at least. Until he finds another chink in your armour.'

But William wasn't interested in hearing any negatives. He wanted to savour the victory. 'I have every good faith that you'll make sure there's nothing to find,' he said. He was full of confidence in Cole now, and suddenly keen to get to know this bright young man better. 'Look, I'm having a small party this weekend, at my estate in Somerset. Why don't you come down and join us? You can meet my wife and daughters.' He saw Cole hesitate and frowned. 'As long as you don't have anything planned, that is.'

In fact, Cole did have plans – plans involving a little cutie named Chenille whom he'd picked up at the Kensington Roof Gardens last Friday. He couldn't think of anything worse than hanging out with William Melville, but he was ambitious enough to know better than to refuse.

'No plans that can't be cancelled,' he said.

'Excellent!' William beamed at him. 'Let me give you the details.'

Chapter 14

Cole let out a low whistle as the taxi turned into Aldringham. 'Fucking unbelievable!' he exclaimed.

Up front, the cab driver smiled to himself. The Yanks were always blown away by this place. It had that old English charm that they couldn't get enough of.

Cole felt his bad mood lift. He'd spent the train journey from London thinking about all the stuff he'd rather be doing than hanging out with William Melville this weekend. Friday nights were sacred to Cole. Working such long hours, he looked forward to letting off steam. Spending two days with the Green Welly brigade wasn't his idea of a good time.

But, now he was here, he didn't feel so resentful. Aldringham was like a palace. *If nothing else, this is going to be an experience*, he thought, shoving twenty quid at the taxi driver.

William came out to greet him personally, pumping his hand and slapping his back like a long-lost friend.

'There are a lot of people I want you to meet this weekend,' he told Cole, ushering him through into the magnificent hall-way, 'and I also have a business proposition I'd like to run by you. But that can wait until tomorrow.'

After the impressive exterior, Cole had wondered if inside might be a disappointment – it wasn't unheard of for these country piles to get rundown. But that wasn't the case at Aldringham. The ground-floor reception rooms were grand and tasteful, with rich wood panelling, ornate hand-painted ceilings and flagged stone floors.

William summoned a maid to show Cole up to his room. When they got there, he tipped her a fiver. Seeing her confusion and embarrassment, he realised he'd made some kind of faux-pas. It was his American mentality: if it moves, tip it. She left in a hurry – Christ, she probably thought he was paying for more than the turndown service.

Once she was gone, he had a good snoop around. Like everywhere else in the house, there were the ubiquitous double-height windows and soaring ceilings. But what set the room apart was the distinctive masculine feel. Neutral tan and ochre walls provided an ideal blank canvas for framed hunt prints and cases filled with revolutionary muskets. Furnishings were at a minimum: a king-sized brass bed dominated the room, along with a free-standing wardrobe and kidney-shaped writing desk, both in rich mahogany. A stag's head had been stuffed and mounted on a wooden plaque opposite the bed. It was all very colonial. Cole flopped down onto the oxblood leather Chesterfield armchair and laughed out loud. This brother sure had come a long way from the Projects.

William had been spot on about Cole's background: he was a *very* poor boy, made *extremely* good. Cole Greenway had grown up in the infamous Soundview section of the Bronx. His childhood home was one of the anonymous high-rise towers on 174th Street and Morrison Avenue. Other than the fact he was black, his father's identity remained a mystery. His mother was a poster child for the disenfranchised African American: five kids by four different fathers and a series of minimum-wage jobs. Soundview itself was a dump, boasting a crack epidemic and twenty homicides a year. Cole was a product of his environment. By the time he turned fifteen, playing truant, drinking all day and jacking cars were all part of daily life.

But then everything changed. One bitter New York afternoon, his best friend became number eighteen in the annual body count. A stray bullet. A life over. Another statistic.

'If he'd been where he was supposed to be, in sixth-period English, it would never have happened,' the dead boy's mother kept saying at the funeral.

It was a wake-up call for Cole. He started attending school regularly, started paying attention. To his surprise, he found he was good at it. At six foot four, he turned out to be good at basketball, too. He tried out for the team and made it. His coach kept an eye on him, recognising raw talent when he saw it. When the time came, he called the scouts in to watch.

A basketball scholarship gave Cole a free ride through Dartmouth. But he was no brainless jock. With a 4.0 GPA he could have made it on grades alone. He managed to play ball all four years, as well as come in the top quarter of his class. There was talk of the NBA, but a recurring knee injury forced him to rethink. It didn't take long for him to decide on his future career. He wanted money. He wanted security. He wanted Wall Street.

He interviewed with all the big banks. Sedgwick Hart was more than happy to recruit him into their Corporate Finance Department. They were paying the most, so he was happy to accept. His fellow trainees eyed him up on the first day and assumed he was there to make up the minorities quota. He quickly proved them wrong.

His first year, he averaged ninety hours a week. He made Vice President at twenty-four. The *Wall Street Journal* ran a glowing profile on him. He was what the American Dream was all about. Last year, at the tender age of thirty, he made Executive Director. The youngest ever ED at Sedgwick Hart.

The day Cole found out about the promotion, one of the senior partners invited him into his plush corner office and offered him a secondment to London. Hints were dropped that he would make Partner within two years if he went. Cole didn't need telling twice. He had no real ties in America.

Women came and went, but right now he was too focused on making it to the top.

Cole took London by storm. He quickly made a name for himself in Sedgwick Hart's Canary Wharf offices as an expert on hostile takeovers. When William Melville contacted the bank looking for an adviser, Cole was the obvious choice.

Cole had seen the look in William Melville's eyes when they first met and knew exactly what he was thinking. He was used to it. Too young and too black – immediate suspicion. But it never took long to prove himself. And then they were all over him. Just like William was now.

The meeting with Grenier, Massé et Sanci had gone well this week. Cole had made it clear to Armand Bouchard that with 60 per cent of Melville's shares in family hands, GMS could never get control.

'We could still build up a stake,' the Frenchman had said. 'Demand a seat on the board.'

Cole had been ready for him. 'You could,' he agreed, 'but we'll go to court and argue that it's a conflict of interest to have representation from a rival fashion group. You'll be left with a two-hundred-million-pound investment that's frankly useless.'

Bouchard had been forced to concede the point – and walk away. William, delighted with the outcome, had been even more insistent that Cole come down this weekend. Cole could already guess why. William wouldn't be the first client to try to poach him. They never succeeded. Nowhere could match a US investment bank in terms of monetary reward. For him, that's what it was all about – the cash. And he was making a bundle of it. Although not enough to afford a place like this, he thought, casting an eye around the exquisitely furnished room. Well, not yet anyway.

He rose from the chair, considering what to do next. He'd already hung up his clothes. It hadn't taken long because he hadn't brought much with him: a rented tux, a pair of chinos and the jeans he was wearing. He checked his TAG Heuer watch, bought with his first bonus. It was only six. With an hour to go until pre-prandial drinks – whatever the hell they were – he decided to go for a walk and check the place out.

He managed to find his way downstairs, and one of the staff pointed him in the direction of the grounds. There was nothing shabby about the exterior either. It was olde-worlde Englishness meets Californian modernity. He passed a huge infinity pool, dipped his hand in and was impressed to find it was heated. He pressed on, down some huge stone steps carved out of the side of the rockface, and on by the grass tennis courts. It was all downhill from there, down the sweeping lawns, down, down, until the manicured gardens ended and met the borders of the wilder parklands.

He stopped still then, shielding his eyes as he looked out across the skyline. A seemingly unending vista of lush fields stretched to the horizon, bordered by a great forest of oak and sycamore trees. There was no one about for miles. Jeez, he'd never seen so much empty space. He breathed in deeply, fresh air filling his lungs. It was the rural idyll and he couldn't help being impressed. And this was someone who'd always been allergic to any landscape devoid of concrete and cars.

He was about to head back in, when a movement in the distance caught his eye. Far away, something or someone had emerged from the thicket of trees that circled the deer park. It was just a blip, a dark blur on the horizon. Cole narrowed his eyes. The blur moved closer and closer, until at last it finally came into focus. It was a horse and rider, galloping across the large open field towards him.

Cole stood watching, transfixed. He didn't know a lot about horses, but he could appreciate the beauty of seeing man and beast together, working in synchronicity. He could also appreciate that the jockey riding that magnificent black stallion was absolutely fearless. Christ, even from here that thing scared the shit out of him, as it thundered across the flat, hooves pounding the ground, soaring over bushes as high as his shoulder. You had to admire the guy . . .

But as horse and rider drew closer, Cole suddenly realised that he'd been mistaken. The jockey wasn't a man after all. It was a young woman. And a hot one at that, he thought with a grin. Dressed in skin-tight jodhpurs, blonde hair flying out from under the black velvet riding hat, a fierce expression on her face, she was like a modern-day Lady Godiva – a fully clothed version, unfortunately.

He stood, hands on hips, waiting for her to draw level with him.

She was even better-looking up close, attractive in that English aristocratic way. In her early twenties, he reckoned, and definitely to the manor born. He could spot class when he saw it. If this was the quality of the booty, then maybe the weekend wasn't going to be such a wash-out after all. Women had never been a problem for Cole and, as the girl pulled her horse up beside him, he got ready to work his magic. Unfortunately, the vision didn't give him a chance.

'I presume you're lost?' Her voice was just as he'd expected, clipped and haughty, full of good breeding.

He grinned easily. 'No, definitely not lost. Just taking a look around—' He was about to say 'before dinner' but she cut him off.

'Well, you really shouldn't be out here, you know,' she snapped. The horse whinnied, reacting to the irritation in her voice. Cole eyed the stallion nervously – that thing was huge. But the girl looked unperturbed, patting the great beast's mane reassuringly.

'I'm sure it's been made clear to you where you can and can't go on the estate. The garden is out of bounds. The kitchen's at the side of the house. If there's any confusion, perhaps you could clarify it with your manager.'

He frowned, unsure of what she was saying. Then it hit him: she thought he was part of the catering staff. Attraction turned instantly to anger. He recognised the disdain in the blonde's eyes; the way she looked down her nose at him. She reminded him of all those Boston Brahmins at Dartmouth – the ones who'd been happy to hang out with him, the big basketball star, during termtime, but still never thought he was good enough to take home for summers in Cape Cod.

He was about to set her straight, but she didn't give him a chance. She whacked the horse's rump with her riding crop. It reared up on its hind legs, nearly knocking Cole in the mouth. Instinctively he ducked away. The girl pulled on the reins, turning the stallion in one smooth move. Cole realised a fraction too late that he hadn't moved far enough away. He stood frozen as the horse's great hooves landed straight in a puddle. Muddy water sprayed up, drenching his one pair of jeans.

'Shit!'

Hearing him swear, the blonde glanced back briefly. Her eyes flicked over the damage.

'Sorry about that,' she called, not looking in the least bit repentant. 'But it's your own fault. You really shouldn't be out here.'

With that, she squeezed her firm thighs against the horse's trunk and cantered away. Cole watched the haughty figure disappear into the distance. Well, whoever she was, he thought, one thing was for sure – she was a bitch.

Elizabeth was in a good mood when she got back from her ride, which only improved when she got a message from Magnus to say that he was definitely going to make it down to Aldringham tonight. That was the main reason she'd come back from university this weekend, on the off-chance that she might see him.

Three years on, they still hooked up whenever possible. Not that they were exclusive – Magnus had made that clear early on. 'We have fun together, Elizabeth,' he'd said, 'but that's all this is. It isn't ever going to be a relationship.'

At first, she'd been hurt. But as time went by, she'd decided he had the right idea. In a few months she would be starting at Melville. She had her career to focus on and didn't have time for relationships. Sex with no emotional attachments suited her. There had been other guys at Cambridge – good catches, each and every one of them – but any time they wanted to get serious, she ended things. Magnus was the only one who had stayed constant in her life.

Now, thinking of him downstairs, she quickly showered and slid into a Ghost dress, a slither of crêpe in purest white to show off the tan she'd earned on the tennis courts. It was a simple, classy look. She left her damp hair loose and slipped into matching heels. Thank God Magnus was over six foot so she could wear them.

As tradition dictated, drinks were being served in the drawing room. Elizabeth was one of the last to arrive. The fifty-foot room was already full of men in black tie, with splashes of colour provided by their female escorts. As a nod to summer, the sash windows had been thrown open and the damask curtains tied back, to allow a breeze to filter through.

Picking up a glass of vintage Krug from the tray of a passing waiter, Elizabeth began to circulate. Working the room came easily to her – a smile here, an empty pleasantry there. As she moved through the crowd, it looked to the outside world as though she was being sociable, but in fact she was trying to find Magnus. For a horrible moment she wondered if he hadn't made it after all. But then she spotted him, standing across the room near the fireplace.

He looked good – more than good, she corrected herself; he looked great. At forty-eight, he was handsome in that intelligent, upper-class way. Still lean, too – no hint of the City paunch that most men developed after a few years of banking lunches.

He must have felt Elizabeth staring at him, because he glanced up and over in her direction.

'Hi,' he mouthed. She made a motion to say that she'd come over to him, but before she could move, her father was by her side.

'Ah, there you are, my dear.'

Across the room, Magnus saw what was happening and shrugged at her, a gesture that said, 'We'll catch up later.' Elizabeth pushed her disappointment aside and gave her full attention to her father.

'Yes, Daddy?'

He took her by the arm. 'I wanted to introduce you to the young man I've been telling you about, the one from Sedgwick Hart.'

That sparked Elizabeth's interest. She had been dying to meet the corporate finance genius that William had been raving about.

She followed her father towards the makeshift bar area, where a group of a dozen industrialists, politicians and City whizz kids were engaged in a heated debate. Elizabeth was already forming a pleasant greeting, preparing to be all charm. But the smile froze on her face as she watched William approach a tall, well-built black man, and lightly tap one of his broad shoulders. *No*, she thought. *No, it couldn't be . . .*

'Sorry to interrupt,' she heard her father murmur, 'but I just wanted to introduce you to my eldest daughter.'

There was nothing Elizabeth could do but wait as William's new boy wonder turned, and regarded her with cold dark eyes.

'Elizabeth,' her father carried on, oblivious to the tension. 'This is the chap I was talking about, the one who helped us out so wonderfully last week. This is Cole Greenway.'

Cole had expected to enjoy this more. He had spotted the blonde rider as soon as she came downstairs. It hadn't taken long to figure out who she was: one of William Melville's daughters. A spoiled brat, born with a silver spoon in her mouth. He'd been looking forward to getting his revenge, seeing the smug smile wiped off her snooty face when she realised the mistake she'd made. But, to his amazement, she didn't apologise. She simply offered him her hand, as though she hadn't insulted him earlier. God, she was one cool customer.

By the time they sat down for dinner, Cole was annoyed again. To his chagrin, William had placed him next to Elizabeth. Cole had a feeling she wasn't too happy about the arrangement, either. As a team of waitresses began serving the first course of wood pigeon, he watched her eyes wander over to a tall, powerful-looking man who sat at the other end of the table – Magnus Bergmann, founder of one of the most aggressive hedge funds on the East Coast. Cole felt a stab of professional jealousy. No doubt she'd rather be sitting next to someone like that, he thought, sawing angrily at the meat – someone of her own kind. But one way or another, he wanted an apology from her.

He cleared his throat to get her attention. 'So, Elizabeth,' he began, 'I guess you weren't expecting to see me sitting next to you tonight?' There was a faint challenge in his voice.

'Excuse me?' She hadn't even bothered to look in his direction, just continued to butter her bread roll. She sounded almost bored. He tried to stem his irritation and failed.

'You know. Earlier – outside in the garden. You obviously thought I worked here.' He wasn't about to let her get away with anything. 'Perhaps next time you'll think twice about your prejudices.'

'What prejudices?' she asked innocently, cutting her roll in half again. 'Against Americans?'

'Oh, don't try and be cute.'

She sighed. But whatever he'd said must have had the desired effect, because she finally put down her knife and fixed him with a cool stare. 'You think *that's* why I assumed you were working here? Because you're –' she paused dramatically – '*black*?'

She said the last word in a stage whisper. Cole had the distinct feeling she was taking the piss.

'Well, wasn't it?' he demanded.

Her pretty pink lips curled into a smile. 'Hardly.' Her tone said *get over yourself.* 'Look, maybe you haven't noticed, but you're the only person my father invited this weekend who's under the age of about a hundred. And most definitely the only one who turned up in jeans. That's why I made the not unreasonable assumption that you weren't one of the guests.'

She paused, waiting for him to say something. He tried to think of a witty comeback, but failed. He saw amusement in her sharp green eyes as she realised she had him. 'Maybe I'm not the one with the prejudices after all,' she said finally. She picked up her glass and took a sip of mineral water. Then she turned back to him, as though she'd had another thought.

'Oh, and if you really want to fit in,' she said, dropping her voice conspiratorially, 'you might want to think about getting rid of the chainstore DJ. Everyone else here has theirs custom made.'

She gave him a sweet smile, then turned to the man sitting the other side of her and struck up a conversation. She proceeded to ignore Cole for the rest of the meal.

For the rest of the weekend, Cole tried to stay out of her way. And when he finally left on Sunday evening, he was quite relieved at the thought of never having to see her again.

Chapter 15

Caitlin's first year in Paris passed quickly. When she wasn't in class or completing assignments, she was working at Café des Amis: that meant most Saturdays and Sundays, as well as week-day evening shifts. She often stayed until well after midnight to lock up, then she would be back in by seven the next morning, to serve breakfasts of croissants and coffee, before heading into the Chambre Syndicale for another gruelling day. It was a tiring routine, but Caitlin was happy. She was doing what she had set out to do when she'd first come to Paris – living on her own terms.

This time she wasn't compromising on anything. The first Friday, after classes, some of the students on her course decided to head out for the evening. They invited Caitlin to come with them.

'We're going to Hotel Costes,' Brooke told her. 'It's meant to be really cool.'

Situated right in the heart of the rue St-Honoré fashion dis-trict, the five-star hotel was renowned for its opulent bar frequented by wealthy jetsetters. As soon as they got there, Caitlin knew the dark, somewhat seedy hangout wasn't for her. A highly-groomed crowd, drinking over-priced cocktails . . . older, predatory men checking out the talent . . . Caitlin had one drink, then left.

That was the first and last time she hung out with her class-mates. They were pleasant enough, but a little frivolous and superficial, obsessed with getting into see and be-seen venues like La Perle or the Buddha Bar. She'd had enough of that at Greycourt, with people like Morgan.

Instead, she found herself getting to know the regulars at Café des Amis. They were an interesting crowd, mostly musicians, writers and artists. Alain always introduced her.

'This is Caitlin. She's going to be a famous designer one day,' he would say, however many times she asked him to stop.

The bohemian crowd was more than happy to assimilate her into their scene, introducing her to the edgy bars and clubs in the converted ateliers of Belleville, Oberkampf and Ménilmontant. They had no idea about her past or her family, nor were they interested. They simply accepted her as one of them. When they asked for her name, she always introduced herself as Caitlin O'Dwyer, and said she was from Ireland. They had no reason to doubt her.

The one drawback to working at Café des Amis was getting hit on. It was an occupational hazard for all the waitresses and one that Caitlin quickly learned to deal with. She always brushed her would-be suitors off, telling them and herself that she was too busy for a boyfriend. Some were more persistent than others, but eventually they got the hint. Alain couldn't understand why she was so standoffish.

'But what is so wrong with him?' he asked, plainly frustrated, as he watched Jules Martel, the lead singer from the Indie band playing at the café that night, slink off after Caitlin had refused to have a drink with him.

Caitlin busied herself wiping down the bar. 'Nothing's wrong with him.'

'Then why won't you have a drink with him?'

'Because I don't want to, Alain.'

The edge in her voice finally made him drop it. But only for a little while. He loved to gossip and was endlessly moving from one romantic drama to the other. Caitlin listened patiently to his stories, with detached amusement. But she never revealed anything about herself. Sometimes he would share confidences, hoping to get her to reveal something in return. But she never did. When he asked her directly, she was always cagey.

'There's nothing much to tell,' she would say, in answer to questions about her family or life in England.

'But what about men?' he parried, returning to his favourite subject. 'Is there someone back home?' He was fishing now, watching closely to see if she revealed anything. 'Someone who doesn't return your affection?'

Caitlin simply laughed. 'No, Alain. There's no one back home. Is it that hard to believe that I'm happy by myself? That I don't need anyone?'

At that, he shook his head. 'But everyone needs someone special in their life, Caitlin. A special man.'

'I have you, don't I?' she said, giving him an affectionate squeeze. 'That's all the man I need.'

That usually shut him up. For a day or so, at least.

When the lease on Caitlin's studio came up for renewal at the end of her first year, Alain suggested that she move into the rather more spacious apartment above Café des Amis.

'I'll give you a good price on the rent,' he said, 'and you can keep an eye on the café for me.'

She was reluctant at first, knowing it would mean sharing with someone; she liked having her own space. However, the price he offered was so ridiculously cheap that she couldn't afford to refuse.

It turned out that she would be sharing the flat with one other girl, Véronique Rideau. A tall, willowy blonde, she worked as an artist's model at École des Beaux-Arts, but supplemented her income by waitressing at the café from time to time. The two girls couldn't have been more different. Véronique was outgoing and flirtatious; Caitlin more reserved and introspective. But despite their differences they got on well – apart from when it came to the subject of men.

Véronique liked to go out and had plenty of male admirers, who all had friends who wanted to be fixed up. She was looking for a partner in crime and her flatmate, Caitlin, seemed the obvious choice. She joined in Alain's quest to fix Caitlin up, forever asking her to make up a four for dinner or drinks. The first few times, Caitlin gave excuses for why she couldn't go. After a while, she stopped bothering.

'Are you *gaie*?' Véronique asked bluntly one evening.

'No,' Caitlin laughed. If she'd thought it would get her flatmate off her back, she would have happily said 'yes'. But she sensed that Véronique would simply start trying to fix her up with her female friends instead.

'But I don't understand.' The Frenchwoman cast a perplexed look around the apartment. 'What are you going to do here all alone?'

'Sketch,' Caitlin replied, off-hand. 'Read. Sleep.'

There wasn't much the other girl could say to that.

During that first year, the Chambre Syndicale didn't get any easier. Caitlin still received more criticism than praise from Madame, and sometimes she wondered if she would ever improve. But she got through the end-of-term exams, and that was all that mattered. William invited her to spend the summer holidays with the rest of the family at Villa Regina, but she turned him down, preferring to stay in Paris and work instead.

Over the past year she had stuck to her decision to stay away from the Melville family. William called her regularly and so did Elizabeth. Since that first term at Greycourt, Elizabeth had continued to reach out to her. In fact, when the older girl had heard that Caitlin wasn't planning to go to Como, she'd offered to come over to see her in Paris instead.

'No one's *that* busy,' she said, half-amused half-exasperated, when Caitlin gave her standard excuse for why it wasn't a good time to visit. But she hadn't pressed Caitlin further, and instead just continued to call her at least once a month.

When college started again that autumn, Caitlin found to her relief that the course began to improve. With the basic skills like pattern cutting under their belts, the class was given the chance to start putting them into practice. They were assigned projects with specific requirements – to design a season, brand or range – as if they were in a proper *atelier*.

Halfway through the term, Madame set the class its biggest assignment to date.

'It will give me the opportunity to see whether you have got to grips with everything you have learned – planning, marking and cutting out the pattern, garment assembly, and finishing processes,' she told the class. 'And, more importantly, it will give *you* the opportunity to explore your creativity, to start finding your own style.'

The students shifted excitedly in their seats, exchanging murmured comments. There was a strong element of compe- tition in the class, and everyone saw this as their opportunity to prove themselves. Madame banged her stick on the ground. Everyone jumped and fell silent, as she had known they would.

'Your brief is to design an evening gown, influenced by a particular historical period of your choosing.' She began to stalk the floor, her limp a little more pronounced than usual.

'Stretch your minds,' she ordered. 'Look for a way to take the historical and update it for the contemporary. Search for inspi- ration wherever you can – in magazines, flea markets, antique shops . . . in the clubs you undoubtedly frequent at night when you should be studying.' A ripple of laughter echoed through the class. Madame silenced it with a look. 'Just remember – there is no wrong answer here. What matters is your creativity.'

Brooke's hand shot up.

'When is this due?' she asked.

'I expect to see a finished product in two weeks,' Madame

said coolly. 'Oh, and you will undertake this work in your own time.'

Caitlin quickly settled on the British Victorian era. She had always been fascinated by the darker aspects of the period, like the criminal underworld in London, with its pickpockets and grave-robbers, the extremes of rich and poor, prudishness and depravity, the violence and the slums.

'This brief is only a springboard,' Madame told the class. 'Think what the period, and the country it is set in, means to you. Find something about it that interests you particularly and run with that. It should not matter what you are drawing or designing. The trick is to make the piece about *you*. Inject your personality into what you are doing. Only then will you suc-ceed in creating something truly distinctive and individual.'

So that's what Caitlin did.

She started by rereading Shelley, Bram Stoker and Radcliffe to get a feel for the mid-nineteenth-century Gothic Revival. And as her research progressed, she began to sketch. Not the dress itself, but rather elements that grabbed her: a horse-drawn carriage on the fog-filled streets of the capital; windswept cas-tles with carved gargoyles, majestic dagger pinions and shadowy archways. The sketches encapsulated the mood that she wanted to convey in her final piece.

As the days passed, Caitlin found there was one theme she kept coming back to: death. The Victorians were obsessed with death, and during their extended mourning periods, widows had worn an elaborate system of mourning apparel. It was an unusual idea for an evening dress, but she felt it could work.

So she went with her instincts, researching the style and materials traditionally used in England at that time for widows' weeds. Then, with the facts under her belt, she had some fun. Taking the basics of the Victorian mourning gown, she slashed the neckline and raised the hemline. Instead of using traditional crêpe, she went for the more decadent material of crushed velvet, in a deep purple with black lace trimming. The result was an ornate costume, lush and sensual, dramatic and extravagant – a kind of glamorous Gothic punk. It was as much a piece of theatre, a piece of art, as a dress. For the first time ever, Caitlin felt she had achieved her best – and, without realising it, she had also found her style as a designer.

But the creative process was just the beginning. Once she had her ideas in place, she then had to start thinking about bringing the garment to life, taking it from 2D to 3D. It was a long, tedious process. In a proper design room, sample machinists and pattern cutters would work with the designer through several stages until the sample garment was ready to be made up in the proper fabric. But, for this exercise, the students were expected to go through all those stages themselves.

'One day you will have a whole design team to help you,' Madame told them, 'but for now you need to be able to do everything yourself.'

It was time-consuming and frustrating, but already Caitlin could see the advantages: using the *toile* – a trial version of the garment in plain-coloured calico – to iron out kinks in the design meant wasting less of the expensive materials that she had bought to make the final garment.

The day for showing their projects came round quickly. The students sat nervously at their assigned workbench, their creations on the mannequins next to them. Madame explained the format of the lesson at the start. Each of them would have to give their own five-minute potted presentation, telling the rest of the class which historical period they had chosen, before explaining the style and materials they had selected for their ball gowns.

Caitlin couldn't help feeling disheartened as Madame began to work her way around the room. She seemed so unimpressed with everyone's efforts. Even the usual stars weren't faring well. Hong Kong-born Kuan Tsang had produced a fitted mandarin dress in black shantung silk, with a red dragon motif, reminiscent of 1920s Shanghai socialites – it was dismissed as cheap and tacky. Brook's antebellum gown, complete with hoop skirt and parasol, was labelled 'more fancy dress than elegant party'.

'Dismal, poor, *penible!*' declared the teacher to a disheartened class.

Caitlin was last to present her piece. Standing back, she steeled herself for the inevitable decimation by Madame. A whisper ran through the class as they studied what she had produced. Everyone turned to the teacher, waiting to hear her verdict. Madame got up, walking slowly over to Caitlin's mannequin, so she could inspect the garment more closely.

'Technically, this still needs a lot of work,' she began, 'but that is not what is important here. I am not looking for a dressmaker,' she told the class. 'I am 'ere to create designers.' For the first time, the cold grey eyes smiled at Caitlin. 'Mademoiselle O'Dwyer, you have created something very special here. Your work has passion, individuality. And *that* is what I am looking for. The rest of you, take note.'

With that, she awarded an astonished Caitlin the highest mark in the class.

Madame stood looking at Caitlin's piece for a long time after the class had departed. She still remembered Caitlin from her interview over a year ago. She had seemed like a quiet girl, but with an interesting portfolio. Her work had shown promise – and it was this same potential that Madame could see today.

There was a darkness in her work, a sense of self that seemed much more highly evolved than in the rest of the class. As she flicked through the sketchbook Caitlin had submitted, which showed the evolution in her thoughts to the final piece, the woman could see exactly where she had sourced her ideas.

The dress was pure Gothic romance, conjuring up images of blood-red lips and ghostly skin. There was also an impressive attention to detail, since with the leftover material Caitlin had made a choker to match – four inches of aged black lace with a draping of jet chains to create an effect like a spider's web. It was all in keeping with the British Victorian era. But despite taking her influence from a historical period, there was also something so very contemporary about what the girl had done. It was, in a word, *impeccable*.

Chapter 16

Elizabeth's final term at Cambridge passed quickly. She worked hard towards her exams, and when the Economics Tripos results were posted at the Senate House, no one was surprised to see that she had been awarded a First.

After indulging in the garden parties and college balls of May Week – confusingly held in June – Elizabeth flew to Italy, where she spent the summer attending an Art History course in Florence. By the time she returned to London in late August, she was already looking forward to moving onto her next challenge, the one that was closest to her heart: going to work at Melville. Although she could have lived with her father in Eaton Square, she decided instead to rent her own place, as she'd always valued her freedom. She found a top-floor flat in a beautiful Georgian townhouse in Mayfair, a few streets from her grandmother and within walking distance of the Head Office.

On her first day at Melville, she was up and ready to go by seven-thirty. She emerged from her flat into the bright morning sunshine. This early, there was still a chill in the air, but she could tell it was going to be another beautiful September day.

As she passed Purdey & Sons, the nineteenth-century gunmakers on South Audley Street, she checked her reflection in the shop window. In her classic charcoal-grey suit, a neat leather briefcase in her hand, she looked the consummate professional. She had made a special effort to look businesslike today, hoping people would see beyond her age and pretty face. Her blonde hair was cut into a sensible bob and she'd kept make-up to a minimum.

It didn't take long to reach Old Bond Street. She passed the shopfront, and then turned down the little alley that led onto Albemarle Street, where the entrance to Melville's Head Office was situated. Like all the other Grade II listed buildings, it had once been a grand residence, but the interior had been sympathetically refurbished inside to a high modern spec disguised in old-fashioned charm. Elizabeth input the security code and the front door clicked open. Feeling a moment of exhilaration, she stepped inside.

In keeping with the essence of Melville, the reception area was all understated elegance, muted colours, thick carpets, fresh flowers. The receptionist knew Elizabeth by sight. She greeted her with a big, fake smile.

'Your father said to go straight on up, Miss Melville.'

Elizabeth took the lift up to the sixth floor, where all the directors' offices were situated. On the way, she fussed with her appearance. She smoothed down her suit, checked that her make-up and hair were in order. Ridiculously, she felt nervous. There was so much to prove. She'd spent her whole life expecting to head up Melville one day. What if she turned out to be bad at it? Elizabeth Melville, who'd never had a moment's self-doubt, was suddenly terrified.

If she had been hoping for words of encouragement from her father, she was to be sorely disappointed. As soon as she got to his office, he started in on a lecture about how she would be treated like every other employee and shouldn't expect special favours just because she was his daughter.

'I've decided to start you off in the Strategy Department,' William told her. 'It's the heart of the business and you'll learn a lot there. I've got a new guy heading up the team. Very smart, very good. In fact, I think you might have met him . . .' A knock on the door stopped him from finishing the sentence. 'Ah, impeccable timing. That must be him now.'

Elizabeth guessed who her new boss was going to be a split second before the door opened. Her heart sank as Cole Greenway stepped into the room. She thought back to the last time she'd seen him, during that weekend at Aldringham, nearly six months ago now. She remembered ruining his jeans and acting like a bitch, and hoped he didn't. From the cold smile he gave her, it was apparent he did.

'Hello *again*, Elizabeth,' he said, in case she was in any doubt. He was just as she remembered: almost threateningly large, with those arrogant dark eyes. To her shame, Elizabeth looked away first.

If William noticed any tension, he didn't show it.

'Good,' he said. 'Well, I'll look forward to hearing Cole's report on your progress, my dear.'

With that, they were both dismissed.

Cole didn't bother holding the door open for her as they left the room. He was off down the corridor, his long legs covering the space quickly. Elizabeth had to run a little to keep up with him. They waited in silence for the lift to arrive. When they got in, he pressed the button for the fifth floor. As soon as the doors closed, she tried breaking the ice.

'I've heard great things about you from Daddy,' she said brightly. 'I'm looking forward to working with you.'

He gave her a cool look. '*For* me,' he corrected.

'Excuse me?'

'You'll be working *for* me, not *with* me.' He said the words slowly and deliberately, as though he was speaking to a child. 'There's a big difference.'

The lift doors opened and he stepped out. She took a deep breath. Right: if that's how he wanted to play it, then she would just have to go along with him – for the moment, anyway.

*

With the exception of Cole, who had his own state-of-the-art office, the Strategy Department was open-plan, with big windows overlooking the bustling street below. It turned out Elizabeth wouldn't be sitting with the rest of the team.

'There's no desk space at the moment,' Cole explained, as he showed her into a small, windowless room at the far end of the office. 'Hopefully in a few weeks' time we'll be able to find you something more suitable.'

Elizabeth looked around in dismay. It was little more than a broom cupboard – with a desk hastily shoved in the corner, facing a wall covered in Blu-tack and drawing pins. The only light was from a single bare bulb hanging in the middle of the room.

'So waddya think?' Cole asked cheerfully.

His dark eyes dared her to complain. Somehow she swallowed down her objections. If this was a test, she was determined to pass with flying colours.

'It's fine, thanks,' she managed.

He gave a faint smile. 'Good. Well, get settled in. Someone will be along to tell you what to get started on.'

After Cole left, she did as he said. She switched on her computer. She familiarised herself with the phone. And then she waited.

After an hour, she was given her first task. A thirty-something, hard-faced brunette came in and dumped a box of magazines on Elizabeth's desk. She introduced herself as Kathleen McDonnell, Cole's second-in-command. Kathleen had a strong Glaswegian accent – she was from good working-class stock – and a chip on her shoulder concerning anyone she felt had got on in the world through nepotism rather than merit. Without any prompting, she ran through her CV, clearly wanting Elizabeth to know how much she deserved her job. Apparently, she had spent the past decade working in marketing, mainly blue chips. Elizabeth thought uncharitably that it looked more like two decades, judging from the lines on her forehead.

After Kathleen finished her spiel, she told Elizabeth what she wanted her to do: go through the pages of every magazine and put a Post-it note wherever there was a mention of Melville or one of its competitors. Elizabeth was mentally calculating how many days that would take, when new faces started barging through the door, carrying more boxes with them. She looked on in dismay as Kathleen's assistants brought in another eight boxes, filled with magazines going back ten years.

'Why does this need to be done?' Elizabeth asked.

'To compare changes in our advertising strategy.' The answer was sufficiently vague not to invite any further questions.

'But it's going to take forever . . .'

Kathleen shrugged and made to leave the room, before turning back to twist the knife in one last time.

'Oh, and before you get started, could you go round the office and take everyone's coffee orders? No one drinks that crap in the machines, so we get the office junior to pop out at eleven and three for everyone.'

Elizabeth stared at her in disbelief.

'You don't have to pay for it,' Kathleen assured her. 'There's a kitty in the kitchen.'

As though money was the problem!

'I'm not getting anyone's coffee,' Elizabeth said flatly.

Kathleen looked peeved. 'Don't get on *my* case. Look, if you have a problem with any of this, take it up with Cole.' With that, she walked out.

Take it up with Cole, Elizabeth repeated to herself. It was obviously the party line that everyone had been told to trot out.

'Fine,' Elizabeth told the empty room. 'I will.'

Cole wasn't surprised to see Elizabeth stalking down the corridor towards his office. He'd wondered how long it would take her to complain. Well, she could go right ahead and moan all she liked. She wasn't going to get any joy out of him. He'd been furious this morning when William Melville had called to say that his eldest daughter was coming to work in the Strategy Department. For six months, minimum.

Cole had been characteristically blunt.

'What the fuck do you expect me to do with her, William? We don't have time to babysit.'

William had laughed. Cole was one of the few people whom he allowed to speak to him that way. Mostly because he didn't want to lose the brilliant man who was such an asset to his organization.

'Elizabeth is a very bright girl, Cole,' he said mildly. 'She won't need babysitting, as you call it. In fact, I think she'll surprise you.'

Cole had snorted. He sincerely doubted that.

But, as usual, William Melville had got his way. Sometimes Cole still couldn't quite work out how he'd ended up working at Melville. After that weekend at Aldringham, he'd got a call from William, inviting him for lunch. He'd gone out of curiosity, nothing more. Having spent a decade in a big, cutting-edge US investment bank, a sleepy English luxury goods company held no interest for him.

But William had been persuasive. To Cole's surprise, the package offered had far exceeded what he was already making. But it was the job itself that had been the clincher for Cole. Melville was facing a difficult period, William had confessed to him. For the first time in years, sales were declining. The company needed a shake-up, but William wasn't sure where. He wanted Cole to tell him. As Head of the newly formed Strategy Department he would have full autonomy for hiring whoever he wanted and for choosing whatever projects he saw fit. Cole was sold.

Apart from the job itself, being headhunted had also given

Cole a kick. He was proud of everything he'd achieved, and liked to be reminded of his success. That was why he had no interest in having William's spoiled brat of a daughter in his department. He'd spent the past few months recruiting some of the smartest people in the industry onto his team. They'd all had to work their asses off to get where they were, and it bugged him that Elizabeth had a golden ticket straight in.

'Fine. Whatever you want, William,' he'd said. 'But, just be warned – I'm going to treat her like any other employee. And that means she's not getting an easy ride.'

To his surprise, the older man had chuckled. 'Believe me, I wouldn't have it any other way.'

Cole was prepared to take William at his word. He'd called his team together, told them the situation – and stipulated that Elizabeth was not to receive any special treatment. And, even though he didn't want her around, Cole couldn't deny that he'd enjoyed this morning. The look on Elizabeth's face when she'd realised exactly who she'd be working under . . . *that* had wiped the haughty smile away. She was no one special here. As she rapped loudly on his glass door, he had a feeling that the message hadn't got through to her yet. Well, he was happy to be the one to deliver it.

He continued to read through the report in front of him, waiting for her to knock a second time, and then finally looked up, as though he'd had no idea she was out there. He beckoned her in, motioning for her to sit down in the chair opposite him. She remained standing. He guessed she thought it made her seem more formidable. He leaned back and looked up at her expectantly, almost pleasantly.

'So, Elizabeth. What can I do for you?'

Up close, she looked even angrier than he'd been expecting. He could see her fighting against it, drawing on all that upper-class English restraint to keep her feelings in check. She tossed her head back, sending her fine blonde hair showering over her shoulders. It was shorter than he remembered. She must have had it cut, trying to look professional for her first day. It looked kinda cute that way . . . Jeez – where had *that* come from? He forced himself away from those thoughts and back to her furious green eyes.

She was blunt and to the point.

'Kathleen came to see me. Told me about the little project she was giving to me.' She managed to make 'project' sound like a dirty word.

'Oh?' he said mildly.

'Oh?' Her voice cracked. 'That's all you can say? I've got a First from Cambridge and you expect me to spend a week going through magazines with Post-its?' There was no mistaking the indignation in her voice.

'And,' she went on, growing shrill, 'as if that wasn't bad enough, I have to go out and get coffee for everyone!'

It took all of Cole's self-control not to laugh out loud. Instead, he rubbed the bridge of his nose, as though this was one problem he felt he shouldn't have to deal with.

'You know, I'm not really sure how much more we'll be able to give you to do at the moment.' He made sure to sound perfectly reasonable, knowing that would irritate her more. 'My department is filled with experienced professionals. We're talking ex-investment bankers, management consultants, senior brand managers. They're the best in their field and they all have something to contribute. You, on the other hand . . .' He trailed off, allowing her to know exactly what he thought of her abilities.

Elizabeth saw the amused look in Cole's eyes and knew she was fighting a losing battle. This was payback for the last time they'd met, pure and simple. She tugged at a button on her charcoal jacket, feeling frustrated. She thought of all the beautiful suits she'd bought the previous week, foolishly excited about starting her new job. If she was going to be sifting through mouldy old boxes filled with dusty magazines, then she might as well put the suits away and come in jeans tomorrow.

'But there must be something else you can give me to do,' she said, a note of pleading in her voice. It was a last-ditch attempt to get Cole to be reasonable.

'Maybe in time,' he told her. 'Once you've proved yourself. But I've been told you start at the bottom, like everyone else.'

'Yes, but—' She stopped abruptly. But what? But the bottom should mean something different for her? Even she could see how ridiculous that sounded.

He saw her floundering and went in for the kill.

'Look,' he said, leaning back in his chair. 'If you gotta problem with this, feel free to take it up with Daddy.'

You'd just love that, wouldn't you? she thought to herself. Well, she wasn't about to give him the satisfaction.

'There's no problem,' she said tightly.

He grinned, letting her know exactly how much he was enjoying this.

'Good girl. Then I suggest you get a move on with those coffees. I'm betting there's an office full of thirsty people out there.'

It took all her willpower to bite back the sharp retort on the tip of her tongue. With as much dignity as she could muster, she turned and walked out of his office, and went to fetch a notebook to take down the coffee orders.

Elizabeth's day didn't get any better after that. By the time everyone went home, she was so fed up that she had changed her mind and was prepared to complain to her father. But when she called his extension, his PA put her through to Uncle Piers instead. Apparently William had headed back to Aldringham to deal with some Amber-related drama.

'Is there anything I can help you with?' Piers asked.

Elizabeth hesitated, tempted to tell him the whole story. He sounded so concerned, and she knew he would listen and sympathise with her. She was aware that some people found Piers a little plodding and foolish, but that's what made him far more approachable than her father. She had always been able to confide in her kindly Uncle Piers – had lost count of the times he had interceded with William on her behalf. But still . . . it wasn't fair to drag him into this.

'No,' she said. 'No. Everything's fine.'

Promising Piers that she would catch up with him over dinner soon, she put the phone down feeling happier. She was sure she could find some way to deal with Cole.

Chapter 17

Amber Melville took a long drag on a Marlboro Light as Perkins nosed the Bentley through the gates of Aldringham. The first thing she saw was her father's Mercedes in the driveway.

'Fuck,' she swore under her breath. She hit the button for the electric window and dropped the cigarette outside. It wouldn't do for him to catch her smoking on top of everything else.

'Fuck, fuck, fuck,' she swore again.

She'd been prepared to deal with her mother, but not him. Frankly, she was surprised he was even here. Maybe that was naïve. She'd just been kicked out of her third boarding school in less than a year. Even Daddy had to sit up and take notice this time. Opening up her vintage handbag, she pulled out some tiger balm and slicked a little under her eyes. Immediately they started watering. It was a trick she'd learned a while back. Tears were always the best defence in these situations. She only hoped no one noticed the intense mentholated smell.

Leaving Perkins to unload her bags, she went inside the house. Mrs Hutchins was there to greet her, thin-lipped and unwelcoming.

'Your parents are waiting for you in the drawing room,' she said stiffly.

Amber heard disapproval in her tone, but didn't care. The old cow needed to mind her own business.

'Could you get me a still mineral water?' Amber said offhandedly as she walked by.

The housekeeper sniffed at her lack of 'please' or 'thank you'. But she did what she was told.

Outside the drawing room, Amber paused to check her appearance in the gilded mirror. She liked what she saw. Adolescence had been kind to Amber Melville. At fifteen, she was all long-limbed coltishness. Tall and slender, with a tumble of platinum-blonde curls and skin like cream, it was already clear that she was going to be the most beautiful of the Melville girls – no idle compliment. Her angelic looks also helped her get away with a lot and she knew it. No one who gazed into her cornflower-blue eyes, wide with childlike innocence, could ever believe she caused the mischief that she did.

She was already plotting how she could talk her way out of this one. She wasn't even sure what all the fuss was about. It wasn't like last time, when she'd got caught smoking pot. She'd only had her belly button pierced – it wasn't exactly the crime of the century. The school wouldn't have known anything about it, if it hadn't been for all the girls crowding round when she was changing for PE, wanting to have a look. Naturally the Gym teacher had felt compelled to come over to see what was going on. But it was ridiculous to expel someone over that, in Amber's opinion – although possibly it hadn't helped that she'd stolen the money for the piercing from her English teacher's purse.

'But you have a perfectly generous allowance,' the Headmistress had said, clearly confused and disturbed by the behaviour of one of her pupils.

Amber had no answer. Stealing the cash had been part of the dare. She hadn't questioned the logic behind it.

She was still surprised her father had bothered coming home to deliver the lecture. Usually he wouldn't have time for something so mundane – he was far too busy running his empire. In fact, Amber could count on one hand the number of times she'd seen him over the past eighteen months. It was nothing new to her. He'd always been a distant figure. She knew, without doubt or self-pity, that she was the least favourite of his children. It didn't take a genius to figure it out. Elizabeth was so similar to him, it was frightening. And everyone could tell he had a soft spot for Caitlin and was tortured by her absence from his life. Whereas Amber . . . well, she was probably most like her mother, and Isabelle wasn't exactly someone he valued. Being bad was all she had.

She hadn't always been that way, of course. When she was little, she had behaved impeccably. But no one except her mother had ever seemed to notice or care. Then one day, when she was five, she'd found some matches to play with. She'd accidentally set light to her granny's favourite Oriental rug and nearly burned down the East wing. Her father had rushed back from London. Afterwards, she didn't remember his anger or the ten minutes of smacking she'd received as punishment. All she remembered was that he had finally noticed her. From then on, acting out had been her way of getting attention.

She rubbed on a little more tiger balm, stinging her eyes until they watered, then knocked on the door. Her father's commanding voice boomed out, telling her to come in. Arranging her features into a suitably contrite expression, Amber pushed open the heavy oak door.

The tableau inside was a familiar one for Amber. Her father sat in the centre of the room, unsmiling, concerned only with the inconvenience of having to deal with his wayward daughter. Her mother was in the corner, crying softly, no doubt concerned with what her friends would think if they found out about this latest humiliation. For the first time, Amber wondered what they were planning to do to her. Maybe send her to the local private school? That wouldn't be so bad. It might be fun to be at home for a change. Or perhaps she would get the rest of the term off . . .

Now that would be a bonus. It wasn't like she needed GCSEs anyway. As soon as she turned sixteen she was leaving school.

You didn't need qualifications to be a model, like Naomi Campbell, Linda Evangelista or Christy Turlington. Amber had pictures of them all on her wall. She spent hours in front of the mirror, copying their poses, and secretly thought she was just as goodlooking as they were. She just needed to survive the next year and then she could do whatever she wanted. And that meant getting through this afternoon as unscathed as possible.

She turned her tear-filled eyes towards her father.

'I'm really sorry, Daddy,' she began, wiping her wet cheeks. Damn – she'd overdone it with the tiger balm.

But before she could get any further, her father held up his hand. 'No, I don't want to hear your excuses. Frankly, I'm fed up with them.'

Amber was used to her father's lectures by now, but even she felt a shiver run through her as she heard his chill voice.

William leaned forward in his chair, his face set in a grim expression. 'We've tried this the easy way, Amber, and it doesn't seem to have worked. So now you've forced me to find a more permanent solution.'

Amber swallowed hard. This didn't sound good.

His permanent solution turned out to be yet another boarding school. Amber didn't even get a chance to unpack. Barely an hour after she arrived, she left again. This time for Beaumont Manor, in Yorkshire.

'Beaumont Manor is an institution designed specifically for discipline cases,' her father had informed her. 'They have vast experience dealing with troubled children. I think this will be the making of you, my girl.'

So much for getting an easy ride.

Amber didn't bother sulking. There was no point. It never worked with her father, only her pushover of a mother. Plus, she wasn't actually that bothered about Beaumont Manor. Her father might like to talk up the harsh regime, but there was always an angle in these places; you just had to know where to look. And she was confident that if anyone was going to find it, then she would.

The North York Moors were as bleak and desolate as Amber had imagined: ruined abbeys and manor houses, framed by barren fields, creepy forests and arid farming country. Beaumont Manor itself was a brooding Gothic castle dating back to the thirteenth century. Perched on top of a rocky cliff, it stood high above the rugged Yorkshire coastline. Exposed for centuries to the driving rain and cruel winds of the English winter, its grey stone buildings were patchy, the gargoyles chipped at the edges. It looked more like a prison than a school.

Inside, Amber was met by a grim-faced Miss Dauston, her Housemistress. Overweight and underloved, she had wound up a bitter spinster – the kind of person who should never have been allowed to teach. Each year, she watched all these privileged young girls go on to lead the kind of life she could only dream about, and it left a sour taste. She was not averse to taking her disappointment with life out on her charges.

She looked Amber Melville up and down. She had seen her type before. The angelic face didn't fool her for a second. Too rich and too beautiful, she needed to be taken down a peg or two. She issued Amber with a three-inch thick, leather-bound rule book – *Beaumont Manor's Code of Honour* – and told her to memorise it.

'Anyone found breaking these rules will be dealt with ruthlessly,' she said in her harsh Scottish burr, as they walked through the labyrinth of corridors to Amber's new room. The words echoed back at them, bouncing off the high ceilings and making the girl jump.

It was only September, but already the place was freezing. Stone floors and a permanent draught from ill-fitting doors and windows didn't bode well. Neither did the tiny radiators.

Amber didn't even want to think what it was going to be like in mid-winter. No effort had been made to create a homey feel. Unlike Amber's previous schools, there were no vases of fresh flowers or noticeboards advertising sports fixtures or clubs. She was actually beginning to worry. Maybe getting kicked out of St Margaret's hadn't been the smartest move after all.

Amber's room turned out to be just as unwelcoming as the rest of the place. It was a tiny, cramped space with high, narrow windows. Peeling wallpaper and a distinctive musty odour suggested there was a damp problem. The furniture consisted of two narrow single beds, two desks and two small wardrobes. The walls were bare apart from two signs – *No Smoking* and *No Blu-tack*. Her roommate didn't look much fun, either. A short, plump girl with huge tortoiseshell glasses and her hair tied back in a severe bun, she greeted Amber with a stony face.

'My name is Eva Mendoza,' she said in precise, over-enunciated English. 'Eet is good to meet you, Amber.'

The accent confirmed what her South-American name and dark colouring had already told Amber.

'Eva is Head of Year,' Mrs Dauston said proudly. Eva dropped her eyes, seemingly embarrassed by the praise. 'She is one of our success stories.'

Amber got the feeling that Eva's behaviour was supposed to be a good role model for her. Oh, great, she thought, eyeing the other girl suspiciously. They'd obviously paired her up with the biggest square in the year. Eva would probably be reporting back whenever she screwed up.

But Amber couldn't have been more wrong. As soon as Mrs Dauston left, Eva's expression relaxed.

'So what are you 'ere for?' she asked, collapsing on the narrow bed. She took off her glasses, shook out her hair and undid a couple of the buttons on her blouse. Within seconds she was transformed from a plain, serious schoolgirl into a

Latin-American minx. Amber realised she'd mistaken to-die-for curves for puppy fat and failed to see through a carefully planned disguise.

'What am I in for?' Amber shrugged. 'Just about everything.'

Eva nodded knowingly. 'Me, too.' She reached under the bed and pulled out a packet of Derbys, offering one to Amber. Amber hesitated. Her gaze moved to the *No Smoking* sign.

'What about . . .?'

Eva gave her a sly smile. 'There are too many rules 'ere. You just need to figure out how to break them without anyone noticing.'

Amber grinned back. This was turning out to be her kind of place after all.

Eva was the ideal role model for Amber – just not in the way Mrs Dauston had hoped. The product of a union between a corrupt member of Brazil's Workers' Party and a voluptuous film star, she had the smarts and body to get away with whatever she wanted. After she turned five, her parents barely spoke to each other or to her. With little parental interest or control, Eva had grown up wild, doing whatever she wanted with little fear of reprisal. It was something the two girls had in common. Being packed off to Beaumont Manor had been her parents' way of brushing an embarrassing problem under the carpet, Eva told Amber, without any sense of self-pity. Amber knew exactly what she meant.

Amber had always thought of herself as fairly savvy. At St Margaret's she'd been cool, the trendsetter, even among the older years. But Eva left her for dust. She was frighteningly knowledgeable about everything. Within a week, she'd introduced Amber to Caipirinhias; the wonders of plastic surgery – 'I 'ad my breasts and nose done before I was fourteen – everybody does in Rio'; and, most importantly and painfully, *cavados* – or, in English, Brazilian waxes.

'Ow!' Amber yelled as the first strip came off. She was lying spreadeagled on the bed, and had never felt so exposed or sore in her life before. She'd always been secretly proud of her white-blonde bush, but Eva had insisted everything came off apart from a small landing strip.

'Sshush,' Eva hissed from between her legs. She handed her a piece of cardboard. 'Here. Bite down on this. You don't want Mrs Dauston to come in, do you?'

Amber bit. It didn't help much. But at least nobody heard them.

It turned out Eva was experienced, too. She'd lost her virginity to an American college boy during last year's carnival. She'd just turned fourteen.

'It was *sheeet*,' she informed a wide-eyed Amber. 'He had a small *cacete*.' She held up her little finger to illustrate. 'But don't worry. It gets better, *saca*?' she said, using the Brazilian slang for 'you know what I mean?' It was her catchphrase.

Amber listened attentively, devouring every gory detail.

'I gave him a *boquete* – you do it like this.'

'He put it up my *cu*. It hurt like hell. Next time – no way!'

It was all news to Amber, who had only ever got to second base with Andy Turner from the boys' school twinned to St Margaret's. He'd been the hottest guy in the Upper Sixth, but barely more experienced than her. After some furtive groping during his Leavers' Ball, she hadn't been especially tempted to go any further. But when Eva talked about it – the different positions, what it was like when a guy went down on you – it made Amber curious to find out what it was all about.

When Amber phoned her mother the first Sunday after she arrived, she was able to truthfully report to Isabelle that she had learned more in the space of four days at Beaumont Manor than she had in an entire year at St Margaret's.

Chapter 18

'*Salut*, Caitlin!'

A dozen voices greeted Caitlin as she walked into the cramped sitting room. She tried to muster an enthusiastic response. It had been another late night at college and she'd gone back to the apartment hoping for some peace. Instead, she'd found Véronique hosting another one of her impromptu parties. Cigarette smoke and laughter filled the air. Empty wine bottles covered the floor. Jules Martel, Caitlin's one-time suitor, had brought along a guitar. He was sitting cross-legged on a cushion, strumming softly, as a girl Caitlin didn't recognise crooned along.

Véronique lay stretched across the couch, her head resting on the lap of Lucien Duval. Caitlin smiled to herself. Her flatmate was a sucker for brooding, tortured artists, and Lucien fitted the bill perfectly. A street photographer, known for his portrayal of modern life in Paris, he was very cool and extremely good-looking. Tall, slender and darkly dramatic, he was a well-known and distinctive figure among the Belleville crowd. Caitlin often saw him in the café, usually with at least one or two adoring females in tow.

Word had got out a couple of weeks earlier that he had broken up with his latest girlfriend, one of the models who worked at l'École des Beaux Arts. Véronique had immediately turned her attention to him. Looking at them now, Lucien stroking her hair, Caitlin guessed she was already halfway there.

Véronique stretched lazily, extending her long legs for Lucien's benefit. 'Grab a glass and come join us, Caitlin.'

Jules stopped playing and scrambled to his feet. 'You can sit here, if you like.'

'Thanks,' Caitlin said. 'Maybe in a bit. I'm going to get some food first.' Seeing the look of disappointment on Jules's face, Caitlin felt bad. He seemed like a nice guy, but she simply wasn't interested.

She disappeared into the tiny kitchen. It was Véronique's week to shop, which meant there was nothing in the fridge – she lived on coffee and cigarettes, so why shouldn't everyone else? However, after a quick rummage in the cupboards, Caitlin found some pasta and an open jar of pesto that didn't smell too bad.

With the pasta simmering nicely, she pulled up a chair to the window and climbed out onto the roof. It wasn't strictly designed to be a terrace, but it was the only outside space the flat had, so the girls made use of it. Véronique sunbathed there whenever she could, while Caitlin often sat out in the evenings, making the most of the refreshing night breeze, drawing and reading in the half-light from the other buildings. Now, she took out her sketchpad to study what she'd been working on earlier that day.

She'd only been there for a little while when she heard a noise from inside. It was the chair creaking. She looked up and saw a man climbing out to join her. At first she thought it was Jules, but then he straightened up. In the half-light from the kitchen, she took in the dark clothes, deathly pale skin and jet-black curls falling over his shoulders. It was Lucien. She couldn't help feeling relieved. She wasn't in the mood to deal with Jules again tonight.

'What're you doing out here?' she asked.

He held up a packet of cigarettes and she smiled a little. He was the only one of their friends who had the courtesy to come out here to smoke. In the grand scheme of things it made no difference – the place stank already. But Caitlin appreciated the gesture.

Lucien leaned against the wall and lit up. He smoked in silence. Not that there was anything unusual about that. He wasn't exactly a big talker. Caitlin reckoned in the year she'd known him he'd spoken a dozen words to her, if that. Which was why she was surprised when he gestured at her sketch-book. 'May I see?'

Usually she hated people looking at her work, but she was so taken aback by the request that she found herself agreeing. 'All right.'

Resting his cigarette on the wall, he took the book from Caitlin and began to flick through her sketches. Her current project was on the influence of film on fashion.

'I'm using *Shoot* as my inspiration,' she said, naming the latest Hollywood blockbuster. It revolved around a gangster living in Chicago in the 1930s, and the movie's presence could be seen in her drawings, which included high-waisted, wide-legged zoot suits adapted into sharp office wear for women, as well as pretty evening dresses inspired by flapper girls.

'Your designs are very theatrical,' he observed. He looked up, seeming genuinely interested. 'Is that what you want to do?'

'Yeah, I guess so. If I can.'

He finished looking through the sketchbook and handed it back to her. 'I am sure you will. From what I have seen here, you have real talent and originality.'

'Thanks,' Caitlin mumbled, feeling a little embarrassed by the praise. But she was pleased, too. It was quite a compliment coming from someone who was acknowledged to be one of the foremost emerging artists in Paris.

Lucien picked up his cigarette, took one last drag, and stubbed the remains out on the wall.

'I'll see you back in there,' he said, before disappearing inside.

As soon as he'd gone, the timer on the stove went off. Caitlin finished preparing her dinner, then brought the plate through to join the others. After a couple of drinks, she quietly slipped off to bed. As she left the room, Lucien had started to give Véronique a foot massage. It didn't take a genius to figure out where the night was going to end.

But the next morning, when Véronique came into the kitchen looking for coffee, she was alone.

'Where's Lucien?' Caitlin asked. 'The way you two were together last night, I thought for sure he'd still be here.'

Véronique gave an unconcerned shrug. 'Me too. But he had to go. Next time, eh?'

Next time wasn't long in coming. A few nights later, the girls were working late together in the café. It was a Tuesday evening and the place was dead. Alain had gone home an hour earlier, leaving them to lock up. There were only two customers left, Lucien and Jules. Caitlin was sitting up at the bar, sketching. Across the room, Véronique had joined the boys at their table. The three of them were drinking pastis, chatting and flirting.

'Come and join us!' Jules called to her.

But Caitlin shook her head. 'I've too much to do.'

By eleven, she was thinking seriously about bed. When Véronique came over, Caitlin hoped she was going to offer to lock up, but her flatmate had other ideas. The two men were heading over to La Flèche d'Or, a nearby club. They had invited her along, and she wanted Caitlin to come too, as Jules's date.

'Please say you'll do it.' Véronique lowered her voice. 'This might be my only chance with Lucien.'

Caitlin sincerely doubted that. In all the time they'd been living together, she'd never known Veronique to not get her man in the end.

'Please,' the girl wheedled. 'Jules is a sweetheart, I promise.'

Caitlin glanced over at Jules, who smiled shyly back. A rather fresh-faced young man, he was far less intimidating than Lucien. Caitlin was sure she could handle him.

'OK, I'll come,' she sighed.

'*Formidable!*' Véronique gave her friend a warm embrace.

Laughing, Caitlin pushed her away. She took off her apron, shoved it under the counter, and ran a hand through her short, dark hair.

'Right. *Allons-y!* Let's go.'

Véronique cast a doubtful look at Caitlin's jeans and tank top, her face devoid of make-up. 'Aren't you going to at least change? I have a dress you can wear . . .'

Caitlin glowered at her flatmate. 'Veronique,' she said warningly. 'Don't push your luck.'

Three hours later, Caitlin wished she had followed her instincts and stayed home. The first part of the evening had been, for the most part, fine. She always liked La Flèche d'Or. Housed in an abandoned railway station, it had been converted into a club by some graduates of the École des Beaux Arts. That meant it attracted many of their artistic brethren, mostly because the drinks were cheap, the live music always cutting edge, and it stayed open until five in the morning.

But while the band had been good, their little foursome had been less of a success. Véronique, used to relying on her looks to catch her man, was struggling to make conversation with Lucien.

She leaned over to him, running her hand along his arm. 'I heard you're opening a new exhibition, *chéri*,' she purred. 'That must be really exciting.'

'Yes,' he said, shrugging her off.

Caitlin bit back a smile. This was typical of Véronique's technique: listen attentively, compliment excessively and make your guy feel like a King. Unfortunately, Lucien didn't seem to be falling for it.

But the other girl wasn't about to be put off that easily. 'So where are you exhibiting?' she persisted.

'Le Nabi.'

Véronique looked blank, but Caitlin's eyes sparked with interest. 'Really?' she said without thinking. 'Le Nabi? That's fantastic!'

Lucien seemed impressed at her knowledge. 'You know of it?' He had every reason to be surprised. Although rumoured to be one of the most dynamic galleries in Paris at the moment, it certainly wasn't in any guidebook – that was because Le Nabi was an illegal squat.

'I've been meaning to go there,' she said. 'I've heard it's excellent.'

Lucien looked amused. 'I only hope you think the same once you have seen my photographs.'

Véronique glanced between Caitlin and Lucien.

'Let's not talk about work,' she pouted. 'It is very dull.'

Caitlin was about to ask Véronique what exactly she *did* want to talk about, but she managed to stop herself. Instead, she decided to leave her flatmate and Lucien alone, and try to get to know Jules a little better. But he was too tongue-tied to answer any of her questions. After a while, she gave up and concentrated on the band. Jules took the opportunity to get plastered. His confidence fuelled by alcohol, he leaned over to put his arm around Caitlin, breathing beery fumes into her face.

'You know, I really like you, Caitlin,' he slurred.

'Thanks.' She pushed him away again. But it didn't seem to have much impact. He was too far gone to notice her mounting irritation.

Jules turned glassy eyes onto Lucien. 'Hey, isn't it your round?'

Lucien nodded at the empty bottles on the table. 'Maybe you have had enough, eh, Jules?'

'Hah! You're just trying to get out of buying.'

Lucien gave a shrug. 'Fine.' He looked over at Véronique and Caitlin. '*Mesdemoiselles*? Same again?'

'Nothing for me,' Caitlin said. 'I'm going soon.'

'*Mon dieu!*' Véronique tutted. 'You can't want to leave already.' She turned to the guys, oblivious to her flatmate's discomfort. 'Caitlin has been single her whole time in Paris, you know. No wonder, when she hardly ever goes out.'

In that moment, Caitlin could have happily throttled the other girl.

Jules was too out of it to process the information, but Lucien raised an eyebrow.

'And why is that, *ma petite irlandaise*? Don't you like Frenchmen?'

She flushed, unsure if he was teasing her, and delivered her standard line. 'No. I'm just too busy for a boyfriend.'

Lucien gave a gentle shake of his head. 'No one should be too busy for romance.'

Before she could reply, Jules leaned across the table, knocking several bottles on the floor along the way. 'What's the hold-up?' he slurred. 'Let's have less talking and more beer!'

Lucien raised an eyebrow at Caitlin, as if to say, *What can you do with him?*

'Whatever you say, Jules.'

Lucien went to fetch more drinks. As soon as he was gone, Véronique left to go to the Ladies room.

'So it's just us?' Jules said. He reached out and gave Caitlin's knee a squeeze. She resisted the urge to kick him. Deciding that if she was going to escape she needed to do it now, before Véronique got back, she stood up, saying, 'I've just spotted some friends I want to say hi to. I'll be back in a bit.'

Jules was too drunk to notice that she was taking her coat and bag with her.

She was almost at the exit when she bumped into Lucien, coming back from the bar with four beers. She couldn't help but feel a little guilty as he looked down at the belongings in her hands.

'Leaving already?' he asked.

'Before Jules gets any worse,' she admitted.

'Ah, I see.' Lucien nodded understandingly. 'Although,' he said after a moment's thought, 'you should of course be flattered by his behaviour.'

'How's that?'

'He only drinks because he is nervous around you. He has been desperate to get you to go out with him, you know.'

Caitlin gave a wry smile. 'Unfortunately for Jules, desperation isn't attractive.'

Lucien laughed softly. 'Yes, you are right about that.'

Caitlin wondered if he was referring to Véronique. For a second she felt pleased that, unlike most guys, he hadn't fallen for her flatmate's routine. Then she felt bad for thinking something so uncharitable about her friend. And when had she started caring who Véronique pulled anyway? It was obviously time to get out of here.

'Please say goodbye to Jules for me,' she said quietly. And with that, she headed for the door.

Lucien stayed at the club a while longer after Caitlin left. He managed to offload Véronique onto Jules, and then set about finding someone for himself, someone not so into him. He liked Véronique well enough, but he was wary of leading her on. Lucien might be a womaniser, but he wasn't cruel – well, not intentionally so.

His eyes settled on a girl, alone at the bar. She was undoubtedly attractive. A true Gallic beauty: long dark hair, skin the colour of warm nutmeg. She also turned out to be on his wavelength. No names, no life story. One drink and they were the best of friends. Two and she was happy to go home with him.

He woke early the following morning. Thankfully, the girl was still asleep. He slipped from the bed, taking care not to disturb her. Ten minutes later, he stood by the window, sipping his coffee, bathed in the glow of the pale early light. It was his favourite time of day, watching the city wake up from the comfort of his Bastille garret. He had just got out of the shower and was naked apart from the towel slung casually around his waist, his damp hair curling down over his shoulders into its trademark ringlets.

He heard a movement and turned to see the girl rolling over in bed, onto her back. The covers had fallen away to reveal one perfectly formed breast, the nipple hard and dark like a raisin. But his mind was elsewhere. He was thinking about the pictures he was going to use in his new exhibition. He had spent the previous day developing his latest rolls of film. Now, he walked over to where he had hung the prints to dry overnight, perusing his work, totally focused on the task at hand.

After a while, his eyes settled on one of the photographs. It was of Véronique's friend, Caitlin. Unpegging the picture, he studied it closely. He remembered taking it the previous week. The café had been quiet that afternoon and she had been sketching up at the bar, so absorbed in her work that she hadn't even noticed him until the flash went off. That was always the best way – to catch the subject offguard. And it had certainly worked this time. It was a perfect profile. She looked deep in concentration, her dark hair falling across her face as she chewed on the end of her pencil. Her expression was veiled; her wide eyes thoughtful, mysterious.

'Who is she?'

The girl's voice broke into his thoughts. He turned to see her standing behind him, wrapped in a sheet, a look of jealousy on her pretty face. He hadn't noticed her waking, crossing the room to peer over his shoulder.

He shook his head slightly. 'No one.' He tossed the photograph onto the table, a deliberately dismissive gesture. But she wasn't going to be put off that easily.

'Are you sure?' Her eyes hadn't left the print. Now she reached down, touching the edge of the picture, frowning. 'She is very beautiful.'

Inside, Lucien sighed. *Merde*. This was turning into hard work. But he showed none of his irritation. Instead, he took her hand – as much to stop her smudging the photograph as to create an intimacy between them – and raised it to his lips.

'You are the beautiful one,' he said, staring straight in her eyes.

The line was obvious, but it worked. The girl's face relaxed into a smile.

'Come back to bed?' she murmured.

She didn't need to ask twice. He gave one last glance at the photograph of Caitlin, and then let the girl lead him over to the bed.

Chapter 19

Piers and Elizabeth were having dinner at Le Caprice. He had taken her there to celebrate her first month at Melville, but the evening wasn't going quite as he'd imagined. Whenever he asked how she had been getting on in the Strategy Department, she avoided the question. He'd expected her to be enthusiastic about her new position, but instead she seemed so subdued.

Finally, over coffee, she confessed how awful it had been.

Piers was appalled when he heard. Elizabeth had always been his favourite. He hated to see her unhappy.

'Do you want me to have a word with your father?' he offered. 'I could ask him to talk to Cole. Or move you to another department, if you like.'

'No,' she said, then seeing the hurt look on his face, hastily added, 'Thanks for offering. But I need to fight my own battles.' She forced a smile. 'Anyway, enough about me. Let's talk about something else. Tell me what you've been up to.'

By the time they finally left the restaurant two hours later, she seemed happier. He insisted on walking her the short distance to her flat.

'We'll have to make this a regular date now you're in London,' he remarked, as they said their goodnights.

She agreed that they would, and he went back to his car feeling good about himself. Seeing Elizabeth tonight reminded him how important he was to the family. He was an integral part of Melville, the glue that held them all together.

Piers's life revolved around being a Melville. It always had.

Growing up, his mother and brother – especially his brother – had been everything to him. They were a family to be proud of. Rosalind was a beautiful and elusive woman, floating in and out of Aldringham in a cloud of expensive perfume, always dashing up to London, appearing in magazines and newspapers. When she was at Aldringham, it was to host elaborate parties with fascinating guests. Meanwhile William, ten years Piers's senior, was inevitably a figure of awe and respect to the younger boy. But, with the premature death of Edward Melville when Piers was just five years old, he also became something of a father figure, too. It was William who taught Piers how to ride first a bike and then a horse; gave him swimming and skiing lessons. He was everything Piers aspired to be and knew that he never would.

One of Piers's earliest memories was, aged eight, accompanying Rosalind to Greycourt to watch William playing in the annual Old Boys versus Pupils cricket match. It was a glorious summer's day, but what Piers remembered most was the pride he felt when he saw William smashing the winning runs to finish with a grand six, and leading his team to its first victory in a decade.

'Aren't you proud of your brother?' Rosalind had said to Piers, as William was awarded Man of the Match.

And he had been able to answer, truthfully and wholeheartedly, 'Yes.'

In his young mind, being a Melville was the most important thing in the entire world. This belief had been reinforced by virtue of the fact that he'd grown up isolated from other children his age. Discovering early on that he was dyslexic, Rosalind had decided against sending him to the local prep that William had attended, and had him home-schooled instead. That meant that by the time he went off to Greycourt, aged eleven, his only major interaction outside the family had been with his ageing tutor.

Needless to say, boarding school proved something of a shock. Although he was an intelligent, studious boy, socially he was clumsy. The other boys homed in on the weakness. His tuck money was stolen; a rotting fish head left in with his gym kit; his homework mysteriously misplaced by the monitors. With his slight frame, he couldn't fight back. Instead, he cried himself to sleep at night, which only made the bullying even worse.

The masters, aware of his problems, intervened where necessary to make sure the other lads didn't go too far, but privately they were disparaging of Piers.

'He's nothing like his older brother,' they would say, remembering William Melville's effortless popularity, his academic and sporting prowess.

Throughout his miserable time at Greycourt, Piers longed to be back at Aldringham with his family. He watched William going to work alongside their mother at Melville and couldn't wait until he was old enough to join them.

After three friendless years studying Natural Sciences at Cambridge, he finally got his wish and joined the family firm. Rosalind started him off at a low-level position in the Finance Department, where he made a slow but steady rise through the ranks to CFO. At last he was content.

The one sadness in his life was that he had never married. He would have liked a wife, children. But it was not to be. While William had courted a succession of beautiful girls in his youth, Piers had always been uneasy around the opposite sex. It was the curse of that same social clumsiness which had plagued him at Greycourt. But he had come to terms with his single status, drew comfort from treating William's family like his own. From the beginning he had welcomed Isabelle, and even though he was a little disappointed that William didn't choose him as best man – Magnus got the job instead – he still threw himself into the wedding plans; and while he wasn't officially named Elizabeth's godfather, he had always made sure to look out for her.

And Piers was content with his bachelor lifestyle. After all, why did he need a wife? Work and family, so seamlessly linked, occupied his time, and on the rare occasions he was alone, he was content to go for long walks or read. A house-keeper and cleaner came in on alternate days to help with the upkeep of his Richmond Hill townhouse. And for nights like tonight, when he was feeling a little lonely, there was always NW8.

NW8 was a *very private*, private members' club. Tucked away in a leafy side street near Lord's Cricket Ground, in a lavish Regency villa, it was frequented by celebrities, politicians and royalty. Discretion was its watchword. There was currently a two-year waiting list for membership and applications were strictly vetted. Visits were by appointment only, to ensure patrons didn't bump into each other. Appointments themselves were made to an unlisted number, always answered by an impassive voice. Every member had a unique pincode, which meant no names were ever used over the phone.

The ladies themselves were of the highest quality: stylish, cultured, intelligent and well-versed in social etiquette. Payments were by bank transfer: thirty thousand up front for Platinum membership, plus fees starting at five thousand pounds for a four hour lunch-date.

In his ten years of membership, Piers had rarely visited NW8's premises, preferring instead to make use of its call-out service. He had always found it to be prompt and reliable. This time was no exception. He phoned from his car and twenty minutes after he got home, the doorbell rang. As he answered it, he saw a sleek black Mercedes pulling away. A driver had dropped the girl off and would remain in the area in case of trouble.

A pretty little blonde stood outside. Fresh-faced, innocent . . .

He stood back. 'Come in.'

The girl did as she was told. Once she was in the hallway, she looked at him quizzically.

'Upstairs,' he directed. 'Third floor, fourth door on the left.'

She was new to the house, and new to him. They always were. Some men liked to be visited by a regular woman, taking comfort in the familiar. Piers didn't. NW8 knew this and much more. His preferences were noted down on a file and adhered to religiously. The girls were always natural blondes, of slight build, never older than eighteen. They were instructed to remove all make-up before arriving, and to wear something girlish and soft. Cotton was preferred, but certainly no heels, leather or latex; colours should be pastels – black, red or purple were to be avoided. The details were strict and specific, and the girls followed them to the letter. The requests might seem odd, but they'd heard stranger.

Upstairs, Piers sat on the bed and watched as the girl unbuttoned her coat and removed the pashmina that hid her face.

'Is everything to your liking?' she asked, still outwardly demure.

Piers wet his lips. 'Perfect.'

And, with that, his loneliness magically disappeared.

Two-hundred and fifty miles north of London, Amber Melville was far from lonely. After all, she had her new best friend, Eva.

After a whole week of sharing a room, Eva and Amber were inseparable. And tonight they were on a mission: to escape Beaumont Manor and have themselves some fun. Amber suspected getting out wasn't going to be easy. The campus had a high wall with locked gates at all entrances. Closed-circuit TV covered every inch of the grounds, and 300 outside lights came on between sunset and sunrise.

But Eva was confident.

'Eet looks more hardcore than it is,' she said breezily, flipping her heavy black hair back from her carefully made-up face. She favoured hot pink Lycra and heavy gold jewellery – like all

Latino *gatinha*s. She wiggled her hips in the mirror, an expert samba move. 'They do not care if we get out, as long as they do not know about eet.'

Lights went out at ten. At ten-fifteen, the girls were out of the door. Stilettos in hand, they tiptoed along the corridor and down the fire escape. Slipping a twenty-pound note to one of the security guards ensured them an escort to the side gate. From the way Eva winked at him, Amber suspected she had slipped him a lot more.

As he closed the gate behind them, Amber's heart was beating hard.

'How do we get back in?' she whispered to Eva.

Eva tossed her head. 'Don't worry,' she said, pulling her faux fur coat closed around her skimpy outfit. 'Eet's all sorted. *Saca*?'

She grabbed Amber's hand and pulled her down the hill.

That first Friday was one of the best nights of Amber's life. Once they reached Whitby, they asked some locals where everyone went for fun. Within ten minutes they were queuing up outside a dingy venue called Cindy's, one of a handful of nightclubs in town. They flashed their fake IDs at the bouncer, deposited their coats in the cloakroom and strutted into the bar. With Amber's pretty face and Eva's silicon-enhanced breasts, they had no trouble attracting attention, in the form of a group of boys from Chatsworth, the local boys' boarding school that stood half a mile away from Beaumont Manor.

The girls perched on bar stools while the guys circled round, plying them with vodka and orange. With the ratio of male to female clearly in their favour, Amber and Eva sat back and let the boys compete for their attention.

As the night wore on, it became apparent that both girls were focusing on the best-looking of the bunch, Jed. But once Amber realised he was having a hard time keeping his eyes off

Eva's chest, she switched her interest to her second choice – Lewis. With the girls obviously having picked out their favourites, the rejected boys sloped off, resolving to try their luck with some of the inebriated locals instead.

It was just past midnight when Jed leaned over to Eva. 'Do you two want to come back to our room for a bit? We've got some CDs you could listen to.'

Eva sprang off the stool. 'For sure,' she said, without bothering to consult Amber. 'Let's go.'

Jed and Eva led the way back up the hill, their arms wrapped around each other, giggling and whispering. They were old pros at this. Amber and Lewis, both less experienced, trailed silently behind them, both increasingly aware of the lack of physical contact between them. But the vodka was beginning to affect Amber. She'd watched the way Eva had acted with Jed, casually letting her breasts brush against him, kicking her shoe off so he was forced to slip it back on her bare foot. Before, it had seemed a little obvious. But now Amber saw it as the height of sophistication. She shivered theatrically, making sure Lewis noticed.

'Are you cold?' he asked unnecessarily.

'Yes,' she said, sticking out her lower lip in the kind of sexy pout she practised in front of the mirror. Tentatively he reached out and put his arm around her.

'Is that better?'

She smiled up at him from under lowered lashes and nodded.

Half an hour later, Amber was in Lewis's bed. Eva was across the room in Jed's. With the 2 a.m. deadline looming, they hadn't wasted much time after they'd got back. Amber could hear moans and furtive rolling around from Eva and Jed. She wondered briefly if they were doing 'it'. She didn't think so. There was something slightly sleazy about all of them going at it in the same room, although the alcohol had done a good job of easing her inhibitions.

She allowed Lewis to pretty much lead the way. At first he just lay on top of her, kissing her slowly. He turned out to be pretty decent at it, not too much tongue. When he started to unzip her dress and unhook her bra, she didn't object. After everything Eva had told her, she was eager to find out what happened next. Her small breasts kept him occupied for a little while. And she was happy, too. She liked the way he sucked on them, rolling her nipples between his fingers.

He slipped one hand under the elastic of her panties. She knew what was supposed to happen next. In the privacy of their room, Eva had introduced her to the delights of masturbation. But, while Amber had enjoyed it very much then, it was somewhat less exciting with Lewis. After a few half-hearted rubs, he seemed to lose interest. So she brushed his hands away and manoeuvred him over onto his back. He needed no further encouragement. He eased out of his trousers, hesitated, and then sensing no objection, took his boxer shorts off, too. She knelt over him, taking hold of his hard-on and caressing him in the way Eva had told her to. She can't have been doing it right, though, because after a while he grabbed her hand, covering it with his, and started rubbing the shaft up and down faster and faster. As they kept on going, he started to groan. Finally, she felt him stiffen and then a long shudder ran through him. The next second a hot, sticky substance pumped out of him and hit her in the face.

She sat there for a moment, unsure what to do. She felt the wetness drip down onto her bare breasts and wrinkled her nose. Lewis reached across to his bedside table and found a box of tissues. He handed her a couple, and they mopped themselves up in embarrassed silence. Thankfully, it was time to go.

'That was the money shot,' Eva told her later, when they were safely in bed at Beaumont Manor.

Amber wasn't sure if she wanted to do that again. Some of

the stuff had got caught in her hair, and strands had dried together in clumps.

'And what about you?' Eva asked.

'What about me?'

'Did you come?'

Amber shook her head. Definitely not.

'Next time, make sure you get yours first,' Eva said firmly. 'Remember – they're never interested after they've had theirs.'

Chapter 20

It was Alain who first told Caitlin that her photograph was going to be featured in Lucien Duval's new exhibition.

'I guess this is his latest attempt to woo you,' he said wryly.

Caitlin concentrated on stacking up the glasses, pretending not to understand the comment. But in fact she was all too aware that Lucien was pursuing her. He had made no secret of it. Since that night at La Flèche d'Or, he had asked her out – once, twice, three times now. So far she'd said no, that she was too busy. It didn't seem to be putting him off.

Going out with him was a bad idea – Caitlin didn't need anyone to tell her that. But they went right ahead and told her anyway.

'Stay away from him, Caitlin,' Véronique warned. After dating Jules for two months, she was a reformed person. 'There are other guys out there. Ones who won't break your heart.'

Alain was equally vocal in letting her know his concerns. He'd spent the past year encouraging her to find a boyfriend – but had never envisioned the urbane Lucien Duval in the role.

'Don't get me wrong, sweetheart. I like the guy very much. But he isn't right for you.'

Caitlin wasn't about to argue. Lucien was everything she had sworn off: darkly, dangerously good-looking, and with a reputation to match. Unfortunately, he was also getting under her skin. She thought about him *all the time*. While her head might still be saying no to him, her heart seemed to have other ideas.

But this time he was way off-base. If he thought putting her photograph in an exhibition was going to win her over, then he didn't know her very well. The thought of all those people staring at her, thinking that she had agreed to be on public display like that . . .

'I can't think of anything worse,' she told him a few days later.

Lucien regarded her for a long moment. He would have happily staked a year's wages that any other girl in the café would have killed to be the subject of one of his photographs. But not Caitlin. She was different. Like the way she kept turning him down whenever he asked her out. Lucien didn't want to sound conceited, but that never happened to him. *Never*. And it had only made him more determined to win her over. He was frankly intrigued by this very reserved, extremely talented girl. And it took a lot to arouse his interest these days.

'Don't refuse me outright, *chérie*,' he said now. 'Come down to the exhibition – see the photograph for yourself. And if you still do not like it, then I will take it down.'

'Oh, come on. You're just saying that to get me to agree.'

He clutched his hands to his heart, feigning hurt. 'I'm insulted that you could think so badly of me.'

She laughed. 'I didn't mean it like that. It's just . . . I'm not sure it's very *me*. Véronique would be far better, surely. She does this kind of thing all the time.'

'But I don't want to use a posed picture. I want this picture of you.' He regarded her intently. 'Would you settle for burlap when you could have cashmere?'

Caitlin blushed a little. It was stuff like this that got to her. The extravagant compliments – even though she told herself it meant nothing, that flirting like that was as much a part of Lucien as his blood or bones.

The French man sensed her weakening and moved in for the

kill. 'Please, Caitlin. I give you my word: if you hate the picture, it will come down immediately.'

She sighed again, this time in resignation. 'OK, fine. You can use the photograph. As long as you promise to remove it if I ask you to.'

He reached out and covered her hand with his. 'Of course. I would never break a promise to you.' His long, cool fingers squeezed hers gently, those intense blue eyes locked on hers.

She drew her hand away and pushed her hair back from her face, something she did when she was nervous or unsure of herself.

'Good. Well, that's settled then.' She stood up abruptly. 'I should go. Get back to work.' She hurried off to the kitchen.

Standing to one side, Alain had been eavesdropping on their exchange. He waited until Caitlin had gone, then leaned across the bar. 'Old friend, I am warning you – take care. Caitlin isn't like the girls you are used to.'

Lucien smiled at his concern. 'I know that.'

'Good.' Alain did not return the smile. 'Because I won't stand for you hurting her.'

The following Friday afternoon, after classes, Caitlin decided to visit Le Nabi, the illegal squat where Lucien was exhibiting. It was one of several in the area, a product of the current art scene in Paris. Lack of affordable studio space and the difficulties of getting exhibited in established galleries had driven many young, innovative artists to start up collectives, taking over old abandoned buildings around the Belleville and Canal St Martin areas.

Le Nabi was the most famous of these. Originally a school, it had closed in the seventies and stood derelict for fifteen years, before a group of artists and photographers had broken in and secretly converted it into an exhibition space. Along with half a dozen other unofficial arts venues in the city, it was rapidly gaining a reputation as a place where collectors in the know could buy work from rising stars before they hit the big time.

Caitlin couldn't help being impressed when she got inside. It was nothing like the term 'squat' would suggest. There wasn't a dirty mattress in sight – the artists didn't actually live there. In fact, it was far bigger and more established than she had imagined: around seventy artists exhibiting over five floors in discreet studio spaces. There was a lot to see – everything from street to installation art, as well as Marcel Duchamp-style sculptures. But Caitlin ignored them all and headed straight for Lucien's exhibits.

She'd asked Alain about his work the previous evening. He'd explained that Lucien used his art to explore the social issues of the time, to show a darker side of Paris.

'His mother was Algerian, his father French,' he'd told her, 'so growing up, Lucien never really felt he belonged to either culture.' Now, looking at his photographs, Caitlin could see how he'd drawn on that – that sense of *alienation* – to highlight the current social unrest in France. He'd taken his camera out to the grubby *banlieues* and here were the results: grainy black-and-white shots of grim public housing and soulless motorways; strip malls and fast-food joints; homelessness and gang warfare. It was a window into the casual violence, poverty and despair of thousands of ordinary lives. It was also some of the most powerful work Caitlin had seen for a while. She couldn't help being impressed by the depth and empathy of his art.

She spent a long time looking at the main collection. Finally, aware that the gallery would be closing soon, she moved through to the smaller annex. The subject-matter was less serious in there – a haphazard collection of moments that had captured Lucien's interest. It was there that she found the picture he had taken of her. It would have been hard to miss, as it took up most of the back wall. For a moment Caitlin felt horribly embarrassed, seeing herself looming so large, until she remembered no one else was here. Only then was she able to relax a little, and finally study the picture that she had come to see.

Lucien had caught her at her deepest moment of introspection, frowning down at her sketchpad, the end of a pencil jammed between her teeth, her short dark hair tucked behind her ears. He was right, she admitted reluctantly. It wasn't so bad. Most people wouldn't even know it was her. She supposed she could let him keep it up, if he really wanted to.

Her decision made, she went to turn away. But something stopped her. She stared at the picture for a long moment. She had the oddest sense of *déjà vu*. There was something so familiar about it . . .

Suddenly something clicked: it was as though Caitlin had been transported back six years, to a Sunday evening in the cottage in Valleymount. She was finishing her homework, while her mother pored over the following week's roster for the hotel staff . . . frowning, totally absorbed in what she was doing. Then it struck her – in the photograph, she looked exactly like her mother!

Caitlin stood there, entranced, unable to tear her eyes away. In fact, she was so lost in the photograph that she didn't notice Lucien entering the room and coming to stand next to her until he spoke.

'Are you OK?'

She started at his voice, looked round and saw that he was frowning down at her. She quickly wiped her eyes.

'Caitlin? *Ça-va, mon amour?*' he asked again.

The genuine concern in his voice made her tear up again.

'I'm fine,' she managed, her voice wavering a little. Then, deciding she needed to offer some explanation, she said, 'It's just . . . well, the picture reminded me of someone, that's all. My mother.'

'And that makes you sad?' he said quizzically.

'Well . . . yes.' She hesitated, and then said in a low voice, 'She died, you see – five years ago.'

Lucien reached out and squeezed her arm. 'I am so sorry to hear that,' he murmured. There was a silence. Another person might have pressed her for more details, but Lucien seemed to accept her need for privacy.

'What did you think of the rest of the exhibition?' he asked instead.

Caitlin was relieved at the change of subject.

'It's brilliant,' she said truthfully. She walked back towards the other room, wanting now to get away from the photograph. Lucien followed. 'This is my favourite,' she said, pointing towards a landscape. 'I love the use of light and shadows. It's . . . superb.'

Lucien looked amused. 'Superb?' He pretended to mull her comment over. 'What an extravagant comment. But how do I know you really mean that? Perhaps you are just being kind.'

She raised an eyebrow. 'And perhaps you're just fishing for more compliments.'

He chuckled softly. 'I have found that you can never hear too many good things about yourself.'

Before she could ask any more about his work, another man appeared in the doorway, interrupting them. He was older than Lucien, maybe in his late thirties, and looked a little more conservative, but still cutting-edge in a black suit and open-necked black shirt.

'Lucien?' He sounded impatient. 'We are all waiting on you – as usual. Are you coming or what?'

'In a bit, Philippe,' Lucien responded good-naturedly. 'Why don't you go on without me?'

The older man looked as though he was about to object, but then his gaze flicked over to Caitlin, and his expression turned from irritation to amusement. He said something else to

Lucien. Although Caitlin's French had improved dramatically over the past year, she still struggled with rapid colloquialisms — but she thought it was something like, '*Instead of standing there flirting all night, why don't you just ask her along?*' Caitlin felt her cheeks heating up. Lucien rolled his eyes, and Philippe chuckled before leaving them to it.

'Well?' Lucien turned to her after the man had gone. 'Would you like to join us?'

Caitlin's instinct was to refuse. She didn't especially like hanging out with strangers. But tonight she didn't want to be alone. After being reminded of her mother, she needed some distraction.

She smiled at him. 'I'd love to come.'

He looked pleased. 'Good. Then we should go before I get into any more trouble.'

Half an hour later, they joined Lucien's friends at a trendy bar-restaurant on Canal St Martin. There were around twenty of them, sitting in a circle on the little plastic seats that lined the bank of the canal. They welcomed Lucien, teasing him about turning up late — something of a habit for him, apparently.

Lucien stayed by Caitlin's side all evening, topping up her wine glass, leaning over to explain in-jokes when she looked a little lost, and introducing her to the designers who worked at Le Nabi. As the night wore on, it grew darker and colder. Lucien noticed her shivering.

'Here,' he said, taking his jacket off and putting it around her shoulders.

It was hard for Caitlin not to be flattered. Lucien was something of a celebrity in the circles they ran in, and clearly popular with everyone here. Even though he sat to the side, quietly sipping his wine and only interjecting with the odd comment now and again, every story and joke seemed to be directed at him. And now here he was, focusing all his attention on her.

Around midnight, there was talk of moving on elsewhere.

'We're heading over to La Flèche d'Or,' Philippe called over. 'Are you coming?'

Lucien looked questioningly at Caitlin. 'I can't,' she said. 'I've got to work tomorrow.'

'I will walk you home then.'

God, no, she thought. That was the last thing she wanted. The romantic walk home, the pause by the door . . . 'Oh, there's no need,' she said quickly. 'It's not far. Really, I'll be fine.'

'But I insist,' he said firmly. 'Not least because Alain will kill me if anything happens to you.'

Unable to think of a logical reason to refuse his offer, Caitlin gave in.

They made the twenty-minute walk back to her apartment in silence. They were both quiet – Lucien, because he wasn't one to make small talk, and Caitlin, because she was preoccupied. She was thinking about the way he had touched her hand in the café last week; of the knowing look Philippe had shot them earlier – wondering what Lucien was expecting to happen when they got to her place. Because that was the last thing she wanted. It was still too soon after . . . well, after what had happened at Greycourt.

Finally they reached the café. At the front door, Caitlin fiddled with her keys. She'd already decided she wouldn't ask Lucien in. That would give the wrong impression, and she had a horrible feeling she'd done quite enough of that already.

'Thanks for walking me home,' she said.

'It was no problem. I will sleep easier, knowing that you are safe.'

She knew then that she had to say something; that this couldn't go on.

'Lucien, please . . .'

He raised a questioning eyebrow. 'Please, what?'

'Please stop saying things like that.'

'Why?'

'Because I've told you before,' she said firmly. 'I'm not interested in going out with you.'

He sounded amused as he asked, 'And why not?'

'Because . . .' she stumbled. 'Because I'm too busy. I've got so much to do for college, and what with working at the café, I don't have time for anything else . . .' She trailed off.

She'd been expecting him to argue back. But instead he reached out and touched her cheek with his long, cool fingers. 'Well, I'll just have to see what I can do to change your mind, *chérie.*'

She didn't know what to say. But he wasn't looking for a response. In that moment, she suddenly became aware of how near he was; the way he had moved towards her without her realising. He was so close now she could feel his breath on her cheek, see the pale moonlight reflecting off his strong jaw as he bent his head, his eyes glittering with something she couldn't quite read. Too late, she guessed his intention. She was still trying to think up a way to stop him as he kissed her.

His lips brushed hers gently at first, so light she wasn't even sure it had happened. Then, sensing no resistance, his mouth found hers properly, his kiss harder, deeper. Then his hands were in her hair, tipping her head back; his tongue prying her lips apart, sliding against hers.

Her eyes fluttered closed and she felt an involuntary shiver of desire run through her body. It had been so long since she had felt like this . . . But as he drew her closer, a memory flashed through her brain, a hazy memory of a darkened room and a bed, and an incident that had started off with a kiss very much like this one; a kiss that had cost her more than she had imagined possible.

What the hell am I doing? The thought flashed through her brain, swiftly followed by another. *This is a mistake.*

She broke away from his kiss, from his arms, pushing him from her. 'Lucien, I said *no!*'

Before he could respond, she fled inside.

She ran to the safety of her bedroom, slammed the door shut and sank to the ground. She noticed her hand was shaking as she reached up to touch her lips, still warm from his. It was a long time before she felt able to pick herself up off the floor.

The following Monday, Caitlin got back from college to find a package waiting outside her door. From the size and shape, it didn't take a genius to figure out what it was. But still, when she unwrapped it and saw that it was indeed her picture from the gallery, she couldn't help feeling touched that Lucien had realised how much it meant to her. All weekend she'd been feeling bad about the way she'd reacted to his kiss. Now she felt even worse.

That evening, when he came into the café, she made a point of thanking him.

'It was my way of apologising for . . .' He hesitated. 'For whatever I did wrong the other night.'

There was a question in his voice, and she avoided his gaze as she said a slightly awkward, 'Thank you.'

He waited until she looked up again and then indicated the chair opposite him. 'Do you have time to join me for a drink?'

Now it was her turn to hesitate. Part of her was terrified of taking this next step, of letting someone in. But there was another part of her, the part that wanted to be with Lucien, that was telling her she needed to grab this opportunity to move on.

'You know,' she said, pulling out the chair, 'I think I'm due a break around now.'

He gave her a slow smile. 'I am very pleased to hear that.'

Chapter 21

Elizabeth gave the fax machine a well-placed smack. She'd discovered over the past few weeks how notoriously temperamental it was. At first, she'd patiently consulted the manual and tried to figure out what was wrong. Now, whenever it wasn't dialling, she resorted to violence. She was about to hit it again when she heard someone call her name. She looked up to see Kathleen glaring at her.

After three months, the uptight Scot hadn't got any friendlier. Elizabeth suspected Kathleen got a secret thrill out of lording it over the boss's daughter. She'd learned not to care. It was easier to be pleasant and bide her time.

She pasted on a smile. 'What can I do for you, Kathleen?'

The other woman glared harder. 'I've left a stack of photocopying on your desk. I'm going to lunch now. Could you make sure it's done by the time I get back?'

'Of course,' Elizabeth said amiably.

As Kathleen walked away, the smile slipped from her face. It killed her to be polite. Every time. But at least it helped cover up how miserable she was, working here.

Unbelievably, it had got even worse since that awful first day. She was given every mundane task in the department. She got sent on all the coffee runs. She covered the phones at lunchtimes; she typed and filed. She stood over the copier for hours, until her back ached and her eyes blurred.

It didn't help that no one seemed to like her. During her first week, she approached Sarah, one of the younger and friendlier girls, and asked if she fancied going for lunch at a new Italian that had opened up round the corner from the office.

Sarah didn't even bother to look up from her computer. 'I don't eat Italian food,' she said.

'Well, we could go somewhere else,' Elizabeth tried again.

'I don't eat lunch.'

A couple of people who sat nearby sniggered. Elizabeth swallowed hard, determined not to let them see how she felt.

'Right, I understand,' she said quietly, turning away.

In the end, she went out on her own at lunchtime, to get some fresh air and grab a sandwich. As she walked along the street, she happened to glance in the window of Bertolli and there, sitting in the window and tucking into pasta, was the whole team – including Sarah. Ducking her head down, Elizabeth hurried on, not wanting to give them the satisfaction of witnessing her humiliation.

That had been three months ago. Three months of photo-copying and filing and being snubbed by her co-workers. For a brief, wild moment, she had considered quitting. She could tell her father that she needed some time elsewhere, perhaps doing an MBA. And she might have gone through with it if it hadn't been for Cole Greenway. She didn't want him to think that he'd won.

The way he'd treated her that first day still grated, and weeks of seeing him stroll self-importantly around the office while she was forced to deal with menial tasks had infuriated her even more. But what made it worse was that every female in the department seemed to have a crush on him. She was in the Ladies one day, touching up her make-up, when she overheard Kathleen and Sarah talking about him.

'Last Friday, I swear I was drunk enough to beg to go home with him,' Kathleen was saying.

Sarah giggled. 'I don't blame you. Do you know if he's single?'

'I don't even care.'

'Kathy!' Sarah giggled again. 'Although I know what you mean. He's really hot.'

Without thinking, Elizabeth gave a loud, dismissive snort. The other two women heard her and turned.

'What's wrong with you?' Kathleen demanded.

Elizabeth shrugged. 'I just don't think Cole's all that great, that's all.'

'Well, honey, you're the only one,' the Scottish woman retorted.

Back at her desk, Elizabeth turned the conversation over in her mind. OK – maybe Cole was good-looking, she admitted grudgingly. But the problem was, he was just so cocksure. Every time he walked by her in the corridor, he would give her a condescending smile, as if to say he'd taught her a lesson. And every time he did that she would vow to herself that one day, soon, she would show him.

She just had to figure out how.

During those first few months, Elizabeth kept her head down and tried to absorb every piece of information that she could. When she wasn't in the office, she devoted hours to reading Melville's annual reports as well as a variety of business journals. It was from one of these that she got the idea to spend a Saturday each month working in the store. 'Time on the shop floor is the best way to keep on top of what's going on in your business,' one CEO of a global retail group proclaimed. Every day she was learning something new about the industry. She stored away her findings and waited for an opportunity to prove herself.

It came sooner than she expected.

Late one Thursday afternoon, Cole popped his head round the door of her office to ask if she would take the Minutes for this month's board meeting.

'I've got loads of stuff to do . . .' she started to say.

'Sorry.' He was curt. 'You're the only one free.'

She sighed heavily. 'Fine.'

'I don't know what you're complaining about,' he said, as they walked along the corridor. 'This has got to be more interesting than photocopying.'

'Plucking my eyebrows is more interesting than photocopying,' she retorted. She sounded so annoyed that he started to laugh. She glowered at him. Then gave in and laughed, too.

In fact, the meeting was better than she'd been expecting. Most of it was routine – going through monthly sales figures. But then Cole tabled a motion that piqued her interest. A Japanese steel magnate was coming to London in a few weeks' time. With a personal net wealth of two and a half billion dollars, he was retiring this year and looking at filling his time with more entrepreneurial pursuits. He was doing a tour of Europe, exploring various investment ideas.

Despite all its expansion, Melville had never entered the Asian market. Cole thought that it was time to go into Japan, and he wanted to meet this businessman. William was more reluctant.

'The economy is terrible over there,' he pointed out. 'Everyone's using the term "Asian Crisis". Gucci issued a profit warning the other week based on the ongoing downturn in the region, and its share price fell thirty per cent. Why invest now?'

'Because this is the bottom – it can only get better from here,' Cole said evenly. 'Demographics are a key factor. The social landscape is changing. Sure, the country's in recession and the traditional breadwinner, the salaryman, is suffering. But the upside is that women are getting more disposable income. And Japanese women love designer goods. Gucci, Louis Vuitton . . . they've been raking it in. We've missed out on a big market so far – let's take the opportunity to get out there now.'

Without thinking, Elizabeth joined in. 'I agree with Cole.'

Everyone turned to look at her. Cole frowned, as though he wanted her to stop, but she had something to say – finally – and she knew her opinion was worthwhile.

'We regularly get buyers in from Tokyo,' she told the board. 'They pick up fifty odd bags at once. I bet they're taking them back home and selling them for a massive mark-up.'

'How do you know that?' William demanded.

Elizabeth met his eyes. 'Because I've been spending some time on the shopfloor.'

The meeting moved on. But Elizabeth's words must have had some impact, because the next day, Cole began to look into opening a branch of Melville in Japan.

A couple of weeks later it was decided that the best way to approach the Far East was to go along with Cole's idea of entering into a joint venture. Mr Yamamoto, the steel magnate, was coming to London the following month to talk to prospective partners. Cole delivered the news to Elizabeth in person. But if she'd been hoping that her support in the boardroom might earn her a bigger role on the presentation team, she was wrong. He made it quite clear that Kathleen was in charge. Elizabeth would simply be helping her put together the research.

'I know maybe it's not what you were hoping to do,' he said, 'but prove yourself on this and I'll find you something else – OK?'

Elizabeth hid her disappointment and nodded. 'OK.'

Of all the people in the Strategy Department, Kathleen had remained Elizabeth's least favourite. The strident Scottish woman, with her no-nonsense attitude and permanent frown, might be a smart, slick ex-McKinsey consultant. But Elizabeth could tell straight off that she was the wrong person to be heading up the pitch to Mr Yamamoto. If Elizabeth had been in charge, she would have sat down and brainstormed what Yamamoto was looking for and how Melville could meet those needs. Instead, Kathleen had taken a more arrogant approach, slanting the presentation towards how great Melville was, compared to its competitors. It all felt too forced, too lacking in subtlety.

At first, Elizabeth tried to voice her concerns, but Kathleen made it clear that her suggestions weren't welcome.

'You're just here to put together the graphs and find out any info I need,' she said nastily. 'If you have a problem with that, tell Cole you want off the team.'

So Elizabeth shut up, got on with what she was told to do and watched the train-wreck unfold. When she saw the new store designs that Kathleen had prepared, she knew that they had already lost the pitch. Yamamoto was looking to invest in a little slice of England, a piece of tradition. But Kathleen's designs didn't play to that at all. Instead they were self-consciously modern: white walls, glass walkways, chrome fittings, lots of light and mirrors. It was the kind of anonymous décor that didn't give any clue to the identity of the brand.

The day for the pitch dawned. Any hope Elizabeth held that Kathleen might work some magic during the presentation faded when she saw what the other woman planned to wear. She'd chosen a navy pinstriped trouser-suit and tied her hair back in a slick bun. It was an aggressive, manly look and all wrong for meeting a Japanese businessman.

Things went from bad to worse. When Mr Yamamoto interrupted Kathleen to query one of the projections on the second slide, she was brisk with him. 'That will become apparent very soon,' she said, as though talking to a small child. 'Why don't you let me get through the presentation and then you can ask me any questions afterwards?'

Yamamoto's brow furrowed for a second. Then his expression cleared. 'Of course,' he said politely. 'Please excuse me.'

Elizabeth could tell he wasn't happy. Kathleen hadn't meant to be rude, but the Japanese style of doing business was simply far less confrontational. Mr Yamamoto listened politely for the rest of the time. But when he left the building, Elizabeth could tell he wasn't coming back anytime soon.

At her desk, she considered the situation. There had to be another way to get Yamamoto on side. That was when she remembered that his wife was over here with him. She picked up the dossier that she'd carefully prepared on Kumiko Yamamoto. She'd spent hours putting it together. Kathleen had barely glanced at it, but Elizabeth thought it held the key to rescuing the situation. No one had asked the basic question about why a steel magnate was bothering to diversify into luxury goods, an area he knew nothing about. Maybe if they'd taken the time to consider that his wife was a fashion icon in her native country, as well as a notorious shopaholic, with an Imelda Marcos penchant for shoes . . .

Elizabeth put a call through to the stockroom. She'd made a point of befriending the guys down there. Everyone assumed because of her cut-glass accent that she was a snob, but she was actually one of the few people who didn't care what level someone was at in the company – as long as they were doing their best for Melville.

'Hey, Gary. It's Elizabeth here. I was wondering about the new lines coming in. I wanted to send a sample to a customer.' She gave a brief description of the kind of thing she was looking for. Then she waited. 'That sounds great,' she said finally. 'Can I come down and take a look?'

Kumiko Yamamoto was in her suite at Claridge's in Mayfair, waiting for her husband to return from one of his interminable business meetings. She had spent the morning shopping in Knightsbridge. She adored Europe and European fashion. Elizabeth's instinct had been right – it had been Kumiko's idea to look into investing in a European luxury goods name. She felt that the right one would impress her circle of friends.

There was a knock at the door. The bellboy stood outside with an unexpected delivery. She remembered to tip him: it wasn't a Japanese custom, but the English seemed to expect it these days. Then she took the beautifully wrapped box inside to the bedroom. In black satin, with a perfectly tied white bow, it looked exciting. Quickly, she untied the ribbon and pulled off the lid. Nestled in folds of white tissue she found a pair of beautiful satin slingbacks.

She took the shoes out to examine them. Whoever had sent these had done their research. Being a whisker short of five foot, she never wore a shoe that didn't have at least a three-inch heel. These, she could tell at a glance, were three and a half. The shoes were red – her favourite colour. And when she slipped them on, they fitted her dainty feet perfectly.

She picked up the With Compliments slip. There was a name and phone number on it. She hesitated for a moment and then started to dial.

When Yasuo Yamamoto got back to his hotel suite late that afternoon, he was surprised to find his wife having tea with Elizabeth Melville. He had already dismissed the idea of investing in her father's company. He had felt insulted today that William Melville himself hadn't come to meet him. And then to send that dreadful woman in his place.

But one of the few people Yasuo Yamamoto paid attention to was his wife, and she persuaded him to listen to what the young lady had to say. Half an hour later, he was a convert. This was exactly what he had been looking for earlier. William's daughter spoke with passion. She truly believed in the brand and she had a vision for the company.

'What about the store interiors?' he asked. 'Are you in favour of what I was shown earlier today?'

This had been a major bone of contention for him. He'd hated the modern designs – there was quite enough of that in Tokyo already.

Elizabeth chose her words carefully. 'Personally, I'd rather go for something more classic, something that epitomises the values that Melville is associated with . . .'

She began to outline the ideas she had for the new store concepts. The look would be expensive and timeless, capturing the quintessential Englishness of the Melville name. Regency wallpaper, rosewood panelling, deep pile carpets so soft you could sleep on them. But there would also be the requisite modern touches to make the stores cutting-edge: voice-activated elevators, touch-button-operated display cabinets, state-of-the-art computerised store directories, so customers could locate and order exactly what they wanted – even if it was in the Paris or London stores. It would be the perfect blend of traditional and contemporary.

As she spoke, Yamamoto began to nod. This was more what he'd had in mind. His wife caught his eye and smiled. As usual, she had been right. This was someone he could do business with.

Two days later, Yamamoto called William to say that he was willing to enter into a partnership with Melville.

'I have one condition,' the steel magnate said.

'Anything,' William told him.

'I want your daughter, Elizabeth, to oversee the store opening in Tokyo.'

It took all of William's control not to sound surprised. 'Elizabeth?'

'Yes, of course. After all, it was she who persuaded me to sign up with you in the first place.'

William wasn't impressed with Elizabeth going behind his back, as he saw it. In fact, he was furious.

'Well, there's no way that I'm allowing her to go,' he said dismissively. 'She doesn't have enough experience.'

William directed his comments at Cole. The three of them were in the Head of Strategy's office. He had already been bawled out for allowing this all to happen. So far, William hadn't addressed one comment to his daughter. It was as though she wasn't there.

'We'll send Kathleen instead,' he proclaimed. 'I'll call Yamamoto and tell him that's how it's going to be.'

Elizabeth looked at her father in dismay. She couldn't believe he was going to take this away from her. It wasn't fair for Kathleen to go, when it was she who'd got the deal in the first damned place.

Cole had stayed surprisingly quiet throughout the whole conversation. Now he raised his head to speak. Elizabeth braced herself. There was no way he'd take her side.

But she was wrong.

'Yamamoto wants Elizabeth,' he said simply. 'If you don't send her, he'll withdraw from the deal.'

That shut William up.

'I can keep a close eye on her,' Cole continued. 'The first sign that she's screwing up, we can get her out of there.'

William regarded his eldest daughter for a long moment. She held her breath. He clearly wasn't happy, but there wasn't much he could do about it. Cole was right: Yamamoto wanted her. It was either lose the deal altogether, or let her go out there.

'Fine,' he said grudgingly. 'We'll do it your way.' With that, he went out, leaving her alone with Cole.

'Thanks,' she said awkwardly. 'For sticking up for me.'

'Don't mention it.' He grinned. 'Hell, I'd do pretty much anything to get you out of my way, right?'

She laughed. Then: 'Do you want to go for a drink?' she asked impulsively. 'You know, to celebrate getting rid of me.'

'Can't.' He was curt. 'I've already got plans.' He nodded through the glass window of his office. She turned to see Kathleen standing outside. With her hair down, make-up on and contact lenses in, she actually looked quite attractive.

Elizabeth tried not to sound bothered as she said, 'Well, maybe another time.'

Cole's mouth twitched. 'Yeah. Maybe.'

Chapter 22

Amber and Eva became inseparable. During the week, they were model students. Eva dragged Amber out of bed at six-thirty in the morning to make sure she was on time for registration at eight; banned her from cutting classes and even had her volunteering to go on cross-country runs across the heather-clad moorland. It was all part of Eva's plan. Her theory was that Mrs Dauston wouldn't bother watching them too closely if she believed they were well-behaved.

'It ees the path of least resistence. *Saca?*'

So during the week they did what they were told. But then every Friday and Saturday night, they got dressed up in all their teenage finery and sneaked out into the nearby seaside resort of Whitby. In sky-high heels, they would totter across the bleak fells of the York moors down into Whitby's old town, and then through the maze of alleyways and narrow streets that led to the busy quayside – and their favourite club, Cindy's. As Amber and Eva stood shivering in the queue, they would look up and see Beaumont Manor perched above them, dark and brooding on the East Cliff, and giggle over their luck at not getting caught again.

Early on they made a pact never to hang out with the same guys twice. The week after their first excursion, Jed and Lewis were back, looking for a repeat performance. The two girls took great pleasure in pretending not to know them.

'I don't wanna steady boyfriend,' Eva said, tossing her great mane of hair. 'This is just for experience, for when I meet someone I really like.'

Amber nodded. She always agreed with whatever Eva said.

But, despite her earlier bravado, Eva didn't seem especially keen on sleeping with any of the guys they picked up. When Amber pressed her on the subject, she said. 'These are only boys. Next time I do it, it'll be with a real *homem.*'

Amber nodded vigorously. 'Yeah, me too,' she said.

It worked out nicely. Each week, they'd pick up a couple of guys, fool around with them for a bit, and then, when 2 a.m. hit, they would scurry back to school and the safety of their own warm beds. Amber had never been happier.

When the Christmas holidays arrived, for the first time in her school career Amber didn't want to go home. The only consolation was that her parents seemed happy that she'd settled in at Beaumont Manor. On her first evening back, her father made her sit in his study as he read out her end-of-term report, rewarding her with a lukewarm, 'Well done,' at the end. Then, later that night, her mother came to her room and gave her a present. It was the DKNY dress that she'd promised Amber if she got through the term without incident.

'Just don't let Daddy know I got it for you,' she warned.

Christmas at Aldringham was quiet and dull. Uncle Piers brought Granny Rosalind down for a few days. Her health was rapidly deteriorating, although she was still as sharp as ever. 'You're turning into a very lovely young woman, Amber,' she observed the night she arrived. 'Just make sure you don't rely on your looks to get you through life. Elizabeth has the right idea – hard work will get you further in the world than a pretty face.'

It was the same lecture as ever, but Amber didn't mind it so much from Granny Rosalind. She could be pretty funny, and had some great stories from when she was young. Unfortunately, Amber hardly got to talk to her over the break, because Piers was always there, fussing over her like an old woman. Even the usually placid Isabelle eventually snapped at him.

'Please, Piers,' she said, rubbing her temples. 'Can't you just sit still for five minutes? You're giving me a headache. And, I would imagine, your poor mother, too.'

For the second year in a row, Caitlin didn't come back for Christmas. It was a shame, because the last time Amber had seen her – about eighteen months earlier – she'd got pretty cool, much cooler than when she'd first come to live with them. Amber had been looking forward to hearing about her fashion course and living in Paris – in fact, she'd been secretly hoping to scrounge an invite out there.

'Why doesn't she ever visit?' she asked Elizabeth one evening.

'You'll have to ask her,' her older sister replied primly, which was *really* annoying as she obviously knew.

Elizabeth was as boring and bossy as usual. The first night she was back, she gave Amber a big sister lecture about getting kicked out of school – God, she sounded *so* like Dad sometimes – and then kept offering to help her revise for the mock exams that were coming up in January. 'If you get a head-start now, it'll save you a lot of extra work in the summer,' she kept saying. *Yawn.*

At least Amber could use revising as an excuse to escape to her room. But, instead of hitting the books, she would secretly call Eva. The girls spoke to each other every day over the break, plotting what they were going to get up to next term. Eva seemed to be having much more fun over in Brazil – out in Rio every night. She talked of her friends back home and a guy she'd met: 'He was gorgeous, so I did *it* with him. He's American. Much cuter than English boys.' Amber couldn't help feeling jealous.

When they arrived back at Beaumont Manor on the eighth day of what must have been the coldest, bleakest January in history, Amber was already looking forward to their first night out at Cindy's. But on Friday morning she woke up with flu.

She spent the day in bed with a hot water bottle, making sure to drink plenty of fluids. But she still wasn't better by the evening. What made her disappointment worse was that Eva was still planning to go out.

'Who're you taking along?' Amber asked in a small voice, as she watched Eva get ready. She couldn't help thinking that her roommate could at least have offered to stay in with her.

'Circe,' Eva replied off-hand.

'Oh.' Amber burrowed further under the covers, feeling even more wretched now. Circe Scott was a new arrival this term. The troubled daughter of seventies' rock star Leonard Scott, she was far higher up the pecking order than Amber, who had a horrible feeling she was about to be replaced as Eva's best friend.

When the Brazilian girl left half an hour later, she bade a coolly polite goodnight to Amber.

For the first time in a long while, Amber cried herself to sleep.

When Amber woke at three in the morning, she was surprised to find that Eva wasn't back. She decided to stay awake, so at least she could find out what had gone on. But four o'clock came and went, and still Eva hadn't returned. Amber watched her digital clock flip round to half four . . . then five . . .

She must have dozed off around six, because the next thing she knew, someone was shaking her awake. It was Eva. Her hands were like ice, and she'd clearly just got back. She was still wearing the same clothes as last night, her hair was a mess and her mascara beginning to run, but she was grinning. Amber's eyes slid over to her clock. It was seven twenty-eight.

'Where have you been?' she hissed. 'You're going to get into so much trouble.'

Eva flipped her hair back. It had frizzed in the early-morning damp, and so the flick wasn't as effective as usual. But she didn't seem bothered.

'No way. No one saw me. And, even if they did, it was worth it. I had the best night ever!'

Amber thought of Circe and guessed that must have been the reason the night was so successful. She was about to be permanently replaced. Hurt and jealousy shot through her.

'Well, I'm glad you and Circe had fun,' she said moodily.

She was about to turn over, putting her back to Eva. But Eva put a restraining hand on her.

'Circe didn't come in the end. She got scared and turned back. She's a *covarde*.'

She spat out the last word. Amber felt her spirits lift. She realised then that Eva had woken her because she missed her partner in crime. And this was her opportunity to get back into Eva's good books.

'So what happened?' she asked eagerly.

Eva grinned. 'First move over and let me under the covers with you. I'm freezing!'

The reason for all the excitement turned out to be a guy. Not a boy this time – a *homem*. Eva had met him in Cindy's. His name was Jack and he was, according to an overexcited Eva, a *total babe*. He was older, but she wasn't sure how old – 'late twenties, I think' – and he had his own business, although she wasn't sure doing what exactly. He also had his own place, a house just outside Whitby, and apparently the biggest stash of weed Eva had ever seen. She'd gone back there with a few others after the club closed. Nothing much had happened between them that night, 'just a bit of fooling around'. But they were planning to meet during the week and she expected they'd do *it* then.

Eva didn't shut up about Jack all week. She sneaked out every night to meet him. By the following Friday morning, Amber realised she was being dumped for him instead of Circe. Eva still hadn't returned from her Thursday-night jaunt by the time breakfast was served. Amber covered for her, saying she was in bed with period pains. As the morning wore on she began to worry that she'd done the wrong thing. Maybe Eva was lying dead in a ditch somewhere . . .

Halfway through Double Maths she finally appeared. There was no time to talk then, but as soon as the lesson ended, Eva grabbed Amber and hauled her to one side.

'You *have* to come out tonight,' she ordered.

Amber looked sceptical. She was getting a little tired of Eva blowing hot and cold. 'What – Jack's not around to entertain you?'

'No. I mean, yes,' Eva said excitedly. 'He's having a party. It's going to be huge. He asked if I had any friends I wanted to invite and I told him about you. He said you can come along!'

All of Amber's earlier irritation at her friend was suddenly forgotten. 'Really? I can come, too?'

'Yep,' Eva said. 'And Jack said he's sure we'll be able to find a guy for you.' It was said slightly pityingly, as though, left to her own devices, Amber would have no hope of finding someone. But she ignored the slight. She was too happy at being included.

Then Eva pursed her lips. 'There's only one thing.'

'What?'

'You can't be so uptight. These are real men. They will expect certain things,' she said, meaningfully stressing the last word. '*Saca?*'

Of course she understood. The last week, without Eva, had been terrible. She was prepared to do whatever it took this time to maintain their friendship.

The night of the party, Amber and Eva caught a taxi out to Jack's house. A twenty-minute drive from Whitby, deep in the countryside, it seemed a curious place for someone young and single to want to live. Amber remarked on the fact in the cab and drew a withering glance from Eva.

'It was his parents' place,' she explained briefly. 'He stays here when he's in the area. He moves around a lot.' The vagueness of the answer set the tone for the rest of the evening.

The drive took longer than it should have. The roads were empty, but they were also rough, unlit and lacking signposts. Eva, who had been out there several times already, was no help finding it.

'I've always been pissed when we've driven here.'

The taxi driver went past the turn-off for Keepers Cottage twice before he finally spotted an old piece of wood with white lettering on it. The first and third e's were missing, so it read K ep rs Cottage.

The cottage itself was at the end of a narrow dirt track, and turned out to be a fifties-style redbrick house with a tiled roof full of gaps. It stood on a patch of grass, which obviously passed for a garden. But instead of flowerbeds there was an upended motorbike waiting to be repaired and a broken swing. It was a stark, empty place. They had passed the nearest neighbour several miles back. A few cars were parked to the side and a light shone through net curtains in one of the small windows. But otherwise the cottage was dark and still.

The taxi driver, a cuddly bear of a man, seemed uneasy about leaving the two young girls there. He looked suspiciously at the dark, looming house. Right now, it resembled the set of a horror movie.

'Sure you'll be all right?' he asked, genuinely concerned. 'I can drop you back in town if you want. No extra charge.' He had teenage girls himself, and there was no way he'd have let them spend the evening here. But Eva was already climbing out of the car.

'No, that will be all,' she said loftily, handing him a fifty-pound note. She didn't wait around for the change.

The taxi driver shrugged. The tip was more than three times the fare. More money than sense. He pocketed the cash and drove away.

Inside, the house turned out to be a typical bachelor crash pad – a hotchpotch of furniture, threadbare carpets and dirty crockery piled high in the sink. It wasn't quite the palace Eva had made it out to be. In fact, Amber was beginning to realise that Eva had exaggerated a lot of things. Including Jack. With a squished nose – the result of a bar fight – and small, piggy eyes, he wasn't exactly Brad Pitt.

'Jack!' Eva squealed when he opened the door, throwing her arms around him and kissing him firmly on the mouth. In her exuberance, she knocked his arm, spilling the can of beer he was carrying. He scowled and pushed her away slightly.

'Leave off, Eva.'

Ignoring the warning tone, she grabbed his hand, staking her claim as his girlfriend.

'This is Amber,' she said then. 'The one I was telling you about.'

Amber blushed as he looked her over.

'Cool,' Jack said, as though deciding he liked what he saw. 'You should meet Billy,' he told Amber. 'I reckon you guys'll get on well.'

Amber wasn't sure what had led him to conclude this, but she followed him and Eva through to the living room anyway. It was as unspectacular as the rest of the house. There were several people sitting around on beanbags and a beat-up sofa, listening to the Prodigy.

'Decided to keep it intimate. Just a few friends having beers,' Jack told them.

It was all much more casual than Amber was expecting. In fact, in her Donna Karan slip dress she was beginning to feel self-conscious. Apart from Eva, all the other girls – well, women to be more precise, because they looked like they were in their late twenties – were in jeans and hooded tops. And that didn't seem like such a bad idea, given that there didn't appear to be any heating.

Jack's friend, Billy, sat cross-legged by a scratched coffee-table. Amber was pleased to see that he was more conventionally good-looking than Jack; tall and well-built, with a grade two haircut and a permanent five o'clock shadow. More of a man than the boys she was used to. He looked up at her with interest.

'Hey.' It seemed to be the standard greeting. He patted the cushion on the floor next to him. 'Sit down here.'

She did as she was told. She was pleased when Eva and Jack sat down too. She wasn't sure she was going to have anything much to say to this man.

Billy handed out beers from the cooler next to him. Amber would have preferred wine, but she couldn't see any around so she took the can he offered. The conversation was a little stilted at first, but after a couple more drinks, everyone relaxed. It turned out the guys weren't around much, which explained the state of the house and the strange musty smell that pervaded it. Jack was a long-distance lorry driver. Billy was 'in-between' jobs.

'I might do some travelling, so I don't want to get tied down,' he explained.

Amber nodded gravely, hanging off his every word. She wondered how old he was. He seemed so worldly. He finished rolling a spliff and held it out to her. She hesitated for a second. She'd smoked weed before, but never with strangers. Then she saw Eva frowning at her. 'Go on,' she mouthed.

Amber didn't want to seem uncool, so she took it. Billy smiled.

'Good girl,' he said.

Billy leaned over and brushed Amber's curls away from her face.

'You're really beautiful,' he told her.

She giggled. 'I'm going to be a model one day,' she said, throwing back her head to pose.

He laughed with her. 'Yeah, I could see that.'

It was a little while later, and Amber was drunk, stoned and having the best night ever. The alcohol and drugs had eased her inhibitions. She felt confident, clever and witty. It was just the four of them left now – her, Eva, Billy and Jack – still sitting in the living room. She didn't remember the others going. The four of them had played some drinking games, the girls deliberately losing because it seemed so amusing to get drunk. Somewhere along the way Eva had insisted on cheesier music – 'Something I can sing to!' Now 'Black Velvet' came on.

Amber squealed. 'I love this song!' She got to her feet. 'I wanna dance.'

She was a good dancer, but before, she had always been too shy to show off the moves she practised alone in front of her bedroom mirror. Now she abandoned herself to the bluesey music. As Alannah Myles's aching Southern voice filled the room, she swayed to the beat, running her hands over her hips. She was aware that both men were watching her, clapping and wolf-whistling encouragingly. She'd never felt so sexy. As the chorus kicked in, she raked her fingers through her blonde curls, then ran the tip of her tongue suggestively over her lips, enjoying having the attention focused on her for once.

As Amber danced, Eva tried to keep the conversation going, but she soon realised neither man was interested in what she had to say. She watched Jack watching Amber, and for the first time felt jealous of her roommate. Before, she'd always had the upper hand because she was confident around guys – and more experienced, too. She had a feeling that was all about to change. For now, though, she wanted to stay in the limelight. So she joined Amber on the makeshift dance floor, and soon the two girls were competing to see who could come up with the most outrageous moves.

Jack leaned over to Billy. 'Hell, this is better than a lapdancing club,' he whispered gleefully.

Billy, who had just caught a glimpse of Amber's pert breasts as she shimmied forward, growled in response.

A little while later, Jack grabbed Eva's hand, and the two of them disappeared upstairs. Amber looked shyly and expectantly at Billy. It was the moment she had been waiting for. She'd hoped they might go up to a bedroom, too. But instead he pulled out the sofabed in the sitting room, explaining that he'd taken to sleeping down here because it was warmer. He sat down on the mattress.

'Come and sit here, sweetheart.'

She did.

It was over very quickly. That was the best thing she could say about the whole experience.

She liked the kissing. And when he reached under her skirt and caressed her through her panties, she'd definitely got turned on. After a little while he sat up and started to take his clothes off. She felt obliged to do the same. Naked and cold, she pulled the sleeping bag over her and waited for him. He joined her a moment later. When he reached between her legs, she thought that the touching might start again. But he must just have been feeling his way, because the next moment he removed his hand and started pushing inside her. He seemed to be having trouble, so she opened her legs wider and lifted her hips up a little, trying to make room for him. He stabbed at her some more. There was a moment of pain, and then finally he was inside her.

It occurred to her then that maybe she should have brought up the issue of contraception. But she didn't want to ruin the mood.

He stopped thrusting for a moment and looked down at her. 'You OK?' he asked.

She bit her lip and nodded, wondering when it was going to

start to feel good. A moment later he shuddered and cried out. Then he slumped on top of her.

Amber lay very still, staring up at the ceiling. Even with her limited experience she could tell that it was all over. But was that really it? Where were the intense waves of pleasure that she'd learned to experience by herself; the slow build-up, that feeling of utter bliss, followed by the aftermath of quiet contentment? She wasn't sure what she'd expected to feel, but it certainly wasn't this hollow emptiness. For one horrible moment she felt utterly ashamed.

He rolled off her and handed her some tissues to mop herself up. Seeing how much stuff was seeping out finally forced her to bring up the sticky subject of contraception.

'Shit. I thought you were on the pill,' he said.

'No. Sorry.'

He got up, walked over to his wash-bag and unzipped it.

'Here.' He tossed her a strip of four tablets labelled Schering PC4. 'Take two now and two more in twelve hours. That should sort you out.'

It wasn't exactly romantic. But then no one ever enjoyed their first time, did they?

Just as it was getting light, the guys called a cab for them. When they got back to Beaumont Manor, Amber offered to pay, as Eva had picked up the bill on the way out. But when she searched through her pockets, she found her purse was missing. A call to Jack from the school's payphone revealed that it hadn't turned up at his place.

'It must have dropped out in the other cab,' Eva said, as they got into bed. 'Bastard taxi driver probably didn't hand it in.'

Amber hmmed her agreement. It was already forgotten. Within seconds she was asleep, dreaming of Billy.

Chapter 23

Caitlin moaned softly. Lucien's lips were on her breasts, his tongue brushing one nipple then the other, his touch tantalisingly light. Tiny frissons of pleasure shot through her. It was a slow build, the kind he specialised in. His teeth bit gently at her, and she squirmed beneath him, feeling a fresh rush of moistness between her legs. Sure now of her arousal, his mouth grazed downwards, trailing hot, wet kisses across her navel, as his hands went for the top button of her jeans. Only then did she reach down to stop him.

'Lucien . . .' she said warningly.

It was the third time she'd pulled back in the past half-hour. The other times he'd ignored her, continued kissing and stroking, until she'd eventually given in. But this time she wasn't going to be persuaded. He could hear it in her voice. It was a tone he was all too familiar with.

Sighing heavily, he rolled away, allowing her to sit up. He stayed stretched out on her bed, watching as she pulled on her T-shirt, ran a hand through her tousled hair. He thought again how much he loved her body, the flawless milky skin, the womanly shape of her with those full breasts and the soft swell of her hips.

She felt his gaze on her and turned to look at him, smiling a little, knowing what was going through his mind. But her eyes remained serious as she said, 'It's late – you should go.'

He pouted a little. 'But I don't want to go, *ma petitette*.'

They had been together for three months now, and he felt

he'd been patient. This was as far as she would ever let things go between them. She was enthusiastic at first, enjoying the kissing, the touching, the stroking. And then, suddenly, something would change. There was always a point where she seemed to shut down, where she stopped feeling and started thinking, where he could feel he was losing her. The first few times he had tried talking to her, asking what was wrong. She'd insisted that she was fine. He never believed her, but he couldn't force it out of her, and eventually it seemed easiest to let it go.

What hurt most was that she wouldn't even allow him to simply stay over, to sleep next to her. Probably because she didn't believe that was all he wanted to do, he admitted. But, in fact, his request tonight had no ulterior motive. He simply liked the idea of waking up next to her. It wasn't something he'd felt with any other girl, and it pained him that she didn't seem to appreciate that it was different with her, that *he* was different with her.

He sat up now, not ready to let it go this time. 'As you say, it is late. Would it really be so terrible if I stayed?'

'I've got an early class tomorrow,' she said evenly. 'I need to get some sleep.'

'What about next Friday, then?' he suggested, unperturbed. 'You could come over to my place. I'll cook dinner . . .' He knelt up on the bed, reached out and cupped her chin in his hand, running his thumb over her soft lips. Instinctively, she parted her mouth, drawing him inside, between her teeth.

'And then,' he continued, encouraged as her tongue caressed the tip of his thumb, 'after dinner is finished, maybe you could stay over. You won't have to get up early the next morning then, and—'

Before he could finish the sentence, she bit down hard on his thumb. He yelped, pulling his hand back.

'God, Lucien.' Her eyes flashed. 'Can't you leave it alone?'

He looked down at the teethmarks on his thumb then back at her. 'I just want to know what the big deal is.'

There was a long pause. She stared at him, and there was an expression in her eyes he couldn't quite read. For one hopeful moment he thought she was about to explain, but then she seemed to change her mind, and looked away.

'I really think you should go now,' was all she said.

This time, he didn't argue back.

After Lucien left, Caitlin went straight to bed. But an hour later she was still awake. Their earlier conversation kept running through her mind.

She knew she wasn't being fair on him. How could he be expected to understand why she kept pulling back, pushing him away? Several times she had been on the verge of telling him about what had happened to her at Greycourt. In fact, she'd nearly caved in again tonight. But something always stopped her. She didn't want him to think differently of her, to treat her differently – to look at her with pity. And she didn't want their entire relationship to be dominated by this one thing that had happened to her.

Instead she had kept hoping that as time went on, as she came to trust him more, it would happen between them naturally. But she still didn't feel ready.

Are you ever going to?

She turned restlessly. The little voice of doubt spoke the question she'd been trying to ignore. More and more lately, she had begun to wonder whether she should just get it over with. She didn't want to be a victim, someone who was going to let one incident rule the rest of her life. Coming to Paris had been about starting over, putting the past behind her. And right now, the way she was with Lucien made it clear that she still hadn't managed to do that.

With that final thought, she drifted into a fitful sleep.

'Mademoiselle O'Dwyer?'

Caitlin jolted out of her day dream and looked up to find the whole class staring at her. She wondered how long she'd been out of it. From the look of disapproval on Madame Tessier's face, it was a while.

She sat up straighter. 'Sorry, Madame. What did you say?'

The old woman's expression darkened. 'I asked you to explain what the major drawback is to CAD and CAM systems. To give you a clue, it is what I have been speaking about for the past half-hour.'

Caitlin's blank look told the woman everything. Computer-aided design and manufacture had never been the most fascinating part of the course.

Madame sighed heavily. 'The drawback – and it is a major one that is worth knowing about,' she said pointedly, 'is that the computing firms have not bothered to fully integrate the design, pattern-cutting and manufacturing sequences. The design stage has simply been left out.'

Caitlin bent her head over her notepad and forced herself to scribble down the words. When the bell went for the end of the lesson, she wasn't surprised that Madame asked her to stay behind.

However, instead of giving her a lecture, Madame wanted to talk about Caitlin's plans after graduation. With only three months now until the course ended, she was speaking to all the students individually. The main message she had for them was that finding a job would not be easy.

'I have been in touch with people I know at Lacroix and Gaultier,' Madame told Caitlin, 'since I think you would be a good fit for those places. Unfortunately for you, no one is hiring at the moment. So I will say the same to you that I have said to your peers. As usual, the three prizewinners at the final show will be awarded a six-month contract at a fashion house. This year it will be more important than ever to win.' She shrugged her thin shoulders. 'If I had to hand those prizes over now, based on what I have seen during the past two years, then you would undoubtedly receive one.' She gave a tight smile. 'That is not something I have said to everyone – and I do not expect it to be repeated outside of this room. Understood?'

'Yes, of course,' Caitlin said quickly.

'But the judging team is made up of industry professionals, so I have no say over who wins. It doesn't matter what you've done these past two years, this final performance is all that counts. That may not be fair on those of you who have consistently performed well, but that is how it works.'

'I understand.'

Madame gave her a hard look. 'I am not so sure that you do. Day dreaming in class today . . .' Caitlin winced. She'd thought she'd escaped this. 'Now is not the time to rest on your laurels. Everyone wants this badly. Your fellow classmates will be doing everything they can to make sure they win this – and you have to, as well.'

Caitlin stared across at her, wondering what Madame had hoped to accomplish by telling her all this. Far from feeling inspired, she was frankly a little demoralised. Right now, it felt as if the woman was telling her she didn't have a hope in hell of winning.

Madame seemed to sense her consternation, because when she spoke again, her voice had softened. 'All I can say is – do your best.' She gave a little smile. 'And make sure you come up with a collection that is worthy of you.'

On the Metro home, Caitlin mulled over those words. The talk of the final show, of life after college, suddenly made the future seem very close. She'd heard rumours about how tough the job market was: too many good candidates chasing too few jobs. A lot of last year's graduate class were still unemployed, apparently. But hearing about it from Madame made it seem more real.

'There's always Melville.' That's what William had said, the last time she'd made her monthly duty call to him. Not that she'd told him about her difficulties getting a job. He'd just slipped the offer into the conversation, let her know that she'd be welcome in Melville's Design Department.

'Thanks,' she'd said. 'I'll bear that in mind.'

What she'd actually meant was that she couldn't think of anything worse. Even if professionally it had been her kind of place – which it wasn't, what with all the beige and navy, and reliance on classic cuts rather than fashion – she would do anything rather than work for William. Even go fulltime at the Café des Amis.

But it wouldn't come to that. She had some more interviews lined up. Plus, as Madame had said, there was the end-of-year fashion show. Scouts from all the major haute couture and ready-to-wear labels in Paris, London, New York and Milan would be there. If they liked what they saw, job offers could be made on the spot. It would be Caitlin's chance to shine, and she needed to make the most of it.

The idea dominated Caitlin's thoughts as she set to work. The biggest challenge was settling on a theme. It was the key to any good collection and never more so than for a student show, when each designer was only allowed to produce six items. A killer theme was key to putting across a consistent and memorable look.

And it just happened to be eluding Caitlin.

'It's so frustrating!' she complained to Lucien, as they ate dinner together late one evening. 'I've never been more devoid of ideas! It's as if Madame's little talk knocked every original thought out of me.' She shook her head despairingly. 'I can't help thinking, What if this is it? What if, after all the hard work over the past two years, I can't pull it off now?'

He smiled gently, recognising her insecurities for what they were. 'That will not happen, *ma belle*. Trust me. You just need to look elsewhere for inspiration.'

Something in his voice made Caitlin look over at him sharply. 'Do you have an idea?'

'Hmmm. Perhaps . . .'

'What?' she demanded.

'You'll have to wait and see,' he said mysteriously.

She opened her mouth to ask another question, but he reached across the table and put his finger to her lips, stopping her.

'You'll not get anything else from me. I want this to be a surprise.'

The next day, he called to check that she was free on Saturday evening. She was.

'Good. Then be ready at six. I shall come to collect you and we can go together.'

'Go where?' Across the line, there was silence. 'If you won't tell me where we're going, then how will I know what to wear?' she said playfully.

'Nice try.' There was a pause. 'Wear that red dress I love.'

The following Saturday, Lucien arrived at her flat at six on the dot, the first occasion she'd known him to be on time. He was looking characteristically flamboyant in a racing-green velvet jacket, with a ruffled shirt underneath, open-necked and hanging loose over black leather trousers. When they left her apartment, he still wouldn't tell her where they were going. He even went so far as to whisper in the taxi driver's ear so she couldn't overhear the destination.

It was only when the cab drew up outside the Opéra Garnier that she finally figured it out. He was taking her to see *La Bohème*. Lucien helped her out of the car in the busy Place de l'Opéra. They stood at the bottom of the opulent staircase, watching the well-dressed crowd streaming up to the entrance.

'So?' he asked. 'What do you think?'

It was the sheer scale that blew Caitlin away at first. At seventeen storeys high on three acres of land and seating more than two thousand people, the Paris Opera House was undoubtedly an imposing building. But there was more to it than that. As she took in the grand neo-Baroque architecture, the gilded statues, it reminded her of the rich history and romance she had read about, and that were integral to the place. With its sumptuous décor – all grand chandeliers and spouting fountains – and its subterranean levels and famous ghost, there was an enduring mystique about the Opera House. It would be an ideal inspiration for her final collection: it was pure Paris and perfectly suited to the dramatic style that she favoured.

She looked up at Lucien and smiled. 'It's a brilliant idea,' she said.

'Good,' he said, looking pleased. 'I am glad to have helped.'

It was then that it struck her. Lucien had gone to so much trouble tonight – so much trouble for her – and it was all because he *cared*. He really cared about her. He made to walk up the stairs, but she reached out and grabbed his arm, knowing that she needed to say this now or she might change her mind. He stopped and turned back, his expression enquiring.

'Lucien,' she said impulsively, 'did you still want to make dinner for me next Friday?'

'Yes, of course I do,' he said simply.

'Good.' It was said decisively. 'Because I thought . . . well, I thought I'd come over then. Like we talked about.'

He waited a beat before asking, 'And does that mean you'll stay this time?'

She took a deep breath. 'Yes, Lucien,' she said. 'I'll stay the night with you.'

He looked so pleased that it was almost enough to convince her that she had made the right decision.

Then, taking her hand, he kissed it briefly. '*Allons-y, mon ange*. We should find our seats.'

Pushing her doubts aside, she followed him up the stairs.

Chapter 24

'Left a little,' Elizabeth instructed. 'And drop it a fraction lower . . .'

There was only a month to go until the opening of the new Melville boutique in Tokyo. It was late Friday evening, it had been a long day and Elizabeth had spent the past half an hour trying to decide on the best position for the Gainsborough. The Japanese decorators who were putting the finishing touches to the store had been patient with her, and for that she was grateful. To the untrained observer, it might seem like she was being fussy. But it was this attention to detail that would help set the store apart.

It had taken three months to get to where they were today. Setting up a new store in a foreign country hadn't been easy, even with Mr Yamamoto's help. Elizabeth had found the perfect site pretty quickly. Naturally it was in Ginza, Tokyo's most elegant shopping district. When the lease became the subject of a bidding war, she'd had to act quickly to secure it. Yamamoto ensured three million yen got to the right people, and soon the site was theirs. That had been the first of many challenges. Settling on a knock-out store design; finding good staff, multilingual, enthusiastic and also cheap . . . the list had seemed endless. But, whatever the problem, Elizabeth had refused to be daunted by it, had always insisted her high standards were met.

Cole had been pretty good about not interfering too much. It had been agreed before Elizabeth came out here that she would provide him with a weekly progress report, and he would then call to follow up on any queries. But, although his questioning was always rigorous, he'd rarely outright vetoed any of her decisions. And where he had, he'd usually had a good reason for doing so, she had to admit grudgingly. His monthly visits to the site had been surprisingly pain-free, too – they'd been mainly observational and, again, any suggestions that he *had* put forward had always been spot-on.

'That's great,' Elizabeth said, finally happy that the painting was in the perfect position.

She left the workmen to hook it up to the state-of-the-art security system. The picture was a quintessential English landscape, borrowed from the family's personal collection at Aldringham.

Elizabeth had kept her word to Mr Yamamoto. The store was a seamless blend of modern and traditional. The building itself was an extraordinary glass tower set over eight floors. Bathed in light, it created a breathtaking effect. Inside, the shopfloor was like a little slice of England. Decorated in a Regency style, tones of cream and navy were complemented by traditional rosewood and gilt. The whole effect was one of luxury and good taste. Elizabeth was sure that it was going to be a hit with the Japanese public. Then, if the Tokyo operation went well, the plan was to continue expanding in the Far East and then into South-East Asia.

But first, Elizabeth couldn't wait for her father to see what she had achieved here, in Tokyo. Maybe it was childish. But he'd been so adamant about her proving herself – and now she had.

It was late by the time Elizabeth got back to her hotel room. She slipped into a silk kimono and mixed herself a G&T from the mini-bar. Swilling the liquid round the glass, she walked over to the floor-to-ceiling windows that lined one side of her room and gazed out across the city.

She was staying in the Presidential Suite of the Park Hyatt Tokyo, in the shopping area of Shinjuku. At over 3,000 square feet, the suite was huge by Japanese standards. Perched fifty-one storeys above Tokyo, it also had spectacular views – to the east, the neon lights of the city, to the south, Yoyogi Park and to the west, Mount Fuji looming in the distance.

She placed her left hand against the cool glass and sighed. Sometimes she didn't understand herself. Everything was going so well. She was on track to make Tokyo a success, and more importantly, to prove her worth to her father. She had achieved everything she had set out to do. So why did it still feel as if something was missing? She had barely had time to think, this past year. Too busy to keep up with old friends, much less make new ones. She hadn't been home to England in months. And men . . . well, there was no time for anything serious, and even the casual flings were a thing of the past. She had always prided herself on not needing anyone, but tonight – and not just tonight, but other times too – she was aware of an emptiness pervading her.

She had an unexpected urge to call someone, to hear a familiar voice. But who? She'd phoned and left a message for Magnus earlier that day, and he still hadn't got back to her. And it wasn't as if there were that many other people she was close to. She spoke to her father on business, and her mother on sufferance; however hard she tried with Caitlin, her efforts were always rebuffed. Amber was too young and silly. Uncle Piers was one of the few people Elizabeth felt comfortable talking to, but right now, it wasn't him she wanted. Then who?

Cole. The idea popped unbidden into her head. Where had that come from? She turned around, her back pressed against the cool window, as she mulled the idea over. She spoke to him a couple of times a week, keeping him up-to-date on her progress. They got on now, bantered a lot. But deep down that was business, nothing more. She'd hardly phone him for a chat.

He no doubt had plenty of friends – plenty of girlfriends – to occupy him. He might even be out with Kathleen.

Elizabeth had wondered if there might be something going on between those two. Before she'd left London, she'd seen them closeted together in Cole's office for hours at a time. She'd considered asking Kathleen if they were an item. But the other woman had barely been speaking to her after losing out on the Yamamoto deal. So Elizabeth had no idea what was going on in Cole's personal life right now.

But still. However illogical it might be, she wanted to speak to him. Elizabeth hesitated for just a moment. Then she reached for the phone and dialled his number.

Unlike her elder sister, Amber had never been happier. She finally felt she belonged. The past few months with Eva, Billy and Jack had been the best of her life. After a while, the sex got better. And so did the parties. Billy and Jack welcomed her eagerly into their little group.

'Amber, you came back!' Billy said the following week when she walked through the door, kissing her full on the lips.

Jack seemed equally pleased to see her. 'Hey, love. Fancy a beer?' He tossed her a can. It was only then that he noticed Eva standing behind her. 'Oh, hi, there,' he said, almost as an afterthought. 'Do you want something to drink, too?'

That was the best part for Amber. For the first time ever, *she* was the one getting all the attention, not Eva. When they'd started going to Cindy's, all the boys had been drawn to Eva's sultry voluptuousness rather than her own waifish looks. But Billy and Jack were different. As the evenings wore on, when it was just the four of them, the guys would always ask her to dance for them. She was happy to oblige. It made her feel special.

Only one person wasn't pleased with all the attention Amber was receiving. And that was Eva.

She nudged Jack moodily. 'Why don't you ever ask me to dance?'

He slung an arm around her, pulling her to him. 'Sure I do.' He went to plant a kiss on her forehead, missed, and got her hair instead. 'All the time.'

She pushed him away. 'No, you don't,' she sulked. 'You prefer Amber.'

Jack sighed. It wasn't the first time they'd had this argument. Usually he tried to placate her, but this time he couldn't be bothered.

'Whatever, Eva.'

He turned away and resumed watching Amber's undulating body, leaving Eva to glare at him through narrowed eyes.

Amber was blissfully happy with the routine they'd fallen into. So she was surprised when one weekend Eva suggested that they do something other than going over to Keepers Cottage.

'I'm tired of those guys,' she said. 'Why don't we go to Cindy's instead? Just the two of us. Like it used to be.'

Amber was standing in front of the dressing-table mirror, straightening her hair the way Billy liked it. She looked at Eva's reflection and frowned.

'But you're the one who said Cindy's was boring in the first place.'

Eva flushed. 'Yes. I know. But—'

Amber's face was blank. 'But what?'

Eva sat up, swinging her legs over the bed. In her uniform, with no make-up on and her hair pulled back, she looked younger than her fifteen years.

'Come on, Amber.' For once, her face was serious. 'We've had some fun. But these *homems* . . . they're bad news. They have no respect for us, *saca*?'

Amber didn't say anything. Assuming the silence meant she was wavering, Eva went ahead and pressed her advantage.

'Don't go tonight. Please. Stay with me. We'll do something together – just the two of us.'

Amber took her time straightening the last section of hair. She switched the GHDs off. Then she turned to Eva.

'I'm sorry if you don't like hanging out with Billy and Jack any more.' Her voice was silky smooth. 'But I do. And, to be honest, I think you're just jealous because they prefer me to you.'

'I'm not—'

'Yes, you are,' Amber interrupted. 'You're jealous that I'm getting all the attention – that's why you don't want to go. Well, I like hanging out with these guys. So don't try and spoil my fun just because you don't want to come along.'

With that, Amber flipped her long, thick hair, grabbed her coat and left a pale-faced Eva sitting on the bed alone.

No one seemed to care that Eva hadn't turned up. Not even Jack, who was supposed to be her boyfriend. It was just the three of them tonight, Amber, Billy and Jack. They sat cross-legged around the coffee-table in the scruffy sitting room, drinking beer.

After a while, Billy pulled a mirror from his rucksack, placed it in the centre of the table and emptied a small phial of white powder onto it. Amber thought nothing of it. Billy and Jack always indulged in a little pick-me-up. As a long-distance lorry driver, Jack had been using it for years to keep him alert on the road. He arranged the coke into three neat lines. But instead of snorting it himself, he looked expectantly at Amber.

She hesitated. They'd offered her coke before, but Eva had always said no, and she had followed suit. Dope was harmless, the other girl said, but you didn't want to touch anything harder. Only now, her restraining voice wasn't here. And Amber wanted to prove that she could do this, that Eva was the coward and she was the braver, more sophisticated one.

'OK,' she said, with what she hoped was an air of nonchalance. Taking the twenty-pound note that Jack offered her, she rolled it up like she'd seen the guys do before. Then she bent over the mirror, put the note to her left nostril and inhaled deeply.

She felt the powder going up her nasal passage, stinging the tender skin, and for a second her face went worryingly numb. But then she stopped caring. Because the feeling of euphoria that engulfed her was like nothing she'd ever experienced before. She felt calm, in control, powerful, confident. As if she could do anything.

Her heart started to beat faster and she felt hot . . . so hot. She pulled off the jumper she'd been wearing. The halter neck top underneath left little to the imagination. She caught Billy watching her and gave him a slow, seductive smile. He leaned over and started to kiss her. She closed her eyes.

The kiss was sweet and tender, the kind she liked. His lips soft, his tongue gently probing. He tasted of cigarettes and beer. Eventually his hand slipped under her top and found her left breast, massaging it in slow, deep circles through the thin material of her bra. It was only when she felt him reach for the zip on her jeans that it crossed her mind to check if Jack was still in the room.

Her eyes flickered open and she stared in confusion. Something wasn't right. It took a moment for her to realise that the person holding her wasn't Billy. It was Jack. She jerked away.

'Billy!' she said, her hand going to her mouth.

'It's OK . . . it's OK,' Jack shushed her, reaching down to squeeze her leg. 'Billy doesn't mind.' He nodded to the side. She followed his gaze and saw Billy sitting across the room, watching them. He got up then and came over to sit behind her.

'Jack's right,' he said, beginning to massage her shoulders. 'I don't mind.'

His lips brushed her neck. And Jack started to kiss her again too, slowly, softly. In that moment, she had never felt so loved, so wanted. This time, when Jack began to unzip her jeans, she didn't object.

And, over the noise of the CD, she also didn't hear the whirr of the video camera perched on top of the mantelpiece.

Chapter 25

Friday night. Caitlin stood in front of the bathroom mirror. A half-drunk glass of neat vodka sat on the side of the sink, where the soapdish should have been. She ran critical eyes over her appearance. Not bad. Nothing like she usually looked. She had made an effort this evening and it showed. She'd gone shopping during the week and spent a month's wages on a vintage dress that she had found in one of the little boutiques in the Marais. She'd fallen in love with the Empire-line gown straight away, had known it was perfect for tonight.

It wasn't only the clothes that were different. She'd gone into Véronique's room and raided her make-up bag. Mascara and eyeliner emphasised her wide, indigo eyes and gave her a look of dark glamour; the deep plum lipstick showed off her full, sensual lips. She hadn't got done up like this in a long time.

'You look good.' Véronique stood in the bathroom door, watching her.

Caitlin gave her a weak smile. 'Thanks.'

'When are you off?'

'Soon,' Caitlin promised. She knew Jules was due round and her roommate was eager to have the place to herself.

Véronique gave a brief nod. 'Give Lucien a kiss from me,' she said, and drifted away.

Soon, Caitlin thought. She would leave soon. She should really have left half an hour ago. Across town, Lucien would be waiting for her. But somewhere along the way tonight her bravado had evaporated. In the end, she'd gone to the freezer, found Véronique's vodka and poured herself a large glass. She was still waiting for the alcohol to work its magic.

She gripped the sides of the hand basin, trying to ground herself. Lucien wasn't Elliott, she told herself again. This was nothing like it had been with Elliott. She was a woman of twenty. She wasn't the same naïve girl who'd arrived at Aldringham all those years ago.

Feeling a little better now, she tossed back the dregs of her drink, wincing as the vodka hit her throat. With one last cursory glance at her appearance, she decided it was time to go. Dumping the glass on the sink, she turned away from the mirror, but as she did so, her hand caught the edge of the empty tumbler, sending it flying. She looked back in time to see it smash onto the hard tile floor, shattering into tiny pieces.

She stared down at the mess and felt a shiver run through her. She hoped it wasn't an omen for the rest of the evening.

By the time Caitlin got to Lucien's place half an hour later, the vodka was finally beginning to take effect. Any last-minute doubts had deserted her. She pushed open the iron gates and walked down the pretty cobbled alleyway to his apartment building. Another resident was on his way out as she arrived. She slipped by him and ran the five flights up to Lucien's top-floor flat.

As he opened the door, looking uncharacteristically casual in jeans and a white smock, his long hair tied back, she felt herself relax.

In turn, Lucien ran his eyes over Caitlin, and decided he'd never seen her look so beautiful. The dress, the make-up, the way her hair fell across her face . . . He was pleased that she had made an effort for him, for tonight.

'*Comme tu es jolie, ma petite.*' He went to kiss her, but she thrust a bottle at him, the cheap Bordeaux she'd picked up along the way.

'I brought some wine,' she said unnecessarily.

'Thanks.' He took a quick look at the label and raised an eyebrow. 'But really, you needn't have bothered.'

Ignoring the sarcasm in his voice, she pushed past him. She always loved coming over to Lucien's apartment. It was open-plan living at its best: beautifully light, with pale maple floors, white-painted beams and south-facing windows. The view outside was a Paris roofscape of chimneypots.

She threw her jacket onto the back of a chair and followed the smell of cinnamon through to the tiny kitchen, where a pan of what looked like stew was simmering on the stove. She ignored the food. Instead, she found an open bottle of wine and poured herself a glass.

'What're you cooking?' she asked as Lucien came in. She leaned back against the counter and sipped her wine.

'El ham lahlou.'

'Sounds complicated.'

'It's sweet lamb. An Algerian dish. One of my mother's recipes.' He took a step towards Caitlin, reaching for her waist, but she twisted away and began opening drawers.

'It smells like it'll be ready soon, so why don't I set the table?' She pulled out some cutlery. When she turned back, she glanced over at the pan. 'And maybe you should stir that. It'd be a shame to let it burn.'

Lucien gave her a strange look as she hurried out of the kitchen, but didn't say anything. By the time she went back in, he was too busy serving up to raise whatever had been bothering him.

The meal was every bit as good as it had sounded. The lamb was sweet and tender, the exotic flavours of North Africa coming through in the orange and cinnamon. But even though the food was delicious, Caitlin found it hard to eat. She pushed the buttered couscous around her plate and hoped he wouldn't notice. Instead, she concentrated on the wine. It was from Algeria, a Château Mansourah, Lucien had explained. Whatever it was, it was exceedingly drinkable. In fact, she wasn't aware of exactly how much she had drunk until she went to pour some more, and Lucien reached out his hand to stop her.

'Maybe you should slow down a little. You didn't eat very much.' He nodded at her almost full plate. 'The alcohol will go straight to your head.'

'I'm fine,' she said tightly.

He peered at her. 'Are you sure, Caitlin? Because if you're not feeling well, I can take you home.'

'No!' Her voice came out more sharply than she'd expected. It was just that now she was here, she wanted to get this over with. She softened her tone as she said, 'I mean, I don't want to go home. I want to stay here . . . with you.'

To prove her point, she leaned over and kissed him. It was a brief kiss, no more than a few seconds, and then she drew away.

Looking over at Caitlin, Lucien hesitated for a moment, torn between his desire for her and his conviction that something wasn't quite right. Her drinking, then making the first move . . . it was so out of character.

Perhaps he might have brought it up with her if he hadn't seen the way her lips were slightly parted; if his eyes hadn't travelled downwards, noticing the way her breathing had quickened, her magnificent bosom heaving, straining against the muslin bodice of her dress. He had never wanted her more than he did right then. So, instead of insisting on seeing her home, he took her hand and led her up the spiral staircase to his bedroom.

She had been in this room many times before, with its white walls, stripped floors, minimal furniture, but only during the day, with the sun pouring through the windows. Now, at night, with the lights down low, it took on a different feel. In the eaves of the building, the slanting roof and beams that ran across it cast eerie shadows. She could feel her heart starting to race as she sat down on the edge of the bed.

Lucien didn't seem to notice that anything was wrong. Instead, he came to sit beside her, stroking her hair away from her face, as he said, 'You can't imagine how much I've been looking forward to this, *chérie*.'

Her mouth felt too dry to respond. Instead, she closed her eyes as he bent his head and started to kiss her. She tried to make her mind go blank, to imagine she was somewhere else. If she could get through tonight, everything would be fine, she was sure of that.

Outside, the weather had turned, and a storm taken hold. As she lay back against the pillows, she could hear the rain beating against the skylight. She was aware of his hands roaming over her body, and forced herself to lie still as he kissed and stroked her. Even then, Lucien didn't notice her lack of response. He was too caught up in his own illusion of how the evening would turn out to see the reality of what was going on.

He was kneeling over her now, pinning her arms back with one hand, while the other started to work on the buttons of her dress. She didn't like that, the feeling of being trapped. The alcohol wasn't helping either – it only made her feel more out of control. She twisted her head away from him, trying to speak.

'No, Lucien . . .'

But he didn't seem to hear her. His lips were on her neck, his body stretched along hers, the weight of him making it impossible for her to move. She started to struggle then, but Lucien seemed to think this was part of the game and gripped her wrists harder.

'Lucien, please!' She bucked under him and he chuckled softly, misinterpreting her resistance for ardour.

Later, she couldn't remember exactly what had happened. One minute they were lying together, making out, the next she had scrambled across to the other side of the bed and was doing her buttons up, while Lucien was sitting back on his haunches, rubbing his cheek, looking at her as though she'd gone quite mad.

'What the hell is wrong with you, Caitlin?' His words tore through her, concern and confusion masked by his obvious irritation.

She couldn't meet his gaze. 'I need to go,' she said quietly, almost absently. She finished straightening her clothes, jammed her feet into shoes, then headed for the stairs.

'Caitlin, wait . . .' He followed her back down to the living room, saw that she was making for the front door, and moved to block her.

'Please, Caitlin,' he implored her, trying to keep calm. 'Tell me what's going on. I don't understand.'

'Get out of my way, Lucien.'

She went to pass him. He grabbed her by the shoulders.

'*Don't!*' She flinched at his touch.

'Jesus.' He dropped his grip and backed away, shaking his head.

Reaching for the handle, she opened the door, then forced herself to look back at him, trying to ignore the hurt and confusion in his eyes.

'This just wasn't a good idea,' she said. 'I should go.'

She could still hear him calling after her as she ran down the stairs and out into the driving rain.

Chapter 26

A week before the Tokyo store was due to open, Elizabeth called her father with a progress report. It was a short conversation, even by their standards. He sounded distracted, and after a while she gave up.

'Are you still coming out next week?' she asked finally.

'I'm afraid I won't be able to make it.' He didn't sound in the least apologetic. 'I'm far too tied up here.'

She was disappointed but not surprised. She'd almost been expecting him to cancel.

'So who's taking your place? Uncle Piers?'

'No. I'm sending Cole.'

Elizabeth sat up straighter. 'Oh, right.' She instinctively pulled a hand through her blonde hair. 'So when is he coming out?' she asked as casually as possible.

Five minutes later, Elizabeth put down the phone. She came out of her office humming. Chihiro, her secretary, looked up in surprise. Elizabeth-san was usually in a dreadful mood after speaking to her father. She wondered what was different this time.

Cole called her later that day. 'Did your dad tell you I'm coming over to check up on you?' he asked.

'He did,' she replied, adding boldly, 'and I'm sure you'll be impressed.'

Her confidence made him laugh, like she'd known it would. 'You know, it takes a lot to impress me,' he drawled.

'Well, I'm up for the challenge.'

'I'm sure you are.'

The comment hung there for a moment, neither of them quite sure what to do with it.

'So,' Elizabeth broke the silence before it became uncomfortable, 'what else is going on in London?'

They talked for a while longer, bantering back and forth. When they finally put the phone down forty minutes later, they were both smiling. They were also both looking forward to the following weekend.

The next seven days were the most frantic and exhilarating of Elizabeth's life. Seeing something she had created come into being trumped every other event, every other achievement.

It helped that Melville's Tokyo store was an instant hit. Elizabeth stuck with her English theme, eschewing the usual champagne and canapé reception for the grand opening, and opting instead for a traditional afternoon tea – cucumber sandwiches with the crusts cut off, freshly baked scones, clotted cream and pots of Twinings tea. The Japanese loved it. With rave reviews in every influential newspaper and magazine, the footfall was ten times as high as even her most optimistic estimates. If trade continued at that pace, the cost of opening the store would be recouped in ten months.

It was good having Cole there to witness her success. After all those months of giving her a hard time, payback felt good. And once the initial furore surrounding the store opening died down, they got to spend some time together.

The night of the store opening, they stayed late – just the two of them – overseeing the cashing up and going through the first cut of numbers. By the time they finished, they were both starving. Elizabeth suggested walking down the street to a nearby *izakaya*, the Japanese equivalent of a tapas bar, where she often went with the store managers.

'I didn't think this would be your kind of place,' Cole remarked, casting an eye around the crowded room. It was noisy and cheap – clearly a favourite of the after-work crowd.

'I do know how to have fun, Cole,' Elizabeth retorted, enjoying surprising him. When the waitress came over, she made sure to order a beer – earning her another raised eyebrow from Cole.

Over a couple of bottles of Asahi and plate after plate of food, they caught up.

'So how's Kathleen?' Elizabeth asked finally.

'Fine.' Cole paused to wolf down the last *yakitori*, and then looked over at Elizabeth. 'You know, we're not an item. And, for the record, we never were. That night after the presentation, it was just a drink between colleagues.'

Elizabeth shrugged carelessly. 'It's none of my business.' But secretly she was pleased he'd wanted to set her straight. In fact, she saw that as her green light. After that, she took to wearing as little as possible. If she was being unprofessional, she didn't care. She wanted Cole to notice her. She was aware that he was only in Tokyo for a limited time. If something was going to happen, it would have to be soon. And she wasn't the type to hang around waiting.

Cole noticed her, all right. It would have been hard not to. He reminded himself that he worked for her father – that one day she'd be heading up the company – and it really wasn't a good idea to get involved. The problem was, however sensible he wanted to be about this, when it came down to it, Elizabeth was smart, sexy and she was throwing herself at him. Ignoring her increasingly skimpy outfits was one thing. Ignoring his raging hard-on was another.

The crux came on his final evening. They were working late in her office, going over the first fortnight's figures. Elizabeth kicked off her shoes, leaned back in the chair and put her feet up on the desk, inches away from where Cole was working.

'God, I'm tired,' she said, stretching theatrically to prove her point, her tiny dress riding up over her firm thighs.

Cole grunted, keeping focused on his computer. He knew it was a ploy to get his attention, and he didn't want to rise to the bait. A moment later, she crossed her slim ankles. He glanced over briefly, taking in the beautifully pedicured toenails, his eyes involuntarily moving up her long, tanned legs.

He forced himself to look back at his screen. It took him a moment to realise he had no idea what he was staring at. Screw it, he thought. He slammed the laptop lid down. Elizabeth looked up, startled.

'Let's get out of here,' he said abruptly.

She raised a questioning eyebrow.

'You're right,' he said. 'I'm tired too. We should go back to the hotel, freshen up, and carry on working there.'

It was a neat little line, to cover his ass. Both of them knew that if they went back to the hotel, the last thing they'd be doing was turning the laptops on. She caught his drift and grinned.

'Yeah,' she said with mock solemnity. 'I'm sure we'll get a lot more done back at the hotel.'

They packed up quickly and grabbed a cab outside the office. It was a short journey to the Park Hyatt Tokyo, where they were both staying. Neither of them spoke the whole way there. To an outsider, it would have seemed like they were two business colleagues sharing a ride. But there was a reason the taxi driver kept looking back at them, as though he could feel the tension. It didn't help that Elizabeth was drumming her fingers impatiently on the leather armrest.

Finally they reached the hotel. Cole threw some money at the driver, didn't bother to wait for change. He held out his hand to help Elizabeth out of the car. Their fingers touched and they both felt the crackle of electricity pass between them.

'Your place or mine?' Elizabeth joked, as they waited for the lift to arrive. They had identical rooms next to each other.

'I'd feel safer on my turf.'

'Then my room it is,' Elizabeth said, smiling sweetly.

It took no time for them to reach the fifty-second floor. Cole murmured something about going to change. Alone in her room, Elizabeth slipped into her silk kimono and opened some champagne, pouring herself a glass.

There was a light knock on the door, and to Elizabeth's surprise, she felt a fluttering deep in her stomach. God, she hadn't expected to be this nervous. It wasn't like her at all. Pulling herself together, she went to let Cole in. He looked good, more his age, in jeans and a sweatshirt. She could tell from his fresh complexion that he'd splashed water on his face.

Cole had hoped that having a few moments alone would give him a chance to compose himself. But that was shot to hell as soon as he saw Elizabeth. He was used to her in work mode. Even the past few days, when she had been deliberately turning up the heat, couldn't prepare him for this, Elizabeth at her most predatory. She struck a pose in the doorway. With her golden hair brushed out, and in the short black kimono, she looked like an expensive call girl. A very expensive one.

'I hope you don't mind,' she said, enjoying the way he was staring at her, 'but I thought I'd slip into something a little more comfortable.'

He cleared his throat. 'No problem.'

She allowed herself a smile as he followed her back along the hallway. After all those months of him treating her like dirt, she liked being back in the driving seat.

'Can I fix you a drink?' she asked, once they reached the living area. 'There's some half-decent champagne here.'

She went to make for the bar, but Cole was too fast for her. She gasped as his hand snapped round her wrist, pulling her back round to face him. Impatience fired his black eyes.

'I don't want a damn drink,' he growled.

In her bare feet, she was suddenly aware of how he physically dwarfed her. She felt unexpectedly vulnerable. In that moment, crushed against his chest, she was reminded of how similar they were. Like her, he didn't enjoy being dictated to. She'd spent the afternoon playing games. Now he wanted to take back control.

He still had hold of her wrist, tight enough to hurt a little, but she wasn't complaining. He was so close now that she could feel his breath on her face, his body warm and hard next to hers. She was about to make her move, but he got there first, reaching down to tug at the belt of her kimono, loosening the knot. She shrugged the robe from her shoulders. The material slid off her, pooling on the floor at her feet. She stood before him then, naked apart from the tiniest scrap of black lace underwear. His eyes swept over her, devouring every inch of her, her strong legs, tight stomach, firm breasts, not a spare ounce of flesh on her.

'Not bad,' he said. 'Not bad at all.'

Elizabeth took a step back. Anger flared in her. 'What the hell's that supposed to mean—' she bridled.

The words died as he reached down between her legs, cupping her in his strong hand. Suddenly she forgot what she'd been complaining about. Through the thin material of her underwear, he could feel she was already wet with anticipation. She pressed herself down against his palm, as if to confirm what he already knew. Slowly, insistently, she rubbed against him.

'Hmmm,' he breathed into her ear, pleased by her reaction. 'So you like that?'

She sighed softly against him in answer. She could see he was turned on too, his erection straining against the heavy denim of his jeans. She went to undo his belt, but he grabbed her wrist, stopping her.

'Not yet, sweetheart.' He was already too far gone. If she touched him now it would all be over in seconds. Not exactly the way to impress her. Instead, he knelt down in front of her, slipping his thumbs into either side of her g-string, slowly easing the black lace down over her ass, her thighs. He waited an agonising moment. Then he lowered his mouth onto her. His tongue licked back and forth, gentle at first and then harder, more insistent, until she started to moan.

'Oh God, Cole,' Elizabeth murmured. 'That feels so good.' She buried her hands in his thick, dark hair, drawing him closer. She could feel her orgasm starting to build, waves of delicious little contractions. He must have sensed it too, because he pushed her back onto the bed and started to undress himself. She waited, naked and impatient for him to join her. When he finally finished undressing, he stood in front of her for a long moment, allowing her to scrutinise him now. He had a beautiful body, taut and firm; every part of him big, larger than life.

Elizabeth couldn't wait any longer. Pulling him down on top of her, she wrapped her legs around his waist, drawing him into her. Cole was impressed with her eagerness. So many girls lay there and expected the guy to do all the work. It was a nice change to be with a woman who wasn't afraid to take the initiative.

He began to move inside her, and she moved with him, her arms tightening around him with every thrust; the soles of her feet pressing against his buttocks, pushing him deeper, as though she couldn't get her fill of him. Oh God . . . oh God . . . She couldn't think any more . . .

She began to cry out first. Then seconds later he joined her.

When Elizabeth woke the following morning, she was surprised and a little irritated to find Cole asleep next to her. She had expected him to leave discreetly, return to his own room. Instead, his arm was thrown over her, as though he didn't want to let her go.

Slowly, stealthily, she slid out from under him, careful not to disturb him. She showered and dressed as quietly as possible. To her relief, he was still asleep when she slipped from the room. Downstairs, her car was waiting. She was at her desk by eight.

An hour later, Cole arrived. She glanced up briefly as he walked into the room.

'Good morning, Cole.'

Her brisk tone must not have registered, because he walked over to her desk and perched on the side. He smiled down at her.

'Hey, I didn't expect you to run out on me this morning. What happened?'

She looked up at him blankly. 'Nothing. I had some work to do.' There was a pause. 'In fact, I'm really busy right now. Is there anything in particular you wanted?'

'I just wondered if you wanted to get some food tonight?' He still hadn't caught her mood. 'My flight's at ten, but we could go out early . . .'

'Why? Was there something you wanted to discuss?'

He frowned. 'Nothing specific. I just thought it might be . . . well, nice to hang out.'

She put down her pen and sighed. 'Is this about last night?' she asked bluntly.

He blinked, taken aback by the question. 'I guess. I just thought—'

'You thought I left early this morning because I couldn't handle the fact that we slept together?'

This time, Cole didn't bother answering.

She gave him a cool smile. 'Then let me save you the trouble of worrying. Last night was just about sex. Two people who were attracted to each other just doing what comes naturally. You know, scratching an itch.'

'Hey, there's no need to talk like that!'

'Yes, there is.' She leaned back in the chair, and he could tell she was enjoying this. 'You see, I just wanted to have some fun, enjoy the moment. And you engaging me in this excruciating post–mortem is really rather ruining that.'

Cole stared at her for a long moment. She could see he was struggling to control his fury.

'Fine,' he said. 'I get it. Whatever you want, Elizabeth.' With that, he sat down, took out his laptop and fired it up.

They worked in silence for the rest of the day. When he left that evening to catch his plane, they said a brief, cool goodbye. Elizabeth stayed at the office for an hour longer and then headed back to the hotel.

It was only then, in the silence of her suite, with another evening alone looming ahead, that she couldn't help wondering if she'd made a huge mistake.

Chapter 27

Rosalind Melville was dying. She knew that with absolute certainty. Death permeated every square foot of her elegantly furnished Mayfair flat, her world reduced to one room now. There were few visitors these days. Most of her friends had already gone. She remembered a time when weekends had been a constant flurry of weddings, followed by the inevitable christenings – and then, before long, the funerals had begun.

Hers should have been one of them. Most people wouldn't have left the hospital after the second heart-attack, but naturally Rosalind had had the best care money could buy. She'd been allowed home, and a team of nurses now monitored her round the clock. They fed her ACE inhibitors and were trained to operate the mobile defibrillator unit that occupied one corner of the bedroom, where the antique dresser had once stood.

It was only family you could really count on at the end, the dying woman realised that now. Her sons were loyal visitors – Elizabeth, too, when she was in London. Today was Saturday, so William was down at Aldringham, but Piers was here with her. Over the years she had often wished that he would marry. Now she was pleased he hadn't. It meant he never minded the hours spent sitting by her bed, holding her hand. He was reading aloud to her from *War and Peace*, but she was finding it hard to concentrate and had lost the thread of the plot.

Feebly, she squeezed his hand. 'That's enough for now, darling.' Even she was surprised by how weak she sounded. It wouldn't be long now, she was sure.

Piers did as he was told. Using a bookmark so he wouldn't lose his place, he put the novel down on her bedside cabinet.

'Did I tell you what that Cole Greenway's been up to?' he asked.

Rosalind smiled faintly. He could never simply sit in amiable silence.

'No,' she said. 'I don't believe you did.'

Without prompting, he started to complain about Melville's Head of Strategy – some minor slight that Rosalind could hardly fathom. She knew what was really eating him. William could be fickle with his affections. This Cole person was his new closest adviser – and that was a role Piers liked to keep for himself. He hated anyone coming between him and his brother.

As he launched into a convoluted explanation of the takeover defences that were being put in place, Rosalind realised she no longer cared. The company she had once loved now seemed so unimportant. All those years spent chasing money and power seemed senseless in the face of death. It was her epiphany; something that had come to her during the long days spent in this bed. All that mattered to her now was dying in peace.

She had been thinking a lot about the consequences of her actions lately – like the changes to her will. She knew how much they would hurt William, and she didn't want that to be her legacy to him. Especially as her reasons for changing, which had seemed so crucial five years ago, no longer felt important. She was also beginning to question the wisdom of giving Amber shares in the company, even if they were going to be held in trust until she was twenty-one.

But resolving her will was only a minor point. There was something else on her mind, too. Something that she should have told William a long time ago. About what had happened all those years ago with Katie O'Dwyer.

Rosalind had planned on broaching the subject with Piers today. She knew he wouldn't like what she had to say. Five years ago, she had sworn to him that she would never utter a word of what they had done, because she knew that it would jeopardise his relationship with William. But now she wanted to go back on that promise. She didn't want to die with a guilty conscience. She needed to make things right with her elder son.

Looking over at Piers, who was still chattering on, she realised she was too tired to tell him today. But she would have to do so soon. Before it was too late.

Chapter 28

Sex was the best sleeping pill Billy Rainer had ever found. There was something about a good, hard shag before bedtime that always made him sleep like a baby. It was all to do with chemicals. Ejaculating released some hormone in the brain that put you out like a light. He'd read that somewhere once, which was surprising, because he didn't read much as a rule. On second thoughts, maybe he'd heard about it on *Ricki Lake*. Yeah, he nodded thoughtfully; that seemed more likely.

He took one last drag on his cigarette – post-coital smoking was a ritual he'd never been able to break – then dropped the butt into the nearest beer can and settled down on the sofabed. The thin covers hadn't seen the inside of a washing machine since he'd moved in, and carried the stale, sweet smell of his semen. God, he was looking forward to getting out of this dump. Once the payment came through next week, he and Jack would be moving onto bigger and better things. All thanks to Amber Melville.

Meeting Amber had been a stroke of luck. He'd known right away she was going to be a little goldmine. Young, naïve and filthy rich: it was like manna from heaven. They'd had some fun with her along the way. There was the night they'd convinced her to come round dressed in her school uniform. Hell, that video was going to make them a fortune. Her angel blonde hair in pigtails; adolescent breasts straining through her too-tight shirt; that gymslip skirt with nothing on underneath . . . He felt himself growing hard just thinking about it. He slipped his hand down the front of his shorts to his semi-erect dick, still wet from earlier. He looked down at the girl sleeping next to him, whose name he couldn't recall, and wondered if she'd be up for sucking him off.

Billy was about to shake her awake when he heard a car coming up the driveway. He looked up to see a beam of head-lights sweeping through the curtains. Straight away he knew that something was off. He wasn't expecting anyone, and as far as he knew, neither was Jack. Maybe the driver had simply taken a wrong turn. Any moment now they'd realise their mistake and turn around.

But that didn't happen. Brakes screeched and the hum of the engine died. The slam of car doors and the crunch of gravel on the path told him there was more than one person outside.

The footsteps stopped at the front door. The bell was out of order. It took a moment for them to figure that out. And then the knocking began. Three short, loud raps echoing on the hard wood, followed by an ominous silence.

Instinct told him not to open up. There were no lights on inside the house; no car in the driveway. As long as he didn't make a sound, then they – whoever *they* were – would assume he was out and give up.

He lay in the darkness waiting. The only sounds now were the insistent tick of the clock and the thump of his heart beating faster and faster. For one hopeful moment he thought they were leaving. But then he heard a hard bang against the front door.

Boom-boom-boom.

His heart contracted. Oh God. They were kicking down the door.

He was on his feet now, searching desperately for the clothes he'd carelessly thrown on the floor earlier. In bed, the girl stirred. 'What's going on?' she asked drowsily. But Billy was too busy panicking to answer. Maybe it wasn't too late. Maybe he could get out the back . . . But then there was one last almighty crash, the sound of wood splintering.

He stood frozen, one leg in his jeans. Jackboots pounded through the house. It didn't take them long to find him – three heavies, with baseball bats and blank expressions. They didn't say anything, they didn't even bother to ask his name. They just did what they'd been paid to do – beat the crap out of him.

The first blow hit him straight in the stomach, winding him. With the second, he dropped to his knees. His resolution to take the beating like a man evaporated when the bat made contact with his face, shattering his left cheekbone. He screamed out in pain.

'Please don't!' he whimpered. 'There must be some mistake. Just tell me what you want – we can sort something out . . .'

But they weren't interested.

The girl was wide awake now. She wasn't known for her brainpower, but even she clocked the situation straight away. Gathering up her clothes, she sensibly slipped out of the door. As she left, Billy finally remembered her name. 'Michelle!' he cried out. But she ignored him. She didn't know him well enough to get involved.

It didn't take long to break him. Five minutes later, the intruders had barely worked up a sweat, whereas Billy was lying curled up on the floor, sobbing like a little girl. The bats were covered in blood and pieces of skin. Two teeth lay on the rug. They looked like incisors, but he couldn't be sure exactly where they came from. Everything hurt like hell.

Finally, the men stood back. He lay quietly, wondering what they were waiting for. And then he heard another set of footsteps in the corridor. A figure appeared in the doorway. Through his swollen right eye Billy saw an older man in a charcoal suit standing above him. Unlike the other three, this clearly wasn't his normal line of work. But there was something about the cold expression on his face that frightened Billy even more. With the others, it had been business. With this guy, it was personal.

The man held out his hand for one of the bats. He raised it up high, and Billy braced himself for the blow. He closed his eyes, hoping that this would be the final one. And then everything went blank.

William Melville nudged the inert body of Billy Rainer with his handmade leather shoe. A low groan escaped from the beaten man, confirming he was unconscious, not dead. William wasn't sure how to feel about that.

His little girl. The things those bastards had done to her . . . He closed his eyes, trying to shut out the thoughts. Luckily, when Billy had passed the tapes onto his contact, he'd been stupid enough to brag about who was playing his leading lady in the movies. The porn distributor – Randy Dickson, if you believed that – had recognised the Melville name, seen a chance to make a quick buck and got in touch with William, guessing correctly that he'd be prepared to pay a small fortune to keep the videos off the market. A little more cash and William had the names and address of the two animals who had orchestrated it all.

He could have gone to the police – but there was no way he would risk the publicity. So instead he'd decided to deal out a little retribution of his own. The Old Kent Road was full of guys willing to do a bit of dirty work for cash in hand, no questions asked.

They'd dealt with Jack first. Caught up with his lorry and left him on the side of the M6, bleeding badly. Then they'd paid this little visit to Billy. William had never considered himself to be a violent man, but he'd got a great deal of satisfaction from delivering that final blow.

Unfortunately, that had been the easy part. Now he had to

deal with Amber. He'd picked her up from Beaumont Manor earlier that evening, having made up his mind that she wasn't ever going back there. Right now, she was outside in the back of the Bentley, crying. He still hadn't decided what he was going to do with her.

Isabelle wanted her home with them for a while. She said that Amber had low self-esteem and that, rather than punishing her, they needed to show her how much they loved her. 'Unconditional love' she'd kept banging on about last night. What nonsense! No doubt that charlatan of a psychiatrist she saw every fortnight had put that rubbish into her head. William didn't agree. In his opinion they hadn't been firm enough with Amber. Now they needed to crack down. 'Before it's too late,' he'd told Isabelle in no uncertain terms. They'd argued about it into the early hours of the morning.

As he walked outside, he caught a glimpse of his youngest daughter in the back seat of the car, her beautiful face red raw from crying. All he wanted to do was pick her up and cuddle her. But he knew he needed to keep his feelings in check; his heart hard, his mind clear. All the way over here, he'd had to listen to her screaming Billy's name, pleading for them not to hurt him, professing to love him. It frightened William that she didn't seem to have any concept of what those bastards had done to her. Even after he'd told her about them selling the tape, she still seemed to think that they cared about her.

She didn't look at him as he got back into the car. At least she'd stopped crying, he thought; her sobs had subsided into a quiet sniffle every now and then. He wanted to say something to her, but he had no idea what. The only way he could think to protect her was to take her somewhere else, somewhere away from here.

He hit the intercom. 'Perkins?'

'Yes, sir?' The answer was brisk and businesslike. No hint of judgement or interest in the evening's proceedings. He was paid not to notice or care.

'Take us to Heathrow. We've got a flight to catch.'

The car started up. William felt himself relax a little as they pulled out of the driveway.

'Where are we going?' Amber's voice shook as she asked.

He didn't reply. In fact, he had no idea where he was sending Amber yet. But he was sure he'd figure it out on the way.

By the time the limo reached Heathrow, Amber felt much better. Although on the outside she remained stony-faced, secretly she'd enjoyed the drama of the evening. Her father still hadn't spoken to her – hadn't so much as looked in her direction – but from the hushed calls he'd made during the journey, she knew she was being sent to New York for the summer. As punishments went, it didn't seem all that awful. A BA representative fast-tracked them through check-in and security, and then escorted them out to the waiting 747. Within moments of taking their first class seats, the plane was on its way.

Amber waited for her father to close his eyes and then signalled the stewardess to pour her a glass of champagne. A businessman in the adjacent seat gave her an appreciative look and she winked at him. Embarrassed, he buried himself in his documents. No, this didn't seem like such a bad deal after all, she reflected, as she reclined the seat. She'd spent the last few hours swearing blind to her father that as soon as she was old enough, she would find a way to be reunited with Billy. But now she was discovering that maybe – just maybe – she wasn't quite so heartbroken over him after all. The weekly parties had grown dull. He never had any money to buy her presents. And Keepers Cottage had been a bit of a dump.

Amber found the headphones in the seat pocket and selected a movie. By the time the plane was halfway across the Atlantic,

Billy, Eva and Beaumont Manor were little more than a distant memory.

William stayed long enough in New York to deposit Amber with the Penfolds, one of the oldest and stuffiest families in America. Charles and Audrey Penfold were old money, blue bloods with impeccable breeding and manners; their name was up there with the Vanderbilts, Kennedys and Rockefellers. Naturally they lived on the Upper East Side, occupying the top floor of a landmark nineteenth-century building on 62nd Street, between Park and Madison Avenues. It was one of those grand old apartments that represented the apex of the late-eighties Louis Quinze style. Every ostentatious detail was beautifully coordinated. The floors were covered in tinted marble; ornamental cornices and friezes decorated the walls; the furniture was carved out of rare woods and inlaid with mother-of-pearl and ivory.

The Penfolds were much like their apartment: perfectly co-ordinated on the surface but with little substance underneath. Amber had met them once before, when she was ten. They were pretty much as she remembered them. Charles Penfold was a Partner in an investment bank. He worked sixteen-hour days – twelve on weekends – voted Republican and had been sleeping with his secretary for the past eight years. Audrey Penfold didn't work, and spent her time doing lunch and her personal trainer. She had been a well-preserved forty-two when Amber had last seen her. Botox and regular trips to the plastic surgeon had made sure she stayed that way.

Audrey and Charles had the perfect Upper East Side marriage: they never shared a bed or a conversation, but were both unfailingly discreet in their extra-marital affairs. Their life together was predictable and well-organised, and they would have preferred not to have to take William Melville's delinquent daughter in. But he was an old friend, who had seen his way to lending Charles money during some lean times a few years back, and so they couldn't very well say no.

William stayed only a few hours. As he left, he promised the Penfolds that once Amber's GCSE exam results came through in August, he would find an appropriate college where she could study for her A-levels, and she could return to the UK. That seemed to pacify the couple. But Amber was less convinced. She remembered little of the exams she had taken a few weeks earlier – apart from English Comprehension, when she'd turned in forty pages in just over an hour, driven on by a coke rush. She suspected yesterday had marked the end of her school career and she wasn't altogether upset by the prospect.

Amber woke surprisingly early the next morning, excited about commencing her New York adventure. It was late June and the city was already stifling. She surveyed her wardrobe. She'd had little time to pack, so she selected the one decent outfit she'd brought with her – a simple white cotton dress. It was imperative that she went shopping as soon as possible, she decided.

She wasn't sure at first how much her father had told the Penfolds about what had happened back in England. But when she went down to the breakfast room she guessed it was pretty much the whole story. Audrey Penfold could barely look her in the eye over her breakfast of black coffee and Prozac, whereas her husband Charles couldn't take his eyes off her.

'Another bagel, my dear?' Charles's deep, burnished voice boomed. He held out a basket of bread and pastries. Amber shook her head – she'd hardly touched the one on her plate. But he seemed not to notice. His eyes were fixed firmly on her chest. She hadn't worn a bra this morning, and under the cool of the air conditioning her nipples had stiffened and were clearly visible through the thin material of her dress.

Audrey frowned. The society matron's sharp eyes missed

nothing. The thought of the pretty young girl spending the summer lounging around the house in the briefest of clothes, showing off her long, tanned limbs, suddenly seemed more of a problem than she had first thought.

By the time breakfast had finished, and Charles had been packed off safely to work, Audrey had decided that it was imperative to find something other than her husband to keep their guest occupied for the summer. Over a fresh pot of coffee, she learned that this was easier said than done. The girl appeared to have no real hobbies or interests. No wonder she had ended up making mischief.

'And what is it you would like to do when you're older, dear?' Audrey asked, thinking that there must be some way – *any way* – to get Amber out of her hair.

'Modelling,' she said immediately.

How original, Audrey thought. She managed a tight smile. 'What a wonderful idea!' She reached for her Rolodex. 'Now *that's* something I may be able to help you with.'

Rich Cassidy was a busy man. As owner of a small but prestigious modelling agency his time was precious. Usually based in LA, he was only in the New York office for the day, holding open auditions to find a fresh face to represent one of his biggest clients, Hiltman jeans. So far, none of the girls he had seen were anywhere near good enough. Hiltman were after a certain look – someone with attitude, someone with unconscious cool.

Rich was stalking back through reception when he spotted her. A stunning young girl, with the cutest white-blonde curls he'd ever seen. She was sitting on one of the low suede sofas, flicking disinterestedly through a magazine while she chewed away at some gum. Rich stared at the girl for a moment, assuming she was a wannabe who had turned up late for the audition. Usually he would have sent her away. He loathed tardiness and hated people chewing gum even more. But this girl . . . she had a look about her – something different.

He headed over to Linda, the receptionist. 'Who's that?' He gestured towards the blonde. 'Someone for Hiltman?'

Linda consulted Rich's diary. 'No. That's your eleven o'clock – Amber Melville.'

Rich raised one effeminately plucked eyebrow. He had forgotten all about his promise to Audrey Penfold. When she'd asked him to meet her unwanted houseguest, he hadn't been keen, but Rich owed her a favour – he'd met his latest boyfriend, make-up artist Louis Kent, at one of her charity dinners – so reluctantly he'd agreed.

He hadn't been expecting anything to come of it. Sure, Amber Melville *wanted* to be a model, but that meant nothing. In his mind, he'd been expecting her to be a typical inbred English aristocrat: mousey hair, long face, thin lips. But in fact, with her crown of tight platinum curls and rosebud mouth, Amber looked more like a wanton courtier from the Restoration Period. Even without knowing her history, he could see exactly what she was: an upper-class slut, rich trash, a spoiled brat who would do anything – and anyone – for amusement. And if she could get that look across on camera, then she was going to make a fortune.

'OK, Linda.' Rich was decisive. 'Get Paul on the line and tell him I'm sending someone down for test shots.' He walked over to where Amber was sitting and squatted down beside her. 'So, Amber Melville,' he began. 'How do you feel about being famous?'

William wasn't happy when he heard that Amber wanted to stay in New York – to model, of all things. 'She should be going back to school this autumn to get some decent qualifications,' he fumed. 'Not gallivanting around with a bunch of strangers.'

Isabelle, who'd spent an hour on the phone the previous evening listening to her youngest daughter's tearful pleas, was more inclined to go along with Amber's wishes. 'They're hardly strangers,' she reasoned. 'I've spoken to Audrey, and the owner of the agency is a great friend of hers. She speaks very highly of him and assures me that Amber will be in good hands. Honestly, I can't see why you have such a problem with this.'

'My problem with this is that she's still only sixteen. Now,' he said decisively, 'that at least means we have the law on our side. She needs our consent to leave home. And I'm quite prepared to use legal means to force her to come back to England.'

His wife sighed. 'Oh, William, she won't thank you for that. This is a great opportunity for her and you shouldn't be the one to take it away from her.' Isabelle shook her head gently. 'Come on, be honest now. Did you really expect her to come back to England, settle down to studying and go on to university? You know that isn't Amber. She's not like Elizabeth.'

That was one point William couldn't argue with.

So once again, with her mother's help, Amber got her own way. She knew that she should have been pleased with the outcome, but part of her was also a little disappointed. Surely, if they'd really loved her, they wouldn't have let her go so easily?

Chapter 29

Elizabeth's schedule didn't get any easier after the opening of the Ginza store. Delighted with the success of the Tokyo operation, Yamamoto was already putting on the pressure to expand, and within a few weeks, she found herself checking out the shimmering skyscrapers and marbled shopping malls of Hong Kong's Central district. Then she was onto Orchard Road in Singapore and the modern shopping district between Sukhumvit Road and Siam Square in Bangkok.

But, even though she had more than enough to occupy her mind, Elizabeth still found her thoughts wandering to Cole and what had happened between them. Late at night, in the understated luxury of yet another anonymous hotel room, she would imagine him there with her: her hands running over his taut biceps and down across his ripped chest; his muscular back glistening with sweat as he knelt above her; those dark, mocking eyes gazing down at her. That was the thing about Cole, it was hard not to feel feminine around him. It was the sheer size of him.

Filled with restless longing, she would toss and turn in bed, unable to sleep. It would have been easy enough to go down to the hotel bar and pick up a nameless businessman for a night of meaningless release. But somehow she knew that would no longer be enough for her. With Cole, it was more than sex. For the first time in her life, Elizabeth realised she was ready to open herself up to someone, to consider a relationship.

After that revelation, she longed to speak to him again. She waited for him to call. Maybe they hadn't parted on the best of terms, but she was sure he wouldn't hold it against her. A week later, when she still hadn't heard from him, she swallowed her pride and phoned him herself. His PA informed her that he wasn't around. She called a couple more times, leaving messages which she was assured he had received. If she hadn't known better, she would have thought he was trying to avoid her. When they finally spoke, for their now monthly catch-up conversation, he was distant, detached. After they'd run through her report, he didn't seem to want to linger on the phone.

'So, any plans to come back out here?' she asked as casually as she could.

'Not at the moment,' he said shortly. 'Hold on a sec, Elizabeth.' She heard him cover the receiver and muffled voices in the background. When he came back on he was abrupt. 'Look, something's come up. I've got to go.'

'Fine,' she said. But he had already put down the phone.

She stared down at the receiver. *I've really blown it this time.*

She was feeling so low after their conversation, that when Magnus Bergman called a week later to say he was in Tokyo and would like to take her out, she forgot all about her resolution to stop seeing men casually and agreed to meet him that night.

Had Magnus always been this dull? Elizabeth wondered over dinner at Hamadaya. She usually loved Tokyo's *ryōtei* – formal Japanese restaurants serving haute cuisine, the favourite of politicians and corporate bigwigs. But tonight, she couldn't help thinking how much more fun she'd had with Cole, when they'd gone out for beers at the *izakaya*. With Magnus, the conversation was polite and formal, there was no flirtation, no intellectual sparring. And yes, he might be good-looking for an older man, but when he put his arm around her waist, there was no strength there, no sense of power. He didn't make her feel safe and protected.

'I'm staying at the Mandarin Oriental,' he told her as he put down his Platinum American Express card to pay the bill. 'It's not far.'

Maybe it was his presumption that she was just going to go along with what he wanted, fall back into their old routine. Or maybe it was because she knew there was someone else she'd rather be with right now. But suddenly she just wanted to get as far away as possible.

'I'd prefer if you dropped me back at my hotel,' she said coolly.

Magnus raised an eyebrow, but didn't make any objection. She had made it clear that whatever had been between them once was over now. He had too much dignity – and no real need – to beg. He was handsome and wealthy. There were plenty of other girls waiting to take her place. Maybe they weren't as special as Elizabeth, but who had he been kidding anyway? That was why he'd never wanted to get serious with her in the first place. He'd always known it was only a matter of time before she came to her senses and found someone closer to her own age. Magnus just hoped that, whoever he was, he was worthy of her.

Chapter 30

The girl gasped. It was somewhere between encouragement and protest, a moan and a sharp intake of breath. Above her, Lucien pumped steadily away, harder and deeper with each thrust.

She had come a while ago; her noisy enthusiasm had let him know precisely when. But he couldn't quite seem to get there. It wasn't usually a problem for him, but lately . . .

He wasn't even aware of how hard he was pounding, didn't notice her gritted teeth or the way she was clutching at the duvet, until she finally choked out, 'Maybe . . . we . . . could try . . . something else?'

He stopped mid-thrust, and she took the opportunity to reach down and give his balls an encouraging squeeze.

'I could suck you off instead?' she offered.

For answer, he grunted. Instead of taking her up on the offer, he withdrew, turned her over and entered her from behind. Only then was he able to close his eyes, allow himself to think of someone else. One final deep thrust and he finally climaxed, quick and silent.

He rolled away from her, slipped the condom off and then reached for a cigarette – another bad habit he'd taken up again. He watched the girl dress as he smoked, aware that he still didn't feel satisfied. Recently he'd begun to doubt whether he'd ever fill the darkness that seemed to be with him these days. He wondered where Caitlin was right now. Wherever it was, he hoped she was feeling even half as shit as him.

*

In fact, across town, Caitlin was at college. She spent most of her time there these days.

It was June in Paris, and for the forty-five students graduating from the Chambre Syndicale fashion school that meant one thing: the final-term show. For Caitlin, it was an excuse not to think about Lucien. She had seen the way he dealt with their break-up: sleeping around, leaving Café des Amis with a different girl every night. She'd reacted by throwing herself into work. It was almost a relief to have the upcoming show to occupy her.

The tension had begun building six weeks beforehand. The show's presence loomed in every lesson, dominated every lunch conversation and coffee break. After a fortnight, any talk of the show was met with theatrical groans from the students.

'I'm sick of hearing about it!' they would say.

But it was all bravado. Everyone was on edge, and understandably so. This was the culmination of two years' hard slog. It was their chance to showcase their work to the Parisian style arbiters — buyers, journalists and, most importantly, designers scouting for new talent to fill their *ateliers*.

Most of the students were preoccupied with their designs, making last-minute alterations or dealing with unforeseen crises. Caitlin had the same nightmares as the rest of her classmates, waking up in a cold sweat from dreams of fashion experts shaking their heads in disgust at her collection, her designs falling apart on the runway, leaving the models naked.

But, as the day drew nearer, she was preoccupied with a more immediate problem: whether to invite Lucien along. She was allowed to bring three guests. William had insisted on coming. She had invited Alain, naturally. That left the third ticket. The ticket that should have been Lucien's.

Caitlin couldn't forget that her collection had been inspired by him and that trip to see *La Bohème*. She had chosen to design evening wear for a young but well-heeled market of wealthy partygoers, and her theme was the Parisian Opera House, during its heyday of the nineteenth century, a grand, extravagant time. The opulent Baroque design and lavish interior could be seen in her colour palette – deep reds and purples, striking black with metallic highlights – and rich textures including brocade, heavy-weight silk and damask. The Gothic grandeur of Gaston Leroux's *Phantom of the Opera* lurked in the background. A feature of Caitlin's work was the attention to detail, and she had trawled the markets searching for appropriate accessories – such as elegant evening gloves and antique pocket watches.

Even with the nerves and self-doubt, she knew she had done a good job. And the work was all her own, of course. But part of her felt that she owed something to Lucien, and sending him an invitation would be her way of acknowledging that. And then maybe, just maybe, they could at least be friends. When she broached the subject with Alain, she had expected him to approve of the idea. But instead he told her to leave well alone.'

'Why?' She asked, confused by his reaction.

Alain sighed. From the beginning, he had been opposed to Caitlin and Lucien as a couple. He had known it would end in heartbreak. He just hadn't expected the broken heart to be Lucien's. He had no idea what had gone on between those two. But his friend was well and truly screwed up over Caitlin.

'If you invite him, it will seem like you want to get back together,' he said carefully. 'And if you don't want to, that would be cruel. Don't you agree?'

Caitlin didn't answer. She knew Alain had never been keen on them getting together. With that in mind, it was hard to trust his judgement. So she put the spare ticket in the drawer and waited for a sign to tell her what to do.

The sign came a week before the show. By then, the students were working at fever-pitch. The classroom at Chambre

Syndicale was buzzing round the clock, filled with the whirr of sewing machines and the nervous chatter of the fledgling designers. Long-limbed models roamed the floor, eyeing up the talent as they waited for their fittings. Even though the students were nobodies now, it was worth being polite to them, as one day they might be somebodies.

Madame took the opportunity to give her last input on the pupils' work. She had driven them hard over the past two years, but now she could look proudly on as they proved that all her nagging had been worthwhile.

Caitlin was busy hand-embroidering beads on a gold brocade jacket when Madame stopped by to see her. She barely looked up as the teacher examined her garments. When she did, she found Madame wasn't just smiling – a rare enough occurrence – she was beaming.

'Well, Mademoiselle O'Dwyer. I see that Paris has worked its magic on you.'

'You like them, Madame?'

'Like them?' The French woman arched an eyebrow. 'Caitlin, whatever – or should I say whoever? – has inspired you in this work, make sure to keep them in your life.' And with a swish of her cane, she walked away.

Caitlin posted the invitation to Lucien that very afternoon. And, even though she got no reply from him, she kept hoping that he would come.

At five to six the following Wednesday evening, Caitlin and the other forty-four graduating students stood nervously backstage in the Salle Le Nôtre at the Carrousel du Louvre, waiting for the show to begin. It was one of the venues used during Paris's main fashion week every year. Tonight, the young student designers were as anxious as the big names always were before a show.

Caitlin watched sympathetically as one of the girls in her class ran off to throw up again. Her stomach was churning too, but at least she'd managed to keep her lunch down. She took a sip of champagne to calm her nerves. Moët had supplied complimentary bottles, and everyone was making the most of them. They were all so high on adrenaline, however, that all the alcohol in the world wasn't going to get them drunk.

The air crackled with anticipation. The next two hours would determine the rest of their design careers, and they all knew it. Three prizes were up for grabs. A jury of twelve fashion heavyweights would decide on the winners, awarding the coveted prizes of six-month internships at Christian Dior, Hermès or Yves Saint Laurent.

Standing behind the huge brushed-cotton curtains, Caitlin anxiously watched the competition. There were some fabulous efforts. A lone bagpipe heralded the entrance of Brooke's models, sporting flirty kilts teemed with pretty knitwear in the softest cashmere. Another scene-stealer was Shay Kestler. As the opening riff of the Jimi Hendrix track took hold, it looked like flower-power fashion had got lost on the way to Woodstock and ended up on the catwalk. Cheesecloth dresses, peasant blouses and beaded necklaces bravely echoed the hippie scene, and somehow worked in all their bohemian ethnicity. They were all so good, Caitlin thought half-admiringly, half-enviously. It was hard to know how she would compare.

Finally her turn arrived. She felt her heartbeat quicken, fired by nerves and excitement. There was a shriek of surprise from the audience as the auditorium plunged into darkness. In the wings, Caitlin grinned. The students were responsible for all aspects of their collection: from lighting to music. Donations from the school's benefactors helped fund the show – the cost of the models, materials and any props – and volunteers from the affiliated drama school lent their services for lighting and stage management. Caitlin had planned her segment carefully, like a piece of musical theatre: as dramatic as the clothes she had designed.

There was a long moment of total darkness, allowing the anticipation to build. Then the lights went up. Through the white screen at the back, the audience could see the shadow of five giant candelabras. A smoke machine started hissing out thick clouds across the floor. A heartbeat later, the aggressive sound of an electric organ tore through the air. And then, as the strong underlying beat of the rock-opera tune took hold, the first model strode out.

Caitlin had taken a chance and led with her menswear outfit. From behind the scenes, she held her breath as Jean-Luc swaggered down the runway, cutting through the clouds of smoke, a modern-day dandy, complete with brocade tailcoat and silver-tipped cane.

The audience exploded.

Caitlin heard the cheers and applause and felt herself finally relax.

In the front row of the audience, William clapped loudly as Caitlin's designs came down the catwalk. He had arrived early, wanting to make sure he secured a good seat, and was pleased he'd made the effort. Sitting in the midst of all the industry experts, he could hear their comments on her collection.

'I adore those trousers!' gushed a journalist from *Paris Match*. 'Such attention to detail.'

'For sure, she will be a big name,' *Le Tribune*'s representative agreed.

Not that William needed anyone to tell him that. Melville might be better known for its accessories than its clothing line, but he had been in the business long enough to know talent when he saw it. Putting his subjectivity as her father aside, Caitlin's garments were by far the best he had seen tonight. He felt a surge of pride, followed by a moment of sadness. He wished Katie could have been here to witness what their daughter had accomplished. Caitlin had come such a long way

from that shy, gauche teenager who had arrived at Aldringham
six years earlier. Now she was a beautiful young woman, with
a promising future ahead of her. No one could ask more for
their child.

After Caitlin's collection, the rest of the show passed quickly.
William watched with detachment, only interested to see how
the others compared to her. They were all good, the standard
high, as would be expected from the Chambre Syndicale. But
none came close to Caitlin, he decided, satisfied. There was no
doubt in his mind that she would get a job offer at a top fashion house. He just hoped she would see her way to choosing to
work at Melville instead. That's what he was going to talk to
her about, after the show.

As William turned away, he bumped into a young man hurrying past. William stopped for a moment, transfixed by the
man's long, flowing dark hair, translucent skin and startlingly
blue eyes. He was like a dark angel, impossible to miss. But it
wasn't just his appearance that made him stand out from the
crowd: it was the way he held himself – that Napoleonic arrogance that seemed to be in every Frenchman's blood.

The two men apologised and then went their separate ways.
Neither of them realised they were there for the same reason.

Backstage, Caitlin was in the midst of what was professionally
the most important night of her life. Scouts from the top couture houses in Paris surrounded her, congratulating her on her
opulent but modern designs, courting her for the future. She
had won the internship at Dior, but once that was finished,
who knew?

When someone tapped her on the shoulder, she turned,
thinking it was going to be one of the other students. But then
she saw the tall, slender man standing before her, his cool blue
eyes fixed on her.

Lucien.

Later, she would tell herself that it was the unexpectedness of him showing up that threw her. And to an extent that was true. It wasn't as if this was the first time she had seen him since the break-up. She saw him around a lot, even if they hardly ever spoke these days. But usually she could prepare herself, close her feelings off. It was the rawness of the moment that had caught her off-guard.

Lucien saw the reaction he was having on her and felt pleased. His ego had been badly damaged by their break-up. It had taken a great deal for him to come here tonight.

'I wanted to congratulate you,' he said, seizing the initiative while she was still trying to compose herself. 'Your collection was truly wonderful. You deserved to win.'

There was a silence as Caitlin tried to think of something to say. But the only thought going through her head was how fortunate it was that she had changed her mind and worn one of the dresses that hadn't made it into the show. It was an intensely feminine piece, with a boned corset, full satin underskirt and a sheer outer coat made of silk organza. She'd let her hair grow out recently, and tonight it was curled into dark ringlets, giving a Gothic romanticism to her look that she knew Lucien would appreciate.

'I didn't think you were going to come tonight,' she said.

He shrugged. 'I thought I owed it to you.'

There was another silence.

'And now I should go.' He bowed his head to her and turned away.

Time slowed. In that moment, seeing him about to walk away from her, she realised she didn't want him to leave. She thought of William, waiting for her outside, even though she had no desire to see him. She thought of the after-party at Hôtel Costes and how she wanted to skip it. And she thought how pleased she was to see Lucien again, that he had come tonight when she had feared he wouldn't.

And that was when she made the decision.

'Lucien?'

There was something in her voice that stopped him, made him turn back and look at her again.

'Yes, Caitlin?'

'Let's get out of here?' It was said tentatively, a question rather than a statement.

A slow grin spread across his face. 'That sounds like an excellent idea.'

Back at his apartment, everything moved quickly. They were in his bedroom and he was kissing her with a feverish urgency. Kissing her mouth, her neck, her shoulders. They were in exactly the same place as they had been all those months earlier. Except this time she wasn't going anywhere.

She heard him murmuring, 'I knew you would change your mind, *chérie*.'

She felt a curious detachment as he unhooked her bra, peeled down her underwear, and laid her on the bed. There was none of last time's panic as he came to join her. Just a quiet determination to see this through.

He was inside her now, and he was saying something, something that sounded like, 'I missed you so much, Caitlin. Every day I missed you.' She closed her eyes, as he began to move in and out, slowly at first, then faster, his rhythm building with his excitement.

Not long now, she thought.

And, as if he'd read her mind, he grabbed her shoulders and her eyes flew open, just in time to see the look of intense pleasure come over his face as he started his climax. And she felt what she could only describe as relief as he buried his head against her neck, so all she could hear was the muffled sound of him calling her name over and over again.

*

Afterwards, she lay in his arms. Gently he kissed her forehead, her nose, her lips. Then he pulled away a little, so he was staring into her eyes as he said, with utter sincerity, 'I love you, Caitlin.'

She reached up and touched his face, wishing she felt the same way. But her only sensation was emptiness. The kind of emptiness that told her it was over between them.

She waited until he was asleep. Then, as quietly as she could, she slipped from his bed, pulled on her clothes and left.

Back at her apartment, she made her preparations. Paris was over for her. She wanted a clean break, a new start.

It was surprisingly easy to pack her life away. She wrote three letters in all: the first to Dior, explaining that she wouldn't be taking the internship after all; the second to Véronique, enclosing enough money to cover the next two months' rent; then the final one to Alain, apologising for leaving so abruptly. She knew she should write to Lucien, too. But somehow she couldn't find the words. Another time – once she had got her head together – she would explain. But, for now, she couldn't think about it.

That night, Caitlin boarded a plane to New York. From her window seat, she watched Paris fading into the distance.

You're running away again, a little voice warned.

And back came her answer:

Right now, I don't care.

Chapter 31

'I've decided to tell William.'

Piers stared down at his mother's hand, clutching his own. It was a Saturday afternoon, and as usual he had come over to the Mayfair flat to keep her company. But instead of asking him to read to her as usual, she'd said that she had something she wanted to discuss with him.

He tried to keep his voice calm as he asked, 'What are you talking about, Mother? What are you going to tell William?' But he was just playing for time. He knew exactly what she meant. It was his worst fear realised.

'Piers,' Rosalind spoke gently. Her watery eyes searched out his gaze, begging him to understand. 'My love, I'm going to tell William what we did . . . what we did about Katie. I'm going to tell him everything. I have to, before it's too late.'

But why? Why do you need to tell him? Piers thought as she continued speaking in her low, broken voice, explaining to him why she felt the need to confess her sins now that she was dying.

'It's time I was honest,' she said. 'For once, I want to do the right thing.'

He rested his head in his hands, his fingers massaging the dull ache that had begun to form in his temples. He couldn't believe how selfish she was being. William's wrath would last for years, and he would be left to endure it.

'But what about me?' His voice was no more than a whisper.

She blinked. 'What about you?'

He looked up at her then. Could she really not see? 'William will hate me!'

There was a silence. 'Yes,' she said calmly. 'He probably will.'

'But that's not fair!' he burst out. 'I only went along with this because I thought it was in William's best interests. I can't be punished for that now!'

'Piers, please.' His mother's voice took on an edge of firmness, the kind she'd reserved for telling him off when he was a child. 'Don't try to change my mind. Nothing you say can stop me from doing what is right.' She paused, took a breath before continuing. 'I know now that I was wrong to conceal the truth from him for all these years.' She stopped again, to take another breath.

Piers looked at her carefully, concern for her health momentarily outweighing his anger over her plans to reveal their secret. 'Are you OK, Mother? Can I get you some water?'

'No, I'm fine.'

'Are you sure? Because—'

'I said I'm fine,' she snapped. 'Just let me finish what I'm trying to say. It's important.' She breathed in again, once then twice. Piers waited patiently for her to continue. 'I'm going to tell him what we did,' she said finally. '*Everything* we did, and then I'm going to ask for his forgiveness. I'm sure if you do the same he'll listen and find a way to forgive you, too.'

'No, he won't!' Piers could hear the whine in his voice and knew it was going to annoy her. 'He'll cut me out of his life – and you know it.'

She looked at him levelly. 'And would that be such a bad thing?'

Piers stared at her. 'What's that supposed to mean?'

'Oh, Piers.' Her laugh was gentle but faintly mocking. 'You know very well what it means. You're nearly forty-five. Isn't it about time you started living your own life rather than hanging off your brother's coat-tails?'

The verbal blow hit hard. He hated his mother when she

was in this mood. She seemed to know exactly what to say to hurt him most.

'Well, I don't think it's quite like that,' he said defensively. 'William appreciates having me around.'

'He *tolerates* you, my love. That's a very different thing.'

'That's not true!'

'Of course it's true,' she said dismissively.

'But—'

'Oh, for heaven's sake,' she interrupted. 'I'm too tired to argue with you.' There was a true weariness in her voice. 'I don't care how you live your life. You're old enough to make your own decisions. As am I.' Her voice sounded hoarse now, her breathing shallow. 'And I just wanted to do you the courtesy,' she stopped, took a breath, 'do you the courtesy of letting you know . . .' She stopped again, wheezing now. 'That I'm going to tell William what we did. And nothing,' she was really struggling now, 'nothing you say can stop me from . . .'

She stopped mid-sentence, as though pausing to take yet another breath. But then she started to cough, a great wracking cough that seemed to rattle her very bones.

Piers stood, paralysed, waiting for her to recover. But instead she kept on coughing, a look of terror in her eyes. That was all he could hear and see – those great shuddering gasps and her wide, staring eyes.

'Mother?' he'd finally found his voice. 'Tell me – what should I do?'

He watched as her hand stretched out, and he followed her gaze to the table at the end of the bed, and finally worked out what she wanted – her nitroglycerin pills. She was having an angina attack. He remembered what they had told them in the hospital, that arguing could trigger an episode.

He picked up the plastic bottle and began to unscrew it, his fingers fumbling with the child-proof cap, losing precious seconds. Finally he had a tablet in his shaking hand. He was about to give it to her when he stopped, remembering suddenly what she had said to him before the choking fit had started.

I'm going to tell William what we did . . . Nothing you say can stop me . . .

Maybe nothing he could *say* would stop her. But now, as though Fate was looking out for him, another way had presented itself. It would be easy, so easy . . . The thought – so abhorrent, so unnatural – had entered his head before he could stop it.

Rosalind's pupils grew larger, as she realised what was going through his mind. Her eyes pleaded with him then, trying to let him know that she wouldn't tell, after all. But how could he trust her?

Later, when he was alone and trying to ease his guilt, he would tell himself that he never really intended for any of it to happen. It was a split second of doubt, a minor hesitation, but one that he was about to rectify. He was, he would tell himself again and again, intending to give her the pill, to get help, to save her after all.

But somehow he couldn't find the strength to move.

She was having a full heart-attack now. And even though he knew he should run outside, call the nurse, knew that if he got her in now, she would probably have enough time to fire up the defibrillator, to resuscitate Rosalind; even though he knew it wasn't too late to do something, instead he stood frozen to the spot.

Finally her eyes closed. Her breathing became shallower. Her face greyed. One last breath shuddered through her. And it was over.

Only then did the enormity of what had just happened register with Piers. He fell to his knees, clutched both hands over his mouth.

'Oh God,' he sobbed through his fingers. 'Oh my God, what have I done?'

*

Lucy Fielding was one of three nurses employed to take care of Rosalind Melville. It was a reasonably cushy number. Every two hours she would check the patient's vitals and administer her medication. That usually took all of five minutes. Then the rest of the time she was free to read magazines or watch TV.

That afternoon, she was on her way to do a routine check when she saw Mrs Melville's youngest son coming out of her bedroom, closing the door softly behind him. Catching sight of Lucy, he put his finger to his lips.

'I think I tired Mother out,' he told her. 'She fell asleep on me.'

Lucy hesitated. The agency was very particular about staff sticking to the planned schedule. But if Mrs Melville was resting, then Lucy didn't want to disturb her. The poor lady rarely got much sleep as it was.

'I'll leave her for a bit longer then,' she said. 'Shouldn't do any harm.'

She walked Mr Melville to the door, sighing as he left. He was such a sweetie – a little shy perhaps, but always polite and appreciative of the nursing staff's efforts, not like that brother of his who was forever finding fault. With that thought, Lucy went to her room and called her boyfriend to recount the events of her day.

Almost an hour passed before she finally went back to check on Rosalind Melville. By then her body was already growing cold. Afterwards, Lucy couldn't help feeling a little guilty. If she'd come in sooner, maybe she could have done something to save the old woman, given her that last medication. But she knew that was silly. Rosalind was old. She'd had a good life. With her heart, it had only been a matter of time. There was nothing anyone could have done to prevent her death.

The funeral took place the last week of August. The weather had been unrelentingly bright and sunny over the past month, and no one relished attending such a sad occasion on an incongruously beautiful day. But thankfully it rained overnight. The mourners woke up to grey skies, although the air was still warm and wet.

The service was dignified, just as Rosalind would have wanted. Her coffin, a solid mahogany casket, was adorned with a single arrangement of lilies. The congregation was like a *Who's Who* of the fashion world: fellow industry executives, designers and models crowded into the magnificent Wells Cathedral. Naturally, the board of Melville were all in attendance.

Elizabeth had come back from Tokyo for the funeral. Of the three grandchildren, she was the only one who would truly mourn her grandmother's passing. Standing by the graveside, she tried to think of the good times – remembering childhood trips to London, Rosalind showing her around Melville's flagship store and recounting stories of her adventures during the war. Elizabeth had visited Rosalind often during her illness. The last few times, the once-great lady had been so pathetically grateful that Elizabeth had felt a mixture of sadness and embarrassment whenever she went to her Grosvenor Street flat.

Uncle Piers had taken it hardest. And understandably so. While William had his own family – a wife and three children – Piers had no one else. Elizabeth knew how devoted he'd been to his mother. She tried to find words to comfort him, but once they got back to Aldringham after the interment he excused himself and went to lie down. Given that he looked as though he hadn't slept since Rosalind's death, Elizabeth could only hope he'd find some peace now.

With over a hundred and fifty mourners thronging the drawing room, no one noticed him go. A buffet lunch was being served, but Elizabeth had no appetite. There was no one she could talk to, no one who would understand. Caitlin hadn't even bothered flying back for today, and in some ways

Elizabeth didn't blame her: it wasn't as though Rosalind had been especially welcoming to her illegitimate grandchild. And Amber was nowhere to be seen. She had come back from New York full of talk about her latest fad, modelling. No doubt she had slunk upstairs to call her friends and tell them all about it. That was the last thing Amber needed – a bunch of people spending the day flattering her. Elizabeth still couldn't quite understand why their father had allowed it.

Their mother seemed to think the independence would do Amber good, teach her some responsibility. But two months abroad seemed to have done little to stem her teenage rebellion. She'd even had the cheek to turn up at the funeral in black jeans, a black T-shirt and oversized sunglasses. Elizabeth had been horrified by the show of disrespect. Then she thought, if Granny could see Amber now, she'd sniff and say that was all you could expect from such a spoiled child, and that made her smile. That was what today should be about, after all: remembering who Rosalind Melville had been.

'That was a beautiful speech you made in the church, Elizabeth.' The girl looked up to see her father.

'Thank you,' she said. Truthfully, she had been surprised when he'd asked her to perform the eulogy today. It had taken a lot for her to get through it without crying. 'I did my best.'

'Yes, you did,' he said firmly. 'She would have been delighted, you know.'

Elizabeth looked away, unsure how to react. These expressions of fatherly pride were so longed-for by her, but equally so rare that she had no idea how to deal with them.

Before she could think of an appropriate response, William had moved off into the crowd, back to playing his role as genial host. Elizabeth walked over to the bar and got the waiter to fix her a gin and tonic. It was Friday and she was planning to stay for the weekend at Aldringham rather than rush back to Tokyo. She heard a shout of laughter behind her and whirled round, prepared to glare at whoever was being disrespectful. But as she surveyed the room, she suddenly realised that no one looked contrite or embarrassed by their humorous outburst. The low, respectful voices that people had used at the start of the day were abandoned now, along with their jackets and ties. Because, deep down, no one really cared about Rosalind. Most of these people were only here to show their faces, to network. Standing there, in the middle of the hypocrisy, Elizabeth felt a sudden desire to be alone.

She got the bartender to pour another large G&T and then took it out onto the veranda. But even there she felt too close to everyone else. She wanted to get right away. So she started to walk, heading down towards the tennis courts. No one would find her there. Only when she was far away from the house did she finally sink down onto the stone steps and rest her head on her knees, pleased to be able to let her public mask slip away.

She'd hardly been there a minute when she heard a cough behind her. She looked up and her heart sank. It was Cole.

'Oh, great,' she muttered. That was all she needed. She'd spotted him in the church earlier, and had managed to avoid his gaze. Now, she quickly wiped her eyes with the back of her hand. She hated anyone to see her looking vulnerable, and it was even worse that it was Cole. However, he didn't seem to notice her discomfort. Instead, he took out a clean hanky from the pocket of his suit jacket and held it out to her. She hesitated for a moment and then took it from him.

'Thanks,' she mumbled, blowing her nose.

'I saw you leaving the house,' he explained. 'Thought I'd make sure you were OK.'

'Thanks. But I'm fine.' She just wished he'd go away.

He didn't. 'You were close to your grandmother,' he said.

It was more of a statement than a question, but she nodded anyway. 'Yes. Yes, I was.' She cleared her throat, fighting to regain her composure. 'But, like I said, I'm fine, honestly. You should go back to the house. I'll be in soon.'

She expected him to take the easy way out and leave then. But instead he sat down on the step beside her and took her hand. They sat like that, not speaking, not moving, but perfectly at peace, for a very long time.

The week after his mother's funeral, when everything had finally started getting back to normal, William made an appointment to see Gus Fellows, his mother's solicitor and the executor of her estate. Afterwards, William often thought that he wouldn't have reacted quite so badly to the contents of her will if he'd had some prior warning; if she'd come to him and said, 'This is what I intend to do with my shares in Melville.' Instead, he had no inkling that anything had changed since that time a decade earlier, when she had made provisions for her entire 10 per cent shareholding to pass to him.

As he sat opposite Gus in the Chancery Lane offices of Fellows & Sons, the last thing he was expecting to hear was that she had made a new will.

'When did she do that?' William asked, already suspecting that any change he hadn't been involved in couldn't be good.

Gus Fellows had the decency to look embarrassed. He pretended to check the date. 'A little over five years ago.'

Five years ago. *When Caitlin had come to live with them*. The significance wasn't lost on William. And he wasn't surprised, although he was still hurt, to learn moments later that Rosalind had elected to leave her shares to her two legitimate grand-daughters – 7.5 per cent to Elizabeth, and 2.5 per cent to Amber.

And William, already feeling aged by the death of his mother, and trying to ignore the niggling awareness of his own mortality, became sharply aware in that moment of the next generation on his tail. Smart, confident Elizabeth, of whom he had felt so proud in the church, whose strength had seemed like such a compliment to him, now looked more like a threat. He knew his eldest daughter well enough to appreciate that she was young, hungry and determined – and that her sights were set firmly on his job. That had always been the case, but at least over the past few years he had been able to control her movements within the company. Now Rosalind had given her the tools to increase her influence within Melville.

It wasn't exactly the legacy William had hoped for.

Chapter 32

Piers jerked awake from the nightmare, covered in a cold sweat. Alone in the darkness, he felt terrified. He reached out for the bedside lamp, fumbling until he finally found the switch. Light flooded the room, and he began to feel a little better.

He lay in bed for a minute longer, waiting for his breathing to slow. Then he disentangled himself from the sheets, stood up and padded over to the bathroom. Under the harsh fluorescent lights, he saw just how bad he looked. His eyes were bloodshot, the skin underneath loose and puffy. It was hardly surprising. He hadn't slept properly for nearly eight weeks now. Not since his mother had passed away. Every time he closed his eyes, he saw her: gasping, choking, dying . . . Whatever he did, he couldn't get that image out of his mind.

The lack of sleep was beginning to take its toll. He'd been walking round in a permanent daze. Eventually, after making a couple of mistakes at work, he'd gone to see a doctor. 'It's perfectly normal, of course,' he'd said, giving Piers a sympathetic smile, 'after the death of a loved one. But I can understand why you might be feeling a bit desperate. Insomnia is a terrible thing.'

That was an understatement, Piers had thought, as the doctor wrote out a prescription. Lying awake night after night, desperate to lose himself in the sweet oblivion of unconsciousness only to find that, whatever he did, he still could not sleep. Sometimes, he felt as though he was going quite, quite mad.

He'd hoped the sleeping pills were going to solve all that. Earlier that night, he had taken two tablets, as instructed, and after thirty minutes he'd felt himself nodding off . . . only to wake three hours later, with that same image in his mind: of his mother reaching out for him, only for him to fail her. And now he felt even worse than before. The pills, which he'd imagined were going to be a miracle cure, seemed more like a curse.

He flushed the rest of the tablets down the toilet. Then he went back to bed, but not to sleep. For Piers, it was a long time until the sun finally came up.

PART III

June 2001 – February 2002

Chapter 33

Caitlin O'Dwyer was nervous, excited and late. Late for the most important night of my life, she thought despairingly, as the limousine inched along Fifth Avenue. Midtown traffic was always a bitch, but this evening it seemed worse than usual. Car horns sounded in an angry symphony. Tempers were rising with the temperature, everyone desperate to escape the claustrophobic heat of the New York summer. Thank God for air conditioning, at least. It was the one advantage of the rock-star car. Tinted windows, TV and fully-stocked bar . . . Caitlin found the bling a little excessive, but her publicist had insisted on it, saying there was 'no way in hell' she could turn up at the CFDA's annual award ceremony in a cab.

The Council of Fashion Designers of America awards – the fashion industry's equivalent of the Oscars. A shiver ran through her. Even now, she couldn't believe she'd been nominated.

She had arrived in New York six years earlier with little money but a big dream – to make it as a designer. Sure, she could easily have got a job at one of the big fashion houses on Madison Avenue, but she'd already decided that she didn't want to spend the next two years doing grunt work – making up patterns of another designer's ideas, overseeing the sample-makers. She wanted to work for herself.

So she rented a dingy set of rooms in a drab tenement on the Lower East Side and started trying to sell the clothes she'd made for her year-end show. Confidently, she booked appointments with buyers at every major department store: Neiman Marcus,

Saks Fifth Avenue, Bergdorf . . . but while the buyers liked her garments, no one was prepared to go out on a limb and stock any.

'Sorry,' she was told time and again. 'We don't take risks on unknowns.'

With funds running low, she invested in a sewing machine and got to work making alterations for half a dozen upmarket boutiques. It was low-paid and technically far beneath her abilities, but at least it gave her time to work on her own designs.

It was a lonely six months. She knew no one in New York, and it wasn't the friendliest city. She also had few opportunities to meet new people. She only went into the boutiques once a week to pick up the alterations, then worked on them alone in her basement. She missed Alain and her friends back in Belleville. She missed Lucien more than she'd thought possible.

But in some ways the loneliness worked to her advantage. She had nothing to do apart from work. And slowly, surely, life got better. She gradually built a reputation for being an excellent seamstress – quick, careful and reliable. That meant she could pick and choose who she worked for. She particularly liked White Heat, a hip boutique on West 14th Street in the Meatpacking District. The clothes were daring, cutting-edge, more her style. Every few weeks she would bring in a selection of her garments, and try to persuade the owner to start stocking them on a trial basis.

'Soon,' he kept saying. 'Once I've shifted some of the stock I've already got.'

But soon wasn't soon enough for Caitlin.

White Heat was popular with the young, rich party crowd. One of its biggest customers was Lena Chapman, a Park Avenue Princess and budding style icon. With her forthcoming debut at the Viennese Opera Ball, she was looking for something other than the traditional meringue dress.

'Something I can make a splash in,' she said.

Two of the shop assistants, Janice and Marie, were tasked with bringing out every white dress in the store for her perusal. Caitlin, there picking up the latest garments for alteration, watched as Lena rejected them all.

'There's nothing special enough, you know?' she complained to Janice, before sweeping out of the store.

'What a pain in the butt,' the girl remarked to Caitlin after Lena had gone.

But Caitlin was thinking something quite different. She had got to know Lena a little over the past few months – knew that she would rather wear something daring and artistically challenging than look just plain pretty. She was Caitlin's ideal client.

Dumping the alterations on the counter, Caitlin ran out after her. She caught up with Lena just as she was about to get into a cab, quickly explained that she was a designer and had a dress that she was sure Lena would love.

'Really?' The girl looked sceptical. 'I thought I'd been shown all the white dresses in the store.'

'It's not in there. It's at my apartment.' Caitlin crossed her fingers, hoping Lena didn't ask why it wasn't in the shop. She didn't want to let on that she was only a seamstress. 'You'd have to come there to see it.'

Fortunately Lena's interest had been piqued. Always up for finding something quirky and unusual, she agreed to come round that evening at seven. At worst, it would be a waste of twenty minutes of her time.

Lena pirouetted in front of the mirror. 'I love it.'

The elegant Art Deco gown was perfect. She had been sceptical about what the softly spoken, somewhat offbeat young woman was going to show her, but it was as though Caitlin had read her mind. Made of white crêpe, the dress was a deceptively simple shift-style garment, given an exotic, opulent look by the handsewn beads that covered it.

A month later, Lena turned up at the Waldorf Astoria looking coolly sophisticated in her Roaring Twenties-inspired cocktail dress. The other girls, in far more traditional gowns, were forced to look on as she effortlessly stole the show.

The following week, Lena's name and picture appeared in the *New York Times* 'Sunday Styles' section. Alongside, there was mention of the young, up-and-coming designer responsible for her exquisite dress – Caitlin O'Dwyer.

The formula for success is one that never changes: hard work, passion and perseverance. But the odd lucky break never hurts. And Lena Chapman was Caitlin's.

After the success of her debs' ball, Lena became Caitlin's first client. More importantly, she passed Caitlin's name onto her friends. Like Lena, they were all young, rich, beautiful and well-photographed. And they all loved the idea of having their clothes designed specifically for them.

Soon Caitlin was running her own couture business.

It was perfect for her, allowing her to create the kind of dramatic, extravagant pieces that were her forte. The young socialites adored the timeless nostalgia of Caitlin's designs: the sweeping strapless evening gowns and delicate cocktail dresses. She would take the time to talk to her clients, find out what they liked, their personal style and what look they wanted to portray at the event they were attending. It was this attention to detail that kept them coming back.

For the first year, Caitlin sketched, cut and stitched every item herself, working eighteen-hour days in her cloth-strewn basement. But as her client list grew she started employing outworkers to help make the clothes. She only used the best. With a service where quality was everything, she couldn't afford for anything to be shoddy. She personally checked every item before it went out – making sure the hand-stitching was perfect.

By year two, Caitlin was doing well, but she was all too aware that couture was time-consuming and badly paid proportionate to the effort involved. She wanted to start designing her own ready-to-wear line, something she could sell into department stores. But to fund a whole collection – with fees for models, showrooms and runway shows – she would need much more cash than she had access to.

Help came in the form of Alexis Reid, a pushy young publicist from Queens. Intrigued by the coverage that the mysterious Caitlin O'Dwyer's work was getting, Alexis made an appointment to see her. She turned up early at Caitlin's dingy walk-up, sat in the corner and watched her conducting a fitting. By the time the customer left, Alexis had made up her mind.

Over a cheap noodle lunch in nearby Chinatown, she laid out the facts. 'Talent is one thing, honey; success quite another. You've got the potential to be huge – but you need my help.' She offered her services in exchange for a share of Caitlin's future earnings.

'You're taking on quite a risk,' Caitlin observed, as they shook on it.

The other woman's eyes glinted. 'Believe me, I'm totally screwing you over.'

Joining forces with Alexis turned out to be the right call. With her power suits and carefully set bright red hair, she was all eighties aggression – exactly what Caitlin needed. Lena and her friends were regulars at every New York party and hip club – and they were attending them in Caitlin's designs. It was fabulous free publicity and exposure, if used properly. Alexis knew how to do that. She kept a list of Caitlin's clients and where they were wearing her clothes, and then she called on whatever favours she could to ensure that a photo of the dress ended up in the papers the next day.

Alexis got the job done any way she could. When it came to the Oscars, she leaked a story that Caitlin had received three commissions to make outfits for the evening. In fact, at that point, no one had asked her to make anything. But by the next morning she'd had four desperate calls requesting her to keep herself available.

Mostly Caitlin let Alexis have free rein. The only time she intervened was when the publicist wanted to capitalise on her links to the Melville family.

'But, honey, it's a fabulous story,' Alexis cooed. 'Like a modern-day Cinderella. And your not-so-ugly step-sister is making quite a name for herself as a model.' She reached into her newly-acquired Hermès Birkin bag and pulled out several glossies, all with Amber's face splashed across them. 'It'd be a big boost to sales.'

'Sales are good enough,' Caitlin said.

'That's true. But they'd be even better if you'd let me leak a little bit of info . . .'

'*No*, Alexis.' Caitlin's voice was uncharacteristically firm. 'And I'd appreciate it if you didn't bring it up again.'

She didn't. After all, it wasn't like they needed the exposure. Caitlin was the darling of the Hollywood A-listers, and the big stores that had once rejected her were clamouring for her to supply them with a ready-to-wear line. Henri Bendel's, known for its innovative women's wear and encouragement to young designers, was the obvious choice to start with. Caitlin poured all her savings into producing a limited collection for the store. Stock was sold out in a week.

Now, as the limo finally pulled up outside the 42nd Street entrance of the New York Public Library, Caitlin felt a prickle of nerves run through her. With the CFDA nomination for Emerging Talent in Womenswear, it seemed all her hard work had finally been recognised. She was on her way to becoming a household name. As long as she won, that is . . .

*

Alexis Reid stood to one side, watching approvingly as Caitlin emerged from the car. She'd been a little worried that her laid-back client might turn up in a long peasant skirt, floaty tunic and ethnic jewellery. But thankfully Caitlin had abandoned her usual breezy bohemian style and pulled out all the stops for the glittering occasion. And doesn't she look glorious for it, Alexis thought, pride mixing with a dash of envy. In fact, in a floor-length gown of midnight blue – one of her own creations, naturally – Caitlin looked downright sensual, the dress showing off her perfect hourglass figure. She was going to steal the show, Alexis just knew it.

Already on the red carpet were Heidi Klum, resplendent in Chanel, and Heather Graham in Dior, with P. Diddy bringing up the rear. But as Caitlin glided towards the entrance, the photographers and camera crews homed in on her.

'Over here, Caitlin!' they called.

Flashbulbs popped. After an hour spent snapping size two models and actresses, it was a relief to see a real woman. And those curves would give J.Lo a run for her money.

Alexis looked on, as Caitlin smiled obligingly for the press. She was a real class act, all old-fashioned glamour. Her gown was cleverly designed to pour over her body, the raw silk clinging to her full breasts, wasp-waist and the gentle flare of her hips, leaving just enough to the imagination. With those smoky eyes, red-lipped pout and her hair piled high on her head, just a few dark tendrils escaping to frame her face, she was every inch the fifties movie star. She had a rare talent for creating a story with her designs. That was why she was such a success.

Although thankfully, that success hadn't gone to her head. Four years on, Caitlin was still the same down-to-earth person Alexis had first met. Yes, she had matured in that time, turned from an endearingly earnest but somewhat clueless twenty-two-year-old girl into a confident young woman. But she hadn't lost her passion along the way. Designing was still at her core; she made no compromises, refused to trade on her name, like others would. That's why she'd been nominated for this award tonight.

Finally, sensing her client needed rescuing, Alexis moved forward. 'That's enough for now, boys,' she said, taking Caitlin by the arm.

'Thanks,' Caitlin whispered, as she allowed Alexis to lead her inside. 'My face was beginning to ache.'

'Well, get used to it,' Alexis retorted. 'You'll be doing a lot more once you've won.'

Protesting that winning wasn't assured, Caitlin followed Alexis through to take their seats in the beautiful Celeste Bartos Forum – just in time, as the awards ceremony was about to start.

In an elegant Yves Saint Laurent tuxedo, Sandra Bernhard played host for the evening. As always, it was a long night – although thankfully not running to the seven hours of the previous year. There were few surprises, with Tom Ford being named Womenswear Designer of the Year, and the Lifetime Achievement Award going to Calvin Klein.

'Now the Award for Emerging Talent in Womenswear,' Sandra Bernhard said. Alexis glanced over at Caitlin, who was trying hard not to look hopeful, but failing miserably. Alexis reached down and took her hand.

'And the winner is . . .' There was a pause. In the vast auditorium the only noise was the rustle of paper as she opened the envelope. 'Caitlin O'Dwyer!'

It was four in the morning by the time Caitlin left the after-party at the Gramercy Park Hotel. The rest of the evening had passed in a whirl of interviews and well-wishing. When her long-time hero Michael Kors came up to offer his congratulations – 'a well-deserved win, darling,' he'd said, kissing her on each cheek – she thought she might die of pleasure.

'The press coverage is going to be unbelievable,' Alexis had said excitedly. 'This could take you international.'

Caitlin thought of all the people she hoped would see her achievement tonight: Lucien, William . . . Childish, she knew, but still. What was the point of success if you couldn't flaunt it?

The journey home was far quicker. Caitlin leaned back in the leather seat, golden trophy in hand, and watched the city slip by . . . past the brownstones of Greenwich Village and the cast-iron façades of SoHo, and onto her TriBeCa loft. She had moved there two years earlier, when she'd started making serious money. Originally a textile warehouse, the building had been converted during the eighties, before the area had made the transition from trendy to exclusive. Caitlin had fallen in love with the duplex the moment she'd seen it. She used the lower floor as her workroom, while upstairs was a huge living-sleeping area.

Inside, she stepped out of her heels, unzipped the gown. It had been fun to wear for one night, she thought, hanging it away carefully. But she was glad to take it off now. Something so grand and formal wasn't her usual choice. She'd only worn it tonight for the publicity shots. Alexis would have killed her otherwise.

Ten minutes later, all trappings of the evening were gone. Dressed in brushed cotton pyjamas, her face scrubbed clean, there was no trace of the sophisticated designer left. Too keyed up to sleep, she made herself a mug of tea and took it outside onto the fire escape. The heat had gone out of the day now, and the air was pleasantly warm. Below her, there were the familiar sounds of the city waking up: a truck delivering to the deli on the corner, an NYPD squad car racing by, siren blaring.

As she sipped her tea, she reflected on the evening. It had been a triumph for her, but still she felt . . . unsettled. Coming back to her empty apartment, it had hit her – how alone she was. All the success in the world meant nothing if you had no one to share it with. Sure, she had friends who had called to congratulate her, who wished her well. Alexis, Alain . . . But she had no family to call, and there was no one special in her life right now. Sure, there had been a few men since she'd arrived in New York. Occasionally she allowed friends to fix her up. She would go out with the guy once, maybe twice. They were usually good-looking men with interesting jobs and the best of intentions. But they weren't Lucien.

Even now, just thinking his name, she winced.

She had thought about him a lot after she first arrived in New York. She'd intended to call, to write, to explain. Once she had gotten her head sorted. But somehow it had never felt like the right time. It was something she needed to do face-to-face. The first chance she'd got was six months later, when she'd gone back to Paris for Alain's fortieth birthday.

She'd spent the weeks beforehand planning what to wear, what to say. Time and distance had helped her realise that she'd made a dreadful mistake running out on him that night.

The party took place at Café des Amis. Caitlin got there early, and spent the first part of the evening catching up with old friends while keeping one eye on the door to catch Lucien's arrival.

It was nearly midnight by the time he finally turned up. She was so pleased to see him, that it took her a moment to register the Icelandic blonde on his arm. Tall and leggy, she was Caitlin's polar opposite. It changed everything. When Caitlin finally came face-to-face with him, they exchanged no more than a polite nod of acknowledgement.

Caitlin was relieved when the party ended and even more relieved to return to New York the next day. She hadn't been back to Paris since then. She wasn't planning a trip any time soon.

So much for her love-life.

With that less than positive thought, she went inside and to bed.

The phone jarred her awake the next morning. Thinking it was going to be Alexis wanting a post-mortem of the evening, she answered. But it wasn't her publicist. It was William.

Caitlin's heart sank when she heard his voice. It had been months since they'd last spoken, even longer since they'd seen each other. She didn't need him ruining her good mood.

'Congratulations on your win last night,' he said, after the preliminary greetings were out of the way.

'Thanks,' she said shortly. She just wanted to get him off the phone as quickly as possible.

'But I'm not just calling to say well done,' he continued. 'I actually wanted to know how your schedule was looking the next few weeks.'

'Busy,' she said automatically.

'Not so busy that you can't manage a trip to London, I hope.'

There was a silence.

'You see,' he went on, 'there's something I want to discuss with you. Something important.'

Caitlin frowned. 'Can't we do it over the phone?'

This time he was firm. 'No, we can't.' There was a pause. 'Caitlin, please. I don't ask much. I would like you to do this for me.'

Reluctantly, she agreed to come over the following week. As she replaced the receiver, she tried to quash the feeling of foreboding.

Chapter 34

Elizabeth padded across the *tatami* mat to where her husband lay sleeping, belly down, on their futon. He was naked, the only way he ever slept during the muggy Tokyo summers, milk-chocolate skin against crumpled white cotton sheets, tight muscles glistening with sweat. She wasn't looking forward to the week apart. Being away from him was torture.

They'd been in the apartment for four years now, ever since their wedding. By mutual agreement, they'd decided against a Western-style block, and chosen somewhere typically Japanese – with sliding *shoji* doors, minimalist furnishings and flexible living/sleeping areas. The location suited them both. In the small, exclusive neighbourhood of Shoto, the flat had easy access to the shopping and restaurants of Shibuya – Cole's choice – but was also within walking distance of Yoyogi Park, Western Tokyo's version of Central Park, where Elizabeth liked to jog at weekends.

Outside in Shoto, dawn was breaking. Early-morning light chinked through the blinds, reminding Elizabeth it was time to go. She bent to kiss Cole goodbye, assuming he was still asleep. But, without any warning, his eyes flew open, he whipped over onto his back and reached out to grab her around the waist. She let out a little yelp of surprise as he pulled her down on top of him.

'Trying to sneak out without a proper goodbye?' In another swift move he flipped her onto her front, so he was lying stretched across her, pinning her from behind. 'You should know better, Lizzie.'

He pressed his weight against her. She could feel his erection through the thin material of her skirt.

'Cole!' Elizabeth did nothing to disguise her outrage.

'Come on, sweetheart.' Beneath him, she'd started to struggle, but he held her fast. 'A whole week without you? You gotta give me something to remember.'

'I can't . . .' she protested. 'The car's outside – my suit . . .'

'Screw the suit.' He was moving against her now, rubbing gently, insistently, back and forth. She could feel herself giving in.

'I don't have time for this,' she objected weakly.

'Don't worry,' Cole murmured, his hands already pushing her pencil skirt up over her thighs. 'It won't take long.'

Elizabeth laughed. 'Just what every girl wants to hear—' But the last word died on her lips as Cole began to ease her panties down.

She felt him hard against her. Anticipation flooded her groin. Instinctively she parted her legs, already wet for him. As she felt him pushing inside her, she forgot all about the plane she was meant to be catching.

Five minutes later it was all over. Mutual satisfaction achieved.

'Bastard,' Elizabeth muttered good-naturedly as she climbed off the bed. She straightened her clothes and then walked over to the dressing-table. Her cheeks were flushed, and she dabbed on some powder, trying to get the heat out of her face. 'It's all your fault if I miss the plane . . .' She snapped the compact shut.

Cole laughed. 'Come on. You loved it and you know it.' He propped himself up on his elbows, watching as she retouched her lipstick, straightened her clothes, gathered her case and passport together.

'It's not too late, you know,' he said, serious now. 'I can still come with you.'

She smiled at his concern. She liked the way he worried about her. Who'd have thought that Elizabeth Melville, who had always prided herself on her independence and strength, would enjoy having a protective husband?

'Thanks for the offer, but I'll be fine,' she said, blowing him a goodbye kiss.

Outside, her driver stood waiting by a black Lexus. He held the door open as she slid into the back seat. Then they were on their way to Narita Airport.

It was still early, so traffic was mercifully light. As they sped along the motorway, Elizabeth thought about how happy Cole made her. A year after Rosalind's funeral, they had married – a quiet ceremony, just the two of them, under the cherry blossoms in Kyoto. They'd kept their relationship secret, only telling everyone after they were wed. Reactions had been mixed. William had been furious, mostly because he still hadn't forgiven Cole for 'leaving him in the lurch' at Melville, after he'd quit to set up his own business. Caitlin had sent a polite card, but had shown no interest in meeting Cole. Amber had arranged for an extravagant bouquet to be delivered – or, rather, her PA had – congratulating Elizabeth on her marriage to *Colin*. That had amused both her and Cole.

Settling in Tokyo had been the natural choice. Elizabeth had spent the past six years growing Melville's Far East and South-East Asia business, opening branches in Singapore, Shanghai and Hong Kong. Six months ago, as head of the most profitable territory in the company, she had finally been awarded a place on Melville's board.

Meanwhile, Cole had opened up Kobe, a chain of sushi and sashimi bars in London. He'd put a strong management team in place, and oversaw the business from Japan, flying back to England once or twice a month.

To say he was doing well was something of an understatement. Turnover had already hit fifteen million and Forbes had recently run a glowing profile on him. He planned to open a more upmarket offering soon: a high-end, upscale restaurant.

Right now, Elizabeth and Cole were the epitome of the young, successful couple. They were also extremely happy together.

But, on a professional level, Elizabeth felt she still had more to achieve – namely, making fundamental changes to Melville's business model. She planned to run the place one day, if her father ever deigned to step down. She just needed to make sure there was still a company left by the time that happened. Because at this rate it looked doubtful.

While Caitlin's star had been rising over the past six years, Melville's had been fading. Elizabeth's side of the business had been doing well, but at Group level, sales were declining. Melville just wasn't drawing in the customers any more. Not that William would admit there was a problem. Elizabeth had tried talking to him about it. The last time she was in London, she had proposed setting up a team to analyse the drop in footfall, but her father had dismissed the suggestion. 'All businesses go through cycles. This is simply a phase. It will reverse itself soon.'

Elizabeth wasn't convinced. Nor was she sure they could afford to take this 'wait-and-see' approach. With sales down, they were struggling to pay suppliers. And employees were beginning to leave. The latest casualty had been Melville's Head Designer the previous month. That's when Elizabeth had suggested asking Caitlin over to meet with them.

Elizabeth had tracked her half-sister's success. Her dramatic designs weren't Elizabeth's style – or Melville's either, which had stayed firmly conservative and classic. 'But she's got talent,' Elizabeth had said to her father the previous month, after the current Head Designer had handed in his resignation. 'And we could definitely use some of that.'

William had loved the idea, mostly because it was an excuse

for him to contact Caitlin. It hurt Elizabeth, the way he lamented her absence from his life. But it was to be expected, she told herself. She was the one he saw all the time, while Caitlin remained distant. And, whatever his motivation for agreeing to ask Caitlin in to see them, it was a step in the right direction. Maybe it would be the start of him agreeing to some of her other suggestions, too.

Cole didn't agree. He thought she was wasting her breath. In fact he wanted Elizabeth to quit Melville altogether. He reckoned William was an autocrat, who was never going to let his little bit of power go. It was the one dispute in their otherwise perfect marriage. And Elizabeth was determined to prove him wrong. After all, she would be running the business one day. She should have some say in the direction it was going now. She just needed to convince her father of that.

A few hours after Elizabeth left Tokyo, Caitlin boarded a plane for Heathrow, too. William had offered to book her flight, but Caitlin had insisted on doing it herself. When was he going to understand that she didn't want, or need, his charity? He had invited her to stay with him at Eaton Square. Elizabeth would be there, apparently. Again, Caitlin had said no. Instead, she'd booked into Baglioni, a boutique hotel in Kensington where she stayed whenever she was in town. She arrived there late afternoon and found a message asking her to phone him when she got in. She had a shower first then made the call.

He sounded conciliatory. 'I thought perhaps we could meet for dinner tonight. Elizabeth's just arrived. You could come over here.'

Caitlin told him she was too tired. Whatever he had to talk to her about, it could wait. She would rather face him when she was fresh.

If he was disappointed, he hid it well. 'Fine. Let's make it tomorrow instead.'

Caitlin agreed to lunch in the Mirabelle. Neutral ground, at least. The thought didn't help her sleep any easier.

The following day, at quarter to one, William and Elizabeth arrived together at the Mirabelle in Mayfair. It was a particular favourite of William's, who never tired of its intimate, clubby atmosphere. Located on Curzon Street, it was conveniently within walking distance of Melville, but still far enough away to mean they weren't likely to be spotted by anyone from Head Office. That was the main reason he'd chosen the venue. That was also why it would just be the three of them for lunch – William, Elizabeth and Caitlin. He had decided against inviting Piers. He wanted as few people as possible to know what they were asking of Caitlin, in case she turned them down.

The maitre d' led William and Elizabeth past the piano lounge and through to the mirrored dining room. As always these days, the restaurant was packed. Businessmen in charcoal suits talked intently over foie gras complemented by Sauternes. William wasn't surprised to see that Caitlin was already there. Experience told him she would want to get this over with as soon as possible.

He hadn't seen her for a while. At – what was it now? – twenty-six she had grown into her looks, developed a strong sense of style. She'd let her dark hair grow out again, and it hung thick and loose around her shoulders. In linen trousers and a billowing sleeveless smock, she looked casual and cre- ative – couldn't have looked more different, in fact, than Elizabeth, in her dark grey Joseph trouser suit, blonde hair tied neatly back from her face.

After rather formal greetings, they busied themselves with ordering. By unsaid agreement, they skipped starters and just went for main courses and mineral water. No one could be bothered to pretend that this was going to be a long, sociable lunch.

Once the waiter had left, an uneasy silence settled over the table. They had never been the type of family to engage in small talk, and no one was about to start now.

It was Caitlin who broke first. She sipped her water, returned the glass to the table, and then asked the question that had been on her mind for the past week, ever since the meeting had been arranged.

'So are you going to tell me why I'm here?'

William and Elizabeth exchanged meaningful glances. It was William who answered.

'Because I have a business proposition for you.' She looked at him warily. He took a deep breath and then said what she'd known he would. 'I want you to come to work as Head Designer at Melville.'

Caitlin sliced into her Dover Sole. She had no intention of eating it – her appetite had deserted her as soon as she'd sat down. It was just to stall for time. She wanted to savour the moment. Revenge didn't get any sweeter than this. To be sitting opposite William, on his turf, having him ask – no, she corrected herself – *beg* her to come and work for him.

She listened patiently, as he tried to put a positive spin on the offer.

'I know you've been making a name for yourself in New York,' he said, 'but heading up the design team for an international fashion house . . . that would be a real opportunity.'

Opportunity? He must think she was an idiot. The fashion community was a small one. She'd heard about the dire situation at Melville – the walk-outs, the decimated Design Department. Right now, no one with talent would go to work there if they could possibly help it.

'So what do you think?' William prompted.

She pushed a piece of fish around her plate. 'Thank you for the offer.' God, it pained her to say that. 'But I don't think it would be the right career move for me at the moment.'

He frowned. 'You're turning us down – just like that? Don't you want to at least take a few days to think about it?'

She shrugged. 'What's to think about? I have my own business – a very successful one. Why would I want to give that up to work at Melville?'

Elizabeth jumped in. 'Well, you wouldn't have to work for us exactly. Perhaps you could design one line, something more youthful, or lend your name to part of the collection.'

'I wouldn't have the time,' Caitlin said. 'I have plans to grow my own company this year—'

'What plans?' William demanded.

Caitlin looked at him coolly. 'They're confidential at the moment.'

William tutted. Ignoring him, Caitlin turned back to Elizabeth. 'I'm going to be working eighteen hours, seven days a week as it is.'

Elizabeth opened her mouth to speak, but William got there first.

'But you haven't even thought about what this could do for you.'

'That's because I don't think it *could* do anything for me. I'm doing very nicely on my own.' Caitlin paused. 'Frankly, I haven't heard one good reason why I should help you out. Because that's what you're asking, isn't it? You want me to do you a favour. Well, why should I?'

'Because we need you, Caitlin.' Elizabeth said it quietly. 'Because things are bad and we need you.'

There was a silence. William flashed Elizabeth a look of fury. But then the fight seemed to go out of him. His shoulders slumped, his eyes lost their spark.

'She's right,' he admitted, and Caitlin could tell it killed him to say it. 'If things go on the way they are, there might not be a business left in a few years' time.'

Caitlin pressed the napkin to her lips before saying, 'Well, I don't really see how that concerns me.'

He looked up sharply then. For a moment he seemed confused. 'What do you mean, you don't see how that concerns you? Didn't you hear what I said?' His voice lowered to a whisper. 'Melville's on the verge of disaster.'

'I heard,' she said evenly. 'But I still don't see how that relates to me.'

Elizabeth could see Caitlin wasn't about to be persuaded. She sat back, ready to let it go. But William wasn't.

'Are you telling me you don't care?' He sounded disbelieving. 'I know you've always wanted to be self-sufficient, but surely you can't stand by while the Melville name is getting dragged down?'

Caitlin gave him a cool look. 'Why not? I certainly don't consider myself to be a Melville. And I never have.'

William stared at her, shocked into silence. As Elizabeth put a pacifying hand on his arm, Caitlin reached for her handbag, found her purse and threw some money on the table. She was on her feet, about to walk away, when William made his last-ditch, desperate appeal. 'Does the fact that we're family mean nothing to you, Caitlin?'

It was the wrong thing to say. She turned slowly to face him.

'Family?' she repeated incredulously. 'You're not my family. You're nothing to me.'

'How dare you be so ungrateful!' he exploded. 'I took you in when you were fifteen. I gave you everything you could want.'

Caitlin shook her head. 'It's always the same with you, isn't it? You think you can throw money at a problem and it will go away.'

'What's that supposed to mean?'

Caitlin hesitated, considering whether to confront him about the cheques she'd found – proof that he'd paid off her mother and known about her existence. But what would be the point? He'd only deny it.

'Caitlin,' he said sharply. 'I asked, what's that supposed to mean?'

She looked him straight in the eyes. 'It means I wish you'd stayed out of my life. You think you were doing me some big favour, bringing me to live with you? Well, I'd rather have stayed in Valleymount and gone on believing you were dead.'

William's face went white. For a moment, she thought he might strike her. 'How *dare* you speak to me like that? I'm your father and you should start showing me some respect.'

All around the room, conversations were stopping, the other patrons turning to stare at the raised voices.

Caitlin realised then that she'd been right all along. She should never have come here today. She had made a life for herself, a good life for herself, and that's what she needed to get back to.

'You just don't get it, do you?' she said. 'You're not my father. You never have been and you never will be.'

With that, she turned and made for the door.

William watched her go. He was furious with her, at the way she had behaved all these years towards him, and the Melville family. But he was also aware that she was his daughter, his only link to Katie, and that he didn't want her to leave like this. He went to stand up, to go after her. But as he did so, a pain shot through his left arm. Wincing, he sat down heavily in the chair.

Elizabeth looked at him with concern. 'Is something wrong, Daddy?'

'I'm fine,' he snapped. He rubbed his arm a little, frowning. It wasn't the first time he'd had that pain. Isabelle had been nagging him for weeks to see their doctor. Someone of his age needed to be careful, she kept telling him.

His age. He hated to be reminded that he was getting old, something the mirror did for him on a daily basis. It only seemed like yesterday that he was taking over the company, with all his hopes and dreams for the future, promising himself that he would grow the business even bigger than his mother had. When had it all passed so quickly?

He opened and closed his hand, trying to shake off the lingering feeling of numbness. It worked – a moment later, the pain was gone. Good. Nothing to worry about. And that tightness in his chest – probably just a touch of indigestion.

'Are you sure you're feeling OK?' Elizabeth was watching him closely now. 'Should I get some more water for you?'

'No.' Why wouldn't she stop fussing? 'I'm going to see if I can catch up with Caitlin.'

He went to stand up again. But as he got to his feet, a second pain shot through him. And this time it didn't go away. Suddenly he was finding it hard to breathe. And now the pain wasn't only in his arm. Clutching at his chest, he saw the alarmed look on Elizabeth's face, knew he should say something to reassure her . . . but instead he was falling, collapsing onto the floor, and dragging the contents of the table down on top of him.

His last thought before he fell unconscious was that he might never get the chance to make things right with Caitlin.

Caitlin was at the door, waiting for the cloakroom attendant to find her wrap, when she heard an almighty crash, the sound of plates and cups smashing on the floor. Instinctively she turned. For the rest of her life she would remember that moment. She would remember how she'd been feeling as she walked away from William, exhilarated by their argument, pleased that she had finally told him what she thought. Then she would remember starting at the noise, looking round and seeing him lying on the floor, eyes closed, face grey, weak, unmoving; feeling confused for a moment, not quite understanding what had happened. Then, all at once, everything clicking into place. And the awful, terrible realisation:

This is all my fault.

Chapter 35

Rich Cassidy was in the Cartier store on Rodeo Drive, trying to decide whether his boyfriend would prefer the watch in platinum or white gold, when he got Amber's page. It was a 911. He sighed heavily. Tonight was his seven-year anniversary. Back in their West Hollywood apartment, Louis had the champagne on ice and the lights turned down low. But their romantic evening would have to wait, because Little Madam – as Rich privately called Amber – sure as hell wasn't going to.

There were times he wished she wasn't quite so successful – then he could tell her to go fuck herself. But six years after he'd first met her, Amber Melville was still a goldmine. Magazine covers, catwalk shows – and, her latest triumph – a seven-figure deal to become the face of Glamour cosmetics. She'd become such a lucrative asset that he was now managing her career full-time. Unfortunately, that also meant he got to deal with all her drama.

He had three more messages from Amber by the time he'd made the short drive to her Beverly Hills mansion. The exclusive gated-community of Summit Circle had multi-million-dollar views across the LA basin and a state-of-the-art security system. The guard checked his ID and waved him through. Rich had his own house key in case of emergencies, which he judged this to be. Taking a deep breath, he opened the front door.

He found Amber in the marble entrance hall, draped over the sweeping staircase and sobbing uncontrollably. A Mexican maid hovered ineffectually to one side. Rich waved her away, making a mental note to slip her a little extra this month so she didn't run to the papers about this. Then he put on his concerned face and rushed over to Amber.

'Petal!' He dropped down in front of her. 'What on earth's happened now?'

Huge, gulping sobs wracked her body, making it impossible for him to understand what she was saying.

'Shush, shush,' he crooned, stroking her hair. 'Tell Daddy all about it.'

It took twenty minutes to get her to calm down enough to tell him the whole sorry story. She was crying over Wallace Marshall, the Lakers' star shooter. The two of them had been hot and heavy for all of seven and a half weeks – a record for Amber. Everything was going fine, until Wallace had been photographed at Teddy's with his hand down the pants of one of the Laker Girls. The first Amber had known about it was when *Star* magazine called to get her reaction.

'How could he do this to me?' she wailed. Another round of tears began.

Rich put his arms around her. 'Oh, come here, petal,' he said, in the baby voice that she seemed to like. Frankly, he found it a little humiliating, but the 30 per cent fee she paid helped him put his personal feelings aside. 'Daddy will make it all better.'

He stroked her hair as she continued to sob, quivering against his chest. Rich flicked a surreptitious glance at his watch, wondering how quickly he could get out of here.

'Come on, angel. He's not worth crying over.' He searched through his pockets and found a silk handkerchief with the Melville monogram on it. Amber had given it to him for Christmas last year. Cheap bitch. He handed it to her. 'Now, dry those tears, pet. You don't want to spoil that pretty face of yours, do you?'

Not that there was much chance of that. Even with her skin

mottled red and nose dripping, Amber still looked good. In fact, perversely, it increased her charm – it was this imperfect, dishevelled beauty that had made her famous.

From the moment Rich had first set eyes on Amber, six years earlier, he had known she was something special. Her launch had been one of those iconic moments that the industry would be discussing for ever – like when Kate Moss had graced the cover of *Face* in 1990, ushering in the heroin chic craze. In Amber's case, the sixteen-year-old heiress had stared defiantly out of the cover of *Style* magazine, rich and bored, with seen-it-all eyes and a cigarette dangling carelessly between crimson lips. Rich had made the stylist play up the sleazy look. They'd taken the photo on an early-morning subway, empty apart from a couple of drunks and a few pinstriped traders on their way to Wall Street. Amber had stood among them, dressed in a lurid gold backless dress, a tatty faux-fur coat thrown over her shoulders. With black eyeliner smudged under her eyes, she'd looked like she was doing the walk-of-shame home after a heavy night. Barely legal and dressed like a hooker, she was impossible to miss.

Her bad-girl image and jailbait looks caused immediate uproar. It was what Rich had been counting on. For a week, no one in Fashion could talk about anything other than Amber Melville. The accompanying article recounted every salacious detail of her brief yet colourful life. The story of English boarding schools, older men, rough sex and hard drugs was too good to resist. Her father wasn't happy; but her own fame – or infamy – was assured.

Rich glanced at his watch again. He sensed the worst of the drama was over. Now he wanted to get out of here as fast as possible.

'Honey,' he said, thinking quickly, 'take my advice. The worst thing you can do is stay in and mope about this tonight.'

Amber turned big, trusting eyes up at him. 'You think?'

'I know,' he insisted. 'You've gotta go out, have fun – show the world that the bastard doesn't matter to you.'

She chewed at her bottom lip, pondering what he'd said. 'Maybe you're right.' She looked hopefully at him. 'You'll come with me, though, won't you? I'm not up to going alone.'

Rich hesitated. He was already late for dinner and he was going to be turning up without that all-important anniversary gift. His chances of getting laid tonight were fading fast.

'I was supposed to be meeting Louis . . .'

Amber's bottom lip began to quiver. That was the heart of Rich's problem. He was the only person she could trust in a crisis. She had an abundance of acquaintances, happy to hang out around her pool or go partying with her, especially when it was on her dime. But she could never let her guard down around them. They were the type to turn round and sell a story about her for the price of an introduction to a casting director. She could trust Rich because it was still in his interests to stand by her.

He weighed up his options – and decided it was easiest to agree to go along. He could always ditch her after they got there. He forced a smile.

'Of course I'll come, poppet.'

'You don't mind?' she sniffed.

'Not at all.'

'Great.' The tears dried suspiciously quickly. She scrambled to her feet. 'I'll go and get ready.'

After she'd disappeared upstairs, Rich looked down at his powder-blue silk shirt. Two big wet patches stained the front of it, where Amber had cried against him. His nose wrinkled in disgust. It was his favourite shirt, and he'd picked it especially for the evening – Louis always said the colour brought out his eyes. And now it was ruined – along with his anniversary dinner. Oh, well. He'd just have to find a way to charge Amber for the cost of making this up to Louis.

*

Three hours later, Amber was feeling much better. She sank down into one of the supple black leather couches that lined the patio at Les Deux, LA's hipper-than-hip nightspot. She'd spent the past hour inside, grinding her body on the intimate dance floor. Out here, the mood was mellower: ambient music mingled with the jasmine-scented air and the soft lighting from the giant candelabras.

The waiter brought over an ice cooler and a couple of bottles of Cristal. Amber slipped her beautifully pedicured feet out of her Jimmy Choos.

'Hey, JB, I want a massage.' She thrust her right foot into Jim-Bob Lewis Junior's lap, burying her toes deep in his crotch and wriggling them suggestively.

He made no move to oblige. Instead, he gave her a slow smile, drawling, 'You gotta ask nicer than that, honey-bunch.'

Jim-Bob Junior – or JB to his friends – was sole heir to a Texan oil fortune and one of Amber's cohorts. With an assured multi-million-dollar fortune, JB had nothing better to do than hang out in the Californian sun. He cruised the Santa Monica pier during the day, hitting on the pretty roller-bladers, and partied all night. It was little wonder he and Amber got on so well. Most evenings they hit Sunset Strip together. It was where Amber had met most of her friends. Wherever she went in the evening, she'd always find someone to hang out with.

Rich had been right, Amber decided as she joked and flirted with JB – she did feel better now that she was here. She wished he was around so she could tell him, but they'd gotten separated in the crowd early on. She'd have to catch up with him later.

Signing up with Rich Cassidy all those years ago had been a stroke of luck. He always gave the best advice. Like his suggestion that she moved to LA. Amber loved it here. A lot of people hated the place, said it could suck the life out of you. But it was ideally suited to young, hot things like her. She especially loved see-and-be-seen venues like Les Deux. It was hard not to feel cool here, surrounded by all the beautiful people: long-limbed girls in skin-tight dresses, accompanied by Armani-clad men who could pump their own body-weight without breaking a sweat. What they all had in common was their bright white smiles, taut, tanned bodies – and the hope that they were either going to make it big in LA or stay big.

Amber's eyes swept the crowd. All the usual suspects were there: the ageing A-list movie star surrounded by girls a fraction of his age, Disney's latest teen sensation, rumoured to be hiding a nasty coke habit, a Hollywood director who had turned Amber down for a role in his latest romantic comedy. She knew people were checking her out, too. And why wouldn't they? In this illustrious but somewhat mainstream crowd she stood out. Wearing a pale pink Babydoll dress, teamed with a black leather jacket and overdone make-up, she was all long legs and peroxide curls. A younger, hotter version of Courtney Love.

She was still scanning the throng when she stopped, did a double-take. A new but curiously familiar face had caught her attention. Her eyes narrowed as she tried to place it.

'Is that Johnny Wilcox over there?' she said slowly.

The others followed her gaze across the room. It was JB who answered, 'Yeah, I think you're right.'

For the first time that night, Amber totally forgot about Wallace.

Johnny Wilcox was one of the members of Brit boy band Kaleidoscope. Their last three albums had gone platinum and they had been considered a hot property – until their surprise split last month. The press announcement had cited creative differences, but media speculation suggested the other three members had gotten fed up with Johnny. Kaleidoscope had built its name on having a squeaky clean image, the housewives' wet dream. Johnny had repeatedly screwed that up. He was perfect tabloid fodder. Slow news day? Johnny always delivered. Every other week the papers were printing photos of him snorting cocaine, rolling around drunk in the gutter or punching out the paparazzi. Girls were queuing up to sell their stories about him: three-in-a-bed kiss-and-tells; all-night sex romps . . . He'd been in and out of rehab for every vice you could name, always falling off the wagon again after he was released.

But, like most bad boys, he was also undeniably sexy, in that dark, mean way – the way that reminded her of Billy a lifetime ago. And now here he was, in Les Deux, surrounded by quite an entourage, even by Amber's standards. She watched with interest as a well-known recording mogul stopped by Johnny's table to pay his respects.

'I wonder what he's doing in LA,' she said, half to herself.

'I heard he's here recording a solo album,' piped up Devon.

Devon Carter was one of LA's manufactured blondes. She also happened to be the star of HBO's hit teen drama *Always & Forever* – or she had been until it got cut halfway through its third season. With no new roles on the horizon, she'd been spending more and more time out partying and trying to forget.

Devon leaned over and stage-whispered: 'Phoenix Records are supposed to have signed him.'

Amber digested the information. Despite Devon's fall from grace, she was still well-connected and her gossip usually spot-on.

JB looked pissed off, as he saw his chances of hooking up with Amber tonight swiftly fading. 'I don't see what's so great about him,' he said moodily.

Amber ignored JB. She was still watching Johnny. He was even hotter in person, she decided. Slumped in a chair, with a beer in one hand and a fag in the other, he had more x-appeal than the rest of the room put together. He smouldered. He had that something extra that you were either born with or you weren't – you couldn't manufacture it. She didn't realise people often said that about her.

Johnny must have felt Amber staring at him, because he glanced over in her direction. She didn't bother to look away. Coyness had never been her style. Their eyes locked, and something passed between them, a moment of mutual recognition. He gave her a slow smile.

That was all the invitation Amber needed. She downed the last of her champagne.

'Guys, I'm going over to introduce myself.' She deposited the flûte back on the low drinks table. 'It's the least I can do for a fellow ex-pat.'

She slipped her feet back into her Choos and stood up, smoothing her tiny dress down over her pert ass, and sashayed over to Johnny. Right now, Wallace's betrayal was the furthest thing from her mind. As Rich always said, the best way to get over someone was to get under someone else. And she had a feeling Johnny Wilcox was going to be that someone.

An hour and a half later, they were back at her mansion. She went through the motions of fixing drinks, and then came to sit beside him on the couch. They were just getting started on the real business of the evening when the phone rang. Johnny was already fiddling with the catch on her bra, so she wisely let the machine pick up. It was only when she heard her mother's tearful voice saying that her father had been rushed to hospital that Amber pulled away and ran to the phone.

Chapter 36

It was lunchtime in London. Seated at his desk, Piers Melville pushed his half-eaten sandwich to one side and reached for his coffee instead. He stared groggily out of the window. If he squinted, he could just about make out his counterpart in the office across the street. Head buried in a file, the stranger looked like he was having a more constructive day than Piers – although that wasn't saying much.

The past six years hadn't been kind to Piers. He hadn't known a peaceful night since his mother's death. He'd lost his appetite, too. The effects of this lack of nutrition and rest were obvious. He wasn't the good-looking man he had once been. His slender figure now bordered on scrawny; his hair had greyed and thinned; his complexion was sallow and his skin seemed stretched over his cheekbones.

He took another sip of his coffee. Not that the caffeine had much effect. He was in a permanent state of exhaustion; most of the time, he felt disconnected from the world, as though his head was in a fog.

The phone rang on his desk, making him jump. Irritated, he looked at the number displayed: it was his PA's extension. He frowned; he'd explicitly told her not to put any calls through for the next hour. Couldn't she follow simple instructions? He took his time answering – throwing his leftover sandwich into the bin and wiping his hands on a paper napkin, before picking up the receiver. 'What is it, Louise?' he said wearily.

As she began to tell him that William had been taken

seriously ill, he could feel the blood draining from his face.

'Piers?' Louise prompted. He was aware that she was looking for some kind of response from him, but he was too stunned to think straight. Sensing he was in shock, she asked, 'Shall I organise a car to take you to the hospital?'

'A car?' he repeated, still dazed. Then 'Yes. Yes, of course. Thank you.' He paused, trying to clear his thoughts. 'Oh,' he said suddenly, 'and do let Elizabeth know what's happened. She'll want to accompany me to the hospital, I'm sure.'

'She already knows,' Louise said. 'In fact, she was the one who called *me*. Apparently she was with your brother when it happened.' She paused and added helpfully, 'I think Caitlin was there, too.'

That brought Piers up short. *Caitlin* was in London? And William and Elizabeth had been having lunch with her. What was all that about? And, more to the point, why hadn't he been included?

It played on his mind all the way to the hospital.

William had been taken to the Wellington, a private facility in North-West London. Elizabeth insisted on riding in the ambulance with him. Caitlin followed in a black cab. On the drive through London, she had one thought in her head:

Please don't die. Please don't die . . .

The Wellington's Cardiac Services Department was one of the largest of its kind in the UK, with some of the country's most distinguished cardiologists leading its specialist teams. That didn't make the news any easier to take. Although CPR had got William's heart beating again, he would need surgery: a coronary angioplasty would be carried out the following morning.

It was Elizabeth who asked the question everyone was thinking. 'What does that involve?'

By then Piers had joined them. Isabelle was on her way up

from Somerset, and Amber catching the first available plane out of LA.

'Angioplasty is surgery to open up a coronary artery,' Mr Davies, the surgeon, explained. 'What we'll do is insert a tiny wire into a large artery in the groin . . .'

As the surgeon warmed to his subject, explaining in minute detail exactly what the procedure entailed, Caitlin began to wish Elizabeth hadn't asked. What she did take away was the important point that the surgery was usually carried out after the patient recovered – but in William's case, because of the severity of the heart-attack, it was going to be performed as an emergency treatment.

Amber arrived from LA the following morning. She stepped off the plane into a sea of flashing bulbs. Rich had called ahead to tip the papers off about her arrival.

'Is it true you're seeing Johnny Wilcox?' the reporters shouted at her.

She stared blankly ahead and allowed the bodyguard to usher her out into the waiting limo. Once inside, she finally let her guard down. It was hard being back in England. After her career had taken off in America, she had been too busy to fly over more than a couple of times a year. And, if she was honest, she didn't particularly like seeing the family. They always made her feel as though there was something a little, well, *unseemly* about her chosen profession.

Not her mother, of course; she was always supportive. Well, when hadn't she been? Amber thought, a touch scornfully. But whenever Amber saw her father and Elizabeth – on the obligatory holidays of Easter and Christmas – they made no secret of the fact that they looked down on what she did for a living. Amber would assure herself it was just because they were jealous that she made her own money and had a life away from them. Being a Melville didn't matter to her. Even if she'd been born a nobody, she would still have made it.

Or would she? There was always that nagging doubt in her mind. The last time she'd seen her father – three months ago on his birthday – they'd argued about a somewhat risqué photo-shoot she'd taken part in for FHM. All she remembered now was him yelling at her, 'The only reason they let you waltz down the catwalk in next to nothing is because you're making a fool of this family, of the family name!'

She'd told him he was talking rubbish, but the doubt had been planted in her mind. Was it true? Was she only in this position because she was a Melville?

As she stared out of the blackened window on the drive into London, she realised just how confused she felt about seeing her father again.

It was a tense forty-eight hours. Lying in his hospital bed, grey-faced and hooked up to bleeping monitors, the great man seemed to have aged immeasurably. The family refused to leave. They watched anxiously as he was wheeled, still unconscious, into Intensive Care, where he would be monitored overnight as he recovered from his operation.

Through the window of the ICU, Caitlin watched her step-mother keeping vigil over William. Even though she had been crying almost non-stop, Isabelle still looked immaculate: make-up carefully applied, clothes unwrinkled. Style and appearance were the two areas where she had every other woman whipped.

Caitlin smiled a little as she watched Isabelle stroke William's hair away from his face. It was rare to see them show each other affection. But then the smile faded as she remembered their argument. *You're not my father.* The words had been said in anger, in the heat of the moment. Caitlin closed her eyes and wished she could shut the memory out so easily.

*

Only one person was allowed into the ICU at a time. With Isabelle inside, the rest of the family had taken up residence on a little row of plastic seats near the room.

Piers, who had come back from the vending machine with coffees for everyone, handed them out before sitting down beside Elizabeth.

'So you were at Mirabelle when this happened?' he asked casually.

'Yes,' Elizabeth said. She was still dazed from what had happened. 'Yes, we were.'

'You and William . . . and Caitlin, too?'

'That's right.'

'I see,' Piers said slowly. 'So, what were the three of you doing there?' The question had been nagging away at him all evening.

'Oh, nothing important,' Elizabeth said distractedly. 'Daddy wanted to see if Caitlin would come over to design for us.'

Piers was speechless. Appointing a new Head Designer was a major strategic decision – he couldn't believe William hadn't seen fit to discuss it with him, nor to invite him along to the meeting yesterday. He wanted to ask more, but looking over at Elizabeth's worried face, he decided this wasn't the time.

Sensing that her uncle was lost in thought, Elizabeth glanced over at him. God, he looked dreadful. Not that he ever seemed particularly well these days. He'd never really recovered from Granny Rosalind's death. 'Why don't you go home and get some rest?' she said gently. 'I can call you if—' She paused to collect herself. 'If something happens.'

Piers shook his head. 'I'd rather stay.' What would be the point of going home? He hadn't slept properly for six years. He was hardly likely to start now.

Amber came out of the Ladies, make-up freshly applied. Seeing her, Elizabeth felt her hackles rise. She was upset about her father, and wanted to take her frustration out on someone.

Right now, her little sister seemed as good a target as any. 'You know, Amber, it's not a fashion show,' she said spitefully.

Amber pretended to look her over. 'I can see that,' she retorted.

Elizabeth bristled. Suddenly she wanted to pick a fight. 'To be honest, I don't even know why you're here. It's not like there are any photographers around.'

This time, the jibe hit home. 'For God's sake, Elizabeth,' Amber said, clearly wounded. 'He's my father, too!'

'You could've fooled me. When was the last time you bothered seeing him? Or called him, for that matter?'

Caitlin, who'd been silent throughout the exchange, now put a restraining hand on Elizabeth's arm. 'Don't.'

Elizabeth glared at her. 'What's it got to do with you? If it wasn't for you, he wouldn't even be here.' She shook Caitlin off and stalked over to Intensive Care.

'What was that about?' Amber asked curiously.

Caitlin merely sighed in answer. Deep down she knew Elizabeth was right. She *was* the one who had done this to him.

Caitlin hadn't been to church for a long time. But, like most people, in the face of death it was easy to find her faith again. On her knees in the hospital chapel, she said a Hail Mary followed by an Act of Contrition, and made a vow to put things right with William if he would just be allowed to pull through.

When she got back to the ward a little while later, the others were standing around outside, preparing to go home for a few hours to rest.

'Has he woken up yet?' she asked hopefully.

'No,' Isabelle said.

'Maybe you should go in now,' Elizabeth said stiffly. 'I think he'd like that.'

Caitlin knew it was the closest her half-sister would get to apologising for what she'd said earlier.

The others left, and Caitlin took up the vacated seat by

William's bed. She remembered suddenly how scared she'd been of him the first time they'd met. It was hard to imagine now, when he looked so weak. Hooked up to a monitor, a drip in his arm, looking as white as the sheet that covered him, he didn't seem so scary. She felt tears sliding down her cheeks and knew she needed to say something, even if he didn't hear her.

Tentatively she took his hand, shocked by how cold his skin felt. That couldn't be good.

'I'm sorry,' she said, her voice barely above a whisper. 'I shouldn't have said all those things earlier. I didn't mean them, not really. Maybe I thought I did at the time, but . . .' She stopped. But what? 'But not now that you're dying.' She thought for a moment, and then tried again.

'I shouldn't have pushed you away all those years. It wasn't your fault what happened. And I—' She stopped, knowing the next bit was going to be hard to say. 'And I promise I'll do what you asked,' she said finally. Her grip tightened on his hand. And was it her imagination, or did he squeeze back? Encouraged, she continued. 'I'll come to work at Melville. In fact, I'd love to work at Melville, to be part of the family. It would be a . . . a real honour.'

There, she'd said her piece. She felt better. For a moment, all that could be heard in the room was the sound of the monitor bleeping. Was it simply wishful thinking, or had his facial expression changed a little? Was it a reflex action, or something more? She stared intently at him. Yes – she felt a surge of hope! There it was again, the same movement.

His eyelids fluttered then opened.

'I'm very glad . . . to hear . . . that you want to work for Melville.' His voice was barely audible. Caitlin leaned forward so he didn't have to strain. He took a couple of breaths before starting again. 'About what you said before . . . your mother . . . I need you to know . . .'

'It doesn't matter now,' she hushed him, seeing him struggling.

Exhausted, he gave in. His eyes drooped closed again. He would tell her another time. The last thing he felt as he fell back asleep was Caitlin squeezing his hand. He felt the love, forgiveness and understanding flow between them, and knew that this was their chance to finally make things right.

The swiftness of William's recovery surprised everyone. By lunchtime the following day, he was fully awake, sitting up and eating. To his family, it seemed like a miracle.

But while he was recovering physically, his emotions were another matter. At first he was in a surprisingly jovial mood, almost euphoric. Having Caitlin by his side when he woke up meant everything to him. It almost made the heart-attack seem worthwhile.

She stayed with him for the first twenty-four hours. They never did speak again about what she had said to him during their argument – anytime he brought it up, she changed the subject. Eventually he let it go, not wanting to disturb the precarious truce between them. The next day she left for New York to settle up her affairs. And after she'd gone, another feeling crept in – an awareness of his mortality.

The heart-attack had given him a scare. Death was a great leveller. What was the old saying? *If you don't have your health, you've got nothing*. Well, once the initial thrill of simply being alive had faded, he began to appreciate what that really meant. He didn't consider himself to be an emotional man but, to his shame, in the privacy of his ward, when no one else was around, he found himself crying. He wasn't ready to die, not yet. He wanted to have his chance to make things right with Caitlin, to see Melville turn around.

During those first few days, his mood alternated between elation and despair. Then, on the third day, he had a visitor who changed everything.

*

Robert Davies, William's cardiovascular surgeon, was one of the top doctors in his field. His nimble fingers had worked their magic.

'You're going to be fine,' he assured his patient. 'As long as you make some changes to your lifestyle, and take the time to recover properly.'

He went on to tell William that he would be allowed home within the next seven days and could start an exercise-based cardiac rehabilitation programme after six weeks. And that was when he dropped the bombshell: William shouldn't even think about returning to work for at least three months.

'You have a high-profile, high-stress job,' Mr Davies said, in his soft, measured voice. 'You must be sensible about this. Take some time to rest. This is your body's way of telling you to slow down.'

As he left his patient to digest the news, William's thoughts immediately turned to Elizabeth. His fiercely ambitious eldest daughter had made no secret of the fact that she wanted his job. With him out of action, she would have a clear run of the place. If it was up to her, he would never be able to return to Melville and he wasn't ready for that. He was only sixty-one; he'd always assumed retirement was still a way off. Now, it seemed closer by the second.

If Robert Davies had hoped that his news would relieve William's stress, in fact it had the opposite effect.

The following day was a Saturday. William asked Hugh Makin, Melville's Chairman and one of his closest friends, to stop by the hospital. He needed to discuss how the company should be run in his absence, and Hugh was one of the few people he trusted. Hugh turned up during afternoon visiting hours with a fruit basket from Fortnum's. He immediately dumped the basket on Piers and came over to give William's hand a vigorous shake.

'You're looking well, old chap! If I didn't know better, I'd say you were faking this whole heart-attack business!' He laughed heartily at his own joke.

William gave a thin smile. 'I can assure you that I'm not.' Then he nodded at the basket in Piers' hands. 'Piers, get that taken care of, will you?'

Every spare space in William's private room was already covered with cards and colourful bouquets from well-wishers. Isabelle had eventually had to tell the nurses to start taking the flowers and gifts to other patients.

'Of course.' Piers made for the door.

'Oh, and while you're at it,' William said, 'could you get Hugh a coffee?'

What he actually meant was that he wanted some time to speak with Hugh in private. He also could do with a break from his younger brother. Piers's fussing was frankly beginning to grate on him. It reminded William of the way he had behaved towards their mother when she was ill, which made him feel even more aware of his age and ailing health. His memories of how the once-strong Rosalind Melville had been at the end were still fresh in his mind: he was far too young to end up like that.

Piers was mildly irritated by Hugh's arrival. He liked having his brother to himself. He was even less happy about having to fetch Hugh a coffee, like some little lackey.

He was on his way down the corridor to the vending machine when he spotted a nurse who had been in to check William's vitals earlier. Piers offloaded the fruit basket on her and then, in a flash of inspiration, asked her to fetch the drinks instead. That way he could get back as quickly as possible and not miss any of the conversation.

He retraced his steps along the corridor. The door to William's room had been closed over. Piers was about to knock and let them know he was back. But the thin laminate door was in no way soundproof. And when he heard what William was saying, he decided to listen quietly instead.

Inside the hospital room, William was explaining to Melville's Chairman that he'd been advised to stay off work for the next three months.

'So what does that mean?' Hugh asked. 'Are you putting Piers in charge?' Along with being CFO, Piers was also Deputy Chief Executive. He was the natural choice to step up into William's role.

But William didn't see it that way. 'Please!' he snorted derisively. 'Of course I'm not putting Piers in charge. I'd like to have a business left by the time I get back. I mean, he may be my brother and he's an adequate Finance Director. But he's hardly capable of managing the company outright.'

Hugh laughed softly. 'I'm glad to hear you say that. We all share that view. But it's obviously hard to say anything to you as he's a relative.'

'Oh, don't you worry,' William assured his friend. 'I'm very aware of Piers's faults. He's the kind of person you carry along. He lacks the intellectual horsepower to ever have proper clout.'

The other man murmured his agreement.

'Anyway,' William said briskly, 'I'll smooth that over with him later. But first I need to ask you a favour.'

'Obviously, if there's anything I can do to help . . .' Hugh assured him.

'There is,' William said. 'I asked you to come out here today because I want you to take over as Chief Executive while I'm away. You've been an excellent Chairman over the past five years, you know the business well, and you have the respect of the board.' There was a pause. 'I know it's a lot to ask, for you to combine both roles. But – will you do it?'

'I'm surprised you even have to ask,' Hugh said, solemnly. 'Naturally I'd be honoured.'

'Good,' said a satisfied William.

Outside in the corridor, Piers leaned against the wall and fought to regain his composure. He was covered in a cold sweat, shaking from the shock of what he'd heard. Hearing William laugh about him like that with Hugh . . . and what had Hugh said? – that they *all* shared that view about him. Could it really be true, that everyone was talking behind his back, sniggering at him?

Just then the nurse appeared with the coffee. Piers knew he needed to pull himself together. He couldn't let either Hugh or William know that he'd heard what they were saying about him.

'I'll take those,' he told her. He breathed in deeply, taking a moment to compose himself. Then he pushed into the room.

'Ah, there you are,' William said. 'I've been waiting for you to come back so we could get started.'

Piers stared at his brother. Liar, he thought.

'Sorry it took so long,' he said out loud. He resisted the urge to throw the hot drink at Hugh, and handed it to him instead.

Then he turned to William. His brother. The man to whom he had devoted his life. And who had now betrayed him. Somehow he managed to smile. When he spoke, his voice contained none of the hatred and bitterness he felt. 'Now, why don't we get started?'

Chapter 37

Early Sunday morning, Elizabeth left the rest of the family at the hospital and headed over to Albemarle Street. At Melville's Head Office, she greeted the night security guard with an easy familiarity. Having updated him on William's condition, she headed inside. As it was the weekend, the place was eerily empty. Trying hard not to feel unnerved, Elizabeth caught the elevator up to the sixth floor – the executive floor. As if on autopilot, she headed down the long corridor to her father's office. Luckily for her, the door was open. With all the confusion and upset, his secretary must have forgotten to lock it. Elizabeth hesitated, aware that she was about to cross a line. After this, there was no going back. She reached for the handle.

Inside, the office lay untouched. Everything was the same as William had left it when they went to meet Caitlin for lunch. Papers and files lay strewn across the floor. Elizabeth knelt down and started to clear everything up.

Only when the office was back in an orderly state did she finally walk over to William's desk. She pulled out his wing-backed armchair. A few years earlier, Occupational Health had installed Aeron chairs in all the other directors' offices, but despite recurring back pains, William had refused to make any concession to modernity. Elizabeth hesitated for just a second and then sat down. She ran her hands over the leather arms, enjoying the feel of being in the driving seat. Then a split second later she remembered why she was here instead of her father, and felt ashamed. What kind of person was she, to be thinking about her own advancement, when he was still so ill in hospital?

But this was no time to be sentimental. Pushing aside her guilt, she swivelled round to the desk, fired up the computer and, after a brief hunt, found her father's passwords written on a Post-it note. Great security, she thought. Within minutes she had accessed his personal files. She called up the address book with the telephone numbers of all the board members and spent a few minutes planning exactly what she was going to say. Then, after checking it was a decent hour, she called Hugh Makin. As Melville's acting Chief Executive, if Elizabeth had any proposals, she would need to get him on side – which was exactly what she intended to do.

When Hugh answered the phone, Elizabeth got straight to the point. She'd given it some thought, she told him, and she wanted to relocate to London. If something happened to her father again, she didn't want to be a twelve-hour flight away. Plus – and this was the part she kept to herself – being at Head Office would make it easier for her to keep a close eye on the business while William was out of action.

Hugh listened as she ran through her carefully thought-out plan. Cole's old job, Head of Strategy, had been vacant for the past few months, ever since his successor had left. She thought it made sense for her to take on that role.

'I'll continue to oversee the Asian operation from here,' she told him. 'To be honest, it's pretty much running itself these days, so I've been looking for a new challenge anyway.'

It wasn't hard to persuade Hugh. Elizabeth commanded a great deal of respect around the company, and he was greatly sympathetic to her wanting to be near William.

'I'm sure your father will be delighted to have you closer to home,' he said.

Elizabeth, who wasn't as certain that he would like the idea of her manoeuvring herself into a position of power, kept quiet as Hugh verbally signed off on her appointment.

It was only once that was all tied up, that she finally got round to calling Cole. He wasn't particularly happy when he heard what she'd been up to. 'You're transferring to London?' he repeated disbelievingly. 'For fuck's sake, Elizabeth! Didn't you even *think* to discuss this with me first?'

London wasn't the only reason he was mad. She hadn't been in touch for the past day and a half. But what with her father's heart-attack . . . after phoning Cole initially to tell him what had happened, she hadn't found time to call again. She felt a twinge of guilt, but quickly pushed it aside. He'd always known her ultimate plan was to come back to England one day.

'Look, Cole, I honestly didn't think you'd mind,' she said, trying to placate him. 'And it makes sense for you to be here, too. You'll be closer to your business and you can start thinking about diversifying into other areas, like you talked about before.'

It was hard for Cole to argue with his wife's logic. But still . . . He couldn't believe she hadn't thought to discuss such a major move with him first. And what worried him most was that she didn't seem to think there was anything wrong with that.

By the time Elizabeth flew back into Tokyo the following morning, he'd calmed down. In fact, overnight the idea of moving to London had begun to grow on him. He'd been suggesting for a while that it was time to put down roots. It was Elizabeth who'd always said that she wasn't ready to give up their hectic city lifestyle. Maybe this would be his chance to get her to settle somewhere.

Elizabeth only stayed a week in Japan. Just long enough to hand over the everyday running of the Asian operations to her trusted assistant. It was agreed that Cole would stay on to organise the rest of their relocation, and then join her in a month or so.

As he watched her getting ready to leave for the second time in a fortnight, he thought how much he wished she didn't have to go again. 'Hey, hun, I'm gonna miss you,' he said impulsively, gathering her up in a bear hug.

She squeezed him back. 'I'll miss you, too,' she said. But he had a feeling her mind was already on everything she planned to do at Melville.

Chapter 38

Back in New York, Caitlin's friends were appalled when they heard her plans. Giving up her business? Moving to London and going to work for her estranged family? It all seemed so sudden.

Alexis tried to talk her out of it. 'It's professional suicide,' she declared.

'It's family,' Caitlin rejoined.

The publicist sighed with frustration. 'But I didn't even think you liked them!'

'Neither did I.'

Alexis saw the steely look in Caitlin's eyes and knew she was wasting her breath. That was the problem with easygoing people. When they said no, they meant it.

Closing up shop in New York was more straightforward than Caitlin had imagined. She finished up her outstanding contracts within a fortnight, put in a good word for her outworkers with other designers and repaid her original investors – thankfully she'd made enough money to be able to do so. Then she arranged to rent out her apartment for the next year.

But, while practically it might have been simple enough to pack up and move her life to London, it was harder to justify to the outside world. Alexis wasn't the only one who thought she was crazy to be going to work for Melville. The company was seen as a dog in the industry. Just when her career was taking off, she was chucking it all in to take an unnecessary risk.

But, to Caitlin's surprise, as the time to leave New York

drew closer, she found she was actually excited about going to work at Melville. Maybe at first she'd agreed to it simply because she felt guilty about William. But lately she had realised this was something she wanted to do – professionally, for herself. While Alexis and all her friends in the business warned that she was ruining her career, she believed this could actually turn out to be her crowning achievement. To revitalise a dying brand like Melville, to do what Karl Lagerfeld had for Chanel, Tom Ford for Gucci . . . Sure, she had enjoyed success with her own business. But this would be on a different scale. This was her opportunity to shape a global brand.

She arrived back in London a month after William's heart-attack. On his suggestion, she'd agreed to move into Eaton Square for the time being. Even though he wouldn't actually be there himself, as he was recuperating down in Aldringham, she sensed that he felt closer to her that way.

The night before she was due to start at Melville, Caitlin stood in the second-floor library, looking out across the street at the park bench where her mother had once sat, and contemplated the task ahead of her. She couldn't wait to get started.

The following morning, her first day at Melville, Caitlin made a point of arriving early so that she could spend some time walking along Old Bond Street. The area had changed a lot in recent years. After falling out of fashion in the eighties, the past decade had seen a renaissance in Bond Street's fortunes, with hip designer stores opening up – the likes of Versace, Lacroix, DKNY. The established names such as Melville looked decidedly sombre and tired next to these stylish young boutiques. As the company's Head Designer, it would be up to her to address that problem.

To Caitlin's surprise and relief, it seemed everyone at Melville was just as enthusiastic as she was about her new role.

That was made evident ten minutes later, when she entered the company's rather grand Albemarle Street headquarters and found herself being treated like royalty. The beaming receptionist knew who she was on sight. She congratulated Caitlin on her recent CFDA win, and offered her tea or coffee, then a magazine – all of which Caitlin declined – before finally calling the design team to let them know she'd arrived.

'Gosh, it's so good to have you here,' enthused Jessica Armstrong, one of the design assistants, who'd been sent down to collect her. She looked more than a little star-struck to meet Caitlin. 'I'll be showing you around today. I hope that's OK?' she asked nervously.

A pretty, petite girl of no more than twenty, she told Caitlin that she'd come to work at Melville straight out of school four years earlier. 'I didn't get the grades to stay on to do A-levels, so I thought I'd get some practical experience instead.' It turned out that, despite her age, she was one of the longest-standing employees. 'A lot of people have left lately,' she explained with a little embarrassed laugh, as they stepped into the lift. 'Although I'm sure that'll change now you're here.'

Melville's Design Department occupied the entire third floor of the Albemarle Street office, which made it sound far grander than it was. A tall, narrow building, in a central London location, space was inevitably limited. Caitlin checked out the workroom first. With its yellowing walls and bare concrete floors, it was a rough, raw space, noisy and crowded, with the design team, pattern cutters and machinists all crammed into the same tiny area.

'It's pretty crazy in here right now,' Jess pointed out unnecessarily.

Caitlin gave a brief nod. With – what was it? – eight weeks to go until the October collection, the workroom was in full swing, the samples already being made for the showing season. Reams of cloth lay rolled out across the cutting tables; the burr of the sewing machines was constant and unrelenting; mannequins stood with half-pinned garments on them.

'And this is the showroom.' Jess led Caitlin through interconnecting doors to the area where Melville exhibited its collections to buyers and the media. Caitlin hated the formal, chandelier-adorned room on sight. It was stuffy and antiquated. Like Melville, she thought.

'Why don't you just show me what everyone's working on?' Caitlin suggested once the tour was over.

The girl nodded, as enthusiastic as a puppy. 'Yes, yes. Of course.'

While she scurried off to get the sketches together, Caitlin went through to her new office – a small section of floorspace that had been cornered off with plasterboard walls. She was beginning to feel the weight of responsibility resting on her shoulders. As she'd walked the floor with Jess, she'd noticed the hope in her new team's eyes. It had suddenly struck her that it wasn't just Melville she was here to save – there were jobs at stake, too. She couldn't let everyone down.

Seeing the plans for the upcoming collection didn't make her feel any better. The team was putting together yet another set of simple, elegant English classics: double-breasted jackets and blazers, tailored trousers and calf-length skirts, silk blouses, complete with heavy gold buttons, and loose jersey dresses. The palette of colours was heavy on brown, beige and cream. It was safe but uninspired, in Caitlin's opinion. A reworking of what had been done before – right down to the scarves, shift dresses and satin shirts sporting the Melville monogram, the interlocking MS. Caitlin knew that it was part of the company's tradition, but *really* . . .

'This is all very conservative,' she said out loud.

Sitting across from her, Jess nodded. 'Yes, I know. I think that's the way William Melville – I mean, your father,' she hastily corrected herself, 'always wanted it.'

Caitlin closed the sketchbook with a decisive bang. There was a hint of a smile as she said, 'Well, then. Maybe it's time for a change.'

That was the problem with Melville's Design Department, Caitlin realised during her first few weeks working there. Change wasn't a word used very often.

A lot of it had to do with the history of the company. Originally renowned for its accessories – shoes and handbags – clothing had never been one of Melville's strengths. Since the ready-to-wear line had been inaugurated in the sixties, the company had tried various approaches, but it had never quite found its niche. After a few disastrous attempts at high fashion, William had decided to stick to a more classic look. The last few designers had been hired for their conservatism, strong tailoring and focus on the older woman.

No wonder Melville apparel was universally considered to be pedestrian, a follower rather than a creator of trends. The target customers were matronly women, fifty-year-old grandes dames who had been shopping at Melville all their lives, and tourists, who saw a trip to the quintessentially English store as being as much a part of their itinerary as the Tower of London or Buckingham Palace. There were never any surprises in the clothes – and that way, Melville gave its two customer groups what they wanted.

Caitlin could see the argument for sticking to the classics. It was safe, never risking a disastrous show. But personally she thought that it was the wrong approach at this point. It was impossible to create an image for the company with a pair of beige trousers or a navy blazer. If William wanted to put the glamour back into the Melville name, then a bolder move was needed.

She would have liked to share these thoughts with her father, but Isabelle had a strict ban on any talk about the business while he was recuperating. Whenever Caitlin went to visit him at Aldringham – which she did every weekend without fail – her stepmother would anxiously remind her not to bother him with any discussions on work.

'How's everything going at Melville?' he would ask as soon as she arrived.

And she would give her standard reply. 'Everything's great. Anyway, you shouldn't be worrying about that now. Just concentrate on getting better.'

He'd wave her concerns away. 'I'm not an invalid, you know,' he'd say gruffly. 'My mind still works perfectly well.' But secretly he was pleased to have her fussing over him.

They never discussed the past. It was enough for William that Caitlin was working at Melville now. She'd had her rebellious stage and he forgave her for it, even if he would never quite understand it. Instead, they spent their time together going for long walks, in companionable silence, through Aldringham's grounds. It was part of William's rehab. And it seemed to be working. At first he had tired easily, only able to go a little way before needing to turn back. But soon he was able to be out for an hour and a half at a time.

He was delighted with the progress. He hated to be stuck out here, away from London, with nothing to do. He missed the buzz of work and it was frustrating not knowing what was going on in the office. He was particularly concerned about what Elizabeth might be up to in his absence. He hadn't been particularly impressed with the way she'd manoeuvred herself into the position of Strategy Director. But Isabelle had stopped him from confronting her about it. It would just have to wait until he got back – whenever *that* might be. Until then, he was content to be able to spend time getting to know Caitlin, and to start making up for all those years they'd missed.

*

A month after she relocated to London, Caitlin presented her proposal for the future of Melville apparel to the board. Having only ever worked for herself, it was a strange concept to Caitlin, seeking the approval of others for her plans. But, to her surprise and relief, all of the directors were on side. They listened attentively as she ran through her proposal to reinvent Melville's image by the time of the next show, due to be held in six months' time at London Fashion Week in February.

'I'd hope to have a first draft of my designs to show you within a couple of months,' she told the room, pleased to see how enthusiastic everyone looked; one or two of the men were even nodding along as she spoke. 'That should give me plenty of time to get everything ready for presenting the Fall Collection,' she concluded.

To Caitlin's embarrassment, there was a spontaneous burst of applause once she'd finished.

After the meeting, Elizabeth made sure to compliment her on the presentation. 'Let me know if you have any problems,' she said. 'Sorry I don't have more time to chat now – I'm rushing off to another meeting. But we should go for coffee sometime soon.'

Caitlin watched her hurry off. Even though they worked in the same building, they rarely got to see each other – Elizabeth never had any time. She was a whirlwind of activity these days, a great ball of energy.

Caitlin had wondered if Elizabeth might question why, after all this time, she had finally made up with William. But if her sister was remotely curious about what had transpired, she never asked Caitlin about it. Always discreet, it wasn't her style to press for information. Instead, she'd simply accepted that Caitlin was now a part of their lives. She hadn't even cared that her half-sister had taken up residence in Eaton Square.

'I'd much rather be in a hotel,' she'd said when Caitlin had asked if she minded. 'I frankly find the house a little stuffy, and I'd prefer to be nearer the office.'

Along with getting to know William, Caitlin had been making an effort to get involved in Elizabeth's life, too. It wasn't always easy, as the older girl was so busy, but Caitlin had at least insisted on meeting Cole properly. As soon as he'd arrived in the UK, she had made a point of inviting him and Elizabeth over for dinner.

It had been a fun evening. They'd all drunk too much, and laughed and debated into the small hours. Caitlin hadn't been at all surprised to find that Cole was just as dynamic and driven as Elizabeth. He was clearly so proud of her – and absolutely crazy about her, too. Halfway through the evening, Caitlin had popped to the kitchen to check on dinner, and had come back five minutes later to find Cole had Elizabeth pressed up against the fireplace. They'd sprung apart as she'd come in, and she'd discreetly looked away as Elizabeth straightened her clothes, half-embarrassed and half-envious that they felt so strongly about each other.

They'd planned to meet up again after that evening, to make a regular fortnightly event of it. But each time they'd set a date, Elizabeth had been forced to cancel at the last minute because she was too busy. Caitlin had no idea what Elizabeth was up to, but she was clearly in her element, full of energy and enthusiasm for her new role. Hopefully, once the craziness of these first few months had passed, they would have more opportunity to spend time together.

After a couple of months back in England, Caitlin's life began to settle into a routine. During the week she worked on her ideas for the next collection, and then Friday night she would drive down to Aldringham to spend the weekend with William. And, if she was beginning to be a little worried about her progress on the new designs, she kept her concerns from her father. She'd come up with something eventually, surely she would. She just needed a little more time. It was just unfortunate that the board meeting, when she was due to present her designs, was imminent. She hadn't expected the creative process to be *quite* so difficult, but – and she couldn't admit this to anyone – she really was struggling. Her initial bravado about being able to reinvent Melville's style was beginning to fade.

It was during a weekend at Aldringham that something happened which took her mind off her difficulties at work. She and William had just got back from one of their walks, and they were in the Georgian Orangerie, reading the Sunday papers before lunch. Caitlin picked up one of the supplements and ran her eye over the contents, spotting an article on London's art scene which sounded interesting. She flicked to it and, as she opened up the double-page spread, she froze.

Because there, staring up at her, was Lucien.

Chapter 39

Elizabeth spent her first month back in England trying to get to grips with what was going on at Head Office. While she'd been in Japan, it had been difficult to keep up to date – William was notoriously autocratic and cagey. And when she finally got all the details, she could see why. The figures were pitiful. Melville was having a hard time keeping up with its payments. Suppliers were fed up. The company was perilously close to breaching loan covenants.

'Daddy, how could you let it get to this stage?' she murmured to herself, late one night as she sat in his office. But there was nothing she could do about that right now, apart from damage control. She set up meetings with key suppliers and cajoled, begged and pleaded for extra time. She undertook a review of creditors and worked with the Purchasing Manager to prioritise payments.

Six weeks after she'd arrived, Cole finally joined her in London. During their time apart, he'd put out feelers looking for a place for them to move into. Through a friend, he'd managed to find somewhere that was fully furnished, vacant and ready to rent. 'It's perfect for us,' he said, after he'd been to view it. 'And the beauty is, we can move in straight away.'

Elizabeth, who'd been living at the Lanesborough for the best part of two months, couldn't have cared less what it looked like – as long as it wasn't a hotel. But that still didn't stop her being a little surprised when Cole took her to see it. She'd been expecting a trendy apartment in the Docklands;

instead, he brought her to a townhouse in Chelsea Harbour.

'This is all very sensible,' she said, as he showed her around.

He looked pleased. 'I knew you'd like it.'

That wasn't quite what she'd meant, but she let it go. After all, even though the gated development might be a little close to suburbia for her tastes, she could understand why Cole wanted to live there. Behind the faux-Edwardian façade, it was a house designed for contemporary living. Decorated in neutral tones, with minimalist furnishings and an emphasis on light and space, there was every mod con they could have wished for: marble bathrooms with Jacuzzi baths; an integrated Bang & Olufsen sound system; even a cinema room in the basement.

Yes, it would make a pleasant enough home. Plus, it wasn't like she had time to find anything herself. 'How soon can we pay the deposit?' she asked.

The week before William was due back at work, he went to see the doctor, who advised him to stay at home for another three months. Although Elizabeth was sorry that her father wasn't back to full health, there was another part of her that felt secretly pleased to have more time without him around. It meant that she could turn her attention to the real problem facing Melville: how to grow sales. The latest Strategy report proved to be 500 pages of detailed analysis, with no overarching conclusions. In other words, a waste of time. Someone had obviously decided that if they generated enough paper, no one would notice that they didn't have a clue what was going on. That would never have happened when the department was under Cole's control. Well, if the analysis wasn't there, then she'd have to do it herself.

She decided to go back to basics. When she'd first joined Melville, she'd found working in the store gave an invaluable insight into the business. So that's what she'd do now. Spend some time on the shopfloor.

It proved to be a gruelling routine. She would get in at seven, spend three hours holed up in her office going through spreadsheets and reports, before starting her shift as a sales assistant at ten. She worked through until six, when her feet were so sore all she wanted to do was collapse into bed. But instead she went back to her desk, pushing through until she could barely keep her eyes open. Then she headed back home, fell into bed exhausted, only to wake up the next morning and do it all again.

It helped that she could survive on four hours' sleep. But she hardly had time to eat, either. She lost a stone in a month.

Cole wasn't impressed – he'd already thought she was too skinny. In desperation, he started sending over deliveries from the restaurant for lunch and dinner – the only way he could make sure she ate. But even then she would get so caught up in what she was doing that she'd push the container away having barely taken a couple of bites. She was surviving on adrenaline alone. And she was loving it.

Working in the store was a real eye-opener. She noticed how shabby the shopfloor was, compared to the Far East stores she'd opened – the carpets threadbare, the cleaners sloppy, leaving dust on top of the glass cabinets. The assistants took no pride in their appearance, chewing gum and showing up with chipped nail polish.

But mostly she paid attention to the customers.

There were a lot of people browsing, but few making the transition to buy. In some ways she was surprised. Clothing aside – that was Caitlin's domain – there didn't seem to be too much wrong with the stock. She could still see the same good-quality workmanship in the accessories lines that had been there for over 100 years. Why, then, was it not as popular as it had been?

Her answer came one afternoon during the second week, when she served a woman who was returning one of the

Devonshire handbags. The Devonshire was classic Melville: a messenger bag of brown calfskin leather, imprinted with the Melville monogram. At five hundred pounds, it was one of the cheaper items in the line. The same version in ostrich retailed at four times that amount.

Elizabeth served the customer silently. It was Melville policy to honour returns without question. The woman was middle-aged and middle-class, obviously on her lunch-break. She seemed a little nervous, as though this wasn't the kind of shop she'd usually frequent. Elizabeth waited until the refund had gone through, and then asked why she was returning the product.

The woman leaned across the glass counter, as though they were discussing some conspiracy. 'Well, to be honest,' she confided in hushed tones, 'I've always wanted one of the Melville handbags. Working in London in my twenties I could never afford one. So my husband treated me for my fiftieth this year. And I was looking forward to showing it off. But . . .' She hesitated.

'But what?' Elizabeth prompted.

'But then I walked into our local Pharm-Mart and saw exactly the same Melville bag for twenty-five pounds. I mean, I know it wasn't exactly the same,' she said hastily. 'It was one of your cheaper lines, and when you looked closely you could see that. But after that I didn't really want the real thing. It had . . . well, ruined the treat for me, I suppose.'

There was silence.

She saw the look on Elizabeth's face and frowned. 'I'm sorry, dear. Maybe I shouldn't have said anything. This doesn't affect my return, does it?'

Elizabeth forced a smile. 'No, of course not.' She paused. 'And thank you for your help.'

After the shop closed, Elizabeth rushed upstairs to change out of her uniform and then took a cab to Oxford Street, heading straight to the nearest Pharm-Mart. She had been shocked to hear Melville was supplying somewhere like Pharm-Mart. A health and beauty retailer, it was a High Street chain known for its rock-bottom prices – people shopped there because it was cheap and cheerful. It was hardly the kind of image Melville wanted to be associated with. Of course, she knew that the Melville Essentials line, which her father had set up in the seventies, catered to a lower price point. But she hadn't pictured it being *quite* that downmarket . . .

The nearest branch was located at the east end of Oxford Street, towards Tottenham Court Road, sandwiched between burger joints and discount stores selling tie-dye. Inside, the shop compensated for its dreary location with bright colours and a forced cheeriness, the products illuminated under harsh fluorescent strip lighting. The aisles were arranged according to product line – skincare, haircare, dental hygiene . . . At the back, next to the pharmacy, Elizabeth found the so-called 'designer' brands. And there, piled high in a cheap plastic basket, were around fifty rip-offs of the Devonshire handbag, squished together under a huge sign proclaiming £25 *each or 2 for* £40.

This was even worse than she'd imagined. She picked one up, a replica of the handbag that had been returned that afternoon. The feel of the plastic material was unappealing; the catch – shaped into the double-M Melville monogram – felt as though it was about to break. The colours were a little too harsh, and when she rubbed hard enough, the tan-coloured dye came off on her skin. She peered closely at the brand and saw that it was, indeed, the one used by the company. These bags were no fakes. Somewhere, somehow, somebody had produced these on Melville's behalf.

And it wasn't only handbags that Pharm-Mart stocked. There were cheap make-up bags, lighters, even combs. All using the Melville name. All poor quality. How on earth could the company retain its glamorous image when it was associated with this kind of cheap, drugstore product?

She bought two of the most offensive bags. Then spent the rest of the evening walking through Oxford Street seeing which other stores stocked Melville goods.

It was nearly nine by the time Elizabeth got back home. Cole was in their state-of-the-art kitchen, preparing dinner. Ever since he'd set up his restaurant chain Cole had really got into cooking. As the owner, it didn't really matter if he knew one end of a saucepan from another, but he'd always been the kind of guy who liked to go into everything thoroughly. He was never going to be content to sit on the sidelines.

He hadn't had a chance to cook for Elizabeth lately – tonight was the first time she'd been home before midnight since he'd moved to London – and she was impressed by how much he had improved. Tender wagyu beef – 'from a shipment we received in today' – was perfectly complemented by crisp Asian greens. Over dinner and wine, she told him about her findings.

'So what do you think?' she asked, once she'd finished.

'Sounds great.' He switched the heat down on the pan of oil, ready for the banana fritters he was cooking for dessert. Then he walked over and took her wine glass, setting it down on the table. He reached up and brushed a honey-blonde lock away from her face, tucking it behind her ear. 'But, given that this is the first time I've had dinner with my wife in weeks, why don't we forget all about Melville for the rest of the evening.'

His hands moved to her shoulders, his thumbs beginning to massage the tender nook above her collar bone. She closed her eyes, sighing contentedly as his fingers worked their magic.

He leaned down close to her ear. 'I thought we could take dessert upstairs.' His voice was low and inviting. 'I could give you one of my special all-over body massages. It's guaranteed to relieve stress.'

Elizabeth sighed again, but this time it was a sigh of regret. Her eyes fluttered open.

'I'm really sorry, Cole. But I ought to get down some thoughts on what I saw tonight.'

'Can't it wait?'

'I need to do it while it's still fresh in my mind.'

He released her shoulders and turned away. 'Fine.' He walked back to the stove. 'Do you still want dessert?'

'Maybe later.'

Cole's back was to Elizabeth, so she couldn't see his face, but she could tell from the set of his shoulders that he was annoyed. Going over to him, she put her arms around his waist. 'I'm really sorry,' she murmured. 'I'll be as quick as I can and then maybe I can join you upstairs . . .' She trailed off and ran her hands over the front of his trousers.

He stood impassively, stirring the pan. She increased the pressure, until finally he groaned.

'OK, OK,' he relented. 'We can finish this off later.' He reached down and removed her hands. 'But you'd better cut that out now, otherwise I won't be able to wait.'

He bent and kissed her lightly on the forehead. Feeling happier, she went off to her study.

Sometime later, Cole woke to find Elizabeth still wasn't in bed. He rolled over to check the bedside clock: it was three in the morning. Jeez. She couldn't still be working, could she? He considered leaving her to it, but knew he wouldn't be able to get back to sleep until he'd made sure she was all right.

As he walked through the house, he remembered again why he loved it here so much: it felt like a proper home. It was funny how he had begun to appreciate that sort of thing lately. He'd even started to think about children. When he'd first looked round the house, he'd caught himself picturing which room would make a great nursery. Not that he'd dared bring it up with Elizabeth. Last time he had, a couple of months earlier, she'd swiftly reminded him that she was only twenty-eight and that for her, at least, children were still a long way off. He guessed she was right. Ten years ago, when he'd been that age, he'd been working every hour to get to the top. However much he might want a more settled life for them, he was going to have to wait for her to catch up.

He found his wife in the study, curled up on the couch, fast asleep. Melville's Annual Report lay open on the floor beside her. She'd obviously lain down to read it and ended up nodding off. Cole thought about carrying her upstairs to their bed, but he didn't want to risk waking her – she needed all the rest she could get. So instead, he went over to the cupboard and found a blanket to keep her warm.

After he'd tucked the cover around Elizabeth, Cole stood for a moment watching her. Asleep, she looked relaxed and content. He didn't get to see her like this very often these days, and he missed it. As much as he loved Elizabeth for her strength and ambition, it was nice sometimes to know that there was a softer side to her, one that was reserved for him alone. Cole hoped William would be back at work soon. Maybe then she'd ease up a bit and finally find some time for them.

After her trip to Pharm-Mart, Elizabeth started to do some more investigation into Melville Essentials. She quickly realised what the problem was. William's brainchild of creating a line of goods at a lower price point had at first increased turnover for the company *without* harming established sales. But, as the years went by, her father had got greedy. At the peak of Melville's popularity, several manufacturers had approached the company, offering to pay an annual fee in exchange for being able to use the brand name. They were then at liberty to put the Melville name on anything they produced – from plastic key-rings to shoddy knock-off bags. These had cheapened the Melville image, so no one wanted to buy the high-end goods.

Having realised just how deep-rooted the problem was, Elizabeth focused on gathering all the necessary information to help support her case to abolish the low-end Melville Essentials. She was certain that this was the only hope for putting the glamour back into the brand, but she also knew that convincing the board wasn't going to be easy. Essentials represented 50 per cent of current turnover – and, more importantly, it had been her father's idea. Thank God, at least, that he wasn't going to be around for the fight.

She thought carefully about how to begin her presentation. She'd got Piers to do some analysis and learned that while Essentials might account for half of sales, margins were so low that the line only represented ten per cent of profits. But she didn't want to start with the detailed analysis. She needed a way of grabbing their attention straight off.

So she decided to gather together products that defined every decade since Melville began. She spent a long time searching – through the stockroom, and charity shops, as well as the stalls of Portobello and Spitalfields markets – until she had everything together: a potted Retrospective of Melville. Every item told a story about the company and how it had evolved. There were the original handmade leather men's shoes from the 1880s; the boots created especially for the Army during the First World War; the first pair of women's shoes designed in the 1920s; a silk scarf made in the parachute factory that Rosalind, her grandmother, had bought after the Second World War; right through to a dress from the first ready-to-wear collection in the 1960s.

When Elizabeth finally stood in front of the board a fortnight later, she spoke passionately about each item as it was passed round the oval table, from one board member to the next, for inspection. They had no idea what the subject of her presentation was – she'd made sure to keep it under wraps. Today, she wanted the element of surprise on her side. She allowed them time to admire the quality of the material, the superiority of the craftsmanship, the intricacy of the hand-stitched seams. And gradually she could see on all of their faces something that hadn't been there for a long time – passion for their product, a belief and pride in their company. She allowed herself a small smile. This was exactly what she had wanted them to feel.

'And lastly,' she said, 'we have the item that I feel defines how Melville is seen today by the public.'

Elizabeth signalled for her assistant to bring over the final box. She had deliberately packed this, like all of the previous items, in carefully labelled, black satin boxes, the kind that the store used to giftwrap purchases. She made a show of untying the white lace ribbon that decorated the box, easing the lid off carefully, then unwrapping the layers of tissue paper underneath until she finally reached the item that had been packed in the middle. Slowly she eased it out, as though it was precious. The board leaned forward, all of them eager to see what required such careful consideration.

Finally she pulled out the item and held it aloft for everyone to see.

In her hands, Elizabeth cradled the cheap plastic copy of the Devonshire handbag. She could see confusion around the table. She glanced over at her assistant, who went ahead and handed out an identical handbag to every member of the board, letting them inspect it for themselves.

'But this is a cheap knock-off,' Peter Harding, the Marketing Director, burst out.

'Yes, Elizabeth,' Hugh Makin joined in. 'We all know that these illegal copies are sold on the market stall. It's something that every company has to put up with, and there's nothing we can do about it.'

There was a chorus of agreement around the table.

Elizabeth placed both hands on the table, palms flat.

'Actually, gentlemen, that's where you're wrong. Dead wrong.' She paused, waiting for her words to sink in. 'This item is being produced courtesy of our licence agreement with Von Welling, a third-rate German manufacturer, who pays us three million pounds a year to produce handbags just like this. It carries the Melville brand name and it has every right to do so.'

There was a stunned silence.

No one interrupted for the next forty-five minutes, as she skilfully argued her case for closing the Melville Essentials line. She talked about how the number of products had grown from three hundred in the mid-seventies to over twenty thousand today; alarmingly, the vast majority of those weren't being produced directly by Melville, but by third party manufacturers who had bought the licence to produce goods bearing the company's brand. She explained that while there were only twenty-five dedicated Melville stores throughout the world, another four hundred outlets were allowed to sell its goods – such as third-rate department stores, pharmacies and duty-free outlets. She showed pictures of brightly lit, garishly decorated drugstores, with basement buckets filled with cheap Melville branded goods. It made for uncomfortable viewing.

'It's no wonder we can't sell this,' she concluded, holding up the five hundred pound Devonshire handbag, 'when we're selling a twenty-five pound version down the road in a cutprice drugstore.'

She paused for a moment. She knew they were all worried about William's reaction if they agreed to abolish Melville Essentials, but she also knew this was the right step.

'*Meliora Conor*,' she said simply. It was the original Melville motto. *I strive for the best*. 'Striving for the best – isn't that what we should be doing?'

Around the table, the men started to nod. There was no question how everyone was going to vote.

Chapter 40

William was fed up. After a series of angina attacks, his doctor had recommended he stay off work for *another* three months – as though the first hadn't been bad enough. 'You have a very stressful job,' he'd said. 'I really think it would be unwise for you to go back into that high-pressure environment at this time.' William would have happily ignored the advice and gone back anyway, but Isabelle had begged him to listen. 'Please do as he says,' she'd implored. 'I couldn't stand it if anything happened to you.'

Usually, Isabelle had a flair for the dramatic – but this time there had been no tears. The plea had been so simple, so heartfelt, that he was moved to give in.

'Fine,' he'd agreed heavily. 'I'll stay off until after Christmas. But then I'm going back, whatever anyone says.'

That may have satisfied Isabelle. But as the days and weeks dragged by, William found himself growing increasingly irritable – snapping at the doctor, the nurses, the staff and his wife – even his daughters, when they found the time to visit or call. Work had been such a big part of his life for so long, that he had no idea how to fill his time when he was away from the office. He hadn't realised how central it had become to his existence – that his status was so intimately linked with what he did. And what worried him most was that the longer he was away from the company, the more frightened he felt about going back.

That afternoon at the hospital had changed everything for Piers. Hearing William laughing at him with Hugh had been a turning-point. It was as if he was seeing his elder brother clearly for the first time. He'd been hurt that William had excluded him from his discussions with Caitlin, but he'd thought it was simply an oversight. Then to learn that William had such contempt, such a lack of respect for him – after that, Piers had begun to realise precisely what a fool he'd been all these years. He had devoted his life to William – had worked under him, had always put his elder brother's needs first. And none of it had ever been appreciated. William didn't care about him. It was exactly as his mother had said – William *tolerated* him. In that moment, Piers suddenly wished that he had listened to her that night. If he had, instead of arguing with her . . . well, then maybe she'd still be alive.

It was a revelation. All that time, he'd blamed himself for what had happened to her when, in fact, it had, at least in part been William's fault.

After leaving the hospital that particular night, Piers had called up NW8 on his way home and had them send a girl over to his Richmond townhouse. She was supposed to calm him down, but, no matter what she did, he hadn't been able to achieve the release he'd wanted. The longer she'd tried, the more anxious and frustrated he'd grown.

'Look, maybe we ought to call it a night,' she'd said eventually, stifling a yawn. 'It's obviously not happening.'

It was the yawn, followed by a quick little glance at her watch, that set him off. He was paying for this – the least she could do was show him some respect. Without thinking, he'd pulled his hand back and struck her once, hard, across the cheek.

'What the fuck?' she'd yelled, clutching her face.

'I'm sorry,' Piers had spluttered, frightened and appalled by what he'd done. 'I didn't mean to—'

But she wouldn't listen. 'Freak,' she'd spat, before grabbing her clothes and rushing out.

NW8 weren't impressed. Piers was not surprised to receive a call from someone at the company. The anonymous voice had demanded twenty grand compensation for the girl, and informed him that his membership would be immediately terminated. Piers apologised profusely, saying it would never happen again. The voice at the other end of the line didn't sound that interested.

The incident was unfortunate, but it taught him one lesson: that it was important to remain calm, keep his feelings in check and not rush into anything. So he put aside thoughts of confronting William, deciding there were subtler ways to get revenge. Instead he kept up his daily visits to the hospital, continued to act the part of the devoted brother, the part he'd played all these years. Then, back at Melville, he took the board aside and told them that the doctor thought it would be best if William wasn't bothered with news about the company. For now, they should refrain from going in to visit.

As the days went by, he could see William fretting about why no one had come to see him. 'Where's Hugh?' he demanded gruffly at the end of the second week. 'I thought of all the buggers, he'd be here.'

Piers feigned embarrassment. 'I'm sure they'll all be in to see you in a day or two.' But there was no conviction in his voice.

William looked at him with shrewd eyes. 'Well, they'll be lucky if I don't sack the lot of them when I get back,' he said with false bravado.

Piers had counted on the fact that William wouldn't call to ask them where they were. And he was right. His brother had too much pride to beg for a visit. And, feeling vulnerable after his heart-attack, he had lost a lot of his old confidence.

As the weeks passed, William moved back to Aldringham. At first Elizabeth and Caitlin had come down regularly to see him, but as the turnaround began to take up more and more of their time, their visits dwindled and William became increasingly isolated from everyone, apart from Piers. He came to rely on his younger brother for updates on the business. And Piers knew exactly what to say to unnerve him.

'You've got absolutely nothing to worry about, old chap. Elizabeth has taken control of everything.'

William scowled. 'Oh?'

'She's doing a fabulous job, everyone says so. Reminds me of Mother in a lot of ways.'

Piers watched William's face turn white.

'Although of course you're missed,' he said quickly – too quickly to give William any real reassurance. He left soon after that, allowing William time to brood.

The following weekend, when he went to visit, the first thing William wanted to know was what exactly Elizabeth was up to.

'Oh, nothing much,' Piers said, deliberately vague. 'I really shouldn't have said anything.'

'Well, you did say something. And now I want to know what's going on.'

This time, Piers tried to be hearty. 'Nothing you need concern yourself with now, while you're still recovering.'

'Piers.' William's voice was firm and threatening. 'Tell me.'

His brother gave a quick, worried glance towards the door, as though expecting Isabelle to walk back in. 'Well, if you insist,' he said reluctantly. 'I suppose the biggest move has been getting rid of Melville Essentials.'

William's hands clenched into two fists. 'Melville Essentials?' he choked out. 'The board agreed to get rid of Melville Essentials?'

'Yes, it was a unanimous decision,' Piers began. Then, seeing the look on William's face, he stopped. 'Oh, God.' He assumed a pained expression. 'I knew I shouldn't have said anything. Now I've upset you.'

William quickly shook his head. 'No, no,' he insisted. 'I'm

not upset. Just ... surprised.' He swallowed deeply. 'Now, come on. Fill me in on exactly what's been happening.'

For the next hour, that was precisely what Piers did.

He had everything carefully planned. If anyone at Melville asked him whether it would be all right to visit William, he gave them the same story.

'Maybe in a few weeks,' he'd say regretfully. 'He's still very weak.'

They'd nod sagely in agreement, relieved that they didn't have to go down to Aldringham. Instead, they'd ask Piers to pass along their best wishes to William – which he always made sure to do, because it reminded his brother that no one had come to see him.

Chapter 41

Caitlin stared down at her sketchpad. It was blank. The bin next to her desk was filled with balled-up sheets of paper, ideas she'd started and then discarded. She had been made Head Designer three months ago. The title seemed to be a curse. From that day onwards, she'd lost all creativity.

Despite her success in New York, working at Melville was a whole different league. Speculation in the press was that she wouldn't be able to pull it off. Tatler had recently run a piece on the company, with the pessimistic headline *The Demise of an English Institution.*

Appointing an untried name like Caitlin O'Dwyer was always going to be a risk, the article concluded. *Let's hope it doesn't turn out to be the final nail in the company's coffin.*

At first Melville's design team had looked hopefully at Caitlin, seeing her as their saviour. But as the days went on, those looks had turned to disappointment and then scorn. Jess was the only one who seemed to have kept faith. Every now and then she would pop her head around the door of Caitlin's office.

'Any luck?' she'd ask.

'Nothing yet,' Caitlin would be forced to reply, trying to ignore the way the girl's face fell.

Caitlin could understand the team's frustration. She'd been doing so well in New York, so what was happening now? Even she wasn't sure. She supposed she had no track record working on something of this scale. But that was no comfort to her team.

Melville was in trouble. Rumours of redundancies grew daily. Already, three of the most experienced design assistants had left for other jobs. She needed to prove herself to the others, earn their respect. And she wasn't going to do that unless she had some damned good ideas. And soon.

But every day she'd sit down purposefully at her desk, get her sketchbook out and sharpen her pencil, poised to go to work and then . . . nothing. She had no inspiration or vision. She responded by pushing herself twice as hard. She was in by eight in the morning and stayed until late into the night. But all she got for her efforts were more and more balls of paper in the bin beside her desk.

Worst of all, there was no one she could confide in. She didn't want to bother William with her problems. Elizabeth was busy with her own work. Her friends were all back in New York and so far she hadn't had a chance to make any in London.

At the next monthly board meeting she presented her first set of designs, cobbled together because she had to come up with *something*. They were passed along the table, submitted to the silent scrutiny of the board members. No one looked impressed.

'They're just a first stab,' Caitlin said, hating the trace of desperation in her voice. 'By next time I should have something more concrete to show you.'

Her platitudes were met with disappointed silence.

After the meeting wrapped up, Elizabeth took her to one side. 'What's going on?' She seemed genuinely concerned. 'Is there anything wrong?'

Caitlin was at a loss to explain. 'No, not really. It's just . . . taking a little longer than I expected to come up with something.'

Elizabeth frowned. 'Right, I understand,' she said, even though it was clear that she didn't. 'Just – well, let me know if you need any help, OK?'

She gave Caitlin an encouraging smile and left her to it.

Caitlin sighed. Her half-sister's patient understanding had made her feel even more wretched. Everyone was counting on her. And she needed to start delivering.

So Caitlin set back to work, feeling even more stress and pressure than before. She made herself a strong coffee and sat determinedly at her desk, waiting for brilliance to strike. At six o'clock, the design room started emptying out. Now, she thought. Now, I'll be able to get down to some serious work.

But two hours later she was about ready to give up. She looked down at what she'd drawn – it was uninspired and unoriginal. In frustration, she stabbed her pencil onto the page, breaking the lead. Great.

She pulled open her desk drawer with such ferocity that it came straight out of its runners. She pushed it back in and started to rifle through the mess for a sharpener. And there, nestling among the papers and pens, as though it had been waiting for a moment just like this, a moment of weakness, was the folded-up article she had torn out of that magazine weeks earlier: the one about Lucien and his current exhibition in London.

That Sunday at Aldringham had been the first she'd heard of Lucien being in England. The article, which she'd just had to read, had told her that he'd moved here the previous year. Apparently the London art scene was far stronger than that in Paris these days, what with the English media and art dealers making stars out of trendy British artists like Tracey Emin and Damien Hirst.

As soon as she'd got back to Eaton Square that night, she'd called Alain.

'Why didn't you tell me he was here?' she'd asked, hurt and upset.

She could almost hear his little Gallic shrug. 'I thought it was for the best.'

Now she stared at the address of the gallery where Lucien was exhibiting for a long moment. He probably knows you're in London, too, the logical part of her brain said. And if he hasn't been in touch, then that must mean he doesn't want to see you.

To hell with it, she decided. It was time she started fighting for what she wanted. Then she glanced down at herself. Her white T-shirt was stained with today's lunch, she wasn't wearing any make-up; and the last time she'd checked, her hair needed a wash.

Standing in front of the mirror in the Ladies room half an hour later, Caitlin wished, not for the first time, that she was more like Elizabeth. Nothing ever phased her sophisticated, organised half-sister. She would have been fully prepared for a moment like this, an unexpected rendezvous with an old . . . friend. Would have had make-up with her, a change of clothes. Or, better still, she wouldn't have left the house looking such a mess in the first place.

Caitlin had improvised as best she could. She'd raided the studio, finally finding make-up and a comb left over from the last fashion show. The blusher and lipstick gave some colour to her otherwise pale, tired face. There wasn't much she could do about her hair, but at least the new cut was meant to look messy.

Clothes were a problem. Curvaceous rather than model thin, none of the samples in the studio were going to fit her. She finally found a black satin shirt from the previous year's collection, which matched her long skirt perfectly. She'd never much liked the loose fit of the shirt before, but because it was made for a model — and was therefore several sizes too small for her — it actually ended up looking OK, clinging to her curves.

Finally happy with how she looked, she went outside to find a taxi.

'Where to?' the driver asked once she was settled.

'The Borden Gallery, in Hoxton.'

At that time of night, it was only a twenty-minute drive to East London and the gallery where Lucien was currently exhibiting. Maybe the cab driver hadn't heard of it, but Caitlin was impressed. Situated on the ever-so-trendy Hoxton Square, the Borden Gallery was small but select. An airy space of white walls, glass corridors and exquisitely lit exhibition halls, the Gallery had made its name from spotting the Next Big Thing. And Lucien was it.

Hoxton and Shoreditch were where the London art scene was centred nowadays. Like Belleville, the area was a former enclave of the working classes and, also like Belleville, it was steadily gentrifying. Avant-garde yuppies and the artistic set had moved into recently renovated warehouses, bringing bars, restaurants and clubs with them, and making Hoxton Square the hub of present-day bohemia. Where else would Lucien be?

'Hi, I'm Zara. Can I help you with anything?'

Caitlin glanced round to see a young, hip assistant flashing a megawatt sales smile. She took a deep breath. 'I hope so. I'm an old friend of Lucien's. Do you know if he's in today?'

The girl's smile cooled several degrees. 'He's around somewhere.' It was said with a total lack of enthusiasm. Zara was used to women coming in here and asking for Lucien. She nodded across the room. 'In fact, there he is now.'

Caitlin felt her heart speed up. She turned . . . and yes, there he was, deep in conversation with a young couple – potential customers, she guessed. Five years and he hadn't changed. He was still dark and dramatic, still the most charismatic man she had ever seen. She hung back, needing a second to compose herself.

He must have felt her eyes on him, because at that moment he looked up. There was nothing for it now, no chance to run away, even if she wanted to. His gaze met hers. For a moment he simply stared. If he was surprised to see her, he didn't show it.

He turned back to his customers, and for a horrible moment Caitlin thought he might ignore her altogether. But then she realised he was simply excusing himself, and the next minute he was walking over towards her.

'Lucien . . .' She stumbled over his name.

'Hello, Caitlin.' He was coolly formal, completely in control, almost as though he'd been expecting her to turn up like this one day, out of the blue.

She couldn't help feeling disappointed by his lack of enthusiasm. She wasn't sure what she'd been expecting. Some grand reunion? Maybe at least a hint of how close they'd once been. But Lucien was all business. They exchanged the prerequisite kiss on each cheek. Caitlin tried not to notice how quickly he pulled away from her. He really didn't seem surprised to see her. He didn't seem . . . well, anything. Not exactly pleased, but not annoyed, either.

'I heard you were exhibiting in London,' she said. He hadn't asked why she was here, but she felt she ought to explain. 'I thought I'd come over and see the gallery . . . and you as well.' She fought the urge to ask if he'd known she was in London. What would be the point? If he hadn't . . . well, they were talking now, so what did it matter? And if he had then it was best not to go there.

He still hadn't said anything, so she rushed on, before her courage failed her and she ran out. 'I wondered if you wanted to go for a drink – you know, to catch up.'

There was a silence. Was he going to tell her to get lost?

But instead he said, '*Oui, d'accord.*' He looked at his watch. 'The gallery closes at ten. There's a bar across the street. Why don't you wait for me there?' With that, he turned and walked away. It wasn't the most promising start. But it would get better. It had to get better.

Caitlin found the bar easily enough. One of the many hip drinking establishments that surrounded Hoxton Square, it had that raw, urban feel associated with the area – exposed brickwork, scratched-up furniture and low lighting. A slice of SoHo cool. It was like being back in Belleville again, except this was a more studied attempt at cool. Friday night and there were probably more lawyers and bankers in the crowd than media and art types.

It took twenty minutes to get served, then another ten to find a free booth – by which time she'd been jostled so much that half the drinks had spilled on the floor. She'd hoped to have some time to pull herself together, but she'd only taken a few sips of her rather warm white wine when Lucien appeared, dark and unsmiling. She'd left room for him to sit next to her, but he slid onto the bench opposite instead.

'You came,' she said.

He raised an eyebrow. 'You thought I would stand you up?'

In fact, it had crossed her mind. 'No, of course not,' she lied.

'Well, it did not even occur to me.' He paused, before adding pointedly, 'But maybe that's because running away has never been my style.'

Ouch, Caitlin thought, as the jibe hit home. It was becoming apparent that Lucien wasn't in the mood to forgive or forget.

Cool air pumped out from huge vents above them, but in the crush of hard, sweaty bodies it still felt hot. Caitlin slipped off her jacket. She felt Lucien's eyes move over her. Because the shirt was so tight across her breasts, the top button kept popping open, and she was suddenly aware of the somewhat plunging neckline. She pulled self-consciously at the fabric, but secretly felt pleased that he wasn't as immune as he wanted her to think.

She pushed the beer towards him. 'Here.' She tried a smile. 'I'm not sure if I got the right kind.'

He gave a curt nod, didn't return the smile. Sensing the conversation was being left up to her, Caitlin searched for something to say. She gulped down some wine and hoped its anaesthetising qualities would start working soon.

'Alain filled me in on what you've been up to,' she said, settling on the most neutral topic she could think of – his work. 'It sounds like you've done very well for yourself.'

He inclined his head in acknowledgement of the compliment. 'You haven't done so badly either.'

So he'd followed her career, too.

'I didn't realise you were in London until I saw that article in the *Observer*,' she said, feeling bolder. 'You probably didn't know I was here . . .'

His blue eyes met hers. 'I knew.'

That put her in her place. The awkward silence returned. She downed some more wine, thought about ordering another glass and then decided getting drunk might not be the best way to deal with the evening.

She searched around for another topic. 'I'm working here now,' she volunteered. 'At Melville.'

'Yes,' he interrupted. 'Your *family's* business.'

Yet another sore point, she thought, trying hard not to feel flustered. 'Oh, right,' she said neutrally. 'I never told you about that, did I? It wasn't a big deal.'

'I'm sure it wasn't.' He paused. 'To you.' He took a sip of his beer. 'And how is it – working at Melville?'

'Not as easy as I thought,' she said with feeling.

'And why is that?'

For the first time since they'd met that evening, he seemed interested in something. Well, if he really wanted to know . . .

She started to talk. And as she talked, she could see him beginning to relax a little. She found herself telling him about moving to London, finding Melville's Design Department in such a mess, getting the go-ahead to make changes, and now the problems she was having seeing them through. He had the implicit understanding of a fellow artist.

'It will come to you in the end, *chérie*,' he told her. 'My advice: relax. Stop worrying. Only then, when you least expect it, will inspiration strike.'

Somehow his understated assurances made her feel better than she could have imagined. After that, conversation was easy. He caught her up on his career, the galleries he was exhibiting in. She knew most of the details already, but was happy to hear it all again. They moved onto mutual friends. Both were still in touch with Alain and a few others from their Belleville days. They reminisced without mentioning what had transpired between them all those years ago.

Despite the quality of the wine, one drink turned into two and then three. By midnight, Caitlin was feeling light-headed and brave.

'Another drink?' she asked, indicating the nearly empty bottle in front of Lucien.

She saw a guarded look come over his face. 'I don't think so, Caitlin.' He waited a beat, then said, 'In fact, I think I should go.'

She chose to ignore the warning tone in his voice. 'Oh, come on,' she chided him lightly. 'You can't leave yet. It's still early.'

'I'm meeting someone,' he said abruptly.

For a moment, Caitlin felt confused. Meeting someone? But it was so late. Then it dawned on her. A girl, of course.

'Right.' She could feel a blush rising in her cheeks, guessed that he could see it too. 'Sorry. I understand. Of course, you should go.'

He stood up. 'Come on. I'll make sure you get a cab.'

She'd been hoping for a quick escape, but it soon became apparent that wasn't going to happen. It was Friday night, as the pubs turned out. There wasn't a black cab in sight. They stood for an increasingly painful ten minutes of silence until a taxi finally, mercifully, pulled up. Lucien held the door open for her. She went to get in and then stopped, not wanting to leave it this way between them.

'Can I see you again?' As soon as the question was out of her mouth she regretted it. Especially when he didn't answer at first, just stared at her, with those piercing blue eyes. She should never have said anything, he clearly wasn't interested. But now that she had started . . .

'It's just that I don't really know anyone here, in London,' she added hastily. 'So if you had a spare evening to go out, grab a drink or some dinner, you'd be doing me a favour—'

'OK,' he cut into her babbling. 'I will call you sometime.'

He slammed the car door closed before she could say anything else. There was a finality to the sound. As the cab drove away, she couldn't help thinking it would probably be the last time she saw him.

It was a week before he called. By then, she'd given up hope that he was ever going to get in touch.

He got straight to the point. 'A friend of mine's performing at Shunt tonight. Have you heard of it?'

'Yes, of course.' It was an off-beat performance art venue, deep in the tunnels under London Bridge station. 'But I've never been,' she said quickly.

'Well, now's your chance. I have a spare ticket for tonight. Would you like to come?'

'I'd love to,' she said warmly.

'Good.' He was brusque. 'I'll see you outside at ten, then.'

With no further pleasantries, he rang off. For a long time afterwards, Caitlin sat at her desk, trying to analyse what the call meant. By the time it got to the evening, she was still no closer to knowing. But it was a start, at least.

Chapter 42

Amber brought her sin red Ferrari screeching to a halt in the Santa Monica beach parking lot. The car took up three spaces, but she didn't care. Driving had never been her forte. She pulled the rearview mirror round to check her appearance – frowning at the dark circles under her eyes and her dry frizz of hair. The bleach she used to maintain the white blonde was doing a world of damage. Making a mental note to book an appointment with Sheri Eskridge at Art Luna to get that fixed, she grabbed her Gucci bag and headed over to where the camera crew, stylists and make-up team were waiting.

She was halfway there when Rich intercepted her. He wasn't in a good mood.

'You're over two hours late,' he said tersely. 'You better get ready to do some serious grovelling. Derek isn't fucking happy – and that's a direct quote.'

She was meant to be filming a TV advert for Glamour cosmetics today. Derek Moss was directing, and he was a stickler for punctuality. The idea was to show her spending a day at the beach, with the highly unoriginal slogan of '*Make-up that lasts as long as you do*'. Derek had run through the images he wanted to use earlier in the week: Amber on the Pier, all popcorn and cotton candy, playing in the penny arcade; then jogging along the South Bay bicycle trail; cooling off in the bluer than blue Pacific waters; shopping in the Third Street Promenade. Then they were supposed to come back tonight at sunset and film her going for a romantic walk along the long, wide beach, sinking her toes into the soft sand.

It was Sunday morning and he'd wanted to start early, before the place started to fill up. The call had been for seven. It was nine now and already starting to get busy. Amber, like everyone else on the shoot, had known it was going to be hard enough filming everything without the usual onlookers gawping at them and getting inadvertently caught in the shots . . . tourists, joggers, bikers and bladers, as well as the LA uptown girls who came to top up their tans. But Amber was damned if she was going to apologise.

She spat her chewing gum onto the sand and Rich frowned. Santa Monica beach prided itself on its cleanliness and there were bins everywhere. But as usual she took no notice.

'Didn't you tell him I was sick?' She pushed her over-sized Chanel sunglasses onto her head.

'Yes, I did.' He waited a beat before continuing. 'Unfortunately, one of the crew saw you out last night with Johnny. So now I look like a liar and you look very not fuck-ing bothered about your contract with Glamour.'

Amber rolled her eyes. Rich had been on her back a lot lately, mainly about Johnny. Her manager wasn't exactly keen on her new beau. In fact, he'd made his feelings on the subject abundantly clear. *Johnny isn't good enough for you. He's dragging you down. You can't keep partying like this for ever. I'm worried about you.*

Bull. Shit.

She knew what was really getting up Rich's nose. He didn't like that she had someone else special in her life. She'd been with Johnny for three months now – in LA that was pretty much a lifetime. That week she'd been in England, after her dad's heart-attack, he'd called her every day. Once she'd got back, they'd hooked up properly, and she'd never regretted it. Johnny was so cool, so sure of himself. And he wasn't tied up in the same old tired scene. He liked to keep it real. The people he invited round to her place weren't the same old faces – they were *ordinary* people, who he'd got talking to in bars, restaurants and clubs. They just wanted to hang out and party. Sometimes Johnny would get his guitar out and they'd start jamming, smoking some of the finest dope Amber had ever had.

He was all about living for the moment, not worrying too much about the next day. So, yeah, maybe they were partying hard at the moment. But what was the big deal? She was still young. Most twenty-two-year-olds cut loose at some point.

But Rich didn't see it that way. They'd had a flaming argument on that very subject last week. He'd been building up to it for a while, and he'd finally exploded when she'd crawled in for a photo shoot at *Vogue* after only two hours' sleep.

'It's un-fucking-acceptable for you to turn up with blood-shot eyes and an acne break-out,' he'd yelled.

'Why don't you stay the fuck out of my business?' she'd screamed back.

The argument had raged on in front of the gruesomely fascinated photographers and magazine staff. It had ended in tears – from both of them. Amber had apologised, given him a huge hug, and they'd sworn that it would never happen again. But now, less than five days later, Amber had a feeling Rich was about to start in on another lecture.

She stifled a yawn. God, she was tired. She'd come straight here from the club. She'd been chewing the gum to hide the smell of alcohol. She put her hand to her hair, matted and tangled after hours on the sweaty dance floor. She knew she didn't exactly look her best this morning, but it was nothing half an hour in the make-up artist's chair wouldn't cure. And Johnny had slipped her some speed before she came out here. It was in her purse, so she could take it later when she started to fade. She had everything under control. Rich was just over-reacting, as usual. And she wasn't in a mood to pacify him.

'Hey, take a Valium, Rich.' Her eyes glittered wickedly. 'Or, should I say, take another one. Who's the star around here? Glamour's lucky to have me. I had lots of other offers and I chose this one because they made it worth my while. What was it they said, to justify how much they were paying?' She pretended to think. Finally, her expression cleared. 'Oh, yes. That's right. "There's only one Amber Melville." And as far as I can see, there still is. So, I'm a little late?' She gave a careless shrug of her petite shoulders. 'What does it really matter?'

She didn't give Rich a chance to answer back. Instead, she tossed her car keys at him, like he was a valet.

'Anyway, can you make yourself useful and get someone to watch the car? I don't want to come back and find scratches all over it.'

With that, she turned and flounced off. If she'd bothered to glance back, she'd have seen the thunderous look on her agent's face. It was going to take all his willpower not to take her stupid keys and scrape them along the length of the bonnet himself.

Johnny stretched out on the sunlounger next to Amber's heated pool. Not that the pool needed heating at this, or any other time of year. It was lunchtime on another scorching California day. The faint breeze wasn't even strong enough to rustle the leaves on the palm trees.

Johnny loved it here in Beverly Hills, with its candy-coloured mansions and manicured lawns. It was all about the image of perfection, which suited him just fine. He hardly ever bothered going back to his comparatively modest Brentwood condo now. What was the point, when this place was so great? There was a tranquil, rarefied atmosphere up here in Summit Circle, with its fresh, pine-scented air and panoramic views of the cityscape below. Even now, despite not having slept for the best part of forty-eight hours, he felt relaxed, chilled.

The maid came over with his Bloody Mary. 'Here you go, *señor*.'

He watched as she set the glass down on the table next to him, complete with a celery stick and Tabasco sauce. It was five-star treatment all the way chez Amber Melville. A cook, butler and fulltime maid – although he would have happily done without the first two and just stuck with the maid, he decided, as she straightened up. With her dark skin, dark hair and dark eyes, she clearly hailed from over the border, down Mexico way. Her Latin American beauty was an antidote to all the pneumatic blondes that were a-dime-a-dozen here.

'Thanks . . .' He paused, waiting for a name.

'Rosita,' she filled in for him.

'Thanks, Rosita,' he said.

She gave him an inviting smile, the kind he could read a mile off, turned and sashayed away. He watched her full, round buttocks undulating beneath the thin material of the maid's out-fit and felt a hard-on stirring in his pants – which was exactly where it needed to stay. He couldn't afford to piss Amber off. Right now, she was his meal-ticket.

Yeah, everyone always assumed he was loaded. He'd made some best-selling albums, so he must be, right? Wrong. By the time everyone else had taken their cut – the record company, the studio, the promoters, his manager, the other band members – there hadn't been all that much left for him. What there was, he'd managed to get through all too easily. Maintaining his lifestyle, keeping up appearances . . . It wasn't like he could check into Motel Six. He was currently forking out twenty-eight thousand dollars a month in rent. That was rapidly depleting his already precarious bank balance. Then there were the nights out. Everyone expected him to pick up the tab. And why wouldn't they? He was the big pop star, after all. It wasn't like he could start asking everyone to chip in for gas.

Even he'd been shocked when his grim-faced accountant had told him how much he had left. It had almost made him think twice about the wisdom of breaking up the band. But he'd wanted to go solo for a while – he'd always been the real star, after all. Like he'd told the guys, 'I want to get away from the Brit Pop scene, do something cooler, maybe some rock, a little soul . . .'

After the band split, he'd got a new manager. His first piece of advice: 'Head out to LA.' Johnny wasn't about to argue. Relaunching himself in the States sounded ideal. Crack the US market and he'd be made.

Life in LA had been great at first. His manager, Brett, had made the appropriate calls, so the right people knew he was in town and looking to cut a deal. Everyone recognised his face, and there was a buzz around him. Sharp-suited record execs took him for power lunches at the Ivy and Spago; girls threw themselves at him – and these were great-looking girls, taut, tanned wannabe actresses and models, not like the English groupies with their cellulite thighs and muffin tops spilling out of their Top Shop jeans. He was invited to all the right parties; when he went into clubs and bars, he was shown to the best seats.

But as the months went on, the invitations began to dry up. It was becoming obvious that no one actually wanted to sign him. They'd all been happy to meet up, but only to suss out whether their competition had seen an angle on him that they'd missed. When his manager had pushed for a commitment, though, the response had been underwhelming. There was a lot of chat about ex-band members 'not always making great soloists', and wanting 'to wait for the dust to settle on the split'. But Johnny – and his bank manager – couldn't afford to wait. He knew his shelf life. He needed to make his move now, while Kaleidoscope was still considered a hot property. Otherwise, he might as well start thinking about alternative career paths, like sweeping floors.

And then he'd finally caught a break: meeting Amber Melville.

He hadn't realised who she was at first. He'd been so wasted in Les Deux that night that he'd assumed she was just another pretty girl giving him the eye. It was only when he'd got back to her place that he'd begun to realise she was worth more than a one-night stand. His manager had been ecstatic.

'Holy shit! Amber Melville! This is the PR coup we've been looking for!'

Under Brett's excited direction, he'd been his especially charming self, got her number and called her religiously while she was in England. When she got back the following week he'd booked a booth at Fred 62 – guaranteed to get you photographed. The next day, pictures of them making eyes over a milkshake were splashed across every celebrity magazine, with the strapline: *Are Amber and Johnny an item?* It kind of bugged him that her name came first, but he'd been able to live with it. After all, this was the most exposure he'd had in months.

Their respective PR machines went to work, with the usual protestations that they were 'just good friends'. It was like issuing a challenge to the vulture press to prove otherwise. An anonymous tip-off to every reporter in town, and Johnny was photographed leaving Amber's place early one morning, in the same clothes he'd been wearing the night before at Teddy's. Later that day, they issued a joint statement saying that they were together, but would appreciate it if the paparazzi gave them their privacy. Suddenly they couldn't move for photographers.

Things were finally starting to look up for Johnny. He was back in the media spotlight. And hanging out with Amber wasn't exactly a chore: she was gorgeous and fun. The record companies had tentatively started getting back in touch. It was only a matter of time before he signed something big. Then he could do what – and who – the hell he liked. He just needed to keep the wolf from the door for now. And that meant finding some way to cut costs, without looking as though he was trying to.

He was still lying outside when Amber got back a few hours later. Stripping off her clothes, she dropped onto the sun-lounger next to him, naked apart from a tiny pink thong, and started telling him about her day – Rich had pissed her off again for some reason. The sooner *that* loser got out of the picture the better, as far as Johnny was concerned. He tuned out until she finally shut up.

'And what about you?' She rolled onto her back and threw a hand across her eyes. 'What have you been up to?'

He propped himself up on one elbow and gazed down at her pert breasts and long, shapely legs. He could live with this, he decided, laying his free hand across her flat belly. 'Actually, babe, I've been doing a bit of thinking while you were out.'

'Hmmm?' It was more of a purr than a word. He grinned, knowing what her answer was going to be even before he'd asked the question.

'Why don't I move in with you?'

Chapter 43

When it came to her designs, Caitlin decided to take Lucien's advice. 'Relax,' he'd told her that night in Hoxton. 'Stop worrying. Only then, when you are least expecting it, will inspiration strike.' She didn't particularly like the idea of taking a break when she was so far behind, but as nothing else had worked, she might as well give that a try.

So the following weekend, instead of heading down to Aldringham as planned, she spent Saturday and Sunday seeing London through the eyes of a tourist. From the National Gallery to the Victoria and Albert Museum, and then onto the Tower of London, she took in the sights, trying to recapture the heart of the city.

Monday morning, she called up Jess. 'I'm not coming in today,' she told her.

'Oh?' The design assistant sounded concerned. 'Nothing's wrong, is it?'

In fact, Caitlin had decided that a day away from the accusing eyes of the workroom staff might help her creative block. So she wrapped up warmly and took her sketchbook to Hyde Park. And there, sitting on a bench by the Serpentine, she managed to achieve something that she hadn't for a long time – she got lost in her drawings. Before, back in Melville's offices, she'd tried to think of a new skirt or a new dress. Now, she drew an impression, a feeling, a mood, not really concentrating on the garments, not worrying about whether it was right for the Collection. She drew for the simple pleasure of creating.

It was only later that night, once she was back at Eaton Square, that she began to realise how good the drawings were. There was something . . . *different* in there, something she hadn't seen for a long time. London played a strong part – but from years gone by. It was a London of masked balls, rakish highwaymen robbing foppish gentlemen and their heaving-bosomed wives, overcrowded streets filled with bawdy wenches, Nell Gwyn and the depravity of Charles II's court. These weren't detailed sketches of garments – they were full pictures, life scenes. But there was no mistaking the presence of the clothing in the background, like a grand costume drama.

Caitlin felt the first buzz of a revelation.

Back at Melville, she called the design team together. Perching on one of the pattern-cutting tables, she watched as they pulled up chairs. Disillusioned, jaded faces stared up at her.

'I know the last few months haven't been easy,' she began.

A few people exchanged knowing looks. Rumours of redundancies had been circulating. They thought that was why she'd called them together.

Caitlin hopped down from the table and stood in front of them, hands on hips.

'Well, today is where that ends,' she said firmly. 'To make Melville Apparel a success, we need to reinvent it as a lifestyle brand. And this is how we're going to do it.'

She had their attention now. Across the room, people were sitting up straighter, removing gum and reaching for a pen and paper as she started to outline her ideas. Back in its heyday, she reminded them, Melville had been the brand of movie stars and jetsetters. She wanted to appeal to the glitterati once again. To do this, she would fuse the past with the present to create a sensual, decadent look; expensive and flamboyant. She summed it up in one sentence.

'When those models come down the catwalk, I want them

to look like Restoration courtesan meets modern A-list celebrity.'

All around her, the design team started to talk at once.

That was the easy part. Now Caitlin had the seed of an idea, she needed to grow that into an entire collection: from clothes to shoes to handbags and other accessories. She had never felt so exhausted and exhilarated in her life. Apart from the help of her small team, she was on her own, designing everything alone. In some ways that was best. It meant she had total artistic control.

She focused in on her original drawings, favouring the ones threaded with the hint of seduction. This idea of the upper-class vamp, the anti-heroine in historical novels and costume dramas . . . she would use that as her springboard and then translate it into a wardrobe for a sensual modern woman.

Caitlin looked everywhere for inspiration, watching old movies again and again, trying to capture the mood she wanted for the fashion show. Film adaptations of Daphne du Maurier's *Frenchman's Creek* and Kathleen Winsor's *Forever Amber*, were among her favourites. Visually sumptuous, the lavish costumes were a constant source of ideas. She fell in love with an emerald-green velvet cape and transformed it into a thigh-length swing coat, complete with faux-sable lining. A cloth-of-gold gown became a cute cocktail dress, retaining the dramatic neckline – low, wide and dropped on the shoulders – while bringing the full skirt up above the knee, so it flared out like a ballerina's tutu.

'I want to create corsets,' she declared late one Friday evening to the design team, who were growing used to her outbursts. 'Proper lace-up, boned corsets – the type that give the wearer a perfect hour-glass figure.'

That weekend, she tasked her assistants with watching the Margaret Lockwood version of *The Wicked Lady* – a movie about an aristocrat who relieves the tedium of her genteel life by becoming a highwaywoman. When the team came in on Monday morning and found sketches of a strapless dress in black leather, with a pencil skirt and lace-up bodice top, they knew precisely where the idea had come from.

At the next board meeting, an uncomfortable silence fell across the room as Caitlin handed round her latest sketches. After last time, no was expecting much. Caitlin didn't say anything about her new designs. She'd decided it was best to let her work speak for itself.

She watched the directors closely to monitor their reaction. Initial indifference turned to interest, followed by murmurs of excitement as they passed the sketches around.

It was Elizabeth who spoke first. Concerned that Caitlin might not be able to pull off a show on the scale Melville needed, she had secretly been putting feelers out, trying to see if she could get anyone decent to take over as Head Designer. Now, thankfully, there would be no need to go down that route.

'These are good,' she said. It was exactly what she'd hoped for – a lavish, upscale collection, dramatic and glamorous – a true break with Melville's current dreary image. There was undisguised admiration in her eyes as she went on: 'I mean, these designs are amazing. Absolutely perfect.'

Caitlin felt a rush of pride mixed with relief. 'Obviously you won't get the full impact just from a drawing,' she said hastily. 'Without the feel and drape of the fabric, it's hard to bring the garments to life.'

No, no, Elizabeth and the directors rushed to assure her; they could see perfectly well what the collection would be like. They might not be fashion experts, but even their untrained eyes could see that they were in the presence of something truly extraordinary. Years of beige and brown were being replaced with blood red and ebony black; tweed and linen by velvet and lace; tailored suits and sensible knitwear were making way for low-slung trousers and lavish gowns.

The board spent another half an hour discussing Caitlin's work before the meeting finally wound up. Elizabeth, rushing off for a conference call, still found time to congratulate her sister. 'You're doing a great job.' She gave Caitlin's arm a reassuring squeeze. 'Whatever inspired you – make sure you hold onto it.'

It was exactly what Madame had said to her, all those years ago when she'd looked at Caitlin's pieces for the final show. Then, as now, Caitlin had Lucien to thank for putting her on the right path.

Collecting up her sketches, she headed downstairs to the workroom. As soon as she got through the door, she was surrounded. After her two-hour absence, the design team had already come up with a hundred new questions.

'OK, OK.' She held her hands up. 'One at a time, guys.' But she was secretly delighted with their enthusiasm. It looked like this might work out, after all.

Getting board approval for her designs was only the start for Caitlin. Now, the sample garments needed to be made up, models selected and brought in for fittings, and a suitable venue chosen to show the collection. Caitlin had already decided against using Melville's showroom as she wanted this to be a firm break with the past. And, even though work was unrelenting, she was happy – because she finally felt as though she was on the right track for Melville.

But while her professional life was going well, her personal life seemed to be as much of a mess as ever. Since that first night at the gallery, she had seen quite a lot of Lucien. They met up once or twice a week, hanging out in the clubs and pubs of Curtain Road and Old Street. But it was always in a crowd, and the conversation never involved anything personal.

Tonight, she'd finally got him to agree to go for dinner with her – just the two of them. They were meeting at CRU, near the gallery. It was casual, a late tapas supper in the bar. 'I can't stay long,' he'd emphasised on the phone when they'd arranged it. But time alone together seemed like a step forward at least.

Caitlin had on her usual workroom attire – jeans and a T-shirt, her battered trainers. In her bag, she'd brought make-up and a change of clothes for the evening. But now she suddenly couldn't be bothered to make an effort. He never seemed to notice how she looked these days anyway. She simply pulled her hair into a loose ponytail, then paused in front of the mirror for a moment, something disconcerting her. It suddenly came to her. With her hair tied back, she looked younger – almost exactly the way she had in Belleville. Well, maybe turning back the clock would help. It surely couldn't hurt.

Three hours later, Caitlin had to concede that the evening wasn't turning out quite as she'd planned. At the last minute, Lucien had cancelled on dinner, telling her that he'd forgotten a prior commitment to meet some friends at Cargo in Rivington Street.

'Can I come along?' she'd asked, unwilling to abandon the evening quite yet.

Lucien had answered with a noncommittal, 'If you want.'

It wasn't the most enthusiastic response, but she'd arranged to meet him there anyway.

Cargo was currently one of the hippest clubs in East London. Built into the railway arches of the Kingsland viaduct, it attracted some of the best DJs in Europe. It was the first time Caitlin had been there, and she wasn't sure she liked it much. She'd hung out with Lucien at nearby 333 before, which she'd loved – it had been very laid-back and low-key. But this place seemed much more self-consciously cool.

Her mood wasn't helped by the fact that the 'friends' Lucien had promised to meet up with included Zara, the snooty gallery assistant. By the time Caitlin arrived, she was already squeezed into a booth next to Lucien.

'It's so lovely to see you again, Caitlin,' Zara brayed. She rested a proprietory hand on Lucien's knee. 'Are you joining us? How wonderful!'

Zara was there with a group of equally Sloaney girlfriends, all wearing low-backed dresses and clutching cute evening bags. Looking around, Caitlin couldn't help feeling under-dressed. Even the girls in jeans had jazzed them up with strappy little tops and pointy-toed shoes.

The evening got more miserable. Zara seemed determined to keep Lucien by her side. She kept dragging him off to dance, or introduce him to someone she knew – 'They've been absolutely dying to meet you, Lucien!' Worse still, he didn't seem to be making any objections.

The crowd was mainly male and extremely pushy. And without Lucien around, Caitlin was an open target. A voice said, 'Can I interest you in a drink?'

She looked up to see a tall, clean-cut man, holding a bottle of Moët. He was in his early thirties, wearing jeans with a smart shirt tucked into the waistband. Management Consultant or banker, she guessed.

'No, I'm fine, thank you,' Caitlin declined politely.

He nudged her arm. 'Come on. Just one drink.' He gave her what she guessed was his attempt at a winning grin. 'I don't bite, I promise.'

The barman came back with her mineral water. She quickly paid. 'Thanks again.' She held up the bottle for her unwanted suitor to see. 'But I'm all set.'

The smile left his face. 'Uptight bitch,' he muttered, as he turned away. *Charming*.

When she walked back to where their group had been

sitting, Lucien had disappeared again. And so had Zara. Caitlin didn't know why she felt so disappointed. He'd been trying to tell her for weeks that he wasn't interested. She just hadn't wanted to see what was in front of her. Well, it was time for that to end. If Lucien wanted her out of his life, then so be it.

Grabbing her jacket, she slipped out of the side door of the club . . . and came to an abrupt halt. So much for a smooth getaway. Because there, standing alone in the alleyway, halfway through a cigarette, was Lucien. Zara was nowhere in sight.

Lucien looked down at the coat in her hands. 'Running away again, Caitlin?' His voice was quietly mocking. 'That did not take long.'

She bristled. He was the one who'd ignored her all evening. 'Well, there didn't seem much point staying around. You were with Zara and—'

'And what?' he cut in. 'We were talking, that's all. And even if there was something more to it, is it really any of your business? I think you gave up your right to have a say in my life a long time ago.'

As he took a step towards her, his face was suddenly illuminated by the streetlight, and she saw something in his eyes that she hadn't been expecting. Anger. It was the first time he'd let his veneer of indifference slip.

'*You* were the one who walked out on *me*,' he hissed. 'On *us*. Twice. For no good reason.'

'It wasn't for no reason,' she protested.

'Then tell me.' He spoke through gritted teeth. 'Tell me, why *did* you leave?'

There was a long silence. Finally she dropped her eyes. 'Lucien, I can't.'

The anger seemed to leave him all at once. He shook his head then, and if she wasn't mistaken he seemed almost sad as he said, 'That's what I thought.'

He stubbed the cigarette out on the wall and walked away. There was a finality to the gesture that terrified Caitlin. She couldn't lose him again.

She opened her mouth to call after him. But the words wouldn't come.

It didn't take Lucien long to get home. His Shoreditch flat was only five minutes from the club. Passing the night porter without a word, he got into the lift and hit the button hard for the top floor.

Usually his apartment was a sanctuary for him. Part of a trendy warehouse conversion, it was a huge open-plan live-work space with floor to ceiling windows. Elegantly furnished in dark wood and fine white linens, it suited Lucien perfectly. But tonight, for the first time ever, stepping inside didn't help him relax.

He went over to the drinks cabinet, found a bottle of whisky and poured himself a large glass. Cradling the tumbler in his hands, he took a sip. It was only then that he saw he was actually shaking with fury. He had never known such rage, never thought he had it in him. He hated that she could do this to him still. With all his strength and anger, he hurled the glass against the wall. It shattered against the brickwork.

'*Putain!*' he swore. *Caitlin, Caitlin, Caitlin.* He put his hands to his temples, wishing he could erase her from his mind. Why did she have to come back into his life now, when he'd thought that he was finally over her?

He found another glass, poured more whisky, and dropped into the armchair. He felt like such a fool. For some reason he had hoped it would be different this time, that she would finally open up to him. How wrong could he be?

Five minutes and another drink later, the intercom sounded. Instinctively, he knew it was her. He didn't move at first. Just sat in the chair wanting to make her wait. Make her know some of the frustration of trying to talk to someone who wouldn't answer.

Finally, three exasperated rings later, he got up.

'Please, Lucien,' she begged. 'Please . . . let me in.'

Against his better judgement, he buzzed her up.

Waiting for her, he paced the floor trying not to think, concentrating instead on the clunk of the old freight elevator as it went down to the ground floor to collect her, hearing it slowly heave its way back up.

The lift arrived. He pulled the heavy grating open, and she was standing there, waiting for him to invite her in. He saw she had been crying and forced himself to ignore the tears, her intense vulnerability.

'What are you doing here?' he demanded.

He watched her take one deep breath followed by another. And then she said the words he'd been waiting to hear for such a long, long time.

'I'm here because I want to tell you everything.'

Chapter 44

William walked slowly into the boardroom. He was the last to arrive. It was his first day in the office after six months recuperating. The board applauded as he entered, each standing to shake his hand as he passed.

'It's good to have you back.'

He gave a weak smile, waving away their enthusiastic greetings. The truth was, he felt disorientated and tired. The doctor had counselled him against returning to work, and Isabelle had begged him to stay at home. But he'd needed to do this. Piers's reports of what Elizabeth was up to had worried him.

Abolishing Melville Essentials . . . 'The vote was unanimous,' Piers had told him. It was hard not to see his daughter's actions as a direct criticism of him. But now he was back in charge, and he didn't plan on going anywhere. Elizabeth would have to accept that.

At least he could rely on Caitlin, he thought, immediately feeling better. She had really come through for him these past few months. He had seen sketches of the designs that she was working on, and he couldn't help being impressed. It was a very different step for Melville, but one that he hoped would pay off.

We'll find out soon enough, he thought. The fashion show was only a month away. Whether employing Caitlin had been the right move would be apparent for the world to see then. But, whatever happened, from a personal point of view he had no regrets – he would always treasure these past few months, having the opportunity to finally get to know her.

Aware of everyone's eyes on him, he cleared his throat, ready to get down to business. 'Now,' he began, 'I'm sure there's an awful lot for me to catch up on. So why don't we get started?'

Sitting across the table, Elizabeth couldn't help thinking how well her father looked: he'd lost weight over these past months, and he had that healthy glow of someone who was watching his diet carefully. She was pleased that he seemed to have recovered, although part of her wasn't exactly happy to have him back at work. Not at this crucial stage.

Change took time. That's what Elizabeth had found. Winning board approval for her ideas had only been the first battle in a long war to turn the company around. Over the past few months, she had been hard at work reducing operations: she'd pared down the product line from twenty thousand to less than a quarter of that size; sliced the number of handbag styles from two hundred to a mere fifty; and reduced the stores stocking Melville items from five hundred to ninety.

'It seems a bit drastic,' Hugh had observed initially, to murmers of agreement from the other directors.

'The company doesn't have time for a piecemeal approach,' Elizabeth had answered. 'We need to see results – and fast.'

You couldn't gradually make a brand cool again. It was the basic principles of supply and demand. For years, Melville had been a luxury name behaving like some pile 'em high, sell 'em cheap outfit. That had to change.

She'd refused to renew contracts for licensing the brand, and sent letters to over a thousand retail clients in the UK and the US announcing that once current stocks of Melville Essentials ran down they wouldn't be replenished. The Sales Director of PharmMart had been the first to complain. 'This is outrageous! We've been doing business for years.'

But Elizabeth was adamant. It had to be this way – all or nothing. It would take another twelve months, but by then

Melville products would no longer be available in chemists and supermarkets; other than the designated Melville stores, only top names like Harvey Nichols or Saks would be able to get hold of Melville goods.

Unfortunately, so far her strategy of removing Melville Essentials from the shelves had succeeded in reducing sales further, without any compensation at the higher end as yet. With every month, there was a new round of dismal figures. Now, as Piers ran through the latest numbers on her father's instruction, Elizabeth could feel everyone staring at her accusingly. But she kept her head up and stayed firm.

'This is a long-term plan,' she told the board confidently. 'Of course you can't expect to see results overnight. We need the customers' perception of the brand to change first.'

In the face of all the hostility, it was getting harder and harder to stick to her beliefs, but somehow Elizabeth managed it. She had to keep any doubts to herself. Because she knew if she showed signs of weakness, the vultures would descend and tear her apart.

'Well, obviously this was all agreed without me.' William made no effort to hide his disapproval. Most of the other directors chose that moment to study their meeting agenda. 'I just hope to God you know what you're doing, Elizabeth,' he said, so no one was in any doubt where he felt the blame lay for the current mess.

In some ways Elizabeth couldn't blame him for being sceptical. But she kept her cool. 'Don't worry,' she said, with a certainty she didn't feel. 'I do.'

'Good.' His tone was brisk. 'Then you won't mind putting together a forecast for how far you expect sales to drop off over the next year, and when you see them picking up again.'

'That shouldn't be a problem,' she replied.

'Excellent. Then I'll expect to see that on my desk tomorrow morning.'

Elizabeth opened her mouth to object. She'd promised Cole that she would be home by seven at the latest, and what her father had just asked her to do would take pretty much all night. But then she saw the challenge in William's eyes; knew the other directors were waiting to hear her answer. If she refused, she would lose face. And she couldn't have that. 'Of course,' she murmured.

Cole would understand that she needed to do this. After all, it was only one more night.

A ten-minute walk away from his wife's office, over in the heart of Soho, Cole was caught up in a meeting about his own business. The kind of meeting that could determine a lot.

He tossed the contract onto his desk. The offhand gesture showed the man who sat across from him exactly what he thought of his offer: twenty million pounds for a 40 per cent stake in his company. Cole had no intention of accepting.

Ed Linton frowned at this outright dismissal. 'Hey, it's a good offer, mate.'

Cole rocked back in his chair, the leather creaking underneath his weight. 'Yeah, I'm sure it is. But I'm still gonna have to say no, Ed.'

The other guy opened his mouth to argue back, and then thought better of it. He'd worked with Cole for long enough to know that once he'd made up his mind, he wasn't going to change it.

The two men had met when Cole first came to England. Ed had been a highflier in the London office of Sedgwick Hart. A few years earlier, he'd left to set up a private equity firm with a couple of other guys. They'd had their eye on Cole's business, Kobe, for a while, and had pitched a tempting offer. But Cole wasn't interested in relinquishing any control – he liked having no one to answer to but himself.

'Well, I'd say that you're foolish to turn me down,' Ed

said. 'But I have a feeling you know exactly what you're doing.'

Cole grinned. 'Always have, always will.'

A tentative knock on the door interrupted them. A moment later, Cole's PA, Sumiko, entered. With the rapid expansion of his company, he'd set up a small Head Office a few months earlier, leasing a modest set of rooms on the top floor of a ramshackle townhouse in the heart of Soho. One of his first tasks after moving in had been to recruit Sumiko. At nineteen, she was young, but had the main qualifications he was looking for – she was native Japanese and also spoke fluent English.

She came over to his desk with some letters, waiting quietly, eyes lowered, as he put his signature on them.

'Would you like me to stay around tonight?' she asked softly once he'd finished.

'No thanks, Sumiko. Have a good evening.'

Ed's eyes followed her out through the door. 'Cute,' he said, once she'd gone.

'Well qualified,' Cole countered.

Ed raised an eyebrow. 'Yeah, I bet.'

'What's that supposed to mean?'

'Come on. She looks like she just stepped out of *Asian Babes*.' Cole scrunched his face in disgust. 'Jesus, Ed. She's nineteen.'

'That old?' Ed shot back, amused by Cole's obvious outrage. 'Hey, buddy, *you* need to get yourself a girlfriend.'

Ed chuckled lightly. 'Believe me, that's the last thing I need.' He took a sip of water. 'So, are you all set for next Thursday?' he asked, changing the subject.

'Pretty much.' It was the five-year anniversary of Kobe's opening, and Cole was planning a big celebration. 'Are you still coming? Or are you too bitter after I turned you down today?'

Ed grinned mischievously. 'That depends. Will Sumiko be there?'

Cole's smile disappeared. 'Hey, Ed, leave it alone.' There was no mistaking the warning in his voice. 'She's just a kid.'

'Yeah, I suppose you're right.' He gave Cole a sideways look. 'And it's not like she'd be interested in me, anyway.'

Cole didn't bother to ask what Ed meant. He was aware that Sumiko had a crush on him, but it was something he was trying hard to ignore. It was harmless enough – more hero-worship than anything else. As long as it wasn't interfering in their working relationship he could overlook it, and she'd lose interest eventually, he was sure.

Ed waited a moment before asking the logical next question. 'And how's Elizabeth doing? Rumour has it things are manic over at Melville.'

'You know Elizabeth,' Cole said evenly. 'She's coping very well.' The answer was vague. But it spoke volumes.

That night, Cole got home to find his elegant Chelsea townhouse empty again. Elizabeth had left a message earlier to say she was going to be late. No big surprise there. He contemplated the long evening ahead. He could hit the gym, but he'd been there every day for the past fortnight. He could see his muscles straining through the sleeves of his shirt – at this rate he was going to look more pumped than the steroid-loaded trainers. Screw it. He'd kick back, crack open some beers, order a pizza, maybe watch some basketball on Sky Sports.

Grabbing a Bud from the fridge, he headed upstairs to change out of his suit. The bedroom, like the rest of the house, looked immaculate, like something out of *House & Garden*. The cleaner was due in tomorrow. What a joke! Kicking the wardrobe door closed, he flopped down on the bed in his boxer shorts and a Knicks T-shirt, and flicked on the television. Elizabeth hated him watching TV in bed – didn't much like him eating and drinking there either.

'It's so *common*,' she'd told him once.

But she wasn't here to nag, so he didn't care. In fact, he half-hoped she'd come home just as he was tucking into his last slice of pizza. Right now, he'd relish a fight. It would be an opportunity for him to get some stuff off his chest.

The truth was, Cole wasn't happy. He hadn't been since they'd moved back to England six months earlier. Elizabeth had always been a workaholic, but lately it had grown ridiculous. They hardly ever went out together, she'd forgotten all about their anniversary dinner, and the other week she had started dropping hints about cancelling their next holiday. He never got to see her. She was always travelling. Three continents, ten countries a month. When they'd run a feature on him in the *Sunday Times* business section, he'd had to ask three times before she'd take a look at it. It was six weeks since they'd last had sex. And this was from a couple who used to do it every night without fail. He'd read the other day that 70 per cent of marriages were sexless. That was one statistic he didn't want to end up part of.

And that was about the time he'd started to notice Sumiko.

He finished the beer, cracked open another.

He knew he'd been defensive earlier with Ed. And there was a very good reason. He was more aware of Sumiko than he wanted to admit.

He remembered the first time he'd met her. He'd been interviewing for a PA all day. He'd seen some good people, but he'd wanted to make sure the chemistry was right. Sumiko was the last candidate to turn up for the job interview. In a formal black suit, she'd been over-dressed and horribly nervous. She'd sat on the edge of her seat, her voice barely above a whisper, as he'd quizzed her about her previous experience and why she thought she'd be suited to the role. Usually he couldn't stand shrinking violets, especially not in his business, but he'd surprised himself by taking a liking to her. He'd offered to make her a coffee, and by the time he came back into the room she'd pulled herself together. Beneath her initial deer-caught-in-the-headlights exterior, she'd turned out to be smart and organised. He'd surprised himself by hiring her on the spot.

She'd worked out better than he'd expected. She was calm and efficient, and more than happy to work late. It hadn't taken long for him to figure out that she had a thing for him. It was also hard not to feel flattered. He was coming up to forty. She was nineteen and hot in that sweet, feminine way: silky dark hair to her waist, wide, soft eyes, and a tiny frame, small but perfect. At five foot three, she made him feel like a giant.

If he was honest, he liked the way she looked up to him, hung off his every word. He'd never really been into submissive types – but lately he could see the attraction of having a girl who'd let you do whatever you wanted with her. There were times he'd be sitting at his desk and his mind would wander . . . he'd imagine calling Sumiko into his office and ordering her to get down on her knees and suck him off. She'd do it right then and there, that curtain of long silky hair falling across his thick, bare thighs. Sometimes he thought about what it would be like to screw her over the desk, imagine her little mew of pleasure as he stuck it into her.

And then he'd catch himself and wonder where the hell those thoughts had come from. He loved Elizabeth, right? He'd made a commitment to her; she was the only woman he should want.

Except lately he hadn't been feeling so guilty when images of Sumiko popped into his head. After all, there was no harm in fantasizing, was there?

He checked the clock by his bed. Twenty minutes until the pizza arrived. He switched off the TV and lay back on the pillows. As his hand slipped down the front of his boxer shorts, he was aware that the woman in his head wasn't a blonde like his wife. In fact, she was most definitely a brunette – a petite, compliant, silky-haired brunette. He tried not to let it bother him.

Chapter 45

The evening started with an argument. Not that there was anything unusual about that. Living with Johnny wasn't quite the fairy tale Amber had imagined. It was more like riding a giant roller-coaster, unpredictable and sometimes scary. Some days, he treated her like a princess. After they'd *made love* – that's how she liked to think of it – he would prop himself up on one elbow, stroke her hair away from her face, and look down at her as though she was the most precious thing in the world. That was when Amber was at her happiest, when she felt nothing could touch her.

But there were the other days, too – dark days, when every little thing she did seemed to irritate him. She lived in constant dread of getting on the wrong side of him, of doing something to set him off. But she put up with it because she loved him. And she knew deep down that he loved her, too. He must do, to have moved in with her. It was the first time someone had made a commitment to her like that.

But that particular Friday evening she had a bad feeling from the start. Johnny got off the phone with Brett, his manager, in a black mood. He'd just found out that the record deal he'd thought was a sure thing hadn't come through. As a consolation, Brett had offered him a two-week stint playing the casinos in Vegas. Johnny reacted by ripping the phone out of its socket and throwing it across the room. 'Fucking useless arsehole,' he screamed.

The receiver landed inches away from where Amber sat

cross-legged on the slip-covered white sofa, flipping through *Vogue*. She didn't even flinch as the phone came her way. She was used to Johnny's outbursts by now. She'd had worse objects chucked at her.

'So are you going to take it?' she asked absent-mindedly. Straight away she realised she'd said the wrong thing.

'Take it?' Johnny's voice came out like a hiss. 'Did you seriously ask me if I was considering taking this fucking shit offer?'

She put down the magazine.

'No, Johnny, of course not.' She sounded nervous now, conciliatory. But it didn't seem to have any effect.

'I mean, is that all you think I'm worth?' He was advancing towards her now. She slunk against the back of the couch, her heartbeat quickening. 'Am I no better than a ten-minute slot squeezed in between a two-bit stripper and an eighty-year-old magician? Do you think that's what I deserve?'

He was a few steps away from her when the anger suddenly left him. His shoulders dropped and he said, somewhat forlornly, 'Hell, maybe you're right.'

Amber hated it when he was like this – it was almost worse than the rages, this defeatism and loss of hope, beating himself up about the opportunities that hadn't come through. It was especially hard for him when he saw how well she was doing. She'd almost been relieved when she'd lost out on the contract to represent Get Fit Sportswear last week.

Jumping up, she went over to stand in front of him, putting her arms round his neck. Standing on tiptoe, she placed a kiss on his unyielding mouth.

'I'm sorry, baby.' She started to cover his neck in tiny little kisses. 'Really, I am.' Then, 'Maybe I could do something to make it up to you . . .'

But he shrugged her off. 'Leave it out. I'm not in the mood, all right?'

As he walked over to the liquor cabinet and poured himself

a whisky, she tried not to feel hurt by his rejection. It wasn't
personal, she told herself. She knew how he got when his
music didn't work out.

'Why don't we go out?' She managed to say it with a bright-
ness she didn't feel. 'That new club, Dynamite, is opening
tonight. Everyone's going to be there.'

Finally he turned round and smiled at her, and even though
she could tell it was an effort for him, she felt a surge of relief
that another full-blown argument had been averted.

'Why not?' he said.

The improvement in Johnny's mood was shortlived. He barely
spoke to her on the ride to the club, and once they were inside,
he headed off to hang out with some of the guys, leaving her
alone. Whenever she went over to him, he would turn his back
on her, as though he hadn't seen her. She chewed her lip. She
hated it when he was like this with her, refusing to touch or
acknowledge her.

'Fancy some blow?'

It was Luke, one of her modelling friends, offering. Amber
hesitated. She'd been trying to lay off lately – in public at least.
Rich was always warning her that it wasn't great for her reputation. Plus, she was already feeling light-headed from all the
tequila shots. But then she happened to glance across the room
and saw Johnny talking to Mercedes Maguire. Rumour had it
that Mercedes was the one who'd swiped the Get Fit contract
away from her. An All-American blonde, with Daisy Duke tits,
a wide smile and tousled hair, she'd swept onto the LA scene six
months earlier and hadn't been off the front pages since. As far
as Amber knew, Johnny and Mercedes had never met. But
maybe she was wrong. They looked pretty cosy together in that
booth.

She turned to Luke. 'Yeah, that sounds good.'

The coke did its job, made her feel confident and powerful

again. She hit the bar with a vengeance. Eventually her old crowd turned up and she started to enjoy herself, dancing with Devon, flirting with Jim-Bob. Unfortunately Johnny didn't seem to have noticed. He was still holed up in the booth with Mercedes. Another tequila shot made her feel better.

'Hey. Take it easy, Amber.'

She laughed at JB's worried expression. 'No, you take it easy.' She slapped at his shoulder, missed, and fell off the bar stool instead, landing straight on her knees. There was laughter all around. Hands helped her up.

Loo. She needed the loo, she realised. She walked unsteadily across the room. People and chairs kept getting in her way. Everything seemed to be tilting at an angle. It was like being on a ship, she thought idly.

Somehow she made it to the Ladies in one piece. There was a long queue. She tried to count how many people were in front of her, but gave up. Damn it. She wasn't sure she could wait. She might end up peeing right here on the floor. She giggled at the thought. The girl in front turned and glared at her, as if to say, What the hell are you laughing at? Amber ignored her. She waited until someone came out of the cubicle and nipped in before anyone else could. There was a cry of complaints from the line. But there wasn't much they could do once she'd locked the door.

It took a surprisingly long time to get her skirt up and her knickers down. She sat heavily on the porcelain seat, resting her head against the cool tiles. She must have dozed off for a little bit, because when she came to, someone was knocking on the door.

'Are you all right in there?' a voice called through.

'Yeah, yeah,' she mumbled, shaking off the tiredness. She struggled to pull her panties back up. Fuck it, she decided finally. She'd just go without. No one would notice. And it'd be a nice surprise for Johnny on the way home.

She left her underwear in a ball by the sanitary bin and headed outside to find him.

She never did. Twenty minutes later, she was rushed to hospital to have her stomach pumped. But not before an off-duty reporter had managed to snap a whole roll of film of her.

She made the front cover of *Celebrity* magazine. A picture of her lying unconscious on the couch at Dynamite, two lines of coke on the low drinks table in front of her and – just in case someone hadn't got the point – white specks of powder dotted around her nose, which she swore had been graphically enhanced. Worst of all, the photographer had aimed the shot straight up her skirt. Although the magazine had blanked out the essentials, it was still pretty damned obvious that she had no underwear on. Underneath the photo, the headline read: *Is This Really the Face of Glamour?*

The magazine hit the stands the day she got home from hospital. Amber was feeling fragile enough and could have done without the extra publicity.

Johnny thought the whole incident was hilarious. 'So you got caught with your cunt hanging out,' he said, throwing the magazine to one side. 'Who gives a fuck?'

He flicked the TV on, signalling the end of the discussion. That made her feel slightly better for a while, until Rich finally returned her call. She could tell from his sombre tone that the news wasn't good. He didn't attempt to sugarcoat it.

'Glamour has terminated your contract.'

'They can't do that!'

He sighed deeply. 'They can. There's a clause saying that if you do anything to embarrass or damage the brand, the contract can be terminated straight away. I wouldn't bother fighting it, if I was you. I've already talked to your lawyers, and they don't think your chances are good. Fifty per cent of Glamour's customers are teenage girls. To be frank, you'll be lucky if they don't sue you for loss of sales after this.' He paused. 'But they've basically said that they won't take you to court if you go quietly.'

For once, Amber didn't have a smart reply. She swallowed hard. She didn't like the way Rich had said 'your lawyers', either; in the past, it had always been 'our'.

'But it was just a stupid mistake,' she said in a small voice. 'I didn't mean to end up in the papers like that.'

Rich didn't say anything. She had a feeling she wasn't going to get much sympathy from him. He'd been warning her for weeks that something like this was going to happen. She cleared her throat.

'Fine,' she said with false bravado. 'It's a shame about Glamour, but there'll be other contracts. Night & Day begged me to sign with them. And what about Hiltman jeans? I'm still representing them, aren't I?'

'Hiltman are cutting you, too.' He sighed heavily again. She got the feeling he was enjoying this, the I-told-you-so call. 'Amber, I don't think you understand the severity of what you've done. I've been on the phone all morning. No one's going to offer you another contract. No one wants to touch you.'

He waited a moment for the reality of her situation to sink in. When he spoke again, his voice was softer.

'There's only one way forward after this, honey.'

'What's that?'

'You've got to go into rehab. It's the only way. And you've got to get Johnny Wilcox out of your life.' He paused before delivering the final blow. 'Otherwise I'm walking, too.'

She refused to go to rehab. She refused to get rid of Johnny. By the time she got off the phone half an hour later, Rich had resigned as her manager. Somehow that seemed worse than losing the Glamour contract. Rich had been there from the beginning for her. She wasn't sure how she was going to get by without him. Maybe he was right and this was the end of her career.

She was still feeling morose when Elizabeth called five minutes later. Apparently the scandal had been reported by *Heat* magazine in the UK, and her big sister had been elected by the family to stage some kind of intervention. Their call didn't last long. Like Rich, Elizabeth was adamant that she needed to get help, and Amber was equally adamant that she didn't.

Elizabeth made no effort to disguise her exasperation. 'For once in your life can you think about someone other than yourself? You know how ill Daddy's been. The last thing he needs is to see something like this.'

Amber slammed down the phone before she could finish. She wasn't in the mood for another lecture. And why should she listen to Elizabeth, anyway? However smart her older sister was, she was still working for their father – and so was Caitlin now. It was only her, Amber, who'd made her own way. They were clearly jealous of her success. But the thought somehow didn't make her feel any better. First Rich, and now Elizabeth. Were they both right? *Was* she making a mess of her life?

Feeling low, she made her way to the rec room. Johnny was there, watching TV on the fifty-inch plasma screen that he'd insisted she buy. She managed to get him to turn the sound down long enough to sob the whole sorry story to him. He was characteristically unbothered.

'Don't worry about it,' he said carelessly, his eyes straying back to the action on screen. 'I've been through loads of stuff like this before. It'll all blow over in a few days.'

'Really?' she sniffed.

'Yeah. Course. Hell, this is probably the best thing that's happened to you. There's plenty of other people who'll manage you. I'll have a word with Brett and see what he can do.'

Amber was on the verge of saying that Brett didn't exactly

seem to be having too much luck finding work for Johnny, but she decided against it. He could be a bit touchy if she brought up the fact that he hadn't secured a record deal yet. Not that it meant anything. He'd explained it to her before. These things took time. He needed to wait until all the furore surrounding Kaleidoscope had died down before starting a solo album. But in the meantime he was coming up with loads of ideas. As soon as he'd signed with a record company, he'd be back in the studio.

Johnny patted the couch next to him. 'Come over here, baby. I've got something that'll calm you down.'

She did as he asked. She watched as he emptied some brownish powder onto a square piece of foil, and then took out his lighter.

'When I heat this up, you wanna breathe the smoke in deep,' he told her.

She eyed it suspiciously. 'What is it?'

'Heroin.' He said it matter-of-factly, as though it wasn't a big deal.

She recoiled. 'There's no way I'm doing that!'

'Relax,' he said soothingly. 'It's no big deal. It's not like injecting, you can't get addicted this way. It'll just relax you, take the edge off a little.' He winked at her. 'Trust me, you'll love it.'

She hesitated. She wasn't exactly a prude when it came to recreational drug use. Since her time back at Beaumont Manor, she'd regularly indulged in coke as a pick-me-up and was partial to the odd joint to mellow her out. Johnny had taken that further. Early in their relationship, he'd introduced her to having sex on Ecstasy, and it had blown her mind: the stimulant heightening every sensation, making her feel a warmth and empathy towards him that she'd never experienced with any other sexual partner. He knew other tricks too – sometimes he'd rub coke on his dick; it acted like an anaesthetic so he could go on and on for hours.

Amber had never had a problem with any of that. But this was different. There was something about heroin . . . the connotations of what it meant, those eighties adverts showing junkies shooting up. But Johnny wasn't like that. And neither was she. If he said it was OK . . . well, she'd just try it once.

He heated the foil and she leaned forward, breathing the fine spiral of smoke deep into her lungs, like he'd told her to.

A wave of nausea engulfed her, and for a moment she wished she'd listened to her instincts and not gone through with it. But then a second later that didn't matter any more because the nausea was replaced by something she hadn't been expecting – a rush of intense pleasure, a feeling of such euphoria that it was like every orgasm she'd ever had, rolled up into one.

Johnny saw the look on her face and grinned knowingly. 'I told you it was good, didn't I?'

Chapter 46

Elizabeth was rarely troubled by nerves. But as she arrived at Melville's first fashion show since Caitlin had been appointed Head Designer, she felt her shoulders tense and a churning in her stomach that surprised her. She was half-expecting no one to turn up tonight.

A month ago, she had asked the PR Department to give her the latest figures for attendance at the show – and had been appalled to see that nearly half the invitations had been declined. Another 20 per cent hadn't even bothered to reply. She'd stormed upstairs to see Chantal, the PR Director's assistant.

'What the hell's going on?' Elizabeth slammed the list down onto Chantal's desk. 'Why's no one coming?'

Chantal's voice shook as she explained, 'We've got the final slot at seven-thirty in the evening. It's after Stella McCartney's show, which is over in W1. Everyone would rather stay in the West End than head over to East London.' The girl hesitated. 'Most of them don't seem to want to make the effort just for Melville.'

It was a disaster. What was the point of Melville having a miracle transformation if no one was there to witness it?

'Chantal, do me a favour, will you?' Elizabeth's voice was softer now, needing to get the other girl on side. 'Find out the shoe size and favourite colour of every influential fashion editor in New York, London, Paris and Milan for me. I've got a way to make sure that everyone comes along.'

The following day, Elizabeth sent out thirty pairs of Caitlin's newly designed Juliet shoes: cute post-party ballet pumps, in softest silver or gold leather embellished with sequins, which folded up into a matching drawstring pouch. Fun as well as practical, Elizabeth felt they showed a more innovative side to Melville, and gave a nice taster of what the new collection would be about. The next morning, the switchboard was jammed with calls from editors who'd changed their mind and now wanted to attend the show. Elizabeth's plan had worked, just as it had with Yamamoto's wife all those years ago.

Of course that hadn't been the end of the problems. It was Sod's Law. She'd woken this morning to find that a blizzard had descended on the capital. As the day wore on, the pretty snowflakes turned to grey sleet and she had spent the afternoon staring out at the dark skies in despair, wondering if the weather would put fashion's great and good off attending tonight. It was bad enough that Caitlin had decided to hold the show way out in Bermondsey, without having to contend with this.

But now, as Cole turned off the road, she saw there was no reason to worry. A line of Bentleys and Jags waited for valet parking. Another queue of black cabs dropped slick media types at the velvet-roped entrance.

Cole glanced over at her. 'Happy?' He'd borne the brunt of her stress these past few days.

She smiled sheepishly. 'Relieved.'

An usher with a giant golf umbrella rushed forward to open the car door. Elizabeth neatly side-stepped a slushy puddle, wondering again why she'd worn strappy sandals on a night like this. They were bound to get ruined. She put a hand to her poker-straight blonde hair. Thank God at least she wasn't prone to frizz.

Cole threw the keys at the valet and came round to join her. He took her hand. 'Come on. Let's go in.'

Elizabeth glanced up at her husband and felt a sudden rush of pride. He always looked good, but tonight he was magnificent, his broad shoulders easily filling out his dinner jacket. He'd had to put up with a lot lately. Once this was out of the way, she would start concentrating on him again.

As long as everything goes well, that is . . .

But there was no reason for it not to. The family had pulled together on this and they were all here tonight, rooting for the evening to be a success. Well, all except Amber. Elizabeth felt the faintest prickle of guilt. Amber's absence was partly her fault. Perhaps, with hindsight, she could have handled their phone call better. She'd just been so upset by those photos of her little sister in the papers that she'd lost her cool.

Once Elizabeth had calmed down, she'd regretted the argument. Wanting to make amends, she had decided the best way to show support would be to invite Amber to model in tonight's show. This time, she'd got Caitlin to call their younger sibling, deciding they were much less likely to rub each other up the wrong way. However, Amber had stubbornly refused, saying she was quite capable of getting work for herself and didn't need their charity.

'She's still angry,' Caitlin had reasoned. 'Give her a few weeks, and we can try again.'

Elizabeth knew she was right. However difficult it was for them, Amber was an adult, and they couldn't force their decisions on her. Now, as she took her place in the front row, she put her troubled youngest sister from her mind, and thought instead of Caitlin and how nervous she must be feeling right now.

Backstage, Caitlin was thankfully too busy to have time for nerves. With only a few minutes to go, she was making a last-minute check of all the models.

'Your tops must have become mixed up on the rail,' she told

two of the girls, standing over them to make sure they swapped back, before turning to another and saying, 'Remember, wait until you get to the end of the catwalk, pause for a few seconds, and *then* take the jacket off.'

She'd peeped out at the audience earlier, and seen the stadium-sized room filling up. So much was riding on tonight, and Caitlin knew it was her reputation on the line. Melville didn't usually hold a show on this scale. For the first time, top models had been hired, and the crème de la crème of the fashion world had been invited to watch. She'd even thought about signing up one of fashion's most sought-after producers to put the show together, but in the end had decided to do it all herself. It was her vision – she didn't trust anyone else.

She'd come up with a list of venues. There were the usual suspects: hotels, museums . . . but she hadn't liked any of them. She didn't want to show her collection in one of the usual minimalist white rooms. Her designs were about London, a fusion of modern and historic London, and she needed somewhere which reflected that. So she'd found an abandoned warehouse in bohemian Bermondsey.

'Why the hell are you holding it there?' Elizabeth had asked when she'd first heard. But as soon as Caitlin had walked into the Listed building, which had once housed spices and teas from the Far East, she had known it was ideal. It had that period feel she had been searching for – huge vaulted ceilings and cast-iron pillars. With those features, she didn't need to think about any further decoration. A runway, seating and lighting had been easy to hire and assemble. And they were all set.

Now, it was up to the designs to speak for themselves. She knew William, Elizabeth and the rest of the family were out in the audience, rooting for her. And Lucien, too. He had sent a Good Luck bouquet that afternoon. It was all in white: white roses, lilies, freesia and gerbera – simple, elegant. Pure Lucien.

If everything went well tonight, she'd finally introduce him to William, she promised herself.

The lights dimmed. And in that moment she put Lucien, her father and everyone else from her mind. Adrenaline coursed through her. This was it. The moment she had been waiting for.

Outside, in the auditorium, the air throbbed with expectation. The momentum around Melville's latest collection had already begun to build even before London Fashion Week kicked off. As journalists, celebrities and fashion commentators took their seats, they chatted and gossiped in excited anticipation.

Usually, the Melville show was a fashion graveyard. But over the past couple of weeks it had become clear that something exciting was happening over at the English fashion house. The pre-show gift had piqued everyone's interest. And then rumours had started filtering out of the Albemarle Street head-quarters – most of them strategically leaked by Elizabeth – of changes afoot. 'There's something going on at Melville . . .'

Now, press and buyers waited in eager anticipation to see if the hype was true.

To set the mood, Caitlin had selected the Prelude to Purcell's semi-opera, *The Fairy Queen*. As the triumphant sound of strings, trumpets and oboes filled the air, everyone fell quiet. Then the formal Baroque music was joined by a driving hip-hop beat booming out of the loudspeakers, a brilliant combination of classical and modern that a friend in the music business had mixed especially for Caitlin.

A bright, white spotlight hit the runway, and model Jasmine Klint strutted out. Laced into a fitted corset in deepest purple, her legs encased in a pair of skin-tight black leather jodhpurs with matching riding gloves, she looked like a modern highway-woman. She cracked a whip at the audience as she stalked by in fuck-me boots.

'This is fabulous!' the senior buyer for Harvey Nichols whispered to her neighbour, but *InStyle*'s Fashion Editor was too busy scrawling down every detail to voice her agreement.

The audience gasped and applauded as girl after girl hit the runway, looking ever-more sensational, in crushed velvet jackets, satin halter-necks and elegant evening gowns made of yards and yards of lace. The collection was sharp, hip and sensual – words no one would have ever associated with Melville.

'The clothes were simply sumptuous!' gushed the Fashion Correspondent for *The Times*, when she phoned in her copy later that night after the show. 'It was costume drama meets contemporary clubland.'

'I haven't seen anything so exciting since Tom Ford took over at Gucci,' the Editor of *Women's Wear Daily* was heard to remark over and over again.

The after-party took place in the swish surroundings of Annabel's in Berkeley Square. The venue was William's choice, a link to the sixties' and seventies' heyday of the company. As the Melville family arrived at the private club, journalists, photographers and camera crews fought to quiz them about the company's new look. Naturally, Caitlin was the focus of their attention. After the show, she had changed into a Baroque-inspired gown of burgundy velvet, complete with fitted bodice and full skirt, trimmed at the bust and sleeves with antique lace. The decadent costume captured the mood of the collection perfectly, and everyone fought to get a photograph.

William stepped forward and put his arm around her shoulders.

'What you have seen tonight is our first step towards showing the world that Melville is still the great company that it has always been. And I'd like you to meet the person responsible – my wonderful, talented daughter, Caitlin.'

He hugged her close, as she smiled up at him. Flashlights blinded them as dozens of photographers immortalised the moment.

Elizabeth stood to the side, looking on, wondering why she didn't feel happier. This was exactly what she had wanted, the kick-start the brand desperately needed. But she was only human, and it was hard seeing Caitlin take all the credit. Especially when she knew that tonight would never have happened without her efforts.

Around midnight, the PR team went out to collect the first editions and brought them back to Annabel's. The fashion and business pages all led with the same headline: *Father and Daughter team breathe life into Melville*, complete with a picture of William embracing Caitlin underneath. There was a look of pride on his face that Elizabeth had always wanted him to bestow on her.

By Elizabeth's side, Piers beamed. 'Isn't this fantastic? Your father's so delighted with everything Caitlin has done.'

On autopilot, Elizabeth smiled her agreement. She was so busy trying to appear pleased for Caitlin, that she didn't notice the appraising look Piers was giving her.

Cole wasn't sure what had got into Elizabeth. She'd been in such a good mood earlier, but now suddenly she seemed irritable and upset, insisting that they should leave right away. 'But I haven't even had a chance to speak to your dad yet,' Cole protested.

'Well, you go and do that,' she snapped. 'I'll see you outside.'

Cole knew she wanted him to follow her, but he wasn't about to go without at least saying, 'Hi,' to William. He knew how easily his father-in-law could take offence.

He found Melville's Chief Executive surrounded by a bunch of the company's directors. It took a while, but finally Cole managed to get him alone. He made the appropriate noises about William looking better. 'And how are you finding being back at work?'

'Good,' William answered a touch defensively. He was always a little wary around his dynamic, successful son-in-law. 'Frankly, I'm not sure how much more of this staying at home I could take,' he added. 'Isabelle was beginning to drive me mad!'

Cole smiled. 'It's definitely an exciting time for the company,' he said generously, happy for once to flatter William's ego. He glanced round the room. 'Tonight was a definite coup for Melville.'

William visibly relaxed. 'Yes,' he agreed. 'I never doubted the show was going to be a great success. But it's exceeded even my expectations.' There was a pause, and both men sipped their drinks. 'And how's everything going with you?' William asked.

'Good,' Cole said, echoing William's earlier sentiment. 'It's been . . . well, pretty hectic since we moved over.'

He hesitated, wondering how to phrase his request. He'd been waiting for an appropriate time to ask William to have a word with Elizabeth about slowing down. Cole had tried to get her to relax, to take work a little less seriously, but he didn't seem to be able to get through to her. But she listened to her father – maybe William would have more luck than him.

Unfortunately, before he could say anything, Caitlin hurried over to them, her date for the evening in tow. 'Sorry to interrupt,' she said to William. Her face was flushed and her eyes glittered with excitement. 'But there's someone I want you to meet.'

Cole looked with undisguised interest at the striking young man standing by her side. With his long, flowing black hair and ghostly skin, there was something almost ethereal about him. He was definitely another arty type. After all, not many lawyers or accountants could get away with dressing like *that* – in black suede trousers and an open-necked black shirt, with a maroon scarf wrapped around his neck. It was all rather too effeminate for Cole's tastes.

Cole could only imagine what William was going to make of *him*. From the little he knew about Caitlin, he guessed she wasn't going to introduce someone to her father unless the relationship was already pretty serious. And from what he knew about William, he wasn't about to give his approval lightly.

He wished he could stay around to see what was going to happen, but he'd left Elizabeth alone long enough. 'I'll leave you guys to it,' Cole said. And good luck, he added silently, as he walked away. You're going to need it.

William assessed Lucien with the wariness of any father meeting his daughter's boyfriend for the first time. Cole was right – the Frenchman was somewhat more *alternative* than he might have liked. But Lucien had stood up under rigorous questioning, answering some rather probing queries about his work and background with an ease and frankness that suggested he had nothing to hide.

'Lucien has an exhibition on at the moment,' Caitlin chimed in, looking anxiously between her father and boyfriend. She couldn't judge how this was going. 'It's at a wonderful gallery in Hoxton.'

'Oh?' William looked unimpressed. He wasn't quite sure what he made of all this photography nonsense.

But if Lucien noticed William's lukewarm attitude, he didn't let on. It was that Gallic confidence; nothing seemed to get to him. 'Of course you would be most welcome to come any time you like,' he said graciously.

William happened to glance up then and saw Isabelle trying to catch his eye. They'd agreed to leave by one, and it was nearly half-past. He put down his drink on the table. 'Caitlin, we're going to push off now,' he said. 'Are you coming, too?'

She glanced around the room. Guests were beginning to drift out, but the party was still in full swing. She wanted to enjoy tonight for as long as possible. 'I think I'd rather stay for a bit longer, if you don't mind.'

'Shall I send the car back for you, then?'

Before Caitlin could answer, Lucien put a protective arm around her shoulders. 'You have no need to worry. I'll make sure she gets home safely, sir.'

William stared at him for a moment, and then he broke into a slow smile. 'Well, thank you, Lucien,' he said. 'And do call me William from now on.'

By four in the morning, the party was almost over. Caitlin sat curled up on one of the plump leather couches, watching the last of the guests. A lone woman moved unsteadily on the dance floor, lip-synching to an old Madonna track; a few of the design team were gathered around a tequila bottle at the bar, noisily doing shots. They beckoned Caitlin over, but laughingly she shook her head. She was enjoying the natural high of success.

Lucien came up to her. 'The car's waiting out front.'

Caitlin took one last look around the room. 'I guess this is it, then,' she said regretfully.

Lucien held out his hand to her. 'Come on, *chérie*.'

He helped her to her feet and they walked outside, arm in arm.

Since that night in his apartment, when she'd opened up to him, everything had finally been going right between them. She'd told him everything: about her mother dying and finding out about William. Leaving Ireland and going to live with the Melvilles. Feeling like she didn't fit in at Aldringham. Then Greycourt and everything that had happened to her there. Escaping to Paris and wanting to start over, to forget the past and her family. But not quite managing to.

'I wish you'd told me,' Lucien had said once she'd finished. 'I would have been more understanding.'

'Maybe, but that wasn't really the point. I suppose . . . well, I didn't want you to pity me.'

He'd lifted her hand to his lips. 'I don't think anyone ever would.'

They were taking the relationship slowly this time. And it felt right. For the first time ever she was able to enjoy them being together as a couple.

They reached the car that would take her back to Eaton Square, where she was still living. The driver stayed discreetly inside, as they lingered by the door. Lucien reached up and touched her cheek.

'*Dors bien, ma petite.*' He bent his head, his lips gently brushing hers, and opened the car door.

She hesitated before getting in. It struck her then, as it had all those years ago when they were at the Paris Opera House – *Lucien was the one for her.* She didn't want to leave him – not now, not ever.

'Lucien?' she said suddenly.

'*Oui, mon amour?*'

'You know, I don't think I'm ready to go home quite yet.'

He raised an eyebrow. 'No?'

'No.' Then she said, almost shyly, 'I think I'd like to come back with you, to your place, instead.'

A look of understanding passed between them. He stared at her for a long moment, before saying, 'I'd like that too.'

The streetlamp cast a pale glow across the room. They stood together in the shadowy darkness, close but not quite touching. Sensing Lucien's hesitation, Caitlin turned her back to him, and said, 'Help me with this?'

Slowly, he unlaced her corset, his fingers brushing her bare shoulders and sending the first flickers of desire through her. Then he loosened the ties of her skirt and the gown fell away.

Outside, a car went by, its headlights illuminating the room. Caitlin caught a glimpse of herself in the mirror, the one that hung on the back of the door: pearl-white skin accentuated by the deep russet colour of her underwear. For the first time ever, she felt no shame. In the reflection, her gaze met Lucien's. He had moved to sit on the edge of the bed, leaving her alone in the middle of the room. The old her would have felt exposed and vulnerable. But now she felt something else – sexual and bold.

She turned to face him, enjoying the way his eyes moved over her body – her heavy breasts and rounded hips – drinking her in. It would have been easy enough to move over to him, but this time she was in no rush. Instead, she reached up and began to remove the combs that held her elaborate hairstyle in place, the ink-black curls tumbling down around her shoulders. When she'd finished, she posed, hands on hips. 'So what do you think?'

'Very nice.' He grinned. 'But you're still wearing too many clothes for my liking, *chérie.*'

A second later, her bra and panties joined the dress on the floor. She walked over and stood in front of him, completely naked now.

'Is this better?' she asked, her voice low and throaty.

A slow smile spread over Lucien's face. 'Much.'

They stared at each other for a long moment, neither of them speaking. Then Caitlin reached down and started to touch herself. She began with her breasts, massaging the soft creamy flesh in slow circles, licking her thumb and fore-finger to better play with her pale pink nipples, tweaking them erect.

'*O, c'est bien – j'aime beaucoup ça . . .*' Lucien was entranced, shocked and delighted by the change in her. His eyes followed her hands as they trailed down across her stomach, lower then lower . . . until she was touching between her legs, stroking herself wet and ready for him.

After a while, she took his hand and placed it there, too. Lucien obliged, mesmerised by her, marvelling at the change in her, happy to take pleasure in her pleasure. Only when he could stand it no longer did he reach up and pull her down on top of him.

By the time he entered her, they were both close to climax. And when, moments later, it finally came upon them in great, shuddering waves, Lucien held onto her tight, knowing that after this he would never let her go.

PART IV

May – December 2004

Chapter 47

Financial Times – Company Watch
London, 2 May
Melville Back in Fashion

English fashion house Melville published another record set of results yesterday. Like-for-like turnover doubled over the prior year, showing how popular the once-maligned brand has become with consumers.

The turnaround is particularly impressive considering that less than three years ago, analysts had written the company off. At the time, the City expected Melville to be the subject of a hostile takeover by French luxury goods tycoon Armand Bouchard. He was only prevented from mounting an outright bid by the company's ownership structure, as the majority of shares remain in the hands of the Melville family. At the time, Bouchard predicted the company's fortunes would worsen until family patriarch and Chief Executive, William Melville, would eventually be forced to sell to him for a much lower price.

He couldn't have been more wrong. After a decade of lacklustre performance, Melville's share price has doubled over the past six months. Yesterday, in the company's analyst meeting, William Melville said that he believed there was still more value to be had from the business.

However, the turnaround has less to do with him than the younger generation who now hold key positions in the business. In particular, his daughter Caitlin, Melville's Creative Director, is said to have played a vital role in reviving the company's ailing fortunes. It is her visionary designs that have wowed catwalk pundits and lured customers back into stores.

With William Melville turning sixty-five next year, many expect him to name his successor from within the family fold. An input of fresh blood could very well drive the share price even further.

Stock Rating: BUY

Caitlin finished reading the article and filed it away in her press-clippings folder. The leatherbound file was nearly an inch thick now, and she felt the weight of it in her hands. Two other folders, of a similar width, sat on the shelf in the corner of her office. The PR Department made sure to send a copy of any articles on Melville to all the directors. It was gratifying to read such enthusiastic coverage. When she'd first started working at the company, it had been a very different story. She remembered the disillusionment and despondency that had permeated every employee. Now, there was a buzz about the place.

The night of the first fashion show, more than two years ago now, it had been obvious to Caitlin that her designs had gone down well. The audience's reception had told her that much. But even she hadn't realised quite how successful the collection had been until she turned up at Melville's showroom the next morning and found the phones ringing off the hook.

She grabbed the nearest handset and found herself speaking to a buyer for Liberty, one of the many who had ignored Melville for years.

'I missed the show last night,' he confessed. 'I'm kicking myself now, because I heard it was fabulous.'

'Oh?' Caitlin couldn't keep the delight out of her voice.

He wasn't the only buyer to call; like him, a lot of them hadn't even seen the show. But they had all heard the same rumour: Melville's Fall collection was white-hot.

As the morning wore on, more and more people phoned, wanting to place orders. Then around midday, Elizabeth appeared. Caitlin had never been so pleased to see anyone.

'Can you believe this?' she asked, somewhere between wonderment and despair.

Elizabeth cast a cool gaze around the busy room. 'Very impressive,' she said shortly. 'But you've got other priorities. Every major fashion magazine and newspaper in the world has been on the phone trying to get an interview with you. I'm handling the PR myself.' She handed Caitlin a sheet of paper. 'Here's a preliminary schedule for the next ten days. You'll fly out tonight.'

'Fly out?' Caitlin repeated. 'Fly where?'

Elizabeth frowned. 'To New York, of course.' She consulted her notebook. '*Harper's Bazaar* and *Women's Wear Daily* are the first names on the list.' She looked over sharply at Caitlin. 'You've created a blockbuster collection here. This is your chance to promote it – and, more importantly, to promote Melville.'

With that, she turned and stalked off.

And that was the closest Caitlin got to a 'congratulations' from Elizabeth.

The next ten days were crazy. Caitlin jetted between cities – from New York to Tokyo, then Paris, Milan and Madrid, answering the same questions over and over again.

'*Tell us about the inspiration behind your collection.*'

'*What's your vision for Melville?*'

'*Why did you decide to go to work for the family company after all this time?*'

She tried to avoid that last question, and anything personal, sticking instead to talking about the clothes.

By the time she got back to London, she was ready to sleep for a week. But there was no time to rest. Melville was suddenly *the* brand to be seen in.

The first sign came one Monday morning, a few weeks later, when Caitlin got into the office to find Chantal, from the PR Department, waiting for her. 'Have you seen *Paris Match*?' she asked excitedly.

'No.'

Chantal handed her a copy of the magazine. The cover showed Hollywood darling Kristina Gates in a black mille-feuille skirt and chequered bustier. They were from Melville's recent collection.

She wasn't the only star sporting Melville apparel. Pop princess Cindy Simon accepted her Grammy for Best New Artist in a slashed-to-the-navel red satin dress; Brazilian Supermodel Alessandra was photographed clubbing in gold hot-pants and matching wedges. And then came the call from the agent of R'n' B singer, Sapphire.

'She'd love it if you could find time to make the outfits for her up-coming tour . . .'

That was when Caitlin knew she'd reached her target. That cool and glamour were back in the brand.

Since then, Caitlin had put out four more collections, each greeted with the same rave reviews as the first. The Design Department had grown. As soon as her budget allowed, she had hired six new assistants. And this time, there was no shortage of applicants – and they were good-quality candidates, too. Last year, William had acknowledged her success by appointing her Melville's Creative Director, which gave her a position on the board.

But, even though the operation was bigger and her responsibilities had increased, Caitlin still kept a firm hand over the design process. Every piece that went out had her stamp on it. Because, when it came down to it, she loved her work – she had a passion for designing that she couldn't explain. It wasn't work, it was a joy.

The only blight on her otherwise perfect world was Elizabeth. Over the past two years, their relationship had deteriorated. From being the member of the family to whom Caitlin was closest, Elizabeth was now the one she felt most distant from. Right now, relations were almost as cool as they had been when she'd first arrived at Aldringham. Everything she suggested seemed to irritate her older sister these days.

That afternoon had seen the latest clash. At the monthly board meeting, Caitlin had been proposing to introduce a Melville perfume.

'A lot of other couture and ready-to-wear houses have branched out in this direction,' she'd concluded her presentation. 'With the lower price point compared to our clothing line, we can tap into mass-market sales and generate significant additional profits by capitalising on the brand.'

Elizabeth had been tutting and clicking her pen throughout the whole presentation. As soon as Caitlin had finished speaking, she'd jumped in.

'There's no way I'm agreeing to this,' she'd said bluntly. 'I've spent the past two years working to rid Melville of its downmarket image! How can you suggest going back to producing lower-priced goods?'

Caitlin had tried to reason with her. 'This wouldn't be anything like what happened with Melville Essentials. Perfume might be lower priced, but that doesn't mean it has to be lower quality. I'm talking about an expensive scent,' she'd said, addressing her comments to the other directors. 'Used in the right way, this could even enhance the brand.'

'How?' Elizabeth had scoffed.

'A well-placed advertising campaign would complement our clothing line and help reinforce the sophisticated image we've been striving for.'

But even when Caitlin had explained that they could avoid making the same mistakes as before, by keeping a limited number of products and selling them only through upmarket outlets, Elizabeth had refused to back down. In the end, the proposal had gone to a vote. Only Piers had supported Elizabeth. Caitlin had seen the resentful look on her sister's face when William had backed her. It had chilled her to see how upset Elizabeth was.

Caitlin had planned to stop by her office before she left tonight, try to smooth her ruffled feathers. But now, as she glanced at the time, she hesitated. It was nearly eight and she wanted to get home to Lucien. Talking to Elizabeth could wait. In fact, weren't they due to attend Cole's restaurant opening next month? Although Caitlin suspected the invitation she'd received that morning was her brother-in-law's idea, she couldn't help feeling that the more informal social situation might be a better place to tackle her. The decision made, Caitlin grabbed her bag and headed home.

Caitlin had officially moved into Lucien's flat six months after that first fashion show, although she'd rarely spent a night away from there in all that time. She had loved the apartment almost as much as he had – it had been frighteningly similar to her own place back in TriBeCa. In fact, when a year later Lucien had suggested they should look round for somewhere larger, it was Caitlin who'd been the one reluctant to move.

'But this is perfect,' she'd said. 'And we're happy here.'

Lucien, always calmly logical, simply said, 'And we will be just as happy somewhere bigger.'

He was right, of course. And buying a home together had been more special and exciting than she had ever thought possible. The apartment would always be *his*, while the place they chose was *theirs*, representing them as a couple.

Fortunately it hadn't been hard to agree on something. They

decided early on that they wanted to stay in the Shoreditch area, near Hoxton Square, Spitalfields and the Columbia Road Flower Market, and luckily they had the same taste in properties, too. As soon as they saw the four-storey, eighteenth-century house, they knew it was the right place for them. It was light, bright and airy.

'Although in desperate need of refurbishment,' Caitlin had told William, the night their offer was accepted.

William had muttered something about not understanding why they hadn't gone for a new build, instead: 'far less work'. But Caitlin and Lucien didn't mind. For the past six months, they had spent any spare weekends and evenings lovingly fixing up the place, starting with redesigning the vaults under the house into a darkroom for him, and converting the attic into a studio for her.

The smell of fresh paint hit Caitlin as she opened the front door. So he had finally got round to decorating the dining room today. Despite their busy schedules, the couple had been determined to do as much of the work themselves as possible, rather than have contractors in. But that also meant it took more time.

Inside, the house was silent.

'Lucien?' she called out.

There was no answer. She went to check the ground floor. But he wasn't there, nor in the darkroom, so she headed upstairs.

She finally found him stretched out asleep on their bed, clad only in paint-spattered jeans, his T-shirt thrown carelessly on the floor. She smiled at the sight of him. There was still paint on his hands and arms, in his hair. He'd obviously planned to take a shower, thought he'd lie down first, and then never made it up again.

Silently, she slipped off her shoes and lay down next to him. It was a warm day out, but their room was refreshingly cool.

The windows had been thrown open, the white gauze curtains billowing gently in the early evening breeze. At first she was content to watch him sleep. But after a while, she couldn't resist moving under the crook of his arm, her head resting lightly on his shoulder. When he still didn't wake, she turned her face to softly kiss his chest, running her tongue over his warm skin. Finally he stirred.

'Sorry,' she whispered, as his eyes flickered open. 'I didn't mean to wake you.'

'I'm not complaining,' he said through a yawn. 'This is an extremely pleasant way to be woken, *chérie*.' He stretched, rubbed his face. His gaze flicked to the clock at the side of the bed, and he groaned. 'How did it get so late?'

'That's what happens when you spend all afternoon sleeping,' she teased.

He pulled a face. 'I think I remember promising to cook for you,' he said apologetically.

'We could go out.'

Her hand lay resting on the flat of his stomach. He reached down, his fingers entwining with hers. His voice was husky as he said, 'Let's stay in instead.'

He pulled her over on top of him.

She sighed contentedly. Life couldn't be more perfect.

Chapter 48

When William came to Elizabeth's office later that night, she thought it was to apologise for supporting Caitlin in the boardroom. Instead, he asked her to take his place on a trip to Tokyo in two weeks' time.

'I wanted to go myself,' he told her, 'but at my check-up yesterday, the doctor advised me not to. And now your mother won't hear of me getting on a plane.'

Elizabeth had been checking her diary as he spoke, and now she groaned. 'Oh, no.'

'What is it?'

'Those dates . . . they coincide with the opening of Osaka.' He looked blank. 'You know, Cole's new restaurant.' His dream to create an upmarket version of Kobe was finally being realised. There was no way she couldn't be there that night. 'Can't I go the week after?' she pleaded.

William huffed irritably. 'It's far too late to rearrange. You know how important this trip is.'

Yes, she agreed, she did know how important it was. And, all the while, she was trying to figure out whether she could somehow find a way to please everyone, husband, father, clients . . .

Half an hour later, having checked meeting and flight schedules, she decided she could just about manage it. She was due to fly back into London the afternoon of the opening, and should still be able to make the party, although she wasn't sure that would satisfy Cole.

She was right.

'Christ, Elizabeth,' he said, when she broke the news to him later that evening. 'I ask you for one night.'

'But you know how important this trip is, Cole!' she said, immediately on the defensive. 'What do you expect?'

He looked at her coldly. 'This is *exactly* what I expect these days. That I come second to that fucking company.'

She changed tack, then. 'I promise I'll be back in time.' She went over to kiss him on the shoulder. 'You know I can't wait to see the restaurant.'

But he wasn't about to be pacified. 'Sure. Whatever.' He shrugged her off, went over to the fridge and got himself a beer. He didn't bother to ask if she wanted anything.

Elizabeth felt suddenly very weary. If the past two years had been the best of Caitlin's life, they had been less kind on Elizabeth. Work had never really eased up. Her home-life had continued to deteriorate – this evening's fight was pretty standard for them these days. And, worst of all, no one seemed to appreciate the effort she was putting in.

Today's boardroom incident had been typical. The directors all credited Caitlin with Melville's turnaround.

'Isn't it so lucky that we have Caitlin?' they had taken to saying.

It was like a kick in the stomach each time, knowing that no one acknowledged the behind-the-scenes changes she had made, which had been just as crucial to the company's recovery. She tried not to let it get to her. She continued on as always, working hard, keeping a close eye on operations, making sure nothing jeopardised the turnaround. But then she saw comments like those in today's *Financial Times*, which glossed over her role in the improved results and even implied that Caitlin would be named as William's successor – and it re-opened the old wounds.

It was ridiculous, of course. Caitlin might be able to put together a killer collection, but there was no way she had the business acumen necessary to be Chief Executive. Elizabeth knew the job was hers. Her father hadn't said anything outright, but there were no other serious contenders. It was what she'd worked for all these years; it was her birthright.

Once William had named her as his successor, life would become better, she was sure. She kept saying that to Cole. 'I'll feel a lot more settled. Then we can get back to normal.'

He always nodded, said that sounded good. But she had a feeling he didn't believe her any more.

A fortnight later, Elizabeth stepped off the plane and into the grey, wet heat of Tokyo. By the time she'd completed the short walk across the tarmac to the terminal, she was already covered in a layer of sweat. It was the wrong time of year to be in Japan. While spring, the famous cherry-blossom season, might be pleasant, summers were notoriously sticky and humid. She would have given anything not to be here – not least because of the strife it had caused with Cole. But unfortunately, backing out hadn't been an option.

After nearly eight years of partnership, Mr Yamamoto wanted out of the Joint Venture. He'd always been an opportunistic investor and, after divorcing his brand-obsessed wife earlier in the year, his interest in Melville had waned. His original investment had increased tenfold, and he wanted to realise the cash and invest it elsewhere. If it had been anyone else, Elizabeth would have called to ask about rescheduling, but she knew Yamamoto too well. He was a powerful man who took offence easily, and they didn't want him black-balling Melville with local suppliers. There was no way he could be put off.

Piers had offered to go in Elizabeth's place, but William wouldn't hear of it.

'Don't be ridiculous,' he'd said dismissively. 'There's no way you could deal with this alone.'

Elizabeth could see how hurt her uncle was by William's

curt tone. Feeling a little sorry for Piers, she cornered him later and said he was welcome to accompany her if he wanted.

'Well, as long as you're sure,' he'd said doubtfully.

'It'll give us a chance to catch up, Uncle Piers,' she'd told him. 'I've hardly seen you lately.'

Their weekly dinners had dwindled recently; if she was too busy to get home for Cole, she could hardly justify spending time with her uncle. And, if she was honest, she would be quite pleased to have Piers along for company. Lately, she had been feeling strangely lonely.

It was to be a whirlwind visit. Elizabeth had organised the trip with military precision, determined to conclude all the business as efficiently as possible in order to get back for the opening of Osaka on Thursday evening. The plane arrived in Tokyo first thing Tuesday morning and they would spend the day at the Ginza store. They were scheduled to have a full meeting with Mr Yamamoto on Wednesday, and their flight was due to leave Wednesday afternoon, landing in Heathrow at four the following afternoon.

'That will leave more than enough time to get back to the house, change and head over to Soho,' she'd assured Cole the evening before she left. He'd merely grunted in response.

When Yamamoto met them for dinner on Tuesday, Elizabeth hoped to save time the next day by getting him to start talking about the JV then. But he waved away her attempts.

'Tonight is strictly for pleasure,' he said. 'Tomorrow is business.'

However much it pained her, she had to accept his wishes. She comforted herself by thinking that at least he seemed in an amenable mood, and that should hopefully make the following day's negotiations quick and easy.

She couldn't have been more wrong. First, he turned up an hour and a half late.

'There was an explosion at my steel plants in Kawasaki,' he explained. 'Naturally I had to deal with that.'

Elizabeth tried to look understanding. 'Of course you did,' she said, thinking that if they started now, she might still just about be able to make the plane.

But it wasn't to be. He kept interrupting their discussion to go outside and catch up on the unfolding crisis. It was impossible to stay focused on the intricacies of the deal when they kept stopping and starting. Worse still, as the hours ticked by, Elizabeth was finding it hard to concentrate. She was so worried about missing the plane that she couldn't keep her mind on what he was saying.

It was Piers who provided a solution. He took Elizabeth to one side after Yamamoto went out of the room for a sixth time.

'There's a BA flight taking off three hours later than the one we were supposed to be on. Why don't I book us on that instead? It should give us time to finish up here and you'll still get to London for the party.'

Elizabeth thought about it for a moment. It wasn't ideal – she'd be a little later and she'd have no time to change, but it seemed like the best solution. 'Yes,' she said slowly. 'Yes. Let's do that.' She smiled at him. 'Thanks, Uncle Piers. I don't know what I'd do without you.'

Piers couldn't help feeling pleased with himself as he went to make the call. He'd been relying on the fact that Elizabeth was so caught up in her meeting that she wouldn't have noticed the news headlines. Along with humidity and heat, Tokyo summers were also known for the typhoons that hit in June and July. Over the past few hours, the weather centre had been warning that one was due tonight. The last few flights were leaving soon, and then the airport would close. That meant he would have Elizabeth all to himself for another evening – which should give him plenty of time to start working on her.

He had waited over two years for his revenge on William.

He had plotted and planned, looking for the right time to move. Now it was almost upon him. He just hoped that he would have the courage to go through with it.

Four hours later, Elizabeth came out of the meeting with Yamamoto in a fantastic mood. They had resolved terms for buying out the JV and there was still plenty of time to catch the later flight. It was only when she tried to order a car to take them to the airport that she realised something was up.

'No airport.' The receptionist pointed up at the weather warnings flashing across CNN behind her. 'No plane.'

Elizabeth stared in horror at the pictures of empty streets, lashed by wind and driving rain. When the hell had that happened? Shut away in Yamamoto's state-of-the-art, earthquake-proof headquarters, there had been no indication of the growing turmoil outside. Now what was she supposed to do?

Cole knew how the night was going to end. He knew as soon as he got Elizabeth's message. She was apologetic, terribly apologetic, if a little defensive. And yeah, maybe the fucking monsoon, or typhoon, or whatever, wasn't her fault. But the point was, she wasn't there by his side, on the most important night of his life. And Sumiko was.

Maybe it would have been different if Osaka hadn't been such an obvious hit. But it was, everyone agreed. It was hip; it was cool; it was now. It was so much more than a restaurant – it was like walking into a chic nightclub: dark, moody, sexy. Everyone kept coming up to Cole to congratulate him – press, celebrities, fellow restaurateurs. They were talking about Osaka being the next Zuma, the next Hakkasan. He felt like King of the World this evening, and he didn't want the night to end.

But by one in the morning, the guests were beginning to disperse. Caitlin and Lucien were among the last to leave.

'We're going to head off now, Cole.' Caitlin kissed him on

both cheeks and then said, in a low voice, 'I know how sorry Elizabeth will be about missing tonight.'

'Come on,' Lucien said, taking her hand. 'Let's get you home. Or you will be too tired to get up tomorrow morning.'

Cole watched as the couple ran up the stairs together. He felt suddenly wistful for a time when he and Elizabeth had behaved exactly like that.

So when sweet, obliging Sumiko came up to him five minutes later, looking particularly pretty in a pale pink shift dress, and asked whether he'd like to go for a drink, what the hell was he meant to say? He thought of his empty house and his empty bed. And he looked at the beautiful young woman in front of him and thought, What's the harm? It's only one drink.

'Where do you want to go?' he asked once they were in the taxi.

Eyes demurely lowered, she said, 'Perhaps you would like to come back to my place?'

She lived alone in a smart one-bedroom flat in Angel. She'd only moved in recently, and it had that new smell about it. By the time they got there, he was already beginning to realise what a mistake this was. They had nothing to say to each other. She just giggled a lot and seemed totally in awe of him. He kind of felt sorry for her. He'd just stay for one drink and then duck out.

'I'll be back in a second.' She giggled again. It was getting pretty irritating. 'Make yourself at home.' Then she disappeared into what he presumed was her bedroom.

Cole paced the floor, swirling the cheap Scotch around the glass, wondering how soon he could get out of here. Once she got back, he'd leave. He waited and waited some more. What the hell was she doing in there? Maybe it was worth making his escape now; it would avoid any awkwardness. He swallowed down his drink.

'Look,' he called out. 'I'd better get going—'

The words died as the bedroom door swung open and she walked back into the room. Suddenly he figured out exactly what she'd been doing all that time. The pretty pink dress had been removed. Now she stood shyly in the doorway, wearing a cream lace negligée and an inviting smile.

Who was he kidding? He wasn't going anywhere tonight.

Over in Tokyo, Piers and Elizabeth had retreated to the safety of the hotel. Even after hearing about the typhoon, she had wanted to head to the airport anyway, on the off-chance that they might be able to get on the last flight out. But Piers had eventually persuaded her there was no hope.

Elizabeth had happily agreed to his suggestion to wait out the worst of the storm together. At least talking to him would take her mind off Cole. Now, they sat in the hotel lobby, along with the other terrified guests. It was still only late afternoon, but outside it was dark and the streets empty, the wind howling and rain beating against the sides of the building.

The waitress came over. Piers ordered a green tea, while Elizabeth went for a brandy. She needed something to help her relax. Cole still hadn't called her back, and she knew he was going to be furious.

Luckily, her uncle seemed to sense her anxiety and kept up a steady stream of small talk, until she started to feel better. Eventually the conversation turned to Armand Bouchard. There were rumours that he was considering making another bid for Melville. Elizabeth had been thinking through their options. Yes, he could bid for the free-float 40 per cent of the company. If he succeeded in getting it, then he could make things difficult for them, pushing for a seat on the board, trying to influence policy.

'It's all going to come down to convincing shareholders that there's still a lot more value in Melville and that we're the management team to realise that,' Elizabeth told Piers.

'Yes,' he agreed, 'but that's going to be difficult, isn't it, with the uncertainty surrounding your father's succession.'

Elizabeth's head snapped up. 'Uncertainty?' She seized on the word. 'Why would there be any uncertainty?'

Piers quickly shook his head. 'I'm sorry. I don't know why I said that.' Seeing her frown, he added, 'Honestly, it's nothing . . . forget I mentioned it.'

But Elizabeth wasn't convinced. 'Piers, if you knew something you'd tell me, wouldn't you?'

He reached across the table and squeezed her hand. 'Of course, my dear. But it's nothing, I promise you. A silly slip of the tongue. I didn't mean anything by it.'

Elizabeth stared at him for a moment. He looked horribly flustered, his cheeks were flushed and beads of sweat lined his brow. Seeing his obvious distress at having upset her, she forced a smile. 'I know you didn't,' she said. 'Anyway,' she went on briskly. 'That's enough business talk. Why don't you fill me in on the plans for refurbishing your house?' She saw him relax and knew she'd been right. Her father *had* said something about appointing a new Chief Executive and it wasn't going to be a rubber-stamp decision to elect her. But who else could it be?

Caitlin.

The name popped into her head. She remembered then that article a few weeks ago, the one that had credited Caitlin with single-handedly turning around the company. But their father knew that wasn't the case, didn't he?

Didn't he?

Elizabeth was quiet for the rest of the evening. She had suddenly realised that Armand Bouchard was the least of her problems. So she was pleased when she finally spoke to Cole the following day and found he wasn't as furious with her as she'd expected. He didn't even mind when she told him that she wanted to change her flight plans and go via LA, before coming back home.

'Daddy hasn't heard from Amber for a while,' she told him, 'so he wanted me to check up on her. I'll only stay there one night and then I'll be back in London.' She hesitated a second before adding, 'That is, as long as you don't mind.'

'No,' he said, 'I don't mind at all.'

His acquiescence was a surprise – and something of a relief, too. The last thing she needed right now was pressure on her marriage. Whatever had caused this new mellowness, she wasn't complaining about it.

Chapter 49

Amber closed her eyes. For a brief moment she was in her Ferrari F430 again, racing through Beverly Hills. Then a horn sounded, dragging her back to reality: a clapped-out Nissan, stuck in a jam on I-405 heading towards Lake Balboa.

It didn't help that it was another steaming afternoon and the air conditioner was out. She cranked down the window, letting in hot, dirty fumes. No wonder the Valley was cheap. The weather, usually a bonus in LA, took on a certain perversity down here, the summers warmer but smoggier too.

Finally the traffic started to edge forward. She took the next exit, following the road signs – helpfully in Spanish – until she turned onto the modest suburban street where she'd moved six weeks earlier. She pulled into the driveway and sat there for a long time after switching off the ignition, just staring ahead. However many times she saw her new home, she still couldn't get used to it.

About six months ago it had become obvious that she had no money left. Her accountant, a fatherly gentleman by the name of Taylor Hammond, had sat her down and explained the hard facts.

'You can't afford this place,' he'd said, nodding at the lavish surroundings of her Summit Circle mansion.

'What about remortgaging?' Johnny, who'd somehow ended up sitting in on the meeting, had asked. 'Raise cash that way?'

Taylor had shot him a disdainful look before turning back to Amber. 'The bank has extended the loan twice already, on the basis that your luck would pick up again. But now that it doesn't seem to be . . .' He'd trailed off then, unable to meet her eye.

Amber got the picture. She hadn't really worked since the Glamour scandal. Neither had Johnny. Two years with them both living off her savings – no wonder she was broke.

Moving was inevitable. Wanting to get as much space for her money as possible, she'd found herself a realtor covering the San Fernando Valley. It had been a rude awakening. After six years living in LA, Amber had seen very little of it. She'd quickly learned to avoid the no-go neighbourhoods – Van Nuys, Reseda. Compared to them, Lake Balboa wasn't so bad. The house itself was nothing special – two beds, two baths, no frills; a small pool in the back yard, just big enough to cool off in. It was the best thing she'd seen in five days' house-hunting. Johnny hadn't been interested in coming with her.

'It's your money, babe,' he'd told her.

As with all the big decisions in her life lately, she'd been on her own.

Moving had been a wake-up call. Amber realised then how arrogant she'd been. She'd had the world at her feet and she'd blown it. After those photos in *Celebrity* magazine, big brands had refused to touch her, and the press had turned against her. Word began to filter out about her turning up late to shoots, and suddenly she had a rep for being a prima-donna.

Johnny couldn't understand why it bothered her so much. 'Fuck 'em all,' he'd said.

Like a fool, she'd listened. Maybe she could have salvaged something of her career after the scandal at Dynamite, but she'd made no effort to do so. It was easier to go along with Johnny's 'fuck 'em' attitude. At first it hadn't felt like much had changed. They'd gotten dressed up, gone out partying to the same places, hung with the same people. But after a while the invitations had slackened off. It wasn't quite so easy to book a table at the

Ivy or Spago; they were no longer on the VIP list for new club openings. Jim-Bob and Devon, and her other so-called friends, had stopped returning her calls. But still Amber hadn't let it bother her. Everything would work itself out eventually, she was sure.

But it hadn't.

Leaving Summit Circle had been the incentive she'd needed to pull herself together. The night that they'd moved, for the first time in a long while, she hadn't touched any alcohol or drugs. She'd even attempted to cook dinner for her and Johnny.

'I need to get my shit together,' she'd told him as they tucked into over-cooked pasta. 'I've got to get work, get some money.'

'Whatever.' Johnny had pushed his half-finished plate aside and reached for a cigarette. 'I don't see what the big deal is. I thought your family was loaded. Why don't you just tap your dad for some cash?'

'Because I want to stand on my own two feet.' *And he won't give me any*, she'd added silently.

Well, that wasn't strictly true. Her family were well aware of how low she'd sunk over the past two years – what she hadn't told them, they'd been able to read about for themselves in the press. But all the talk of drugs had made them wary about offering a financial lifeline. Her father had taken a 'tough love' approach. 'Come home, get the help you need, and I'll happily support you. But while you insist on staying out in that *place*' – he made no secret of his contempt for LA – 'you're on your own.' He'd pretty much stuck to his word. There were the odd hand-outs, and presents at Christmas and birthdays – mostly she asked for jewellery that she could sell on – and she could still wangle money out of her mother or Caitlin if she tried hard enough. But she didn't want to take the easy way out this time.

Amber had never been one for soul-searching, but over the past few weeks she'd begun to think about what exactly she'd achieved in her life. And the answer was a big, fat zero. It was a sobering thought: twenty-five and nothing to show for it. Oh sure, she'd been a model, a global name. But that had been through luck more than anything. This time she wanted to figure stuff out on her own.

Easier said than done.

Last month, she'd managed to get herself signed with some third-rate agent, who'd sent her on her first casting today – an advertising campaign for *Break*, the casualwear brand. It hadn't gone well. She'd had to queue with 150 other girls to audition, waiting over three hours only to be told that she didn't have the 'fresh' look they were after. Maybe next time it'll be better, she thought, as she got out of the car.

She let herself into the house and saw immediately that Johnny hadn't accomplished the one task she'd asked of him today – to clear up. She sighed heavily as she bent to pick up a bucket of KFC that lay on the floor in the still bare hallway. The furniture from her old place had been too large and opulent to bring here, and she hadn't had the time or cash to shop for anything new yet.

Out in the back yard, she found Johnny with eight of his cohorts, most of them strangers to her. They looked like they'd made an afternoon of it – pizza boxes lay around, and someone had stacked the empty beer cans into a pyramid. Amber's eyes narrowed as she spotted Johnny rubbing suncream onto a blonde girl's back. Sheri, a Texan beauty queen, had arrived on the bus six months earlier. She attended acting classes during the day, and worked the bar at a club on Sunset most evenings. That's where Johnny had met her. A big fan of Kaleidoscope back when she'd been a kid, Sheri had been suitably impressed to meet *the* Johnny Wilcox. Johnny, who never tired of having his ego massaged, was happy to have her join his dwindling entourage.

Neither of them had spotted Amber, so she hung back and

watched as Johnny massaged the cream into Sheri's skin, his hands lingering a fraction longer than they needed to.

Amber cleared her throat to let them know she was there. Johnny looked up.

'Alright, darling? How did it go?'

He didn't look remotely ashamed to be caught with Sheri. It irritated Amber. He knew she didn't like the other girl – who was nineteen and full of herself – but he went ahead and invited her round anyway.

'Fine,' she said, coolly. She wasn't about to let on how humiliating the whole experience had been in front of Sheri.

Sheri sat up. She was wearing the briefest of string bikini bottoms, in metallic silver. She'd dispensed with the top, so that she didn't get strapmarks, but she made no effort to cover up her silicone breasts.

'Was that the *Break* audition?' she asked, sticking out one long, tanned leg to admire the colour. She didn't wait for Amber to answer. 'I heard there were a ton of people there.'

Amber frowned. She suddenly realised why she recognised the bikini – it was one of her own. Sheri had obviously gone into her room and helped herself. She wanted to say something, but knew she'd sound petty.

'I've got a headache,' she said instead, 'so I'm going inside for a nap. Maybe you could keep it down,' she added meaningfully.

But Johnny either didn't catch the tone or chose to ignore it.

'OK, babe. See you later.'

As she walked across the patio towards the house, she heard him laughing with Sheri. It was the perfect end to her horrible day.

She waited until the others left before coming out of her room. She'd been fuming in there all afternoon, and she had to say something to Johnny about it. She found him in front of the TV, lying on the sofa watching some music channel. He'd managed to get himself another beer, she noted, but hadn't thought to come in to see how she was doing.

'Does Sheri have to hang out here all the time?' she asked, going to sit down by his feet. 'You know I don't like her.'

He threw a peanut in the air and dropped his head back, catching it in his mouth.

'Why's that?' He chewed down on the nut. ''Cos she's better-looking than you?'

She recoiled at his words. He saw her reaction and rolled his eyes.

'It was a joke, Amber. You can still take a fucking joke, can't you?'

'It didn't sound much like a joke,' she said in a small voice.

'Oh, for fuck's sake, leave it out, will you? As if I don't have enough to worry about.'

She wanted to make him understand how much his comment had hurt. But she'd got to know that tone of voice all too well and didn't want to push her luck. So she let it go, like he'd known she would.

'I'm sorry,' she said, although she wasn't quite sure what she was apologising for. 'It's just the audition didn't go too well today.'

He gave her a cold look. 'Yeah? Well, at least you had an audition, Amber. You know, I've had jack shit for months. There's no need to fucking rub it in.'

'I didn't mean it like that!'

He threw the remote down and swung his legs off the couch, narrowly missing her head. 'Fuck it. I'm out of here.'

Amber scrambled to her feet and followed him outside. 'Please, Johnny. Don't go. I didn't mean it.'

But he wouldn't listen. He got into his car, slamming the door hard. She watched helplessly as he roared out of the driveway.

*

Amber waited up for him. She waited all night, until dawn finally broke. She was terrified that he wasn't coming back, all because she'd been in a bad mood about that stupid audition. Because however much her head told her that being with Johnny wasn't good for her, her heart was telling her that being without him would be worse.

Somewhere between the tears and the worry, Amber must have eventually dozed off. She woke up to find Johnny climbing into bed next to her. She waited for him to reach for her. When he didn't, she turned over to face him. He was on his back outside the covers, hands tucked behind his head, stark naked like always. She could tell from his breathing that he was still awake.

'I'm sorry about last night,' she said quietly.

He yawned. She smelled whisky.

'No worries.'

At least he wasn't angry with her any more. Eager to make it up to him, she reached down between his legs. She rubbed a little, but got no response. He pushed her hand away.

'Not now, darling.' He turned away from her.

She settled for spooning against his back instead. And, if she could smell Sheri's perfume on him, she chose not to think about it. She was just happy he'd come home to her.

Elizabeth called a few days later to say that she was going to be in town for a night – would Amber like to see her?

Amber jumped at the invitation. 'Oh, yes,' she said, surprised at how pleased she was to hear from her elder sister. 'I'd love to.'

Elizabeth wanted to come out to see her new place. But Amber, suddenly aware of just how ashamed she was of the grubby little house, suggested meeting for brunch at the Hotel Bel-Air, where she was staying, instead.

When Amber walked into the dining room, Elizabeth tried hard not to show how appalled she was by her little sister's appearance. It wasn't just that her hair was lank and her skin had the greasy look of someone living off junk food; what upset Elizabeth most was that Amber had lost her sparkle. She had that defeated look of someone who had been disappointed one too many times. It took all of Elizabeth's willpower to greet her as though everything was normal.

They went through the motions of catching up. Amber asked how Cole was – 'Fine,' Elizabeth answered tersely; then she asked after Johnny, whom she'd met once and hated on sight. 'He's fine, too,' Amber said, her eyes firmly fixed on the menu. After that they moved onto safer topics, gossiping about mutual acquaintances and the rest of the family.

It was only once they had finished eating, and the plates had been cleared away, that Elizabeth grew serious. 'You know, it was Daddy who suggested I come over here,' she said.

Amber looked guarded. 'Oh?'

'Yes.' On the plane over, Elizabeth had planned a whole lead into this. But now she simply said, 'He's worried about you, Amber. We all are. Please, come home.'

The younger girl felt a sudden rush of tears. She'd been expecting the usual lecture from Elizabeth about her lifestyle, her total lack of direction, what a disappointment she was. That she'd been prepared for. But this . . . well, she hadn't anticipated this stark, unconditional plea from her sister.

Heartened by the fact that Amber hadn't rejected her straight off, Elizabeth talked on. 'All you have to say is yes, and I can book you on a flight straight away,' she continued earnestly. 'We can leave tonight. Mummy and Daddy would love to see you.'

Amber didn't know what to say. It was *so* tempting – to go back to Aldringham, to stay in her old room, to let someone else take care of her for a change. But then, wouldn't it be like admitting defeat? She wanted to show them she could pull herself together, that she didn't need their help.

Somehow she swallowed down her tears and managed a

smile. 'Look, it's good of you to worry, but I'm fine. Maybe things were a bit difficult for a while, but everything's starting to pick up now. Did I tell you about this movie role I'm being considered for?'

Elizabeth sighed. 'No, you didn't.'

'Well, I'm not sure whether it's *totally* in the bag,' Amber said brightly, 'but everything's looking good . . .'

Elizabeth listened as Amber chattered on. She was aware that her sister was lying, but it seemed kinder to go along with the story. She'd said what she'd come here to say. It was down to Amber to take her up on the offer.

In the weeks after Elizabeth's visit, Amber tried to stick to her good resolutions. She started taking care of herself, kept off the drink and drugs, got early nights instead of going out partying with Johnny. But it was a constant battle. Every day brought new levels of personal humiliation followed by knock-back after knock-back. She'd gone from Hot to Not, Hero to Zero, and it seemed everyone wanted to remind her of that.

'What am I doing wrong?' she begged her agent.

Zena DeLaney was a gum-chewing, chain-smoking, middle-aged woman, past her prime in every way. Her offices currently comprised one room above a Laundromat; she didn't plan to move out anytime soon.

Zena shrugged carelessly. 'Who knows?' she said, in her nasal voice, mentally putting a black mark through the English girl's name. Zena had thought she was onto a good thing when the striking heiress had walked into her office. But she realised now that Amber was a dead end. 'Making a comeback's never gonna be easy at your age.'

Amber walked out feeling completely demoralised. Too old at twenty-five. She wasn't going to have the longevity of Cindy Crawford or Naomi Campbell. But what else could she do? She had no training, no way to make any money. She suddenly felt exhausted. Rising to the occasion looked easier in the movies.

It didn't help that Johnny wasn't exactly being supportive.

'Face it, love,' he said that night, taking a long drag on his spliff. 'You're past it. Happens to the best of us. I've had to get used to it. So should you.'

She was tempted to remind him of what had happened eighteen months earlier when one of the other band members, Dave Ridwell, had released his first single – and it had gone straight to number one. Johnny had gone on a bender that lasted two days. Since then he hadn't spoken about trying to get a record deal.

But was he right? Did she just need to resign herself to the inevitable?

As if sensing her resolve weakening, Johnny held out the joint to her. 'Here. This'll make you feel better.'

She stared down at it. She could think of nothing better than to lose herself in the sweet aroma; to forget cold, hard reality for just a little bit, to let the edges blur, to feel the peace and calm descending on her.

Finally, with a show of willpower she hadn't thought she possessed, she shook her head.

He shrugged. 'OK. Your choice.'

Amber felt proud of herself. She wasn't ready to give up quite yet.

For the first time in their relationship, Johnny was the breadwinner. He never seemed short of cash now. Amber had a good idea where it came from, although she pretended she didn't. People turned up at the house all hours of the day and night, strangers with hold-alls and backpacks stuffed full of God knows what. They would follow Johnny into the back room, never staying for long.

Business was always conducted behind closed doors. Amber

never asked what went on and Johnny never volunteered any details. She always stayed out of the way when Johnny's 'business associates', as he called them, were around. She didn't like the way they looked at her, especially Weasel.

Weasel was a Whigger – a tall, skinny white boy who thought he was black. He wore his jeans baggy and low, had an array of wife-beaters and a tattoo of a weasel smoking a joint on his scrawny right bicep. He didn't smile often, but when he did he displayed a set of yellow-brown teeth, apart from the very front incisor, which was solid gold. What annoyed Amber most was how he liked to talk ghetto.

"S'up, my niggaz?' He'd high-five Johnny, while looking at her, his eyes crawling all over her body. Amber always reached for something to cover up when he was there. She hated him being around. The house wasn't exactly big, but Weasel always seemed to disappear into dark corners, pouncing whenever she walked by.

'Does he have to come round here?' she asked Johnny once.

'If you want to keep eating.'

There wasn't much she could say to that.

One night, she got home from another disastrous casting, for a walk-on part in a TV advert. She'd waited in line for two hours. She'd kept her head up and tried to ignore the bitchy comments from the other girls. But when it got to six and the runner had come out to say that they were finished for the day, and everyone left would just have to come back tomorrow, she'd felt her resolve slipping.

She'd rushed home, hoping that Johnny wouldn't have any friends around and they could spend the evening alone together, like a proper boyfriend and girlfriend. She knew as soon as she got back that he wasn't there. It was dark and there weren't any lights on. She let herself in, trying not to feel disappointed. A note on the kitchen counter said he'd gone out with Weasel and would be back soon. She crumpled it up.

With Johnny, she never knew what 'back soon' meant.

The hours crawled by. She didn't want to eat – someone had told her last week that she was carrying a bit of weight on her hips – so she put on the TV, but she couldn't concentrate. She kept looking at her watch, feeling anxious and tense, wondering where Johnny was.

By midnight, he still wasn't home, so she went to bed. He'd be back by the next morning, she was sure of it.

Two days later, he finally walked through the door, as casually as if he'd popped out to fetch milk. By then, Amber was beside herself.

'Where were you?' she cried hysterically, rushing into his arms. She'd called every hospital and police station looking for him. 'I thought something had happened!'

'Hey, hey.' He pushed her away. 'I'm here now, aren't I? Quit your whining, woman.'

'But where were you?' she sniffed.

'With Weasel. We went down to Nuevo Laredo.'

'Oh.' She wanted to ask what he'd been doing at the Mexican border town, why he hadn't called. But she knew he wouldn't like that so she kept quiet.

'I was worried,' she said instead, feeling a fresh batch of tears start to run down her face.

Johnny shook his head. 'Jeez-us. You need to chill.'

He was right, she realised. She felt exhausted. She hadn't slept for nearly forty-eight hours, but it was more than that. She was tired of trying so hard; she was tired of constant rejection; she was tired of feeling so aware of her misery. And she knew there was one thing that could make her forget all that.

'Yes,' she agreed. 'You're right – I do need to chill. What exactly did you have in mind?'

Chapter 50

It was early morning in Paris. Sitting in his top-floor office at Grenier, Massé et Sanci's headquarters, Armand Bouchard's thoughts were across the Channel, with his English counterpart, William Melville.

Along with every other major fashion house, GMS was based on rue du Faubourg St-Honoré. Renowned for being one of the most fashionable streets in the world, it was a prestigious location. Even though being based there was expensive, Bouchard was happy to put up with the extra cost for the cachet. Whenever he looked around GMS's headquarters, he could feel proud of what he had achieved. There was nothing like being able to see a lifetime's achievements every day to make you feel good about yourself.

Of course, even the most successful businessman made mistakes along the way. For Armand, Melville was one of those. He could see that now. Eight years earlier, he'd known the English fashion house was in trouble. He should have moved then, but he'd hesitated. It had been hard to see any value in the business, and he'd thought that by waiting a while, he could pick it up at a bargain price.

Well, he'd been wrong. Now the company was worth three times what he would have paid for it then. But he wasn't going to beat himself up about it. William Melville might be driven by pride and arrogance, but Armand Bouchard was cold and logical. It was how he had got his nickname – Napoléon – in the press. Sure – he wished he'd moved sooner with Melville, but that didn't mean he would walk away now. Quite the opposite, in fact – he still saw value there.

'But surely nothing has changed since last time, Armand,' his second-in-command had challenged him at the last board meeting. 'With sixty per cent of the shares in the family's hands, how can you hope to get control? None of them will sell to you.'

The other directors had murmured their agreement. A week earlier, Armand would have conceded that they were right. Except they hadn't been privy to the phone call he'd received, out of the blue, the other day. A phone call that suggested the family wasn't quite as unified as everyone assumed.

Lately – well, ever since she'd moved in with Lucien, really – Caitlin had found herself thinking about having a baby. Perhaps it was something to do with finally being in a stable relationship, or perhaps it was simply that she wanted a family of her own, something she had missed out on during most of her adult life.

At first, she tried to put the idea from her mind. Naturally they'd talked about having children at some point, but she'd imagined that time was still a few years from now. And it seemed something of a cliché – wanting to be a mother to make up for the loss of her own. But, however hard she tried to forget about it, she simply couldn't.

'I know it's a silly idea,' she told Lucien, after finally confessing how she felt to him one evening, 'and that there are so many reasons to wait. We're both so busy at the moment, and we haven't even been together that long . . .'

Lucien nodded solemnly. 'You're right,' he agreed. 'There are a million reasons why this would be a terrible time to have a baby.' Caitlin felt a twinge of disappointment. But then he leaned forward, and she saw his eyes were dancing with amusement. 'But who cares about that?'

She drew back, startled. 'Really?'

He gave her a slow smile. 'Really, *chérie*.'

Two months later, to their delight, Caitlin found that she was pregnant.

The following weekend, she and Lucien went down to Aldringham to tell William their news. To Caitlin's amusement, he looked a little shocked and embarrassed at first. She had expected as much – he was terribly old-fashioned, after all. 'Not that he can say very much,' she had reassured Lucien on the drive down there. 'Not after what happened with my own mother.' But it still didn't stop him frowning disapprovingly at Lucien. Although once it was clear they intended to marry before the child was born, he seemed a lot happier.

In fact, William was thrilled at the thought of becoming a grandfather. He'd been saddened by Elizabeth's report of her meeting with Amber. He had no idea how to reach his troubled youngest daughter after she'd rejected his overtures again. But the news of his first grandchild cheered him.

He'd been thinking for a while that he wanted to make a gesture towards Caitlin, to reward her for all her hard work at Melville and to signify that she was part of the family. Now seemed like a good opportunity to do that. So, the following Monday, he asked his solicitor to start drawing up the papers to transfer 5 per cent of his shares in the company to Caitlin. 'You don't have to do that,' she protested, when he told her of his intention.

'But I want to,' he said firmly. 'Elizabeth and Amber both have a stake in the company. It only seems right that you do, too.'

He also insisted on throwing an engagement party. At first he wanted to make it a grand occasion, but Caitlin persuaded him not to – she had already agreed with Lucien that they would keep everything low-key. So instead, the following week, they gathered for an informal drinks party at Eaton Square and broke the news to the rest of the family and a few select friends.

Mostly, everyone was pleased for them. Elizabeth was the only one who seemed a little off, her congratulations forced, her questions about their plans rather sharp.

'So where are you planning to tie the knot?' she asked.

'Aldringham,' Caitlin told her. 'It's going to be very small—'

'Aldringham?' she cut in. She downed her wine and held out her empty glass to a passing waiter. 'How lovely. I bet Daddy's delighted.' She gave a thin smile. 'It seems like everything's turning out *perfectly* for you at the moment.'

'Elizabeth,' Cole said warningly.

She rounded on him. 'What?'

He nodded at the wine glass in her hands. 'Don't you think you've had enough to drink?'

'No, I don't actually,' she retorted, and walked off.

Caitlin watched as Cole followed her out to the terrace, where they continued their argument away from the party. She couldn't help remembering how in love the two of them had been. What on earth had happened?

'I hope we don't end up like that,' she said to Lucien later that night, as they lay in bed together.

He turned over and hugged her gently to him. She had noticed him doing that a lot lately, treating her as though she was glass, liable to break at any second.

'Of course we won't, *chérie*. We will always be as happy as this.'

She closed her eyes, feeling tiredness wash over her. Right now, when everything felt so perfect, it was easy to believe him.

The following Monday, she arrived at work to find a message saying that there was an emergency board meeting starting at ten. With only five minutes to spare, she grabbed her camomile tea and headed upstairs.

'Any idea what this is about?' she asked Douglas Levan, as she slipped into the seat next to him. She usually didn't like the slimy Sales Director, but today nothing could spoil her good mood. She was successful, pregnant and in love – what could go wrong?

Douglas pulled a face. 'How the hell should I know? It's not like anyone tells me anything.'

Caitlin ignored the jibe. She was feeling too happy to let him get to her. In fact, Caitlin was so caught up in her own little world that she hardly noticed the grim expressions on the faces of Elizabeth and William as they walked through the door. It was only when her father stood to speak, and the room fell into an uneasy silence, that she felt a prickle of concern. As far as she knew, Melville was doing brilliantly: all the numbers coming through were good, the commentary in the press was excellent. What on earth could be going on?

'I hoped we were out of the woods with this,' William began. 'I thought with the recovery . . .' He came to a halt.

Everyone in the room was frowning, confused. Caitlin suddenly noticed his ashen face. Whatever this was about, it was bad.

He coughed a little, clearing his throat. 'It's just been announced to the market that someone has built up a five per cent stake in Melville.'

'Who?' demanded Douglas Levan.

William gave a derisive snort. 'Armand Bouchard, of course.'

The room exploded, everyone talking at once.

William lifted his hand for quiet. 'I know, I know. It's a terrible shock. But make no mistake – we will fight this.' He drew himself up to his full height, warming to his theme. 'I've already been on the phone to our bankers. We're going to set up a war room, get our defences in place.' He turned to Caitlin. 'I want you to sit down with an HR specialist to go over your contract – they're going to insert a clause that says you can walk out in the event of a third party acquiring over thirty per cent of the share capital. Elizabeth, you'll come with me to talk about shoring up our financial position.'

'Do you want me along, too?' Piers asked.

William looked over at him briefly. 'That won't be necessary.'

'But—'

'Piers, please.' William didn't bother to keep the exasperation out of his voice. 'This is important.'

Piers watched them go. He'd given William one last chance to make him part of his inner circle. And he'd been rejected again. If he'd been at all undecided about whether to go ahead with his plan, that exchange had made up his mind.

The house looked ordinary enough. It was an anonymous semi on a busy road in Hounslow, West London. Sullivan Road itself was that odd mix of commercial and residential, with a Chinese takeaway, dry cleaners and DVD store at one end, and tired housing at the other. The residents were mainly low-income renters and council tenants. That meant no one stuck around long enough to notice the goings-on at number 32.

Irina Serapiniene had been living at number 32 for five months now, but she still didn't know much about Hounslow. The one important detail she did know was that it was only a twenty-minute drive from Heathrow, where she had arrived twenty-three weeks, five days and seventeen hours ago. From there, it was only a two-hour flight to Lithuania. That knowledge, the proximity of home, was what kept her going as she looked out of the top-floor window – nailed shut so she couldn't escape – and at the busy junction below.

Irina knew now that she had been stupid. Back in her home town of Vilnius, the Lithuanian capital, she had always been on the lookout for adventure. At fifteen, she was a pretty girl, with her fair hair and slight build, and vivacious too, the most daring of her friends, going to new places and staying out after curfew.

So when she got chatting to a woman at a nightclub, who said she could organise work in England over the summer, Irina jumped at the chance.

'What would I be doing?' she asked eagerly.

Her new friend, Sonja, was vague. 'Probably waitressing in London – it'll be fun and well-paid. Oh,' she added as an afterthought, 'and your flight will be taken care of, too.' Later that week, Irina forged her parents' signature on the document allowing her to leave Lithuania unaccompanied. Then she packed a small bag, left a hasty note for her mother, and went off to meet Sonja at the airport.

It was only when they got to Heathrow that Irina began to feel nervous. Sonja asked for her passport, and they were then joined by an older, thickset man, an Albanian named Bedari.

'He's a friend,' Sonja told Irina. 'He'll take you to your accommodation.'

That was the last time Irina ever saw Sonja.

Irina grew increasingly apprehensive on the journey. The man didn't speak once. When they finally arrived at number 32 Sullivan Road, she followed him inside and up to a small, shabby room on the first floor. She had barely put her suitcase down when he knocked her to the ground and proceeded to rape her.

'Getting you to England cost twenty thousand pounds,' he told her once he'd finished. 'This is how you'll pay that debt off. And if you try to escape, I'll kill you.'

Then he left her alone, turning the key in the lock so she was in no doubt that she was his prisoner.

Over the next week, Bedari and three other men took turns to condition her. After a month, Irina ran out of tears. She was expected to service twenty to thirty men a day, and she learned to do it without complaining rather than risk Bedari's fists. The men themselves disgusted her. Sometimes they were rough; sometimes they paid more for anal sex so they didn't have to use a condom. She was terrified of getting sick, of getting pregnant. She wasn't allowed out by herself. The girls rarely got to speak to each other, but what Irina heard terrified her – some of them had been sold to three, four, five different people. She hoped that wouldn't happen to her. At least here she knew how close she was to the airport. It was something to hang onto.

And now there was a bigger reason for not wanting to be sold on. *Hope.* Someone had promised to help her. One of her regular clients, a man called Matthew. He was quietly spoken, shy – in his late twenties, she guessed – and kind, too. He had started coming to see her regularly and seemed to have taken a shine to her, bringing her little gifts of soaps and chocolate. Even Bedari had joked about it.

'This one, he might marry you, hey, Irina?' he'd said, nudging her in the ribs.

She'd wondered sometimes why Matthew didn't have a girl of his own; she guessed it was because of his weight. But underneath he was a nice man. On his third visit he had started asking her about herself, asking where she had come from, if she was OK. Her English wasn't good, but he'd seemed to understand that she was here against her will. And he had promised to help her escape. Next Thursday. Only four more days. After all this time, she could last that long.

The key turned in the lock and Irina's heart jumped, as it always did at that sound. Bedari appeared in the doorway. He said something to the man behind him, who moved forward to take a look at Irina. This must be the client Bedari had told her about earlier. He was rich, apparently, with very specific requests.

'He like natural yellow hair,' Bedari had said. 'None of that dye shit.' The Albanian had brought clothes for her, too. She wasn't to put on the short, tight skirt or garish make-up like usual. Instead, she wore a floral dress with long sleeves and a demure neckline. Her face was scrubbed clean and her fair hair brushed until it shone. Irina tugged nervously at the collar of the dress. Anything out of the ordinary worried her now. The stranger looked her over, then turned to Bedari and said something. She understood enough to know that the man was pleased with her. Money was exchanged, and then a happy Bedari left the room, locking the door behind him.

Once they were alone, the man indicated for her to sit on the bed. She did as she was told and he smiled a little at her. She began to relax. He was different from her usual clients, better dressed, clean and close-shaven. He sounded a little like Matthew, she decided. She wondered why he came to a place like this, when surely he could have many women.

He came over to sit beside her on the bed. He was still fully dressed and seemed to have no interest in taking her clothes off, either. He simply stroked her blonde hair away from her forehead, tracing the contours of her face with his hand. There was something almost tender in the way he touched her. After months of being starved of affection, it took Irina by surprise. For some reason, she had the strangest urge to laugh. A giggle rose in her throat. She tried to swallow it back, but failed. As the man bent to kiss her, a strange, high-pitched titter bubbled forth from her, a nervous, involuntary sound.

Her hand came up to cover her mouth, but it was already too late. In that split second, the man's expression changed. For a brief moment he looked hurt, and then his eyes hardened, his lips tightened. She could tell that he thought she was laughing at him, mocking him.

After all this time, Irina had developed a sixth sense for danger. The alarm sounding in her head reminded her of when she'd first met Bedari all those months ago. She saw the blow coming even before the man had raised his hand.

'*Ne* . . .' she implored, as his open palm connected with her cheek. If only she knew the words to explain that she hadn't meant to be disrespectful. '*Prasau!*' she cried. 'Help!'

But he wasn't listening. He had stood up now, so he could put more power behind his fists. Irina had seen men like this before, and knew there would be no reasoning with him – just as she knew that her screams and anguished pleas would be ignored by everyone in the house.

The back of his hand struck her other cheek. Weighing 90 pounds to his 160, she was no match against the full force of his rage. The impact of the blow split her skin open and knocked her off the bed. She put her hands out to break her fall. But as she went down, she cracked her head on the bedside cabinet. Her neck snapped back and she felt something break inside her.

She must have been drifting in and out of consciousness. The next thing she knew, she was lying on her back, staring up at the ceiling. The man was kneeling over her, and he no longer looked angry, only scared. And he was shouting at the door – calling for help, she imagined. But it was already too late. She could feel herself fading now, slipping away for good.

It was so unfair, she thought dreamily. A few weeks ago, this might have seemed like sweet release. Now she'd had an end in sight – only four days until Matthew came to rescue her. But she wouldn't be here for him. Would he notice? Would anyone care that she had gone?

That was the last thought that went through her head.

Chapter 51

Tokyo had been playing on Elizabeth's mind. It was Piers's comment on the uncertainty surrounding her father's successor. Something that had seemed so implausible when she'd first read about it in that newspaper article all those weeks ago suddenly appeared more likely.

It didn't help that everything seemed to be about Caitlin at the moment. Elizabeth was so fed up with celebrating her half-sister's achievements, her wonderful, perfect life. And now her father was planning to give Caitlin five per cent of the company. Maybe, like he said, it was simply to bring her closer to the family. But maybe there was something more sinister behind his actions.

Elizabeth brought up her concerns with Piers, who seemed to be the only person on her side at the moment. He tried to reassure her that she had nothing to worry about. But finally, when she wouldn't let it go, he sighed and said, 'If you're really that worried, you should talk to him. Ask him outright what his plans are. That way you can set your mind at ease.'

That evening, Piers was due to have dinner with William. The ten-year age gap between the two men had never been so obvious. The stress of Armand Bouchard's takeover bid had caused another angina attack. Piers sensed that the episode had upset his brother, reminded him again of his own mortality. It was the perfect time for him to raise the subject of Elizabeth.

'So did Elizabeth get round to speaking to you in the end?' he asked.

William looked up sharply. 'No. Why?'

'Oh!' Piers feigned surprise. 'Oh, it's nothing.'

William scowled. 'Come on. Spit it out.'

'Honestly, William. It's nothing. She's just worried about you.'

'Worried about me?' William was on the defensive now. 'In what way? What did she say?'

Piers pinched the bridge of his nose. 'She simply mentioned that she's concerned about your health, especially now that this Bouchard mess has reared its head again.'

'Concerned about my health? What's that supposed to mean?'

Piers looked uncomfortable. 'Well, she thinks we need a strong management team if we've got any hope of seeing his bid off.'

William's eyes narrowed. 'And she doesn't think I'm up to it, is that what you're saying?'

'Heavens no!' Piers protested. 'She's just worried about the strain all this is putting on you.'

William's voice was cold as he said, 'Well, you can tell her from me that she's got nothing to worry about.'

A few days later, Elizabeth finally managed to get an appointment with her father.

'Daddy,' she said immediately, 'I think we need to have a serious chat about your succession plans.'

William was immediately suspicious. 'What plans?'

'Well, I assumed—'

'I wouldn't assume anything, Elizabeth,' he interrupted. 'As you can see, I'm fit and healthy and have no intention of going anywhere.'

'But the other week—'

'The other week was nothing. It was just a small episode.' He gave a wry smile. 'Would you jump into my grave half as quick?'

'Daddy! I didn't mean it like that! I just think that your choice of next Chief Executive is something we ought to talk about.'

'Why? What's it got to do with you?'

Elizabeth felt confused. This wasn't how the conversation was supposed to turn out. 'I would have thought it had everything to do with me,' she said. 'I've spent the past three years sweating blood, getting this business back on its feet!'

'Don't exaggerate,' William said icily. 'You're not the only one who cares about this business, and you're not the only one who helped turn things around.'

'Oh, yes? And who else helped? Caitlin, I suppose.'

He looked at her levelly. 'Now you mention it, Caitlin has played her part.'

It was precisely the wrong thing to say. 'Oh, please,' Elizabeth scoffed. 'She might be good at designing, but that doesn't mean she's got what it takes to run a major company. She doesn't have it in her, and you must be losing it if you think she has!'

'Don't talk about me or your sister like that!' William thundered.

'*Half*-sister, Daddy,' she shot back. 'You might want to remember that.'

'And *you* might want to remember that I am still in charge of this company.' His voice was cold, his eyes like flint. 'For now, what I say goes.'

She stared at him for a long moment. 'That's what I'm worried about.'

It was the worst outcome Elizabeth could have imagined. But she didn't realise that her life was about to disintegrate even futher.

Elizabeth would always remember the exact moment she realised Cole was having an affair. It was the night of his birthday, and he'd decided to hold a dinner in the private dining room of Osaka. She was late as usual, a last-minute crisis at the office. She rushed into the restaurant, flustered, knowing she didn't look her best, wishing she'd had time to get her hair done and change into the new outfit she'd bought.

Dinner was already underway by the time she reached the dining room. Cole was at the head of the table and his PA, that mousey little Japanese girl, was next to him. Elizabeth was about to walk over but something stopped her. She'd never really bought into that women's intuition nonsense, but somehow she sensed something wasn't quite right.

She lingered in the doorway for a moment, watching Cole and Sumiko together. It wasn't that they were doing anything obvious – holding hands or whispering to each other – they were simply eating sashimi, like everyone else round the table. But when some wasabi sauce escaped from the side of Cole's mouth, Sumiko giggled, and then reached up to wipe it away.

And that's when Elizabeth *knew*.

It was like a physical blow. She faltered on her feet, had to grab the doorframe to steady herself. She felt the bile rise from her stomach, as she remembered how Cole had joked about Sumiko's crush on him, how she had teased him about it. But there was no time to feel sorry for herself. People had begun to notice her. She couldn't run away and cry – and God, that wasn't her style anyway. She had no choice but to go over to face them.

As she crossed the marble floor, the conversation at the table faded as the guests turned to watch her arrival. They were all waiting to see what she was going to do, she realised. Well, she wasn't about to give them the satisfaction of causing a scene. Instead, she pasted on a smile and walked over to Cole.

'Happy Birthday, darling.' She leaned down to kiss him lightly on the mouth. 'Sorry I'm late.'

'Don't worry about it.' And he meant it, too.

She realised then why he hadn't been mad at her for missing the opening of Osaka; why he'd stopped bugging her about the hours she was working.

Elizabeth was still standing. Cole had made no move to find her a seat. There was a spare place at the other end of the table, but she was damned if she was going to sit there.

'Sumiko, would you mind,' she said, pointing towards the empty chair. 'I'd like to sit next to my husband.'

'Of course, Elizabeth.'

The words were said politely enough, but Elizabeth couldn't miss the touch of insolence in her eyes. It took all of her self-control not to slap the girl – and God, she was a girl, too – as she took her time gathering her belongings and vacating the seat.

Dinner was terrible. Elizabeth could feel everyone looking over at her, assessing her mood. Somehow, she kept up a steady stream of polite conversation. She stuck to mineral water, apart from a sip of champagne for the birthday toast, worried that alcohol might make her say something she shouldn't.

The party broke up around midnight. She watched Cole kiss Sumiko briefly on the cheek, his hand lingering a fraction too long on her arm, and wondered how much more of this she could stand.

Husband and wife didn't say much to each other during the taxi-ride home. Throughout the meal, Elizabeth had envisioned confronting Cole when they got back, but once they were there, she couldn't find the words. They went straight up to the bedroom, undressing silently, backs to each other. How long had it been like this between them? Elizabeth wondered.

Once they were in bed, the lights out, she reached for him. She felt his reluctance at first, knew he wanted to pull away, but she was insistent, bringing her mouth down hard on his, making it clear what she wanted.

He gave in, but on his terms. There was no romance, no

affection. He turned her over, so they couldn't kiss, then mounted her, thrusting into her fast and hard. There was silence throughout the whole act, the only sound a low grunt when he finally came. Then he rolled away from her, still saying nothing.

She waited until his breathing deepened and she knew he was asleep, before stealing out of bed and going over to the ensuite. Locking the door behind her, she sat down on the edge of the bath and finally cried. She cried so long and hard that it was as though she'd never cried before, biting down on her hand so he couldn't hear the huge, great hulking sobs that racked her body.

A long while later, she washed her face and headed back to bed.

She planned to say something the following morning, but she still couldn't find the words. And as the days and weeks passed, she realised she wasn't going to. She was surprised and appalled at herself. All those years she'd scorned her mother for sticking by her father, and now she was doing exactly the same thing. But the truth was, for the first time in her life she had no idea what course of action would be for the best. Because, when it came down to it, she still loved Cole.

She wasn't sure what she was waiting for. But then Fate has a habit of throwing in a catalyst, a wild card, a curve ball – something you'd never expect. For Elizabeth it was the third morning in a row when she found herself on her hands and knees, heaving over the toilet bowl. As she sat back on her haunches, wiping her mouth with a piece of hastily grabbed toilet paper, she remembered how preoccupied she'd been six weeks earlier. Preoccupied enough to forget taking her birth control pills around the time of Cole's birthday. And preoccupied enough not to notice what she'd done until now, when it was far too late.

*

Getting through the days was an effort for Elizabeth. Everything was piling up on her, and she was waiting for something to crack. The situation still hadn't improved with her father. She was terrified that he was seriously considering making Caitlin the next Chief Executive.

Elizabeth was sick of hearing about Caitlin. She remembered when the girl had first arrived at Aldringham, shy, naïve and awkward. How was it that now she seemed to have everything – the company, as well as a man who was madly in love with her, and a baby on the way – when she, Elizabeth, the original golden girl, had nothing?

She'd never really thought having a child was important to her. But now, in the position where she had no partner to be happy with her, to share in what should be a joyful occasion, she realised how much she wanted it. With no one to tell, she had never felt more on her own.

The only person who seemed to be on her side was Piers. It was in him alone that she confided her fear that William was favouring Caitlin. They spent long evenings closeted in his office, as she ranted about the unfairness of it all.

'It's ridiculous!' she declared, for what felt like the hundredth time. 'I deserve this! I've given up everything for this business – all my time, my energy. Even my . . .' She had been about to say 'even my marriage', but managed to stop herself.

'I know, I know,' Piers commiserated. 'I'm on your side. I think your father's on the verge of making a terrible mistake. I don't want to see you cheated out of your inheritance, either.'

Suddenly all the fight went out of her. Between Cole and this . . . she just didn't have the energy any longer. 'But I suppose if Daddy wants it that way, there's nothing I can do, is there?'

It had been a rhetorical question. But she saw the look that crossed Piers's face – thoughtful, calculating – and the spark in his eyes. 'What is it?' she said slowly. 'What are you thinking?'

'I *might* have an idea how to get around this, to make sure you get what you deserve, after all.' He was studying her carefully as he spoke, as though looking for her reaction. 'It's not perfect, of course,' he continued. 'But it might well be our only option.'

Elizabeth felt a prickle of unease. The way he'd said it, she sensed whatever he had in mind was going to go against her father's wishes. But what choice did she have?

'Tell me,' she whispered.

Piers's suggestion was for them to stage a management buyout – effectively an acquisition by executives within the company. He wanted to pool their shares – his 5 per cent and her 7.5 per cent – then launch the takeover bid together. There was one main complication – as they wouldn't have the personal funds to acquire the company outright themselves, they'd need to find an external backer.

'How hard would that be?' Elizabeth asked, both thrilled and terrified by what Piers was suggesting. Was she seriously considering this? Did she dare?

'I've been looking into it,' he said, a touch enigmatically. 'I think there are a couple of private investors who might be willing to put up the money.'

His arguments were clear and concise. With two members of the family working together, their bid would be viewed favourably by the market – especially if they emphasised her part in the turnaround. He'd even put together a spreadsheet showing the price they could offer to buy at. If she was a little surprised that he'd gone so far on his own, she didn't dwell on it. At first glance, the numbers looked good; they would be offering 40 per cent premium to where the shares were trading. Of course, it was easy with a management buyout to put together a fair price – they were both insiders who knew the business well.

As Elizabeth studied the figures, she realised it might just work. At the level they were offering, it wouldn't make much financial sense for Armand Bouchard to top that. And William wouldn't be able to amass the sort of backing he would need in order to counter the bid.

'And with his ill health lately, I don't think any bank will see him as a good risk,' Piers concluded. 'Of course, I know neither of us wants to hurt your father,' he said hurriedly, 'but it does seem to me that he isn't thinking straight at the moment. Maybe in the long run he'll even thank us for this.'

On her way home that night, Elizabeth wondered if she dared talk Piers's proposal over with Cole. Usually she liked to get his opinion on any major decision within the company, since he often saw something that she didn't. Maybe this would be a good way to get them talking again. But as soon as Elizabeth walked into the house, she knew it wasn't to be. Two brown leather cases stood by the front door. Cole was leaving her.

She found him in the lounge, sitting in the dark. A bottle of whisky sat in front of him on the coffee-table – it was hardly touched. Elizabeth stopped still, a cold feeling sweeping through her. She was surprised how strong her voice sounded as she asked, 'What's going on, Cole?'

Cole ran the tumbler of amber liquid between his hands. He couldn't even look at her.

'I'm moving out,' he said finally, stating the obvious. Slowly he raised his gaze to meet hers. 'There's no point in me being here. I haven't been happy for a long time and I don't think you have either.'

She walked over to the chair opposite him and sat down. 'How can you know what I feel when you haven't bothered to ask?' she said, more calmly than she felt.

'I have been asking, Elizabeth. You just haven't noticed. I've tried talking about this.' He leaned forward, clasping his hands together. 'I've been trying for months. But you don't seem remotely interested in making things work.'

'And you are?' she retorted. 'Because tell me, please – how exactly is screwing your secretary helping our marriage?'

The words took a moment to sink in. She saw the look of surprise cross his face and almost enjoyed it.

'Yes, that's right,' she said softly. 'I know all about Sumiko.'

He had the grace to look ashamed. 'Look, it just happened, OK? You were never here . . .'

'Oh, so this is my fault?' Elizabeth broke in. 'I drove you to it, did I? Let me guess, I don't understand you the way she does.'

'That's not what I meant.' He ran a hand through his short, dark hair. 'It just . . . wasn't the same between us. And Sumiko – well, she flattered me, paid me a lot of attention, I suppose.'

'Yeah, I just bet she did.'

Cole winced at the venom in her voice. Elizabeth saw his reaction and wished that she could take the words back. Why did she always find it easier to make a quick retort than say what was in her heart? She wanted to start this conversation over, only this time she'd tell him how she really felt: how she hated what he had done, how she had cried for hours over his affair . . . how she still loved him and wished she'd listened to him months earlier, so that it hadn't come to this.

But when she closed her eyes, she couldn't get that image of the two of them out of her head. She wasn't sure she ever would. Sumiko: soft and obliging, sweet and exotic . . . everything that she, Elizabeth, wasn't.

'I guess it was handy for you,' she said sharply, suddenly wanting to pick a fight.

He looked at her wearily. 'What's that?'

'That I was working so hard. I guess it gave you a lot of free time to see *her*.' Elizabeth couldn't stand to say her name again. 'I mean, how long has it been going on for? It must have been a while. I figured it out a few weeks ago, and what do they always say – that the wife is the last to know.' She gave a short, bitter laugh. 'So it must have started a long time before that.'

Cole looked pained. 'Elizabeth, please. This isn't getting us anywhere.'

'Well, I think I have a right to know the details. Like, when did it start between you? And where exactly did you conduct your little trysts?'

'Elizabeth, don't!'

But she wasn't listening. 'Did you go to a hotel? Did you bring her back here?' She could hear her voice growing shrill, a note of hysteria creeping in, but she continued with her rant. 'Does everyone at your office know? Have they all been laughing behind my back?' She stopped abruptly, aware suddenly of how overwrought she sounded.

Cole stared at her for a long moment. 'Maybe it's best if I go,' he said quietly.

'Go where?' she snapped. 'To be with *her*?'

Sensing the conversation was going nowhere, Cole got to his feet. It struck her then. He was going; he was really leaving her. She desperately wanted to say something to stop him. She knew this was the moment, if ever there had been one, to tell him about the baby. But her pride intervened. If this was really it, she didn't want his last image to be of her begging him to stay.

So she said nothing and instead watched as he walked away from her.

At the door he stopped, turned back. 'This isn't about Sumiko, Elizabeth. It never was. She's the symptom, not the cause, of what's been going wrong.'

With that, he was gone.

Chapter 52

Amber was feeling no pain. She was happy, oh so happy. There was nothing like it – sitting cross-legged around the flame, that long moment of anticipation as the brown powder melted into a ball of fluid, and then leaning over greedily to breathe in its magical perfume.

Over the years, she'd indulged in everything from alcohol and marijuana to ketamine, coke, Ecstasy and speed. But, for her, nothing beat the heroin rush: that first burst of euphoria as the drug crossed the blood-brain barrier, the intense explosion of pleasure in her gut that slowly melted into a feeling of warmth and well-being, as though she were floating away on a cloud where no one could touch her. There were no worries with heroin, no nagging self-doubt – only sweet release. And that's what Amber craved.

Of course, she'd dabbled with H over the past two years, ever since that first time Johnny had introduced her to it. But this time it was different. Somehow it had become a regular part of her routine. And she would be concerned about that, except most of the time these days she was in a happy place, where there was no need to worry.

The only drawback was that Weasel seemed to be around more than ever.

'Do you *have* to bring him here?' Amber complained one time. 'I don't like the way he looks at me.' She shivered just thinking about him. 'It gives me the creeps.'

Johnny shrugged disinterestedly. 'Yeah, so he fancies you,

princess. You should be flattered.' He gave her a sly look. 'In fact, maybe if you were a bit nicer to him, he'd be nicer to us.'

Amber recoiled. 'What's that supposed to mean?'

Johnny quickly shook his head. 'Nothing. Just kiddin' round. Forget it already.'

And Amber found it easy to forget once he started heating up the silver foil.

Except, as the weeks went by, it was getting harder and harder to achieve that same feeling of euphoria. She was doing more and more hits a day, but it just didn't have the same effect.

'I know how you can feel that good again,' Johnny said whenever she complained. And she knew what he was talking about. The syringe he kept offering. The promise he made that it would hit the spot much faster, give her that same rush as the first time. Her mouth went dry, her palms sweaty, just thinking about it. It was taking all her self-control to say no.

One night Johnny brought home some extra-good stuff, 'Real pure,' he assured her. He was right. It was so good that Amber stopped minding that Sheri and Weasel were there too. As the hit took hold, she sank back on the cushions spread out across the floor of the sitting room. Still no furniture, but who cared? She felt so mellow, like she was seeing everything through a haze. Life was good.

Sheri stood up and held out her hand to Johnny. The rest of them had stuck to snorting coke, so they weren't as out of it as Amber.

'Why don't we go in there?' Sheri nodded at the spare room.

Johnny took one look at his girlfriend, decided she was too far gone to notice and followed Sheri inside. As he closed the door, he saw Weasel moving towards a drowsy Amber. The two men exchanged looks. Johnny didn't feel bad about their little agreement. It wasn't as if she had any idea what was going on right now. And it was about time she started paying her way.

Through the haze, Amber watched Johnny and Sheri go. She felt drowsy and wondered if it was time for her to sleep, too. But she didn't want to be alone just yet. Weasel was here, though, to keep her company. She held out her arms to him.

'Wee-zel,' she sang drowsily. 'Love-ley Wee-zel.' She giggled. Then she promptly passed out.

Weasel looked down at the unconscious girl. He had been looking forward to this for a long, long time. He'd had to put up with her high-and-mighty ways for months. But now everything had changed. She was the dirt and he was in control.

He licked his cracked lips in anticipation, watching her stretch and smile in her sleep. She was in a good place, having good times. He felt his hard-on deflate a little. In his fantasies she'd always been fully aware of what he was doing to her, that was part of the turn-on.

Bitch, he thought. Fucking bitch. Well, she wasn't going to cheat him out of this. He had the whole night to do whatever he wanted with her. Maybe he just needed to get creative.

Feeling better, he leaned down and picked her up, fireman's lift over his shoulder. He wasn't a strong guy – but she weighed pretty much nothing, and it was easy enough to carry her through to the bedroom. He kicked the door shut, dropped her on the bed.

By the time he'd taken her clothes off, he was geared up and ready to go. He quickly got undressed himself, catching sight of the condom that had fallen out of his jeans pocket. God, how he hated those things. Everyone made you use one these days – even the hookers. Well, not tonight. The thought made him even harder. He turned Amber over and ran his hands over her skinny, white buttocks.

This was going to be great.

*

Amber woke in her bedroom the next morning. Her first thought, as it was every morning, was that in five minutes she could have her first hit of the day. Tears sprang to her eyes. God, she felt low. It wasn't a new feeling. She often woke miserable and depressed. Sometimes it was so bad that she just wanted everything to end. But Johnny seemed to sense those days and knew exactly what to do. The H usually cured that, made all the bad thoughts go away. But today Johnny wasn't there with her. She was alone. And something wasn't right.

She couldn't remember how she'd got here, for one thing. She was on top of the sheets. Her clothes were on, but not right. Her T-shirt was inside out, the buttons on her jeans done up wrong. She tried to remember the night before. They'd been in the lounge, her, Johnny, Sheri and Weasel. She remembered taking some stuff, some great stuff, and then . . . She must have passed out. She'd had a horrible dream. About Weasel.

She felt a chill descend on her. There was no air conditioner on, the room was like an oven, but her body was covered in goosebumps. She suddenly became aware of the pain between her legs and in her back, as if someone had tried to split her open. Her eyes strayed to the baseball bat in the corner. There was blood on the handle.

Her screams brought Johnny running in.

'What did he do?' she kept yelling over and over again. 'What did you let him do to me?'

She was sobbing hysterically. Johnny kept trying to take her in his arms, to calm her down, but this time she wouldn't be pacified so easily. Over the tears and shouting, she thought she heard the front door click closed.

'What was that?' she demanded, suddenly alert. 'Was that Sheri? Did you spend the night with her while that sicko . . .?' She stopped talking then because she couldn't breathe, she was almost hyperventilating. 'Oh my God. Oh my God,' she kept panting over and over again.

'Fucking calm down, Amber!' Johnny yelled at her. Then he slapped her across the face hard: once, twice. He'd read that shock like that could snap someone out of their hysteria. It was a risky approach, but it paid off. Amber finally stopped screaming. The crying and shouting subsided, and soon she was just sitting on the edge of the bed, sobbing quietly.

'But you don't understand,' she whimpered. 'The stuff he did . . .'

Johnny was kneeling in front of her now. He grabbed her shoulders and shook her a little. 'Don't be stupid. That never happened. It was just a dream.'

Amber felt confused. It had seemed so real. But it couldn't have happened, right? Johnny wouldn't have let something like that happen to her.

He was speaking to her in low, reassuring tones. 'I've got something for you. Something that'll make you forget everything. Does that sound good?' She nodded numbly, knowing what he was going to do and no longer having the energy to argue. She wanted to put those horrible thoughts out of her mind.

She held out her skinny arm for him.

After that, she was mainlining three times a day. And Johnny was right, it wasn't like all the scare stories. Life was the same as always – just so much better because whenever things got bad she knew there was that sweet release available.

Sometimes she wondered why she'd been so afraid of the syringe. She wasn't a junkie – someone who would steal a TV for a fix, rob a pharmacy without considering getting caught. She was a functioning addict, someone who was able to hide the dilated pupils, needle scars and ferocious hunger from everyone who knew her. For now, at least.

Rich came round to see her. He'd surprised her by keeping in touch.

'Jesus, Amber!' he said when she opened the door. 'What the hell's happened to you?'

He frowned at the long-sleeved shirt she wore even though it was hitting ninety degrees outside. That was a stupid move, she realised. People noticed stuff like that, something out of the ordinary. She'd have to be smarter.

Even she was surprised at how sneaky she could be. She learned to disguise the needle marks with make-up, and cover up her weightloss by wearing baggy clothes. If anyone asked why she was so thin, she was quite happy to hint that she was anorexic. She didn't care what anyone thought of her, as long as they didn't find out about the precious H and take it away from her.

Johnny Wilcox had gone out that night with the express intention of getting good and drunk. He'd ended up in a bar in Reseda, one of LA's shittier neighbourhoods. It was a typical sleazy establishment, complete with pool table, rednecks and a beefy bartender hiding a Glock under the counter in case of trouble. And alcohol, of course. Cheap alcohol.

Except the alcohol wasn't having the desired effect. He owed money to men who frankly scared the shit out of him. And that was keeping him sober.

The empty-eyed waitress saw he'd finished his drink. 'Can I git you anything else?'

'Yeah. Why not?'

They'd told him yesterday that he had a week to come up with the cash. There was no way. He wasn't even sure how he'd gotten himself into this mess in the first place. When his record deal hadn't come through, he'd started dealing on the side. It had seemed like easy money at first. He had good connections in the music industry, which meant a ready supply of customers who had the means to pay.

But then that deal Weasel had set him up on had gone bad.

He'd turned up at the meet as usual but, instead of the regular buyer, a Hummer had drawn up. He hadn't been able to make out any faces – he'd been too busy staring at the submachine pistol. He'd had no choice but to hand over the stuff. It was a set-up, he reckoned. And he suspected Weasel had something to do with it.

'One hundred thousand dollars, Johnny,' an anonymous voice had told him down the phone last night. 'By the end of next week.'

It might as well be one hundred million. The only major asset Amber had left was the house, and there wasn't enough time to sell that. You'd think with all that money her family had, she'd be able to lay her hands on some cash.

The only option left was running – but he'd been assured that if he tried anything like that, it would end badly for him. He wasn't inclined to put the threat to the test. Especially since on the way down here he was almost sure he was being followed. Maybe he was being paranoid, but a black Mercedes had been on his tail. Granted, it had sped on when he pulled over, but still . . .

He downed a final shot, threw twenty dollars he couldn't afford on the table, and headed for the door.

Outside, the alleyway that ran along the back of the bar was deserted. He pulled his baseball cap down and hurried towards his car. Sirens wailed as two cop cars and an ambulance sped by on the main street. Another busy night in downtown LA. He jumped as a bin lid crashed to the ground behind him. Then he heard a cat screech into the darkness and relaxed a little, hurrying on.

He was nearly back where he'd parked when he noticed that another car had pulled in front of his. As he got closer, the headlights came on, hitting him in the face.

'Hey!' he protested. He held up his hand, shielding his eyes from the glare. As he became accustomed to the light, he realised the car was the black Mercedes he'd spotted earlier. The windshield glass was tinted so he couldn't see inside.

He stopped still, thought about turning and running. But he had no idea where he'd go.

One of the car doors opened. A man he didn't recognise got out.

'Mr Wilcox?' He spoke in a cultured English accent. 'I have a business proposition for you.'

Chapter 53

Caitlin always loved visiting Lucien's parents. Going to Aldringham was such a sombre affair, even now, after her reconciliation with William. The Duval household was the diametric opposite – large, noisy and haphazard.

'You have such a wonderful family,' she'd said to Lucien, the first time he'd taken her to meet them. It was how she'd want her home to be.

After Lucien's father, Stéphane, had retired from teaching, he and his wife had moved from the *banlieues* of Paris to the pretty village of Saint-Robert, in the *département* of Corrèze in the Limousin region. They had gone there to be closer to Lucien's older brother, Émile, who lived nearby with his wife, Sophie, and their three children.

'Although since then we've realised there are far better reasons for being here,' Lucien's father was always fond of joking. Not least the fact that Saint-Robert was picture-postcard perfect. In a commanding position above the surrounding valleys, it was made up of small streets of medieval houses, built around a Romanesque church. There was a strong sense of community in the village, the shops and restaurants always bustling, especially in the sunshine. It reminded Caitlin a little of Valleymount.

Lucien's parents lived in a splendid old farmhouse, a convenient walk into town. Caitlin and Lucien tried to visit every month or so, but this time they had come out especially to tell his parents in person about the baby and forthcoming wedding.

'Ah!' Stéphane cried when he heard the news. He embraced Caitlin warmly. 'Now I can officially welcome you to the family!'

Lucien's mother was next. Farida took Caitlin's hands and said very solemnly, 'I know it will be difficult for you, without your mother around. So let me know what I can do to help. You are already like a daughter to me.'

Caitlin felt tears spring to her eyes.

An impromptu celebration spilled over into the evening. When it came time for dinner, the men carried a table outside onto the grass, and they whiled away several more hours, the adults drinking, eating and laughing, as the children played among the fruit and nut trees.

By the time Caitlin and Lucien finally retired for the night, to a beautifully converted outbuilding that stood adjacent to the farmhouse, she was ready to drop. She was at that early stage of pregnancy, where she seemed to be in a permanent state of exhaustion.

But once she got into the big brass bed, she found she was unable to sleep. Something was unsettling her. Perhaps it was the silence – the nights were so still and dark here, so different to London, where there was always noise and light: streetlamps, traffic, rowdy passers-by. But here, when she opened her eyes, it made no difference. It really was pitch black; silent, too, apart from the occasional hoot of an owl.

'Trouble sleeping?' Lucien's voice came to her from the dark.

She felt, rather than saw, him roll over onto his side to face her. As always these days, his hand went instinctively to the small bump of her stomach.

'What's wrong, *chérie*?' he murmured.

'Nothing.'

'If it was nothing, you would not be awake,' he observed.

She laughed softly. 'I'm fine. Honestly.' After a pause, she added, 'Just thinking about tonight, I suppose.'

When she didn't elaborate, he said, 'You know, I do not believe you for a second. But when you want to tell me, I'm here to listen.'

She smiled into the darkness. She felt better now that she could feel him close, the warmth of his hand through her thin cotton nightdress. But the truth was, she was having a hard time herself, figuring out what was wrong. Despite her excitement about the wedding and the baby, something had been bothering her. She felt very . . . alone. And tonight, seeing Lucien with his family – *her* family now, she reminded herself – well, that had brought her loneliness to a head. Seeing his mother in particular, happy for him, fussing around her, asking about her wedding dress and pregnancy – it had reminded Caitlin that she wouldn't be able to do that with her own mother.

She was thinking about her mam a lot these days. Maybe it was something about getting married and expecting a child of her own that made her want to lay the past to rest. Whatever the reason, she found herself longing to know what had transpired between William and Katie, all those years ago.

She had never talked about it properly with her father. When she'd first come to Aldringham, she had been too terrified of him to ask questions; once in Paris, she hadn't been interested in anything he had to say; and then, after his heart-attack and their reconciliation, she hadn't wanted to bring the subject up, to disturb the fragile peace between them.

But now she needed answers. She was an adult, and she could deal with hearing about what had happened between her parents, however upsetting it might be.

When she got back to England, she would speak to her father. With the decision made, she was finally able to sleep.

William guessed what Caitlin wanted to talk to him about as soon as she asked whether they could meet one evening for dinner. He wasn't sure what exactly gave it away. Maybe it had been on his mind too, the need to clear the air, now that she was going to be a wife and mother herself.

He was about to leave his office to meet Caitlin when his phone rang. It was Elizabeth, wanting to know if she could see him.

'Are you free for dinner tonight?' she asked. 'I have a few things I need to discuss with you,' she told him. In fact, she wanted to speak to him badly. The speed with which Piers was progressing with the buyout frightened her. She kept thinking that if she could have one last attempt at reconciliation with her father, then maybe she wouldn't need to go through with the takeover after all. It still wasn't too late to call it off.

'I'm sorry, Elizabeth,' he said shortly. 'But I can't tonight.'

There was a pause as she waited for him to elaborate. But he didn't.

'Call Sheila tomorrow morning,' he said instead. 'Get her to put something in my diary for later this week.'

Disappointed, Elizabeth decided to pack up and head home. She left the building ten minutes later, which was unfortunate, because she was just in time to see William walking along Albemarle Street with Caitlin.

William took Caitlin to the Ritz for dinner. He hadn't been there for years, but it seemed appropriate for the evening.

'This is where I first took your mother,' he said, once they were seated.

Caitlin looked up at him, surprised that he had been the one to bring the subject up first.

He gave a wry smile. 'Well, that's what we're here to discuss, isn't it?'

'Yes, it is,' she admitted. She glanced around at the ornate Louis XVI-style décor, trying to picture her very humble, down-to-earth mother in these elaborate surroundings. 'Did she like it here?'

He smiled a little at the memory. 'Oh, yes. Very much so, I think.'

The waiter came over then to take their order. Once he was gone, William resumed the conversation, more businesslike this time.

'So tell me, my dear, what do you want to know?'

'I want to know what happened between you,' she said bluntly. 'How it ended.'

William took a long sip of wine, travelling back in his mind to thirty years earlier. He remembered the first time he'd met Katie in his office, and how he'd been immediately drawn to her, captivated by her quiet, gentle manner. He'd felt compelled to see her again – and, despite his best efforts, found himself falling for her, the first time he'd ever felt that way about anyone. And he remembered the last time he'd seen Katie, the night before he'd left for Lake Como. He had spent the whole fortnight thinking about her, missing her more than he'd imagined possible. In the end, he'd come to a decision: it would mean leaving his little daughter Elizabeth, too. But he couldn't carry on like this.

'I was so tired of sneaking around,' he told Caitlin. 'I wanted your mother and me to be together properly, whatever the consequences.'

He stopped talking then, stared off into space, thinking about what could have been.

'But?' Caitlin prompted.

He snapped back to the present. 'But she had already left,' he said brusquely. 'I went to her flat the night I returned. The landlord told me she'd gone, left no forwarding address. The next day at Melville, I went to the shopfloor, and she wasn't there either. It turned out she'd resigned just after I'd left for Como.'

He hadn't believed it at the time, that she had gone, left his life forever, without so much as a word, a letter. He'd been alternately furious with her and then worried for her, out there, alone. At one point he'd even considered hiring a firm of private detectives to trace her. But in the end he'd thought it best to respect her decision to go.

'And that's the truth,' he told Caitlin sadly, once he'd finished his side of the story. 'That's exactly what happened.'

Caitlin said nothing for a moment. Of course she wanted to believe him, but . . .

'But I don't understand,' she said. 'What about the cheques?'

William looked confused. 'What cheques?'

She explained about the cheques that she had found among her mother's belongings. 'I assumed you knew about me, and that you'd been the one sending them all those years. I thought Mam had lied to protect you.'

'No!' William's denial was so vehement that patrons at the adjacent table turned to see what was going on. He apologised, and when he spoke again, his voice was lower, although his eyes still flashed fiercely. 'I promise you this, Caitlin – I *did not* send your mother away. And I certainly *did not* know anything about you.'

There was a silence, and then Caitlin spoke. 'But what did she say when she wrote to you about me?'

William sighed. 'By the time she contacted me . . . well, it was very near the end. She must have thought she had more time.'

'Yes,' Caitlin said quietly, tears in her eyes. 'She went downhill very quickly in those last few days.'

'She just wrote a couple of lines telling me that I had a beautiful fifteen-year-old daughter and hoping that I would be there for you after . . . after she'd gone.'

Caitlin shook her head. It was all so frustratingly vague. 'So the two of you never spoke, then?'

It was William's turn to shake his head. 'No. All I had time to do was leave a message at the hospital, letting her know that

I was coming. I caught the next plane over, but . . . it was already too late.' He wiped his eyes.

Caitlin turned everything over in her mind. 'Where *did* those cheques come from, then?' she pondered. 'Who else could have known about me?'

'Honestly, I have no idea.'

Caitlin could think of only one person who might have the answer. She looked up at William and said, 'I think I should go back to Valleymount and speak to Nuala.' She waited, wanting William's blessing for what she planned to do, but knowing she would go even if he didn't give his approval.

Slowly he nodded.

Elizabeth chewed at her lip. It was a nervous habit she'd developed lately.

'I wonder what they were talking about,' she said to Piers. First thing that morning, after a sleepless night, she had come to his office and told him about seeing William and Caitlin leaving together the previous evening.

Piers watched as Elizabeth's lip split open and a little blood seeped out. She was looking dreadful these days. Her hair was scruffy, as if she hadn't had time to style it properly, and her roots needed doing. For the first time, he could see wrinkles on her forehead, her brow furrowed from frownlines. She looked her age. Stress had done that to her. *He* had done that to her. He felt a pang of guilt. He'd always liked Elizabeth, and hated using her. But she was crucial to his plan. That night in Tokyo, he had placed the first seed of doubt in Elizabeth's mind. Now he could see it growing, nurtured by her long-held fear that William favoured Caitlin.

'Do you have any ideas?' she asked Piers for the twentieth time. Her imagination was clearly on over-drive.

'I honestly don't know,' Piers said slowly.

Elizabeth got to her feet. 'Well, I want to know. I have a

right to know,' she said aggressively. 'I'm going to ask him straight out.'

Piers watched her make for the door. The usually haughty, poised heiress was paranoid and skittish. 'Wait,' he said now. She turned, frowning. He moved towards her. 'Why don't I have a word with your father instead? He might be more likely to open up to me.'

Usually Elizabeth would never let anyone tell her what to do. But now she hesitated. In the past few weeks, she had started to doubt herself, and it was making her weak.

'OK,' she said finally. 'Maybe that's a good idea.' She gave Piers a sad smile. 'Thanks, Uncle Piers. It's good to have some-one I can count on.'

The last part was said with a touch of wistfulness. Piers patted her arm. 'That's quite all right, my dear. You know I'll do anything I can to help you.' He paused and asked, 'And what about that other business?' He was referring to the buyout plans. He'd taken on the organisation himself – finding the financial backer and preparing the legal work. Everything was nearly in place. He just needed Elizabeth to give the go-ahead. 'Have you made a decision yet?'

She looked away. 'No I haven't.' Her voice broke a little. 'I can't decide what to do.'

Piers sensed the worst thing he could do was pressurise her. 'You take whatever time you need,' he said gently. 'You have to be sure about this.'

Piers didn't ask William about Caitlin straight out. He was a master at extracting information and knew the best way to approach the matter was to bring it up casually, as though it meant nothing to him. He waited until he was about to leave his older brother's office and then, almost as an afterthought, said, 'I called up here last night but you'd already left – with Caitlin, as I understand it. Is everything OK?'

William took a moment to consider his answer. He and Caitlin had agreed that they would tell no one about her trip. But he didn't like lying to his brother.

'She's going back to Valleymount, where she grew up,' he said truthfully. Then he told Piers about the mysterious cheques that had turned up in Katie's belongings. 'She wants to speak to Nuala in person,' he told him, 'and try to find out the truth about what happened to make her mother leave London all those years ago.'

William saw the blood drain from Piers's face as he spoke. 'Are you all right?' he asked, concerned.

Piers forced a smile. 'I'm fine. Absolutely fine. Just the beginnings of a migraine. I've got some tablets somewhere. If you'll excuse me . . .'

Back in his own office, Piers shut the door, leaned against it and closed his eyes. He'd thought the secret was well and truly buried. But Nuala knew just enough for Caitlin to connect all the dots. He would need to step up his timetable and put everything in motion before she had a chance to go back to Valleymount.

Chapter 54

When Caitlin stepped off the plane in Dublin, she felt a rush of bittersweet nostalgia. For a moment, she was fifteen again, grieving for her mother and being packed off to live with a family who she was certain didn't want her. She'd come a long way since then. Ireland had, too. Over the past decade, the Celtic Tiger had woken, stretched and roared. Eire was no longer the butt of Europe's jokes — it was a thriving, prosperous country, a desirable place to live.

She got through the airport quickly. William and Lucien had both offered to accompany her, but she had turned them down, explaining that this was something she needed to do herself. Her fiancé hadn't been happy about her undertaking such a stressful and emotional trip.

'I don't want you upsetting yourself, *chérie*.' His gaze had instinctively moved to her stomach. 'Not when it could be bad for the baby.'

She'd smiled softly at him, touched by his concern, but not swayed by it. 'Lucien, I know you're worried. But this is something I need to do.'

He'd wanted to argue back. But seeing the determined look in her eyes, he'd known she would not be dissuaded.

Outside the airport, she found the car that she had booked to take her out to Valleymount. As she settled into the back, she was surprised at how nervous she felt. She had kept up her annual pilgrimage to her mother's grave, scraping together the airfare even during the lean times in Paris and then New York.

But she had always stayed in Dublin and made the trip up there for a day, never dropping in on the people she had once known.

That's why the call to Nuala had been so difficult. But if she'd been worried that her mother's old friend might not be pleased to hear from her after all these years, she couldn't have been more wrong. In fact, the woman had sounded delighted, saying that she'd followed Caitlin's career in the paper.

'We're all so proud of you,' she'd said. 'And your mam would be, too.'

Caitlin had choked up at that.

They had spent some time on the phone. Roisin was no longer around – she had moved to Australia with her husband and two children.

'And all the others have moved out too, so there's plenty of room for you to stay.'

'Oh no,' Caitlin had said quickly, not sure if she could handle the memories. 'I don't want to put you out.'

'Ah, sure.' Nuala had sounded embarrassed. 'You'll be wanting to stay at the hotel.'

That had done it for Caitlin. Snobbery had been the furthest thing from her mind.

'Well, if it's really no trouble, then of course I'd love to stay,' she'd said warmly.

Time hadn't changed Valleymount. The pretty stone cottages looked the same; the neighbours had aged but not altered. Caitlin couldn't help wondering what her life would have been like if her mother had lived, if she'd never found out about her heritage or the Melville family.

Nuala still lived at the same house. Apart from a lick of paint, that hadn't changed either. She opened the door covered in crayon and with two grandchildren hanging off her. They belonged to Roisin's elder sister, Evelyn, Nuala explained; she babysat while her daughter was at work.

'There's another asleep in the cot upstairs,' she told Caitlin, inviting her in. She smelled of warm milk and talcum powder, and looked perfectly happy about that.

Nuala settled the children in front of the TV – the sitting room still had the same floral wallpaper and brown velvet couch, Caitlin noted fondly – and then the two women went through to the kitchen. While Nuala boiled the kettle, Caitlin sat at the old farmhouse table she remembered from when she was a child.

They made small talk as Nuala bustled around the kitchen.

'So what's this all about?' she said finally, as she poured two large mugs of tea. 'It's your mam, isn't it?' She saw the look of surprise on Caitlin's face and smiled shrewdly. 'I guessed that was the reason for you coming here again after all these years. You've got questions about what happened to her, am I right?'

'Yes. Yes, that's exactly it.' Caitlin frowned a little. 'I found something – some cheques – among her personal effects. It was a few months after I'd moved to England, just after she . . . after she died.' She cleared her throat. 'And I wondered if you knew anything about them – and about what happened between her and my father.'

Nuala stared at her for a long moment. 'Yes,' she said. 'Yes, I do.'

Then she proceeded to tell Caitlin what she knew.

Piers's eyes were grave. 'You need to make a decision,' he told his niece.

It was Friday evening and Elizabeth was exhausted. The strain of the past few weeks had taken its toll. Cole had called her a few times since he'd moved out, but so far she'd avoided talking to him. She'd dialled the landline number he'd left her once – out of curiosity – ready to slam the receiver down if a female voice answered. But, to her relief, it was just a politely indifferent hotel receptionist. Although Elizabeth had felt happier – at least he wasn't living with *her* – she'd refused to leave a message. She was still too hurt and angry to even talk about their marriage – or to tell him about their baby.

She'd been for her first ante-natal appointment that morning – alone. She was ten weeks' pregnant and the cheerful midwife had confirmed that mother and baby were both doing well. She'd quickly glanced at Elizabeth's left hand, and then asked chirpily, 'So no Daddy today, then?' Elizabeth had answered with a curt, 'He's busy.' After that, the midwife had been a little more subdued for the rest of the appointment. She'd advised Elizabeth that she would need up to ten check-ups, as it was her first pregnancy. For a brief moment Elizabeth had wondered what it would be like, turning up to each of them by herself. Then she'd decided to put it from her mind.

She'd considered taking the rest of the day off but, unable to face going home, she'd come back to the office and spent the rest of the afternoon sitting at her desk, daydreaming about nothing in particular. Then at seven, after everyone had left, Piers had come by to ask whether she'd decided to go ahead with the buyout – as though today hadn't been stressful enough already.

Elizabeth stared down at the documents in front of her. She felt uncomfortable signing away her shares like this – even though she knew it was necessary if they wanted to go ahead with the acquisition. As an individual couldn't launch a takeover, they'd had to set up a holding company, through which they would pool their shares and make the bid. The documents Piers had had drawn up provided for them to exchange their shares in Melville for a proportional stake in the holding company. This would give Elizabeth 60 per cent of the voting rights and therefore overall control of the takeover vehicle.

'Can't we hold off for a little while longer?' she asked.

Piers shook his head. 'We risk losing the financial backer if we do,' he said regretfully. 'They want to either move on this or look around for another investment opportunity.'

Elizabeth chewed at her sore lip. That was the crux of the problem. This backer was giving them great terms. It was a private equity investor, investing anonymously through a shell company set up in Luxembourg. Usually private equity would insist on taking a stake in the holding company, and want to get involved in the day-to-day running of the business. But these guys were prepared to finance it all through debt, and just take a healthy interest rate in exchange. There was a profit-share clause as well, but that meant nothing compared with the benefit of not having to give away any control.

Elizabeth stared down at the documents in front of her, ready to be signed. Part of her felt guilty, as though she was betraying everything she'd ever held dear. Another part of her blamed her father. If he'd believed in her . . . if he hadn't favoured Caitlin . . .

And at the back of her mind was the thought that she couldn't lose the company, not after all of this. She had lost Cole. She needed something to show for her life.

'Elizabeth?' Piers prompted.

She made a decision.

Piers watched Elizabeth scrawl her signature and felt a huge rush of relief. Finally it was going ahead. He had organised every detail perfectly. His plan was so smart and so clever that it seemed almost a shame not to be able to tell everyone about it. While the family held 60 per cent of the share capital, it was impossible for an external bidder to get the majority necessary to take over the company. Elizabeth had now broken that stranglehold. By manipulating her, using her jealousy and insecurities, he'd managed to get her to agree to the management buyout – which was going to facilitate Armand Bouchard's takeover.

Elizabeth had trusted Piers to work out the details of the contract. Because of this, she had neglected to read the small print, which stated that the financial backer – in fact, Bouchard – was allowed to convert his financial stake to equity if the takeover vehicle held more than 20 per cent of Melville's share capital. As Bouchard now owned Piers's shares plus another 10 per cent he'd picked up in the market, he would have a controlling two-thirds stake in the holding company. Elizabeth had effectively signed away her shares and her future in the company – as well as facilitating the takeover, as she'd now broken the family's controlling stake.

In order to conclusively seal Melville's fate, Piers had wanted to get hold of Amber's shares, too. That part of the plan had taken a little longer to figure out. He'd known enough about her problems to realise that she would be an easier target than Elizabeth. But he'd needed to find a weakness, a way to get to those shares without her realising, so he'd hired a private investigator to probe into her life. Once he'd found out about Johnny and the money he owed, he'd known that was the way in.

'One hundred thousand dollars will be yours, if you get Amber to sign these documents.' Piers had allowed Johnny to push him up to one hundred and fifty thousand, although he'd been quite prepared to pay more. By signing, Amber would be agreeing to transfer ownership of her 2.5 per cent stake in Melville to him, Piers. Then he would in turn sell it on to Armand Bouchard.

Piers had opened the back door to allow the wolf in. From there, it would be up to Bouchard to offer sufficient money to get the rest of the shareholders to sell out to him. But, with the financial might of the GMS Group behind him, Piers was in no doubt that he could do it. William would never see it coming.

Amber needed a fix. As she sat on the floor of the sitting room, arms wrapped round her knees, rocking back and forth, she craved that hit more than anything in her life. Where was Johnny? He had promised to take care of her.

'If you're nice to me, then I'll be nice to you,' he'd said.

Well, she'd done what he wanted – signed those damned papers. Now he should keep up his end of the bargain.

He had been on at her for the past couple of weeks about signing her shares over to him. At first, she'd told him no. Even in her state, she knew her father would be furious.

'But you don't understand,' he'd said, close to tears. 'These people I owe money to, they're going to put me in hospital.'

'I'm sorry,' she'd told him. 'We'll have to find some other way.'

But then he'd turned nasty – started withholding her stuff. Eight hours without a fix, and she hadn't given a shit who owned the shares. After ten hours, she'd been begging to sign them over.

And Johnny had promised that afterwards he'd sort her out. But he hadn't. Instead, he'd disappeared into the bedroom and hadn't come back out. It wasn't fair. She needed her stuff now or she was going to die, she just knew it.

She got up, stumbled over to the bedroom. She was about to go in when she heard him talking. So that's what he was up to. He was on the phone, arranging to meet someone. It was Sheri, she was sure. Not that she cared who he was sleeping with, but if she caught him, she could tell him off – use that as a way to get him to give her something more special than usual.

Slowly, quietly, she picked up the extension, covering the receiver with her hand so he couldn't hear.

But it wasn't Sheri on the other end. Amber blinked in surprise as she heard a familiar voice. It took her a moment to place, but then she realised – it was Uncle Piers. Why on earth was he calling? Through her haze, Amber felt a flash of excitement. Had Daddy asked him to see if she was OK? There had been times over the past few months that she'd wished with all her heart that she'd gone back home to England with Elizabeth. Now, maybe she'd have a second chance.

She was about to speak, to let him know that she was on the line, but some instinct stopped her. There was something about the conversation between her uncle and her boyfriend that didn't quite make sense.

'My representative is waiting at the hotel,' Piers was saying. 'Once you bring the papers, and he has confirmed that they have been properly signed, I will transfer the money direct into your account.'

Johnny coughed nervously. 'And this is all legal, right?'

'Perfectly legal,' Piers agreed. 'Amber has simply signed a contract authorising the custodian to sell her shares. No one can dispute that.'

'Fine,' Johnny said, still sounding unsure. 'Good. Just tell me again where I need to meet this bloke of yours.'

As carefully as she could, Amber replaced the receiver.

As soon as Johnny left, Amber called her father. When he wasn't around, she tried Elizabeth, then Caitlin. But she got the same answer every time. They were all unavailable.

'But it's an emergency!' she pleaded with William's PA.

The woman sounded unimpressed. 'As I said, I'll pass on your message.'

The problem was, she'd cried wolf too many times. They were used to her calling with one crisis after another. She couldn't rely on them getting back to her anytime soon. There was only one thing she could do. Go to London herself. She couldn't help feeling a moment's exhilaration – her first natural high in a while. This was finally her chance to prove herself.

She booked herself on the next flight. First Class was out of her reach, and she maxed out three other cards paying for a last-minute economy fare. While the cab waited outside, she took one last hit – she'd made Johnny show her his stash before he'd left the house. But that wouldn't be enough. There was the flight, then once she got to London . . . She needed to take something with her.

Amber emptied her Chanel compact, replacing the make-up with a different powder. She hesitated for a second, staring down at the solid silver case – she knew it was risky. Then the cab beeped again outside and she made her decision. Quickly slipping the compact into her make-up case, she zipped it into her handbag. She probably wouldn't use it, but she felt better knowing it was there.

'Are you OK, miss?'

Amber opened her eyes and looked up at the concerned face of the air stewardess. She was very far from all right. It was halfway through the thirteen-hour flight to London and, more pressingly, eight hours since her last fix. Withdrawal had set in. Her body was covered in a cold sweat and she was shaking uncontrollably. She looked like she was carrying every major tropical disease.

'I'm fine,' she managed through chattering teeth. 'Flu.'

The stewardess gave her an odd look. 'Would you like me to get you a blanket?' she asked.

Amber nodded to get the woman off her back. What she needed was to land. Once she got off the plane she could find a Ladies room and sort herself out. She shivered her way through the next six hours, getting increasingly worse. When the plane landed, they were kept waiting for twenty minutes before finally being allowed to disembark.

Amber was the first off. As she descended the steps she saw three uniformed policemen with a large Alsatian waiting at the bottom of the stairs. There was nothing she could do except continue. She reached the last step and moved to walk by, pretending she hadn't seen the stewardess point her out. But a man in a dark suit, who was standing next to the policemen, stepped forward and placed a firm hand on her shoulder.

'Miss, would you mind coming this way?'

'So it's true?' Caitlin said. She felt so disappointed. She hadn't wanted to hear this. 'William had her sacked?'

Nuala looked at her sympathetically. 'That's what she told me. While he was away, the Store Manager, Miss Harper, asked your mam to leave – and she made it clear that the orders had come from his office.' She reached out and squeezed Caitlin's hand. 'But you can't hold it against him now. It was such a long time ago.'

'I understand that.' Caitlin was silent for a moment. There was something troubling her about the whole story. 'But what I *don't* understand is how he found out about me?'

Nuala sighed. 'You see, your mam had no one to confide in about the baby, except me. I wanted her to tell William about you. She refused at first, but I finally bullied her into it.' The older woman paused to sigh again. 'Unfortunately, the night she went to his house . . . well, she saw him with his wife. After that, she decided it would be best to leave well alone.' Nuala bit her lip, knowing that the next part wasn't going to be easy for Katie's daughter.

'Go on,' Caitlin said steadily. 'I need to hear this.'

'It was difficult back then, for someone like your mam, on her own,' Nuala explained. 'Unwed mothers in Ireland – you'd be lucky not to have the baby taken away and be sent to the Magdalene Laundries. Katie knew all that, of course. She thought about having you adopted at one point, thinking it would be for the best. But she couldn't do it, God love her,' Nuala added hastily. 'I remember telling her she was mad, but she insisted she was going to keep you.' The woman looked guiltily at Caitlin then. 'It was only because I was worried about her, about how she was going to cope with no money, that I did it.'

'Did what?' Caitlin prompted.

Nuala took a deep breath. 'I'd left Melville by then. I was married and pregnant with Roisin; we were talking about moving back here, and I wanted to help your mam. So I went into Melville the week after you were born, and asked to see that woman, the Store Manager. Right there, on the shopfloor, I told her what was going on and demanded to see Mr Melville . . . your father.' Nuala's eyes glistened with regretful tears. 'Of course, Miss Harper couldn't stand the fuss in front of the customers, so she took me upstairs to her office, and told me to wait there.'

Caitlin shook her head, unable to believe what she was hearing.

Nuala snorted. 'Well, as it turned out he was obviously too busy to see me. It wasn't *him* who came in twenty minutes later – it was old lady Melville with her youngest son. Your man William must have sent them down in his place.'

Alarms began to sound in Caitlin's head. 'You mean, it was Piers and Rosalind you talked to? Not my father?'

'That's right,' Nuala confirmed. 'They addressed me very formally. They'd obviously discussed the situation and decided what they were going to say so that they didn't implicate themselves in any way. They wouldn't admit that you were anything to do with William – and, remember, these were the days before DNA tests. But they said that,' Nuala affected an upperclass accent, 'as Katie had been a valued employee, they felt for her plight, and as a token of goodwill the company would be happy to send a cheque every year on your birthday.' She shook her head in disgust. 'A token of goodwill, indeed. Anyway, at least I'd got something out of the scuts, or so I thought. But your mam was a proud woman. She was furious when she found out what I'd done, of course. And she refused to ever cash that money. Every year those cheques came, and every year she ignored them.'

Caitlin's heart was beating faster. Nuala might not have understood the significance of what she'd said, but she did. 'But did it never occur to you that Anne fetched them down to see you because they were the ones who'd told her to get rid of my mam in the first place? I mean, that would make sense, wouldn't it? After all, she was told to go when William was away on holiday. Maybe it was them all along.'

Nuala stared at her for a long moment. 'Sweet Jesus,' she breathed. 'I'd never thought of that.'

Caitlin called William to tell him what she had found out.

'My mother and Piers?' he repeated disbelievingly. '*They* knew about you?'

'Yes,' Caitlin confirmed quietly.

'But . . . all these years and they never said anything!' He sounded in shock. 'Even last week, Piers could have confessed. I told him that you were going back to Valleymount to see Nuala and he didn't say a word.'

There was silence. Caitlin didn't know what to say – she knew how close William and Piers were. 'Do you want me to fly back tonight?' she asked finally.

'No,' William said. 'No, there's no need for that. I think I should try to find Piers and see what he has to say about this. I still . . . well, I still can't quite believe it.'

It was nearly midnight by the time the police allowed Amber to use a phone. She was thinking more clearly now. The on-duty doctor had given her some methadone, which had calmed her down. It wasn't the same as a hit, but it would do. She didn't even know who to call first. She plumped for Elizabeth. She dialled the number, expected to get an answering machine, and couldn't believe it when her sister actually picked up.

Amber quickly explained what was going on, that Piers had tried to get her shares.

'But don't worry,' she said proudly. 'I took the papers from Johnny's bag. I've got them with me.'

There was a long pause at the end of the phone. When Elizabeth finally spoke, Amber had already guessed what she was going to say.

'It's too late. I've already signed mine over.'

Chapter 55

Armand Bouchard and Piers Melville launched their takeover bid on Monday morning. Even without Amber's shares, Bouchard now had 22.5 per cent of the share capital. If all the public shareholders decided to take up his offer, his holding would rise to 52.5 per cent – a controlling majority.

The pieces of the puzzle had begun to fall into place over the weekend. After Elizabeth had spoken to Amber, she'd finally worked out that Piers had tricked her. She'd called William and left a calm, dignified – if slightly shaky – message, explaining exactly what had happened and resigning from the board. Since then, no one had been able to get in contact with her. Piers had also gone to ground.

By ten in the morning, the Melville board – with the notable exceptions of Piers and Elizabeth – had all gathered to discuss Bouchard's offer. Caitlin took her place beside William.

Hugh Makin kicked off. He had obviously been elected to speak on behalf of the other directors. 'The majority of us feel that we should recommend the offer to our shareholders,' he said, making it clear a secret meeting had already been held this morning.

Everyone looked to William. The fight had gone out of him. His shoulders were slumped, his head bowed. The betrayal by both his daughter and brother had taken its toll.

'Perhaps you're right,' he murmured. 'Perhaps it's time to give in.'

'*No.*' Caitlin's voice was loud and clear. She was damned if she was going to let Piers win.

The Sales Director, Douglas Levan, glared at her. 'I hardly think you're in a position—'

'Let her speak.' William's voice was weary, but he still had enough command to make the other man fall silent.

'The family still has forty-seven and a half per cent of the shares,' Caitlin began. 'That means we're playing for the remaining thirty per cent, which is publicly owned. All we need to do is convince shareholders that there's more value leaving the company in family hands—'

'The offer is at a forty per cent premium to where the shares are trading at the moment,' Douglas interjected.

'Yes, but we're still putting through big changes. There's potentially a lot more value to be had.' She paused to let her words sink in. 'Bouchard is trying to get the company on the cheap. And you guys are going to let him.'

There was silence as the men around the table digested what she had said. It was William who spoke up. 'She's right,' he acknowledged, 'We can't give in at the first bid. The least we can do for our shareholders is put together a decent defence. Who knows, maybe we'll win. But, if not, at least we'll have made the bastard pay through the nose.'

No one could argue with that. As directors, they had to act in the best interests of the shareholders. They would fight, at least for now.

After everyone had gone, Caitlin looked over at William. So much had happened that weekend. By the time they had dealt with Amber and figured out what Bouchard and Piers were up to, they hadn't had time to discuss what had happened with her mother.

'Look, I want to apologise for not believing you,' she began.

William held up his hand. 'Let's not worry about that now.' His voice was gruff. 'I want to focus on saving the company.

We can put the soul-searching on hold for when we've got ourselves out of this mess.'

Caitlin waited for a second, and then asked, 'Does that include Elizabeth? Because if we've got any chance of winning, we're going to need her help too.'

It was eleven in the morning, and Elizabeth was still in her dressing-gown. She hadn't opened a paper today and was avoiding the news programmes. She couldn't believe how stupid she'd been, trusting Piers. She had been so desperate to be made Chief Executive that she had lost everything. She'd betrayed her father and Caitlin, destroyed the company and, worst of all, pushed Cole away.

The doorbell interrupted her self-flagellation. Part of her hoped it might be her husband, but deep down she knew that was ridiculous – and she was only mildly disappointed when she opened the door and found Caitlin standing there.

'So what do you think?'

It was an hour later, and the two women were sitting in Elizabeth's kitchen. Caitlin had just outlined her idea for saving the company.

Under the takeover rules, Melville had forty-two days to mount its defence against the bid. When the rumours of a possible takeover had first started, William had insisted on inserting 'poison pill' clauses into both his daughters' contracts. That meant if anyone outside the family acquired over 30 per cent of the share capital, both Caitlin and Elizabeth could leave the company immediately. Caitlin's idea was to leverage this for all its worth.

'Our strongest argument is that Melville is essentially a family company and that, as a family, we're best equipped to run it,' she told Elizabeth.

Under takeover rules, Melville could hold a meeting to explain to investors, analysts and the media why the company was worth more than the takeover bid. This could act in two ways – to either push up the offer price or encourage investors to reject the bid outright. At the meeting, Caitlin wanted to put on a new fashion show – in lieu of showing the October collection.

'It's a little unorthodox, but I think it's our best shot,' she said. 'I can work on it in secret – just me and a few of the design team that I trust.'

Elizabeth thought it through. 'So you'd have – what? – forty days, tops, to pull together a collection. Can you do it?'

'I'll give it a go.'

Elizabeth nodded, and then fell silent. 'Well, it sounds like you and Daddy have it all under control,' she said stiffly. 'I hope it all works out.'

Caitlin smiled gently. 'Come on, Elizabeth. I'm here because we need you on board, too. It's only going to work if the whole family pull together.'

Elizabeth didn't answer at first. There was only one thing preventing her from saying yes. 'What does Daddy think of all this?' she asked tentatively. 'Of me being involved? I can't imagine he's very happy about what . . . what I did.'

'I think right now that's the least of his concerns,' Caitlin pointed out.

Elizabeth thought about it for a moment, and then said, 'Fine. Just tell me what I need to do.'

With Caitlin designing a killer collection, and most of the board ambivalent about the outcome of the takeover, it was up to Elizabeth and William to do everything possible to combat Bouchard.

William took on Piers's role as Finance Director and set to work coming up with new, robust forecasts for the next five years. Once he was happy with those, he got together with a team of corporate brokers from Sedgwick Hart, Cole's old firm, to determine how far they could stretch the valuations.

Elizabeth assumed a more public-facing role. 'I know I'm not at my best right now,' William admitted to her. 'I think you'll project a more vibrant image, and that's what we need to get across.' That meant she had to meet up with all their key shareholders and present their ideas for the business. With the top fifteen investors scattered across four continents, it was a punishing schedule. Every night, she fell into bed completely wiped out. But in a way she was grateful for the distraction of work. Cole had called wanting to meet up, but she had put him off.

'I need some more time before I make any decision,' she'd told him.

He'd seemed to accept that. She hadn't asked if he was still sleeping with Sumiko. At the moment, they were separated. It wasn't really any of her business. But she was beginning to realise how much she missed him. At night, she came home to an empty house where there was no one to listen about her day, to talk through the good points and the bad. It made her think about what it must have been like for him, when she'd been working so hard, always putting Melville first. It didn't excuse what he'd done. But it did help her see his actions in a different light. Inevitably, her family had asked after Cole. She'd kept her explanation brief. 'We were having some problems and so he's moved out for a while.' She didn't volunteer any further details, and her demeanour didn't invite enquiries.

In her Hoxton home, Caitlin was also working every hour she could, under Lucien's watchful eye. Usually she would spend months planning and researching a collection – now she had mere weeks. But that could be no excuse for slacking on quality. The sharp eyes of the fashion and financial worlds would be looking for any hint of weakness.

The theme had been easy to settle on. She wanted to emphasise patriotism, the Englishness of the brand. So many small and midcap UK companies had been bought up by foreigners recently, French and Spanish conglomerates on the acquisition trail – so the idea was, let's keep Melville independent. To Caitlin, the Second World War seemed to capture perfectly that combative spirit.

Initially Elizabeth and William weren't impressed with the idea. Caitlin wasn't particularly surprised. In many ways, the forties had been an austere period for women's fashion, what with rationing and government regulations on the manufacture and distribution of clothing. But then that had simply encouraged designers to be more innovative: shortening skirts to make the most of restricted fabrics, and introducing the concept of mix-and-match separates to create the illusion of a more extensive wardrobe. If she worked with that, put her own unique spin on it . . .

'We're in your hands,' William said.

Elizabeth agreed. 'Do whatever you think is best.'

Caitlin did. She recruited Jess and two more of her trustworthy design assistants and set up HQ at her house. With the question mark over the company's future, the Design Room at Melville was in a demoralised slump, so when everyone was officially told that the three had left the company, no one questioned the lie.

Luckily, Caitlin's lounge and dining area was open-plan, thirty feet long and flooded with natural light. They cleared the furniture into one of the spare bedrooms and made it their workroom. Sewing machines, mannequins and drawing boards were brought over in the dead of night from Melville. Caitlin was on good terms with the suppliers, so she could just call them up, say what she wanted, and it would be with them the next day, no questions asked. After all, they only needed enough for the showing samples.

It was a ridiculous set of circumstances, but the four of them had never had more fun – working to the absolute max, bent over a sewing machine until their backs ached, alternating the pizza, Chinese and Indian takeaway menus, mainlining coffee.

Two weeks before the clothes were due to be shown, Elizabeth came to look at what Caitlin had achieved. She couldn't help being impressed.

'I had doubts at first,' she admitted, 'but you've absolutely nailed it. This is going to blow them away.'

'Thanks.'

Then Elizabeth frowned. 'But who are we going to use to model the clothes? If we go to any of the usual agencies, word will leak out about what we're up to.'

Caitlin smiled mysteriously. 'I've got an idea about that, too.'

The next day, Caitlin and Elizabeth went to visit Amber at The Causeway Retreat, England's most exclusive private rehab clinic. William had booked her in there after picking her up from the police station the night she'd landed in England. Rehab was one of the conditions of her release. It was fortunate she only had enough drugs for personal consumption on her – it meant the authorities could be lenient, as long as the family took responsibility for her.

She had been at The Causeway for a month now, and everyone was keen to see how she was getting on. They'd been shocked by her appearance the last time they'd seen her: the skeletal body, unwashed hair and grey complexion.

It was a thirty-minute helicopter flight from Central London to the 350-acre private island off the coast of Essex – the best way to get there, as the road was only accessible four hours a day at low tide. Amber was in a group therapy session when they arrived, so an orderly took Elizabeth and Caitlin on a tour of the grounds. It was more like a five-star hotel than a clinic, with a gym, swimming pool and games room. After they'd finished looking round, they sat in the lush, landscaped gardens waiting for her.

She finally came out, carrying a jug of orange juice with her. After a month in rehab, she looked back to her old self. The most severe physical withdrawal symptoms had hit forty-eight hours after her last dose and had lasted a week.

'It's the psychological demons that are going to be harder to combat,' she told them. The deep, overwhelming depression had gone, but the cravings hadn't. They never would, the clinical nurse had explained. The hunger would always be there, the dream of the next fix. It was up to her to want to stay away from it.

'But let's talk about something else,' she said hastily. Shut away from any news, she was eager to hear what was happening with the takeover bid. Elizabeth quickly explained what they'd been up to.

'I wish there was some way I could help,' Amber said, once she'd finished speaking. She saw Elizabeth and Caitlin exchange a look. 'What is it?'

'Actually,' Elizabeth said slowly, 'there is something you can do. That's why we came to see you.'

'But it would mean leaving here,' Caitlin interjected, 'and we don't want you to do that unless you feel ready.'

In some ways, Amber didn't want to. It was easy to stay clean in such a peaceful, isolated environment, with a strong support network in place and no temptations for miles. The thought of leaving the safe cocoon terrified her. But she also knew she couldn't stay here for ever. She had already discussed a home aftercare plan and seeing a psychotherapist in London. At some point, she was going to have to stand strong.

She took a deep breath. 'Tell me what you need me to do.'

While Melville got its defences in place, Armand Bouchard started turning the screws. Piers had undoubtedly helped pinpoint areas where the company was vulnerable. Melville's main loan was due to run out a few days before the defence meeting, and the bank that controlled it began to make noises about withdrawing their financial backing. Bouchard's GMS Group was a corporate behemoth, and its influence in financial circles far exceeded Melville's. No one wanted to alienate a potentially lucrative client.

Elizabeth hit the phones. But everywhere, doors were slammed shut in her face. None of the banks she normally dealt with wanted to know. They were all too frightened of Bouchard. She couldn't even get them to return her calls. Furious after being told that another Corporate Lending Director was in a meeting of indeterminate length, she slammed down the receiver and looked at her list. His was the last name. She crossed it through.

'Shit,' she swore under her breath. She was out of ideas.

When the phone rang a second later, she jumped, wondering if it was one of the banking executives finally returning her call.

It wasn't. Fortunately it was something even better.

'Hello, Elizabeth,' said a familiar voice. 'I hear you're looking for a hundred million pounds. And I think I may be able to help.'

The contract was signed quietly three days later. When Cole had heard the news about the loan, he'd called his old banking contacts. Within hours he had a syndicate of five US investment banks willing to come in on the deal. As they were spreading the risk between them, he'd even managed to negotiate a lower interest rate than Melville had had with the original loan.

William came to Elizabeth's office to deliver the news that the money was theirs. 'Cole really pulled through for us, didn't he?' he observed, walking over to sit at her desk.

'Yes,' she said shortly.

'I hope you've called him to say thank you.'

Her mouth tightened a fraction. 'I will.' There was a silence. Then: 'Was there anything else?' she asked.

William sighed. 'Look, my dear,' he began, 'I don't know what went on between you and Cole, nor do I want to. Obviously, whatever it was, he hurt you very badly.' William stopped, clearly waiting for an answer. Elizabeth stared down at her desk.

'Yes,' she mumbled. 'Yes, he did.'

Her father nodded. 'Now, I understand that you're the only one who can choose whether to give him a second chance. But whatever you decide, make sure you do it for the right reasons. It's far too easy to act out of spite or stubbornness.' He stood up and made to leave. At the door, he turned back. 'Just remember – there's no weakness in forgiveness.'

Elizabeth debated with herself for a long time after he'd gone, and then finally phoned her husband.

'I just wanted to let you know again how grateful we all are here, Cole,' she said. Aware of how stiff she sounded, she tried again. 'You don't know what this means to us . . . I mean, to me.'

'I do. More than you realise. I just wish you'd felt you could call me to ask for help.' He waited a beat, then said, 'Elizabeth . . .'

She closed her eyes. 'Please, don't—'

'No.' He was forceful now. 'Let me say this one thing.'

She waited.

'I miss you, Elizabeth.'

There was a long silence. All that could be heard was their respective breathing down the phone.

'Well, that's what I wanted to tell you,' he said gruffly. 'I know you've got a lot going on now, but maybe in a few weeks' time . . .'

'I miss you, too,' she said suddenly.

'You do?' He sounded pleased.

'Yes, I really do.' She looked at her watch. It was nearly eight in the evening. She thought of all the work she still had to do tonight. And she made a decision.

'Cole?'

'Yes, Elizabeth?'

'Are you free for dinner?'

It was after nine before he reached the house. They greeted each other awkwardly, with a brief, almost platonic kiss on the cheek.

'I'm really glad you called,' Cole said for the fourth time since he'd arrived. She was relieved that he seemed as nervous as her.

They went through to the kitchen. He'd brought a vintage Taittinger with him, and while she called to order Chinese, he cracked the bottle open.

'None for me,' she said, as he went to the cupboard for glasses.

He looked disappointed – he'd obviously been hoping the alcohol might loosen them both up. 'I thought we were celebrating?'

She took a deep breath. This was it. 'Well, you see, I would, but . . . but I'm not drinking at the moment.'

'Oh, right.' He frowned. 'I guess you need to keep a clear head with everything that's going on.'

'Well, yes, I do,' she said, carefully. 'But . . . but that's not the reason I'm not drinking right now.'

It took him another moment to process what she'd said. Then she could see his expression change as he finally got it.

'You're pregnant,' he said, almost a whisper.

She couldn't tell if he was happy or not about it. He looked kind of stunned.

'Yes,' she said. 'I'm pregnant.' She waited a second. Then, when he *still* hadn't said anything, she added in a small voice, 'Is that OK?'

She watched as his eyes moistened with tears. 'OK?' he choked. 'It's only the best damn news I ever heard.'

Matthew Monroe stared down at the phone number of his local police station. He was trying to psych up the courage to make the call. He knew it was the right thing to do, that he owed it to Irina. But he was also worried about what might happen to him. Matthew was basically a good guy. At thirty-eight, he led a stable if unexciting life. He held down a good job and owned his own home. He had a wide circle of friends, and most evenings he could be found at one of the many pubs by the river in Kingston. Every Sunday he had lunch with his mother; once a month he took her to visit his father's grave.

But, despite the fact that he was a nice person, and solvent to boot, Matthew had never had a girlfriend. And he guessed he never would. The problem was a thyroid condition that made him clinically obese. People might claim that beauty was only skin deep and to never judge a book by its cover, but Matthew knew differently. Since he was a child, he'd been stared at in the street and called names.

Over the years, he'd learned to accept himself and was a much happier person for it. But, while he had plenty of female friends, he knew that however much they liked him, he would only ever be the guy they told their men-problems to.

He'd visited his first prostitute at the age of twenty-seven, when he'd despaired of ever finding a woman who'd want to be with him. It was an experience he'd repeated sporadically since then. It wasn't something he was proud of, but everyone deserved some comfort.

He'd met Irina the first time he'd gone to the house in Hounslow. He'd known straight away that she was there against her will. Her English wasn't good, but he'd got the gist of what had happened to her. He read the papers, all those stories about girls forced into prostitution over here.

Together, they'd planned her escape. But something had gone wrong. When he called to book an appointment with her – what would have been the final one – he was told that she had gone back to her family in Lithuania. He'd pretended to accept that, but his gut told him something wasn't right. From what he'd understood, she was a prisoner. Why would they suddenly let her go back home?

He knew what he needed to do. He picked up the phone and dialled.

'I'd like to report a missing person.'

Chapter 56

The financial world had never seen anything like it.

Exactly forty-two days after Armand Bouchard launched his takeover bid, all interested parties were invited to attend Melville's defence meeting.

'Why is it so last-minute?' everyone wanted to know.

Investors were frustrated; the financial community sceptical. The share price had stabilised around Bouchard's offer price, which meant that the market had assumed that his bid would be successful. But still there was a buzz in the air as shareholders, journalists and analysts gathered at Somerset House to see what Melville had to offer. The family had managed to pull off a major turnaround two years earlier. Perhaps they would surprise the world again.

Behind the scenes, Caitlin had that cold feeling in the pit of her stomach, the one she always got before a show. Once again, the whole future of Melville hinged on her pulling this off. That knowledge weighed heavily on her.

Elizabeth glanced over and smiled reassuringly, as though she could guess what was going through her sister's head.

'Don't worry. This is going to be brilliant.'

Caitlin managed a smile back. Deep down she knew Elizabeth was right. With her two sisters' help, Caitlin had pulled together what she thought was going to be her best show ever. Instead of holding the meeting in a stuffy bank, they'd opted for Somerset House. Situated on the Embankment, with views of the Thames, there was nothing that epitomised London more. A marquee had been erected in the central courtyard, where the ice rink stood in winter, with the beautiful backdrop of the neo-Classical buildings.

'If nothing else, it'll give the bankers a break from the City,' Caitlin had reasoned when suggesting the venue.

She was right. As the sober-suited analysts, investors and financial press took their seats, the air crackled with anticipation. They were used to sombre presentations – this looked like it was going to be fun. Alongside them, select members of the fashion world were also taking their places.

'Inviting them will show we've got confidence in the collection,' Elizabeth had pointed out.

Inside, the marquee had been decked out like a forties' dance hall. There was a big band in the corner to play wartime classics; Union Jacks and gas masks hung from the ceiling. As usual, every little detail had been attended to.

Caitlin looked out into the crowd, searching for Lucien's face, knowing that would calm her. She caught a quick glimpse of him, gave a wave, and then there was no more time to worry.

William tapped his watch. 'Let's get started.'

Caitlin made her way to the control booth. It was only six in the evening, but it was November and already dark. When the lights fell, the marquee plunged into blackness. It was the technique she'd used at her graduation show in Paris, and she'd thought it would work well here, too – adding extra drama to the occasion. A second later, an air-raid siren howled through the air. Everyone jumped in their seats; one woman screamed, then there was nervous laughter as the audience realised the blackout was part of the show. Caitlin exchanged a grin with the sound man. That was the impact they'd been aiming for.

As the wail of the siren died away, it was replaced by the sound of the band striking up, playing a medley of wartime swing classics. Amber stalked onto the catwalk, looking dramatic in a black leather trenchcoat and matching thigh-high boots, her hair slicked back from her face Gestapo-style. She had pulled through for them, not only agreeing to model but also roping in old friends to take part, too – all fellow celebrities who had fallen out of favour with the fickle media and been labelled has-beens.

'Maybe it'll help relaunch some of their careers, too,' she'd said, when Caitlin first suggested the idea.

Amber strutted down the catwalk to rapturous applause. But that was only the start. Caitlin's forties' theme had paid off, making for another stunning collection. There were high-waisted, wide-legged trouser suits in tweed; pencil skirts worn with seamed tights; Land Girl jodhpurs and loose cotton dresses. A strong military theme pervaded, with aviator jackets, smart naval coats and military boots. Key colours were deep plum, bottle green, rusty orange, black and navy.

'Most of my friends aren't models,' Amber had warned at the beginning, but that had worked to Caitlin's advantage, as the clothes flattered more well-endowed women. Her evening dresses in particular worked best on hour-glass figures, with padded shoulders, bodices and full, gathered skirts emphasising the slimness of the waist. Sewn-in cummerbunds were intricately embroidered with beads and jewels to add glamour.

It was a strong, ladylike look, full of drama and whimsy. But, as always, it was Caitlin's attention to detail that set her show apart. She'd briefed the style team the week before.

'Forties' women compensated for the limited availability of new clothes and fabrics by splashing out on striking hair and make-up,' she'd told them.

The models reflected this, sporting big barrel curls and elegant chignons. Complexions were creamy, cheeks rouged; lips were slashes of crimson and scarlet, and eyebrows arched. Accessories included neat hats, leather gloves and elegant clutch bags.

The analysts and investors went crazy with every new outfit. They might not be fashion experts, but even they could tell that what they were seeing was something very special. Pound signs flashed before their eyes. Everyone had their BlackBerries out, and the share price was already on its way up, sailing past Bouchard's bid.

After the final applause died away, William took to the podium. He had never looked better, a true English gentleman in his Savile Row suit, dignified and authoritative. He began speaking in his strong, burnished voice. It was a rousing address, which he and Elizabeth had co-written the night before. It went back to the roots of the company, the original John Miller and his shoemaking background, and carried on through the years, emphasising how Melville's fortunes had waxed and waned.

'Melville has always been a family company,' he concluded. 'Despite what recent press reports may have said, we are still as united as ever. And, to prove that, I'd like to introduce to you my daughters, who together have made this wonderful day what it was.'

He beckoned Amber over. 'I think you'll all be familiar with my beautiful daughter Amber.' He bent to kiss her. She looked fabulous too, the image of Veronica Lake in a split-fronted evening dress with a dangerously low back.

Then he turned to Caitlin. 'And, of course, the talented designer of today's show – Caitlin.' He clasped both her hands as she joined him. When the applause finished, she went to stand over beside Amber, the two girls linking arms.

And then he turned to Elizabeth. For a moment, she wondered if he'd acknowledge her, after what she had done. But then he was smiling at her. He held out his hand and she joined him on the podium. She was almost shaking, fearful of what he would say. But he embraced her just as warmly as the other two girls, before turning back to the audience, his arm around her shoulders. It was an unfamiliar gesture from someone who had never been especially tactile around his children.

'And this is my eldest daughter, Elizabeth,' he said, and there was no mistaking the pride in his voice. 'She has done more for this company in the past decade than I have in nearly thirty-five years of being Chief Executive. And, with that in mind, I'd like to announce today that I will be recommending to the board that she takes over from me when I retire next year.'

Elizabeth stared at him, stunned, as the hall exploded. 'But after everything I did,' she whispered to him. 'I nearly lost the company for you – and I thought you'd want Caitlin.'

He shook his head. 'Caitlin's an excellent designer, and we're very lucky to have her. But you've proved time and again that *you're* the one who has the vision to lead the company. If I haven't always said that, it's because sometimes I worry that you're going to show me up!'

'But the takeover—'

'I know that wasn't your fault. I know now how manipulative Piers can be.' He took her hands in his. 'You still deserve to be the head of Melville. I can't think of anyone who would do a better job.'

They were the words she had been waiting her entire life to hear.

Later that evening, William cracked open a bottle of champagne to celebrate. He and his three daughters had gathered in his office at Melville's headquarters to digest the events of the day.

'None for me,' Amber said, as he took out glasses from the cabinet. She'd spent enough time out of it over the past few years.

'None for me either,' Elizabeth said.

Everyone looked at her quizzically.

Amber asked the question first. 'I know why I'm not drinking, but why aren't you?'

But Caitlin had already got it. 'Oh, Elizabeth, you're pregnant, too. Of course!' she said, her eyes going to the thickening waistline. She felt tears gathering in her eyes. 'Congratulations! Cole must be so excited!'

Elizabeth was frankly surprised no one had noticed sooner. At nearly four months, however cleverly she dressed – wearing empire-line frocks and long jackets in dark colours – she'd known that she couldn't disguise the bump for much longer.

She thought back to the night she had told her husband. 'Yes,' she said, answering Caitlin. 'Yes, you're right, Cole's delighted. He can't wait for us to be a family.'

William ended up pouring a glass just for himself. 'Another grandchild,' he said, shaking his head in disbelief. 'I guess it *is* time I retired.'

Outside on Albermarle Street, Piers stared up at Melville's headquarters. He could see a light on in William's room. He knew that they were all up there celebrating, laughing at him. He had watched this evening's meeting on the live webcast, and it had eaten him up to see their success. Despite his best efforts, it seemed William would be keeping his company. He'd already got an earful from Armand Bouchard, but he didn't care about that. He never had. What he cared about was that William had bested him. He had staked everything and lost. But he wasn't out yet. He was still going to make William pay. After all, he had nothing left to lose.

Getting out of his car, he went to the boot, removing a large hold-all. Inside, he had his favourite hunting rifle. With the bag in his hand, he crossed the street to the front entrance. He'd deliberately waited until the security guard had gone on his patrol of the building. He took his key out and found it still worked. Just as he'd thought, no one had bothered to change the locks.

He had the door open and was about to step inside, when he

felt a heavy hand on his shoulder. He turned to see a tall, burly man in an ill-fitting suit.

'Piers Melville?' the man said. 'I'm DC Rob Lumes. I'd like to have a word with you about the disappearance of Irina Serapiniene.'

Epilogue

Piers was arrested for Irina's murder. At his trial, his legal team entered a plea of not guilty by reason of insanity. He was sentenced to twenty-five years in Broadmoor.

Caitlin and Lucien were married on a crisp winter's day at Aldringham. Caitlin's wedding dress was cleverly designed – by herself, of course – to disguise her rather advanced pregnancy. Three months later she gave birth to a little girl. She named her Katie.

Two months after that, Elizabeth had a little boy. She called him Edward, after her grandfather. The night he was born, mother and father spent a long time debating whether he would one day head up a fashion or a restaurant empire.

The following year, Melville announced another positive set of results. The share price hit a record high. Finally convinced that his stewardship would be remembered as a success, William officially retired. He reiterated that his successor would be Elizabeth.

To his surprise, he didn't miss the office. He and Isabelle had both mellowed with their advancing years, and they finally found common ground living together at Aldringham, doting on their grandchildren.

Elizabeth was acknowledged to be the strongest Chief Executive Melville had ever seen. But she also made time to be a good wife and mother. Two afternoons a week, she left the office at lunchtime. She also introduced flexi-time and crèche facilities for mothers who worked at the company.

She and Cole had never been happier. When the following year he was named Ernst & Young Entrepreneur of the Year, she was by his side at the award ceremony. Later that night, they celebrated his win in bed. Nine months later she gave birth to her second child, a little girl named Ella, after Cole's mother.

Following the fashion show, Amber had a number of modelling offers. She turned them all down and instead joined Melville's Marketing Department. To everyone's surprise — especially her own — she actually enjoyed working there. Focusing on her career helped her take a well-earned break from drugs, alcohol and men.

Caitlin's innovative collections continued to define the Melville brand. For their belated honeymoon, she took Lucien and little Katie on a tour of Ireland. They went back to Valleymount and found a pretty cottage on the outskirts of the peaceful village, which they decided to buy on the spot.

They spend most weekends and holidays out there.

Simon & Schuster proudly presents

The stunning second novel from Tara Hyland

FALLEN ANGELS

Coming soon in hardback

Turn the page for a preview . . .

Prologue

Sister Marie scurried along the dark corridor, as fast as her pudgy little legs would carry her. Even though she would never admit it to the other nuns, alone in the cloisters at night, she often got scared. This evening was worse than usual. An earlier storm had knocked out the electricity again, and the flame from her candle cast eerie silhouettes on the stone walls, as though shadow demons lined the path on either side, lying in wait for her to pass.

'The Lord is my shepherd, I shall not want,' she murmured under her breath, trying to draw courage from the words. 'He makes me lie down in green pastures.'

As she continued to recite the Psalm, Sister Marie shivered, this time from cold rather than fear. Even the heavy wool habit couldn't keep her warm at this time of year. With less than a week to go until Thanksgiving, the weather had finally turned. The cold, bright sun set earlier these days, and then the infamous San Francisco fog rose up from the sea, covering the thick legs of the Golden Gate Bridge before rolling in towards the shore, the white mist creeping across the city and snaking its way up here, to the Sisters of Charity Orphanage on Telegraph Hill. Sometimes, lying awake in her eight-by-ten-foot cell, Sister Marie imagined the fog oozing in through the keyholes and under the doors, like something from one of those monster movies her younger brother liked to watch.

Stop that, she scolded herself. It was this overactive imagination that had led the Canoness at her last convent to suggest that she might not be suited to life as a nun. But even though she had struggled through her postulancy, the six-month period to determine whether she should take the veil, Sister Marie hadn't wanted to give up. It had finally been agreed that she should be allowed to continue with her novitiate, the training to take vows, but on the condition that she went outside of the closed order. Moving to the orphanage had seemed like the best option. She adored children and had always known that motherhood would be the hardest aspect of secular life to renounce. Now she wouldn't have to.

The Orphanage had been founded by the Sisters of Charity back in the nineteenth century, funded with donations from the city's upper-class Catholics. At present there were ninety-seven children in the institute's care – and tonight there was about to be one more. A call had come through late that evening, just as the nuns were about to retire, asking if they had room for another child. It was a baby apparently, only a few days old. Apart from that, no other details had been imparted about the new arrival: not its sex, nor the reason for it being abandoned here. It was most curious.

Sister Marie had been assigned to stay up with Mother Superior while she waited for the child. But as the hours dragged on, she'd begun to grow bored. Tired of her fidgeting, the Reverend Mother had eventually sent her to fix them both a late-night supper. It had been bad enough getting down to the kitchen in this creepy building. Now, on the return journey, the nun's progress was slower, as she was carrying a tray laden with mugs of cocoa and a plate of thickly sliced bread, spread with butter and jam. It would have been slower still, if a gust of wind hadn't blown through the corridor at that moment, extinguishing her candle and plunging the cloisters into blackness. With a little squeal of fright, Sister Marie let go of the tray. The crash of metal and china on the floor echoed around the vast walls, sending her scuttling the last hundred yards to Mother Superior's office.

She burst through the door without knocking. 'Reverend Mother,' she panted, hardly able to get the words out, 'you'll never guess what happened . . .' Without pausing for breath, she launched into an explanation of her adventure. It was only as she started to calm down that she took in the scene properly: Mother Superior was on her knees, clutching a string of rosary beads, and had been in the midst of praying. 'Oh, my goodness!' A hand fluttered to her chest. 'I interrupted you! I'm sorry, really, I am. About supper, too . . .'

'Enough of your apologies, my child.' Mother Superior's voice was low and calm. 'I have no need for refreshment. Just in future perhaps you could make your entrance a little less dramatic. My old heart can't take the excitement.'

There was the barest hint of amusement in the rheumy eyes – the novice was renowned throughout the Order for her histrionics. Using the desk, the old nun hauled herself up, her joints creaking as she stood. She winced.

'Are you alright, Mother?' Sister Marie rushed over to take her elbow.

''Tis nothing.' She waved the younger woman away. 'The cold brings out my arthritis.' She lowered herself slowly and painfully into the wooden chair, and then nodded at the seat opposite. 'Sit yourself, child. We still have a long wait ahead of us, I fear.'

With that, Mother Superior bowed her head and fell into a contemplative silence. Sister Marie opened her mouth to speak, and then closed it again, knowing she ought to resist the urge to talk. That was something else she found hard to deal with – only speaking when she had something worthwhile to say. A natural chatterer, these periods of quiet went against her nature. It was so much easier for the Reverend Mother, she thought enviously. There was a stillness about her, a sense of serenity that the novice was certain she would never possess, no matter how many years she was here.

In the dim candlelight, Sister Marie studied the older woman's face, soft and lined, as fragile as crepe paper. She was well over seventy now, and still going strong. She spoke little about herself, although there were rumours of a decade spent in the Missions in Africa, her time cut short after contracting a disease that weakened her heart. But despite her physical fragility, there was an unmistakable inner strength about her.

Sister Marie sensed that, like the Abbess at her last convent, Mother Superior had doubts about her suitability to take the veil. Secretly she did, too. Life as a nun was even harder than she had imagined. The tiny cell, starkly furnished with only a wooden bed, writing desk and dresser; rising every morning at five-thirty a.m. to go to chapel for an hour of prayer. But although the Superior was free to dismiss a novice at any time, Sister Marie guessed that the decision of whether to continue would ultimately be left to her. The Reverend Mother was one of those rare people who did not sit in judgment, and truly believed the words, 'let him who is without sin cast the first stone'.

The two women continued to sit in silence, with the younger nun trying hard not to fidget, alternately wishing for the visitors to hurry up and arrive so that she could go to bed, and feeling guilty for the thought crossing her mind. Eventually, she must have nodded off in the chair, but the sound of a car drawing up on the outside street jerked her awake.

Sister Marie jumped to her feet. 'That must be them.' She couldn't keep the relief out of her voice.

A moment later the bell rang, confirming she was right. Only then did Mother Superior stand, too.

Outside, whoever had rung the doorbell had retreated to the warmth of the car. It was a fancy car, too, Sister Marie noted. Black and sleek, a Lincoln Capri, and this year's model, 1958.

That the car was expensive surprised her. Usually when a new-born came to the orphanage, the mother was an unmarried girl who'd got herself in trouble, and the baby would simply be left on the doorstep. But this was clearly a very different situation. Sister Marie wondered if Mother Superior knew any of the details – unfortunately even if she did, she was unlikely to divulge them to her gossipy underling.

Sister Marie looked on with undisguised curiosity as the driver stepped out of the car. He was a tall, distinguished man in his late forties, with dark hair, dark eyes and a navy cashmere coat that must have cost more than it did to feed the entire orphanage for a year. The collar was pulled up, as though he wished to disguise his identity – or maybe she was just being fanciful again. He walked round to the back of the car and opened the rear door, reaching in as though to retrieve a bag. From her position on the stone steps, Sister Marie couldn't see inside, but she thought she heard a woman weeping softly. Perhaps she was mistaken and it was just the newborn though, because a moment later the man emerged carrying a small bundle of blankets, which promptly started to howl.

Without making any attempt to soothe the crying child, he crossed the drive to where the Reverend Mother stood. His face was blank and he didn't say a word, leaving Sister Marie to assume that all relevant information had been imparted over the telephone earlier. Mother Superior took the child from the man's arms. The baby was obscured by the blanket it had been wrapped in, so the older nun pushed the material back. As she caught her first view of the child's face, she frowned, as though something wasn't quite right, and then a moment later her expression softened.

'God love you,' Mother Superior murmured tenderly. Her composure recovered, she looked up at the man and said, 'You can be sure that the child will be raised as a good Christian.'

The man nodded once, to acknowledge her words, then headed back to the car.

Sister Marie followed the elderly nun inside. Goose bumps covered her arms, and the hairs on the back of her neck were standing on end. She still hadn't laid eyes on the baby, but she sensed that something was amiss with the child. Whatever was wrong, it had been enough to unsettle the normally unflappable Mother Superior. And that knowledge disturbed her more than anything else.